Praise for
Jaclyn Reding's novels

The Adventurer
Book Two in the *Highland Heroes* Quartet

"A fine Scottish plaid expertly woven of romance, history, and legends, the second book in Reding's *Highland Heroes* . . . is sheer magic. Readers who enjoy such books as Connie Brockway's *McClairen's Isle* series and Diana Gabaldon's *Outlander* (1991) won't want to put this one down." —*Booklist*

"Exciting . . . a delight. . . . Jaclyn Reding shows she is no pretender, but a contender, to the . . . throne."
—*Midwest Book Review*

The Pretender
Book One in the *Highland Heroes* Quartet

"A hero who is a heartbreaker—ruthless, dangerous, and so sexy you'll want him for yourself." —Catherine Coulter

"Delicious blend of humor, history, and adventure—a story readers will truly savor." —*Booklist*

"The tables are turned on an unconventional heroine. . . . Colored with drama and humor, this one is a winner."
—*Rendezvous*

"[I am] looking forward to Jaclyn Reding's tales starring Elizabeth's four younger siblings." —BookBrowser

continued . . .

S0-AGX-550

White Mist

"The queen of Regency-era Scottish romance . . . enticingly portrays a compellingly evoked wild landscape and its resilient denizens."
—*Booklist*

"This is an exceptional book, one that ranks high . . . a truly wonderful tale."
—*Rendezvous*

"Explore the history and drama of the Scottish Clearances. [A] must."
—*Publishers Weekly*

White Knight

"I'd be a damsel in distress any day if this white knight was in the vicinity. Don't miss Reding's latest goodie."
—Catherine Coulter

"Jaclyn Reding spins a tale of love like no other! Highly recommended!"
—Under the Covers Reviews

White Magic

"With her superb knowledge and admirable skill, Reding captures the romance and grace of Regency England."
—*The Literary Times*

"This very satisfying historical romance runs the gamut of emotions; it also leaves just enough unsaid to make you want to read the next book in the quartet."
—*Rendezvous*

White Heather

"Captivated me from the start . . . a charming combination of mystery, murder, romance, intrigue and legend . . . a magical journey to romance." —*Scottish Radiance*

"Rich in historical detail, endearing characters, compelling stories—Jaclyn Reding has it all. This is a writer to watch." —Linda Lael Miller

HIGHLAND HEROES:

The Secret Gift

JACLYN REDING

A SIGNET BOOK

SIGNET
Published by New American Library, a division of
Penguin Group (USA) Inc., 375 Hudson Street,
New York, New York 10014, U.S.A.
Penguin Books Ltd, 80 Strand,
London WC2R 0RL, England
Penguin Books Australia Ltd, 250 Camberwell Road,
Camberwell, Victoria 3124, Australia
Penguin Books Canada Ltd, 10 Alcorn Avenue,
Toronto, Ontario, Canada M4V 3B2
Penguin Books (N.Z.) Ltd, Cnr Rosedale and Airborne Roads,
Albany, Auckland 1310, New Zealand

Penguin Books Ltd, Registered Offices:
80 Strand, London WC2R 0RL, England

First published by Signet, an imprint of New American Library,
a division of Penguin Group (USA) Inc.

First Printing, November 2003
10 9 8 7 6 5 4 3 2 1

Copyright © Jaclyn Reding, 2003
All rights reserved

 REGISTERED TRADEMARK—MARCA REGISTRADA

Printed in the United States of America

Without limiting the rights under copyright reserved above, no part of this publication may be reproduced, stored in or introduced into a retrieval system, or transmitted, in any form, or by any means (electronic, mechanical, photocopying, recording, or otherwise), without the prior written permission of both the copyright owner and the above publisher of this book.

PUBLISHER'S NOTE
This is a work of fiction. Names, characters, places, and incidents either are the product of the author's imagination or are used fictitiously, and any resemblance to actual persons, living or dead, business establishments, events, or locales is entirely coincidental.

BOOKS ARE AVAILABLE AT QUANTITY DISCOUNTS WHEN USED TO PROMOTE PRODUCTS OR SERVICES. FOR INFORMATION PLEASE WRITE TO PREMIUM MARKETING DIVISION, PENGUIN GROUP (USA) INC., 375 HUDSON STREET, NEW YORK, NEW YORK 10014.

If you purchased this book without a cover you should be aware that this book is stolen property. It was reported as "unsold and destroyed" to the publisher and neither the author nor the publisher has received any payment for this "stripped book."

The scanning, uploading and distribution of this book via the Internet or via any other means without the permission of the publisher is illegal and punishable by law. Please purchase only authorized electronic editions, and do not participate in or encourage electronic piracy of copyrighted materials. Your support of the author's rights is appreciated.

For Steve . . .

. . . and another twenty years

Chapter One

She'd been looking over their most recent acquisition, a rare first edition of Anne Bradstreet's *The Tenth Muse,* when the call had rung in on the shop phone.

Their Wednesday afternoon clerk, Rosalia, poked her head around the doorway of the book-crammed office a moment later, something she would do any number of times on any number of Wednesday afternoons, usually to ask things like:

"Want a coffee, Lib?"

"We're sending out for Chinese, Lib."

"Who the heck wrote *Highland Heroes: The Adventurer,* Lib?"

Her face this time, however, wasn't its usual sunny self.

"It's for you, Lib. It's . . ." Rosalia hesitated, bit her bottom lip. "Um, it sounds important."

Libby didn't even ask who it was. She fished for the receiver hidden beneath the nest of packing material that littered the desk in front of her. Her heart actually thumped as she put the phone to her ear, her voice breathless when she spoke her name a moment later. It was as if she already knew, which was impossible, given the fact that the words she would hear had been so utterly, so absolutely unexpected.

"Isabella . . . this is Dr. Winston. I'm calling about . . . I'm afraid . . ." He paused. "It's Matilde."

From that moment, and for the rest of Libby's life, the poetry of Anne Bradstreet would be synonymous with her mother's death.

That had been a week ago. In truth it felt like a lifetime must have passed since she had received that terrible phone call.

Libby was no longer sitting in her cluttered office at Belvedere Books, at Fifty-eighth and Lexington on Manhattan's East Side, where she spent her days cataloging their newly acquired titles and listening as Rosalia recounted her latest dating disasters. Instead she was standing in the parlor of her mother's Victorian house, high above the historic fishing village of Ipswich-by-the-Sea on Massachusetts's North Shore, where she had spent the past three hours accepting condolences from the people of the town in which she'd grown up.

It had been a long and emotionally draining day. Stealing a quiet moment when there was a lull in the gathering of mourners, Libby wandered over to the tall front windows to look out at the expanse of the gray north Atlantic. The glass rippled in the light reflecting off the sea, washing the cozy parlor with a pale autumn blush.

She'd almost forgotten how much she loved this place. The house had stood on its rocky cliff for some one hundred and sixty years, an idyllic sea captain's house complete with a widow's walk and rusted sea gate. Inside, the faded walls were papered in huge cabbage flowers, a delicate backdrop to the collection of antiques placed about the room. Books were arranged both vertically and horizontally along the far wall, while potted plants flourished underneath the bay window. Lace doilies, like intricate spiderwebs, stretched along the arms of the wing chair and the velvet sofa's curving back. On the mantel were photographs, Libby building a sand castle, Libby being pushed on the old garden swing by her father, displaying the happy lives that had been lived there.

It wasn't until she turned from the window that Libby happened to notice the cherry cabinet clock standing in the corner. It had stopped at precisely ten minutes after twelve, having been left unwound since the very morning her mother had passed away. It was sadly symbolic, that unticking clock. The room, after all, had always been the very heart of the house.

In that same parlor, Libby had played as a child, had had tea parties with her mother on summer afternoons. Every year they'd celebrated Christmas before the warmth of the small hearth, decorating a huge fir tree with garlands and lights and bright tartan bows. There was the carpet where Libby had learned to dance, standing on her father's great feet as he had waltzed her around the room. And in the corner, the piano where she'd practiced her scales stood, just by the entryway where her height over the years of her childhood had been chinked into the doorjamb with her mother's favorite paring knife.

Standing there now, Libby felt her gaze turn toward that doorjamb; the marks still visible even from across the room. She gave in to a small smile as she remembered how she had always tried to lift her heels a little off the hardwood floor to make herself taller than she really was. She remembered, too, how her mother had always caught her.

"Flatten those feet, Isabella Elizabeth Mackay Hutchinson," she would say, her voice carrying the soft Scottish lilt that had remained with her long after she had crossed the ocean to America. "There's naught to be gained from trying to be a tree."

How Libby had always hated the fact that she hadn't grown tall and lanky—and blond—like her friend Fay Mills, who had become a runway model at the age of sixteen, had left high school in Ipswich to move to New York, and now had her face beaming out from countless covers of newsstand magazines. Fay had always had the perfect face, the perfect body, and even the perfect name for it. Try as she might, Libby had never been able to think of a single fashion model named Libby.

Libby was, had always been, *average*—average height, average weight, average black hair and eyes that were more smoky than blue. She made an average salary, lived in an average studio apartment on West Seventy-sixth that needed far more redecorating than her average salary would allow. And since she spent most of her time surrounded by musty, aging books, she wore average clothes, comfortable khakis and chunky over-sized sweaters that she ordered from the L.L.Bean catalog because she was too busy most of the time to go shopping herself. Even her shoes were average, with only a hint of a heel, best suited for climbing the rickety ladders that stretched to the highest of the shelves at the shop.

So she supposed her name fit her.

Libby.

Average.

Boring.

Her mother, however, hadn't agreed.

"You'll ne'er be average to me, Isabella Elizabeth. To me you'll always be my one and only . . ."

The one and only child Matilde Mackay Hutchinson had ever had.

Closing her eyes against the sting of tears, Libby took a deep breath and tucked the memory back into the farthest corner of her thoughts. She felt more alone at that moment than she could have thought possible. She let the breath go slowly.

Dishes, she thought as she opened her eyes. There was a sink full of dirty dishes in the kitchen waiting to be washed, and food enough to feed the whole town lining the counters, waiting to be put away. Everyone who had come to pay their respects had brought something in covered casserole dishes and linen-lined baskets. If she had six months, she could never eat it all, so she planned to wrap it in plastic and distribute it the next day to various homeless shelters in Boston. Her mother, she knew, would think that "grand."

Libby started for the kitchen to tackle the mounds of ham salads and baked beans—but stopped, hesitating, when she caught the whisper of voices coming from the other side of the arched doorway.

"A shame it is, poor child."

Libby heard a responding sigh.

"Oh, yes. Libby's all alone now. No brothers or sisters to comfort her. Not even a husband . . ."

She recognized the voices. Mrs. Phillips and Mrs. Fanshaw had been two of her mother's neighbors who for as long as Libby could remember had made it their business to comment on the business of others. Libby should have expected they would have an opinion this day.

"And how old is she now—Libby? Must be nearly thirty."

Thirty-one, Libby wanted to say, but bit back the words when the other one spoke again.

"Goodness! But I was wed and had three children before I was thirty. At this rate, by the time little Libby finds herself a man, it'll be too late for her to have any children to leave this place to."

"This is true . . ." Another sigh. Mrs. Fanshaw was excessively fond of sighing. "If only things could have been different last April . . ."

She didn't finish the thought. But she didn't have to. Everyone in Ipswich-by-the-Sea would have known what she meant.

"And to think," she said instead, "all those bedrooms

upstairs, empty still. Poor Matilde and Hugh never had any other children."

"You know, I wonder if Libby would be interested in selling the place. It isn't as if she'll move back here now that Matilde is gone. Charles Derwent had always told Matilde she need only name her price and he'd buy it from her. The view from the porch is simply the best anywhere on the North Shore."

Libby stiffened. Sell her mother's house?

"Of course she'll have to sell," Mrs. Fanshaw persisted. "What other choice will she have? Living so far away now in that city?"

That city. As if New York was akin to Sodom and Gomorrah.

"Oh, yes. Though she never let on, I know Matilde was simply shattered when Libby moved away. Oh, she tried to put on a brave face. Matilde always hid her sorrow well, but look how Libby came to visit less and less often these past months. Poor Matilde. At her age, a woman should have been surrounded by the laughter of grandchildren, instead of sitting on that porch alone each night, staring out at the sea."

Libby turned, leaned against the wall. She looked toward the windows and caught a glimpse of her mother's rocking chair there, its wooden spindles bleached and cracked from years of sunlight and the harsh sea air. Seeing it empty now, she felt something unpleasant twinge deep in the bottom of her stomach.

Was it true? Had her mother felt as alone as they'd said? Neglected by Libby after she moved to New York those five years ago?

Libby thought back to the day she had told her mother of the position she had accepted with Belvedere Books, Manhattan's oldest and most prestigious antiquarian bookshop. For Libby, it had been the opportunity she had always dreamed of, a chance to spend her days immersed in her love of old books. And Matilde had been happy for her. At least it had seemed so . . .

Libby had only answered the advertisement on a lark, had never dreamed she would be asked for an interview, let alone offered the position of acquisitions assistant.

But she had.

Most of the time she wasn't even in the shop. She could spend days, even weeks traveling to estate sales and out-of-the-way bookshops, in search of those editions that were most rare. She had an eye for it, and George Belvedere had told her it was the reason she'd been offered the job.

Quite often her travels had brought her through New England, and she would stop and spend a long weekend with her mother, just the two of them. But truth be told, those weekends had come fewer and farther between in recent months, ever since . . .

April.

It had just been too hard, coming back, having to face the memories, the looks on the faces of the townspeople. In fact it had been a full two months since Libby had been to Ipswich-by-the-Sea at all. Instead she'd kept in touch with her mother through a series of less and less frequent phone calls.

And now, because of that, her mother had died alone, sitting in the very parlor where Libby now stood, only to be found by one of the neighbors, who had grown worried when Matilde hadn't shown up for the weekly meeting of the Ipswich-by-the-Sea Gardening Club.

Dr. Winston, the family's physician since Libby had been a child, had said she'd had no symptoms, no episodes that would have warned of such a thing coming. Her mother's heart had simply quit.

Just like the clock in the corner.

He'd said it, Libby knew, to try to comfort her, to ease the guilt he obviously knew she must be feeling. His kind words and gentle smile had done nothing, however, to lessen the harsh truth that Libby should have been there with her.

"I'm here now, Mother," Libby whispered, even though she knew it was too late. She could only close her eyes and wait out the churn of her emotions before turning once again to the kitchen.

Three hours later, the house stood empty.

After the last of the mourners had left, patting her hand and pitying her with their eyes, Libby had curled up in her mother's rocking chair on the porch. It was a cool autumn night, and she'd wrapped herself in the weathered folds of the woolen throw Matilde had kept there, watching the darkness of the October night steal over the star-filled Atlantic sky.

Libby pressed her nose into the scratchy blanket and breathed deeply, seeking her mother's familiar scent. Lilacs. Always lilacs. Would she always remember that scent, Libby wondered. Or would time diminish it, fading like the autumn leaves until it was simply gone forever? Libby felt the sea wind blow across her face, pulling at her hair, heard the fallen leaves toss about at the bottom of the garden steps. Her heart twisted in her chest just like those leaves, roiling on the swirl of her emotions, and she wept into that blanket as she wished—just wished—she could see her mother's face once more.

All day, even as she was surrounded by the residents of the town, Libby had felt utterly alone. She'd been lonely before. Living on her own in a city the size of New York where most people didn't know their neighbors did that. Yet she'd never felt as alone as she did now.

Growing up an only child, Matilde had always made certain Libby had never felt the isolation of it, keeping her busy with reading or baking or repainting the kitchen a different color, as she had done nearly every year of

Libby's childhood. There must be at least fifteen different shades beneath the current sunny yellow.

Matilde had been so much more than a mother to her. She had been Libby's best friend. Libby had never realized, had never once considered what her moving to New York must have done to her mother.

Shattered, Mrs. Phillips had said.

Yet Matilde had never made Libby feel guilty for having gone. It was as if she had known, had understood Libby's need to try her wings and fly. Matilde had taken whatever she had been able to get, those random weekends, those rushed phone calls whenever Libby had been particularly buried in her work, and she hadn't raised a fuss even when Libby had had to cancel her last visit to attend an estate sale in upstate New York instead.

Had she known then? Libby wondered, reflecting back on that not-so-recent phone call. Had her mother somehow sensed they would never see one another again? She remembered that her mother had sounded breathless when she'd answered the phone that day. When Libby had questioned her, she'd waved it off with the excuse that she'd been in the cellar and had hastened up the stairs to catch the phone, rushing, it turned out, to learn that her daughter wouldn't be coming to see her that weekend.

Oh, God . . . why? Libby closed her eyes as she felt, truly felt, her heart splintering inside her chest. Why hadn't she just taken the time to make the drive?

She had always intended to make it up to her mother, take her to Boston for the symphony and dinner in the North End. It had been one of their favorite outings together, a mother-daughter date of Mozart and Antonio's spinach manicotti. But somehow the days had turned into weeks, and Libby just hadn't been able to get away. She was just always so damned *busy,* working until late, burying herself in her work, getting home at an hour when she feared she might wake her mother if she called. She'd even tried to give her mother her old laptop, the one she'd used before Mr. Belvedere had bought her the more up-to-date model for her work on the road, thinking they could keep in touch by e-mail more easily.

Her mother, however, would have none of it.

"A person writes a *letter,* Isabella Elizabeth, using pen and paper and proper postage. A letter is composed, with rhythm and thought, like a piece of music. E-mail is nothing more than fast-food correspondence. A takeaway window sort of way to dash off a few lines, using as few words as possible and even fewer thoughts. It's detached. It's impersonal."

She had been so very, very right.

It was dark when Libby finally got up from the rocking chair and walked the length of the wraparound porch to the screen door. She closed her fingers around the latch and found a small sense of comfort in its familiar, strident creak as she opened the door and headed inside. She went to the kitchen to make a pot of tea, taking the time to use loose leaves like her mother always had, not her usual quickly steeped muslin bag of whatever happened to be handy. She chose her mother's favorite tin from the tea rack, a blend that she had sent to her from London each month, and even heated the Brown Betty pot with a dash of boiling water before adding the leaves and filling the pot to steep, just as her mother had taught her.

Libby opened the cupboard and started to reach for her favorite mug, a clunky oversized thing emblazoned with an image of the Statue of Liberty. She had sent the mug as a gift to her mother shortly after she'd moved to New York, but Matilde had never used it and it had become Libby's mug whenever she visited. This time, however, her fingers fell short of it, and Libby reached underneath it instead to one of the dainty porcelain cups and saucers painted with bright flowers that her mother had always insisted upon using for tea.

Libby gave in to a smile as she splashed the steaming orangey-brown brew into the cup, remembering how she used to heckle her mother about the cups whenever they would have tea.

"Teacups like this are for decoration, Mother. Or collecting. They should be on display on a shelf, not used for drinking. They hardly hold more than a sip."

Matilde had simply shaken her head, her eyes lifting heavenward behind the round lenses of her reading glasses. "'Tis a far sight more proper than that basin of a thing you insist upon drinking from."

Setting the saucer and cup, and its matching pot, on a tray, Libby walked carefully up the curving stairwell to her bedroom. She stopped before opening the door, and after a moment's hesitation, continued down the hall until she had reached the door to her mother's bedroom.

Libby had only to nudge the panel with her knee and it swung easily over the polished hardwood floor. She stood for a moment in the doorway, staring at the room that was awash with the moonlight coming in through tall, gossamer-curtained windows.

Her mother's lilac scent wafted over her, welcoming her. How many times had Libby spent the night in that tall four-poster bed with its pristine white linen duvet that felt just like a cloud when you slipped underneath it? On stormy summer nights, and sometimes in winter with the fire glowing in the bedroom grate, she had come tiptoeing inside, more often after her father had died when she had been just seven. They would sit together, Matilde and Libby, and Matilde would brush out Libby's dark hair, back when it had been long and straight and pulled back in its usual ponytail.

It was after she had moved to New York that Libby had had it cut to her shoulders—a city-girl hairstyle for a city-girl life. But instead of sleek and fashionable, Libby's life was more suited to alligator clips with pencils stuck in at odd angles. She kept her hair styled simply, parted on the side and tucked behind her ear in a manner that had it flipping up under her chin whenever she was bent over the pages of a book.

The tea set clinked softly as Libby crossed the room. She set the tray on the folded coverlet that stretched across the foot of the bed. It was a high bed, made all the more so by the thick feather-filled pillowtop that layered the mattress. Libby used the small bed step and sank slowly into the down-filled covering. She lay there for several quiet moments, letting the softness embrace her, staring at the ornamental trim on the ceiling as through the open windows she heard the sea tide break softly on the shore beneath the house. Instead of comforting her, however, the sound only made her realize how silent the house now stood.

Libby clicked the bedside lamp on, taking up the teacup for a quiet sip as she eased back against the feather-filled pillows. She had changed earlier that evening out of her black suit into her favorite flannel lounging pants and oversized Boston College sweatshirt. She had pulled her hair up into an unruly knot of a ponytail and had removed her contact lenses from eyes that were red and irritated from crying, wearing her wire-framed eyeglasses instead.

She could imagine her mother at that very moment, sitting at Heaven's tea table, shaking her head in dismay. Libby had a dresser drawer full of crisp linen nightgowns that her mother had given her every Christmas, but somehow they had always been too pretty, too pristine for her to wear. Libby vowed that as soon as she returned to her apartment she would start to wear them.

She finished the tea, poured another cup, but she wasn't tired. She should be exhausted, having slept so little in the past week as she'd made the arrangements for her mother's funeral service and burial, and then met with the family lawyer, John Dugan, to discuss the details of the estate.

Even he had suggested she might sell the house, thinking it would make a fine B and B. The truth was, Libby didn't know what she was going to do with it. It was a big place, with some five acres of land that ran down to its own private stretch of shore. Her father had bought it for her mother as a wedding gift, to replace the home she'd left behind in Scotland, and Matilde had loved the house, even naming it in the old Scottish tradition, Thar Muir—Across the Sea. If Libby sold the place, the land might be broken into lots, divided up, and developed. A boat jetty with kayaks and sailboards would overtake the shoreline. Condominiums would replace the grand oaks and maples whose leaves now blazed with fall color.

Restless now from the conflict of emotions that came with her thoughts, Libby reached for the drawer in the nightstand in search of something to read. Her mother had always kept whatever book she was reading there, and Libby smiled to herself as she recognized the weathered leather cover of one of Scott's Waverley tales tucked away inside.

It was from a set that Libby had given her mother for her birthday just a few years earlier, a complete centenary edition collection that Libby had found at a Hudson River estate sale. This particular title was *Castle Dangerous,* one of her personal favorites, and Libby opened the book, looking for the usual ribbon that marked Matilde's reading place.

But it wasn't a ribbon pressed between the heavy vellum pages. It was an envelope . . .

. . . an envelope addressed to Libby, written in her mother's hand.

My dearest Isabella, began the letter she found inside,

*if you are reading this then I am well and truly
gone. I have felt it coming some time now, not in
my physical health, just a sense of knowing, which
is why you find this letter here, waiting for you.
Please don't despair over my passing. I have had a
full and wonderful life, blessed with so much joy.
My dearest joy, my daughter, has been in having
you.*

The page began to blur, clouded by Libby's tears. She
blinked, took a breath, read on.

*With my passing, the time has come for me to
tell you something of a family secret. Do not be
angry that I did not choose to share this with you
before now. In time, you will understand. If you
will look underneath the lamp on my nightstand,
you will find a key. The box that the key will open
is contained in my armoire, on the very bottom, behind my slippers. It is my gift to you. Look closely
at what it holds, and I promise everything will become clear to you. Just know that I love you more
than I ever thought it was possible to love. You are
the very best daughter a mother could ever hope
for, my dearest Isabella Elizabeth.*

Libby's hand trembled as she set the letter aside. She
sat for a moment, just staring at it, feeling as if she had
stumbled into a dream. Finally, she slid off the bed and
lifted the lamp. She found the key just as her mother had
written, waiting underneath. It was a small key, the old-
fashioned skeleton type, the sort they used only for decoration anymore or in late-night mystery movies.

She walked to the tall mahogany armoire, opened its
double doors. Her mother's blouses and skirts hung
neatly inside, crisply pressed, with tissue paper separat-
ing each one. Surrounded by her mother's scent and the

whisper of her last words, Libby knelt and searched the bottom of the compartment, reaching to the very back of it, behind her mother's row of slippers until her fingers found the shape of what felt like a small wooden chest.

Libby pulled the chest out, looked at it in the light. It appeared to be very old, made of a dark wood and carved with the symbol of two thistles entwined. Libby ran her fingers over the carving. She knew that design. It was the same symbol her mother had always stitched onto the handkerchiefs and tablecloths she had worked while rocking on her porch.

Libby took the key, fitted it inside the lock. She turned until she heard it click, then slowly lifted the chest's lid.

Her breath caught when she saw what lay waiting inside.

A large, rounded crystal, about the size of a small walnut, was tucked against the box's silk lining. It was attached to a long silver chain, and Libby lifted it to watch the stone dangle in the lamplight. Despite its unusual shape, the stone sparked, seemed to grab the moonlight, reflecting a misty, milky blue. It was a most remarkable thing, the way the stone seemed to hold the moon's light deep inside.

Libby slipped the chain over her head and let the weight of the stone hang around her neck. As it nestled against her chest, the light seemed to reflect, change, warming to a soft pink.

But how could that be when moments before the stone had shone blue?

The time has come for me to tell you something of a family secret, her mother's letter had said. *It is my gift to you. Look closely at what it holds, and I promise everything will become clear to you.*

But nothing was clear. Nothing at all.

Libby searched further inside the chest and found what appeared to be a photograph, black and white and tucked beneath the tattered cloth where the stone had lain. She picked it up. A man, his handsome face smiling toward the camera, stood leaning against the trunk of a tree. His eyes were light, his hair dark, and his smile lifted higher on one side than the other. He looked familiar somehow, but Libby didn't know why. She knew she had never seen him before.

She turned the photo over. On its back was written simply, "Wrath Village, Scotland."

Libby sat back, studied the man in the photo. Who was he? Why had her mother left her such a mysterious gift?

Matilde had rarely spoken of her life in Scotland before she'd come to America. Whenever she did, it was only to say that there was nothing to tell, that she'd left for the promise of a better life. Once, when Libby had been in the sixth grade, she'd been given an assignment at school to draw a "family tree" with the names and dates of her parents, her grandparents, her great-grandparents. All of her classmates had had full, abundant trees with many branches filled with photographs of brothers, sisters, aunts, uncles, and grandparents stretching back for generations. Libby's tree, however, had only resembled the sad little tree Charlie Brown had chosen in the *Peanuts* Christmas cartoon, with only three branches; one for her, one for her father, Charles Hutchinson, and one for her mother, Matilde Mackay.

Matilde had told Libby that she'd never known her husband's parents, as he'd been rather older than she was and his parents had died before they'd met and gotten married. When Libby had questioned Matilde about her own parents, she had simply given their names— Hugh and Catherine. There weren't, she'd said, any pictures for her to paste on her tree.

But there was a photograph.

This photograph.

The man pictured in the photograph was someone

from her mother's life in Scotland, someone whose memory she had kept all these many years. Whoever he was, he had to have meant something to Matilde, something very special. Perhaps he was still alive, still living in Scotland. If so, he would want to know that Matilde has passed away. Perhaps he could even tell Libby something more about this mysterious stone her mother had left to her. But without a name, how could she possibly track him down?

All she had was the name of a village.

That was, at the very least, a starting point.

Chapter Two

Dusk had fallen by the time British Airways 7946 touched down at Inverness's Dalcross Airport. The sky was leaden, a curtain of clouds blotting out the ebbing daylight and a fine, spitting mist sheened the plane's window, casting Libby's first sight of her mother's homeland in a dim haze.

As they taxied to the terminal, the pilot's voice came over the loudspeaker, announcing that it was a "brisk seven degrees Celsius." Libby didn't know whether that meant it was cold or not, but as everyone else seemed to be donning their overcoats, she did the same.

She'd taken the 8:20 p.m. flight from Boston the night before, with what should have been a brief stopover in London that morning. But she'd extended the stopover, opting to remain in London for the day, taking a connection on to Scotland later that afternoon.

It was the first time Libby had been to the United Kingdom, and London was too much of a temptation to simply pass through. All the way from Paddington Station, she'd had her face pressed to the window of the black cab as they rolled past the golden gates of Buckingham Palace and inched their way through the swirl of traffic at Piccadilly Circus with the tall tower of Big Ben standing sentry in the distance.

Any other time, she would have stopped to watch the Changing of the Guard, or have a stroll along the banks of the sleepy River Thames. But Libby had only six hours before she had to make her connecting flight, and London to an antiquarian bookseller was quite a bit like the Saks Fifth Avenue annual sale to a compulsive shopper. There were more bookshops, book fairs, and auctions on tap than in any other city in the world. And there was one street in the center of London on which a good many of them could be found.

Charing Cross Road ran from St. Giles Circus all the way to Trafalgar Square, and Libby spent the day peeking in its shop windows and browsing through its book-crammed stalls. She even passed by the famed number 84, which was, she was saddened to discover, now a Pizza Hut and no longer the quintessential shop immortalized in print by author Helene Hanff. She met colleagues she'd only ever spoken to on the phone or by e-mail, and even treated herself to a purchase or two for her own modest collection. She passed hours digging through shelves, perched on ladders, and sitting cross-legged on the floor, losing herself in the imaginary lives she discovered hidden away between the weathered cover boards.

It wasn't just the stories, but the books themselves, the texture of the thick vellum pages, the earthy scent of the seasoned bindings. Libby read inscriptions written decades, even a century, earlier and daydreamed about the people who had composed them.

To Dorothea, Remembering Paris . . . With all my love, Spencer.

Aunt Freda, With love from Ros—Christmas 1927.

William Seton, Esq.—135 West Regent Street, Glasgow, 1862

If she took a moment, Libby could just imagine Ros and Aunt Freda, sitting with their family and basking in the warmth of a Yule log while that very book lay wrapped and waiting for Christmas morning. Wouldn't it be wonderful, she mused, to travel to Glasgow, to seek out 135 West Regent Street, and to see if perhaps a descendant of William Seton, Esq., could still be living there? And what of Dorothea and Spencer? They could today be an elderly couple, married some sixty-plus years, with a glimmer in their eyes whenever they remembered their time in Paris.

It was the sort of thing that usually had her purchasing the book for herself. It was almost as much a pleasure for Libby to imagine their lives as it was to read the lives of the characters contained inside the books. She didn't care if it was a cookbook or a treatise on vegetable gardening. She'd even once spent nearly half her monthly paycheck for an eighteenth-century Voltaire written completely in Russian, simply because the inscription had read "For Catherine, Empress of my Heart . . . Gregory." Libby never could quite convince herself that the book hadn't once been a gift to the Russian czarina from her favorite lover.

All too soon the hour for her connecting flight approached, and Libby found herself leaving London aboard the express train bound for Gatwick Airport, her suitcase comparatively heavier than it had been upon arriving.

The airport at Inverness was small, plopped in the middle of what appeared to be little more than a farmer's field, with huge rolls of shorn hay lined up along one end. Libby followed the other passengers as they disembarked directly onto the tarmac, claiming her bag on her way inside the terminal. She'd already gone through customs in London, so within an hour of landing, she was tucked inside a rented, semicompact Vauxhall Astra and was rolling west along the A96. She knew this because

as soon as she had turned onto the roadway, a computer-
ized voice barked at her from inside the dashboard.

"You—are—on—the—A96—traffic—flowing—
freely."

It had scared her half to death. In America, cars didn't
typically talk.

She found a button just above the radio and just below
the small speaker from which, it had seemed, the voice
had bellowed. The button bore a question mark with the
letters NAV. She pressed it.

"You—are—on—the—A96—traffic—flowing—
freely."

She pressed it again.

"You—are—on—the—A96—traffic—flowing—
freely."

The motorway (not, she'd been informed by the rental
car agent, the *highway*) bypassed the city of Inverness,
taking her over a stretch of bridge that crossed the
Moray Firth. Even at dusk it was a lovely sight, the waters sluggish and everything limned in a hazy aura of
light. As soon as she reached the opposite side of the
bridge, the navigational voice inside the dashboard
barked again.

"You—are—on—the—A9—traffic—flowing—
freely."

Safe in the knowledge that she had taken the correct
route off the roundabout, Libby eased back in the driver's seat, trying to accustom herself to driving on the
left side of the road. Behind her, the lights of Inverness
glimmered in the mist.

At first, Scotland appeared rather like her New England home, with miles of drystone walls that ran along
the roadside, laundry hanging from wind-lashed lines,
and boats bobbing in lonely shadowed harbors. It was
greener, perhaps, with far fewer trees, and hills that
rolled and stretched into the horizon. Instead of steeply
pitched Cape-style houses, there were stone cottages

with dormer windows and pristine whitewashed walls. The road, too, seemed to grow narrower the further she drove, winding and twisting past a succession of different villages with charming names like Dingwall or Strathpfeffer or even Dornoch (pronounced "door-knock" by the rental car agent).

It wasn't until the map led her onto the A836 that Libby began to realize just how different Scotland could be.

Her first clue was the SINGLE-TRACK ROAD sign, which she'd barely had time to glimpse before a pair of head-lights came tearing straight at her. A flash of panic had her swerving for the side of the road to avoid the oncoming car, but, not quite accustomed to driving on the left, she headed for the right and nearly collided with the other vehicle head-on.

She skidded to a stop, trying to calm her panicked heartbeat while praying that another car didn't approach. She glared at the dashboard and that button with the question mark.

"You could've warned me," she muttered, then tore through her carry-on bag for the travel guide she had picked up the day before leaving. She vaguely remembered having seen something in it about driving when she'd flipped through the pages during her flight.

Yes. There is was. Page 214. "Survival Guide; Practical Information."

Whilst driving through Scotland, you may chance to encounter what is referred to as a "single-track road," particularly in the Highlands region. Single-track roads should be treated as you would a double-track, or divided road. First thing to remember is to be certain to stay to the left side of the road! Avoid pulling into passing places on the right-hand side when passing oncoming vehicles.

Oh, well. Rule #1 broken. Libby read on.

> *On a single-track road you will find small lay-*
> *bys (areas to pull over) that you can use to let an-*
> *other car to pass if you should meet. Remember*
> *that whoever is nearer to the passing place has to*
> *reach it in order to allow the oncoming vehicle to*
> *pass. The Scottish are generally a friendly sort and*
> *will usually greet the other driver when encounter-*
> *ing a vehicle on these roads.*

Libby rather doubted that the other driver's "hand sig-nal" had been his idea of a friendly greeting.

After a quick study of the road signage illustrated at the bottom of the page, she decided to give it another go. She certainly couldn't sit there all night. She edged the car back onto the roadway, knuckles tight on the steering wheel, and watched the path before her as if at any mo-ment an eighteen-wheeler might appear, heading straight for her.

Blessedly, none did, and as the miles began to pass without another car in sight, Libby's confidence slowly returned. She even started to relax and picked up a little speed.

The first mileage sign came into the light of her head-lights moments later.

WRATH VILLAGE—67 MILES

That wasn't so bad. If the road stayed clear, she would be there in an hour, hour and a half tops.

Libby had never seen dark *this* dark before.

It had been well over two hours since she'd seen that first mileage sign, and she was now beginning to panic. She had no clue where she was, or if she was still in Scotland, for that matter. The saner side of her knew she

must be. After all, she was on an island, and she hadn't
driven into the ocean yet, but the last mileage sign she'd
seen had read WRATH VILLAGE—18 MILES, and that had
seemed like at least an hour before. She'd been punching
the little NAV button over and over, but had received only
a sort of empty hum in response. Apparently even the car
didn't know where they were. She supposed, however,
that the empty hum was decidedly better than being told
"You—are—in—the—middle—of—nowhere—traffic—
flowing—freely."

The driving was torturous. The narrow road wound
and wandered its way through steep hills and along
straggling loch lines so close to the water's edge that she
daren't blink for fear of driving straight over.

"You—are—at—the—bottom—of—the—loch—traffic—flowing—freely."

Along one particularly grueling stretch, she'd had to
come to a tire-screeching halt when an indistinct figure
had suddenly emerged into the glow of her headlights.

It turned out to be a sheep that had had no intention, it
appeared, of moving. It merely stood, staring back at her
while chewing its midnight snack, leaving her little
choice but to edge the car around it.

There were no streetlights, no traffic lights, no lights
of any kind, only the occasional lamp glow that she
could just make out coming from some remote cottage
window. Even the moon seemed to have gone into seclusion.

At one point, some distance back, she'd passed a red
phone box and for the next several miles had seriously
considered backtracking to it, to call someone—anyone—to come and rescue her. She would have, except
that she had no earthly idea how she would ever tell
them where to find her.

And she'd never been so tired in her life.

The fatigue of the past days and the stress of the past
weeks had been steadily winning the fight to overtake

her. She could sense herself starting to slip in her efforts to fend it off and had even felt her eyes begin to close as she drove. She had opened the car windows to the bitter chill of the outside air and blared the only station she could get on the car radio, a static mixture of Celtic folk and accordion-ridden country dancing music.

She hadn't slept a wink during the flight from Boston, had been restless the entire flight, out of balance, with no clue what she was going to find on the other end of her journey.

Had her mother felt the same when she'd made her trip all those years before? Had she been excited? Frightened? Matilde had come to Boston, she'd told Libby, to marry Charles Hutchinson, an American who had apparently swept her off her feet, for she'd had Libby almost immediately after. What a rare thing their love for one another must have been, to have brought her mother so far from everything she had ever known. Matilde had always told Libby she didn't regret having gone to America, and she'd never once returned to Scotland, not even to visit. In fact, throughout her childhood, Libby could remember no letters, no phone calls ever having come from that corner of the world.

Then why? Why the peculiar crystal stone and the photograph of a man Matilde had never mentioned? And why would her mother have waited until after she was gone to reveal it to Libby?

There was an answer, Libby knew it. And there was only one way—and one place—to find it.

Wrath Village.

If she ever got there.

Just a few more miles, she told herself. She punched the gas as she started to climb a steep rise. Surely she had to be almost there.

Just as she reached the top of the hill, a scattering of cottages appeared in the distance, and a modest black-and-white sign came into view.

WRATH VILLAGE—3 MILES.

She had made it. Somehow, remarkably, unbelievably, she had found it.

As she rolled along the sleeping street, past a post office with its red-and-yellow ROYAL MAIL sign, Libby began to look ahead, envisioning the soft bed she would collapse into, imagining the warmth of the toasty fire that awaited at the quaint B and B she'd found when she'd begun researching the village on the Internet.

She nearly shouted out loud a "hallelujah" when a short while later she saw the second, smaller sign, which directed her off the main road and onto what amounted to little more than a pathway, so obscure that it didn't merit an A, a B, or, for that matter, even a Z.

Just a few minutes more, she told herself, and she would be at her mother's childhood home.

But twenty minutes and two dead-end turns later, Libby was still driving.

It took everything she had just to keep from falling over the steering wheel and weeping.

"This . . . is . . . ridiculous," she grumbled aloud to the windshield wipers that were intermittently sweeping away the faint drizzle that had begun to fall. She backtracked yet again and yanked the steering wheel to the right, encouraged when the isolated road passed a stone cottage, its windows as dark as the moonless sky. It was the first dwelling she'd seen since the post office earlier. No one seemed to be at home, but a cottage was still a good sign. Surely the village must be just ahead.

Libby pressed on, slowing the car slightly when the road entered a thicket. Suddenly there were trees where moments before there had been nothing but open, empty moorland, with huge limbs gnarled from decades, even centuries, of growth. They weighed in on either side of the car, bringing to mind the apple orchard in *The Wizard of Oz*. Any moment now she expected to hear one of them grumble, "She was hungry!" before reaching out its twisted branches to whack her.

Okay, now she really was beginning to lose it.

That was it. She was just going to turn around, head back the way she'd come, and spend the night in the post office parking lot if she had to. Libby slowed the car to a halt, yanked the gearshift into reverse. And then . . .

What was that?

She squinted through the drizzle dotting the windshield. Was that a light she saw ahead?

Shifting into first gear, she inched forward. She could hear the wheels crunching on gravel, and the rain pelleting the windshield. She scanned the gloom before her. It was so unbelievably dark. She was just beginning to believe she had imagined it when, suddenly, she saw it again.

A flash of light.

Libby slowed the car, stopped, and flicked the headlights to high beam, then back to low, once, twice, hoping to draw the attention of whoever it was lurking ahead.

Success!

A light flashed in the distance, pointing in her direction and holding steady. Stifling the urge to giggle like a lunatic, Libby rolled forward to meet her rescuer.

Twenty seconds later, she was slamming the brake pedal to the floor.

She opened her mouth to scream, but nothing came out. Not even a gasp.

Standing before her was a man. She didn't notice his face, his hair color, or even his height. She couldn't have said with any certainty later whether he'd been wearing jeans, a kilt, or, for that matter, a taffeta ball gown.

There was only one thing she could describe in clear detail.

And that was the gun he had pointed at her windshield.

Dear God, she thought fleetingly as she waited for her life to begin flashing before her eyes, *I've just driven into some horrible reality television show . . .*

She realized then that she could do one of three things. She could floor the gas pedal and run him down, although given the fact that he was about twenty feet from her and aiming a shotgun right at her nose, his first reflex might be to fire. That wouldn't be very good.

She could jam the car into reverse, but without any light and the glut of trees she's just crawled through, she would no doubt ram herself straight into a tree trunk.

So she did the only other thing she could think of. She put both hands on the steering wheel and blasted the horn.

The sudden blare, however, didn't send him fleeing into the night as she'd hoped. Instead he walked straight for her and yanked open the car door. Libby was still leaning on the horn, leaning on it for dear life, staring at him in the way a hapless Transylvanian held up the sign of the cross before an advancing Dracula in the old black-and-white films.

Very calmly, and without saying a word, the man wrapped his fingers around both her hands and lifted them off the steering wheel.

The horn went silent.

He simply stood there, holding her hands and staring at her.

Libby was too paralyzed to speak. She opened her mouth, but the words wouldn't come. She stared back at him, at the hardest pair of eyes she'd ever seen, and waited for him to do whatever he intended to do to her.

And since she had no one left in the world, her absence would scarcely be noticed.

He let go of her hands. "Get out."

Libby jumped at the sound of his voice and fumbled with the seat belt. She tried to unhitch it, but her hands were shaking, trembling, and she couldn't work the button.

"I said get out."

His voice was deep, terrifyingly calm, and his face was without expression.

"I'm trying to get out, but I can't—"

"I mean get out of here. Turn the car around. And leave. Now."

"I—" she stammered, "I was just looking for—"

"I know bloody well what you were looking for. You're not the first, and I'm reasonably certain you won't be the last. So let me save you the trouble. I'm not interested."

"I beg your—not interested—in what?"

"I'm not interested in *you*."

"But I'm not—"

"You're right, miss. You're not. You're not going to get what you came here for, so why don't you save us both a lot of trouble. Turn your car around, drive back the way you came, and never come back again."

Libby just stared at him, blinking, trying to think of something to say. A moment later, everything, the exhaustion and stress of the past few hours, the emotion, the grief, the confusion, the terrible loneliness she had been buried beneath the past weeks, all of it came bursting out in a sudden shower of sheer, utter hysterics.

"But that's what I'm trying to do! I have been driving for three hours, and now I don't know where in the world I even am. I mean, what is wrong with your roads? None of them have names, only numbers, and some of them don't even have that. There are no street signs anywhere. The roads just turn and twist till I have no idea what direction I'm going. I don't even know where I am. There aren't any houses. Where do people live? Where do you buy food to eat? The sign said three miles! Are miles longer in Scotland than everywhere else in the world? Or do you just make up fake villages and distances to confound drivers for your own personal entertainment?"

By the time she finished her tirade, she was crying. *Damn it!* And what was worse, she couldn't seem to stop herself. Her shoulders were hitching, and her breathing was coming in strangled little sobs. Then she started to hiccup. She couldn't imagine how pathetic she must look, strapped in her little Vauxhall Astra with its worthless NAV button, exhausted, flight-haggard, bawling her eyes out and hiccuping like a drunkard. She half expected the dashboard voice to suddenly scold, "You—are—making—an—idiot—of—yourself—tears—flowing—freely."

Libby put her head in her hands and just let it go. She cried for her mother, for the loss of her, for the horrible guilt she felt over not having been there for her in her last days. She cried for the sheep that had stood in the middle of the road, refusing to budge. She cried for the fact that while she lived and worked in one of the largest, most complicated cities in the world, she couldn't follow a simple road map to a Scottish village. She cried for the disaster of that April day. But mostly she cried for the fact that at that very moment, this lunatic with the gun could kill her and no one, not a single soul on the face of the earth, would ever even realize it, because there was no one. No one in her life anymore, no one but her.

It had to have been several minutes later when Libby finally managed to collect herself. He was still standing there, next to the open car door, saying nothing, just looking at her with that same bland expression that wasn't even an expression at all. Libby turned her head, peered up at him. She could barely see him through the smear of tears that clouded the lenses of her eyeglasses.

He said nothing, but he reached into his pocket and took out a handkerchief. He offered it to her. Libby took it, cleaned her glasses, dried her tears, wiped her sniffly nose.

"Thank you."

"Keep it."

Then he said, very quietly, "If you are looking for the village, it is just down the drive, past the gatehouse, and to the right. You'll have to go down a steep hill and across the stone bridge. It may seem like you're driving straight into the sea, but it is the right way, I assure you."

Libby simply nodded. She knew exactly where he had directed her. She had already gone that way twice before and had indeed assumed she was driving straight into the sea. So she had stopped, and turned around, and on the third try, had ended up there instead, with his gun pointed at her face.

"There's a turnaround just some ten feet ahead." He pointed down the drive into the uncompromising darkness.

"Thank you," she said again, hanging her head in embarrassment as she reached for the door to close it. She just wanted to get away, and she prayed she would never see him again.

Libby pulled the car forward and swung into the turning place, switching into reverse so quickly that she didn't even notice the hulking towers that loomed in the glow of her headlights. She didn't see the gate with its emblem of two thistles intertwined. Nor did she see the sign, nearly obscured by ivy on the pillar beside it.

A sign that read, CASTLE WRATH.

Chapter Three

Graeme Mackenzie stood watching as the Vauxhall Astra and its weepy American occupant vanished into the night.

It wasn't until the red of the car's taillights had faded into the night that he turned and headed back down the drive. His black-and-white collie, Murphy, blinked at him with his one blue eye and one brown eye, then walked quietly along beside him.

It was a dark night, unfathomably, impenetrably dark, and so he'd mounted a light onto the sight of his shotgun to help him find his way. He'd been out doing a little target shooting and had just been heading back to the house for the night when the unexpected beam of a headlamp had blinked from up the drive.

Of course he'd immediately assumed she was just another one of *them.* Why the hell wouldn't she be? So he'd turned his light onto the figure of the car, lifting the shotgun as if to scare her, to teach her a lesson for all the others who had come before her—and all those who would no doubt come after her, too.

What he hadn't counted on was finding that she was some wayward American tourist lost in the Highlands, and a wayward American who had burst out crying the moment she'd seen him.

Graeme didn't know what to believe. If she was just another one of *them*, it certainly wouldn't be the most inventive excuse he'd come across in the past eight months. That distinction would have to go to the lass who had hidden herself away in his shower stall, complete with a big red bow tied around her—

—package.

He'd come across virtually every ruse there could be since he, Graeme Arthur Frederick Mackenzie, had been endowed with, in a tragic twist of fate, on the very same day, the titles of Viscount Kintail and the Marquess of Waltham. In the blink of an eye, it seemed, he'd become the unanticipated heir to both his mother, a countess in her own right, and his uncle, the very illustrious Duke of Gransborough.

It should never have happened. For the first thirty-five years of his life, Graeme had been perfectly content filling the role of the youngest son's youngest son. As such, he'd had it pretty easy. He was connected to one of the most highly regarded families in the United Kingdom without really having to face any of the obligation of it, save the odd appearance at the Chelsea Flower Show or the Queen's Regatta whenever his mother asked him to attend with her. Otherwise, he had been virtually overlooked. *The spare.* Not considered worthy of the rest of the world's attention, which had suited him just fine.

Until February 12 of that year.

Before that date, there had been three reasons why Graeme had never dreamed he would find himself in the position he was now in. They were his cousin, Winston, his father, Maxwell, and his older brother, Thaddeus.

Fate had snatched two of them, Teddy and Wins, in a tragic bit of skiing high jinks at the Klosters in Switzerland. Three weeks later, on February 12, Fate saw fit to take his father, too, by the delivery of an aortic aneurysm in his sleep.

"You'll be the heir now," Graeme's mother, Gemma,

the Countess of Abermuir, had said to him. They had
been walking together from the family burial ground at
Gransborough House, the ducal estate in Durham. Until
she'd said it, Graeme hadn't really considered it. He
could have no inkling of the consequences this chain of
events would bring him almost immediately later.

It had begun with only a small item in the tabloids announcing his assumption of the hereditary lesser titles of
viscount and marquess. Soon after, there appeared a
snapshot of him buying a latté at the Starbucks in
Leicester Square. Unfortunately, it had attracted the attention of a more notorious London talk show host, who
had proclaimed him across the BBC television waves as
"rather dishy."

Very soon, he couldn't stop for a copy of *The Times* at
the corner newsstand without a camera lens pointing and
clicking his way. Next, one of the other city publications
came out with its annual "Most Eligible Bachelor" feature. Topping the list had been Graeme's name, with a
description of his family connections, his occupation and
place of work, even his favorite city haunts. A veritable
fortune hunter's shopping list.

At the Ascot Races, one of those events he'd attended
with his mother each year, Graeme had been leaning to
tell the woman beside him the time, and the image of
them, her face discreetly hidden beneath the deep brim
of her hat, appeared in the tabloids the following week,
under the headline

GRANSBOROUGH HEIR
ALREADY LOOKING FOR LADY RIGHT?

After that, young British women began "turning up"
wherever Graeme went. In the park when he walked
Murphy, when he'd been buying groceries at Mark's and
Spencer's, he'd once been out with a group of business
associates during which the meal had been constantly in-

terrupted by the constant stream of drinks being bought for him by young women at the bar. That had been bad enough. The paparazzi, however, became positively rabid in their bid to get the latest snapshot of the heir to the dukedom of Gransborough, the young, *eligible,* thirty-six-year-old heir to a title that combined, among other things, prestige, wealth, history, a town house in London, and forty-five thousand acres of prime British real estate.

Graeme had eventually left London because of it, retreating to the ducal country seat. But that hadn't deterred them. They'd simply followed him there, watching from behind the topiary or "happening upon" him in the local village.

So he'd left Durham and taken a flat in Hampstead Garden outside London. Eventually they'd found him there.

They'd found him in Surrey.

They'd found him in Edinburgh.

They'd found him on holiday in Spain.

Everywhere he turned, there were young, single women wanting him to cure them of their singleness—and with them, the paparazzi, hoping to catch him on celluloid with someone, *anyone* they could allude to a connection with.

Once, he'd been helping his housekeeper, a woman of fifty-two years who was married and had grandchildren, to bring in groceries. The image of them had appeared on the front page of *The Buzz* tabloid the following week, above the caption "Waltham Setting Up House With Mystery Woman."

His own mother had called asking when the wedding was.

So when Graeme had learned from a colleague of the proposed sale of a remote Highland castle that had been standing vacant for the past three decades, he'd jumped on it.

Perched on a steep cliffside hundreds of feet above the North Sea, Castle Wrath stood at the very northwestern tip of the Scottish mainland. It was surrounded on three sides by the sea, on the other by miles and miles of empty, abandoned moorland. Except for the local village, there wasn't a settlement for a dozen miles.

It was paradise.

Thus far, he'd managed to remain anonymous. He dressed casually, making himself as unassuming as possible whenever he had to go into the village for supplies. There they knew him only as Graeme Mackenzie, resident caretaker of the castle. Its new owner was officially the Countess of Abermuir, his mother, so that no record of the sale could be traced to him by the more diligent of the media watchdogs. When he needed to travel to London for his business as an architect, which he did sometimes weekly, he went by private jet or helicopter, which came to retrieve him at a remote spot on the estate. He'd been so very careful this time, doing everything humanly possible to keep himself concealed.

Or so he'd thought.

"Here you are, love. Have a sip of Miss Aggie's tea. 'Twill chase that chill off straightaway."

Libby smiled dimly at the woman, one of two spinster sisters who were the proprietors of the Crofter's Cottage B and B. They were twins, they'd told her almost immediately upon her arrival, as if that hadn't been obvious the first moment she'd seen them. They were virtually impossible to tell apart, with matching silver blond curls, lively pale eyes and parchment-like skin. Their eyes crinkled at the corners in exactly the same fashion, and their mouths made identical welcoming smiles. They even wore the same style of eyeglasses, round and wire-rimmed, and Libby couldn't help but wonder if their prescriptions matched, too.

They called themselves simply Miss Aggie and Miss

Maggie, and they had lived in the village, running the Crofter's Cottage, for the past twenty years. Before that, they had lived in London, in a modest South Kensington Victorian flat where the most exciting thing that had happened had been the day they'd watched the carriage carrying Diana Spencer pass by as it had made its way to St. Paul's Cathedral for a royal wedding. The soon-to-be princess, they'd told Libby gleefully, had even waved to them from inside the carriage.

Since they were twins and so very identical, when they had been girls, their mother had taken to dressing them in different colors in order to make it easier to tell them apart. Aggie was in yellow, and Maggie wore pale green. It was a custom they continued to the present day in their matching night robes and slippers.

Libby took the teacup Miss Aggie had offered and closed her fingers around it. It was the same flowery sort of cup her mother had always favored. She lifted it to her lips for a sip, relishing the warmth of it, a warmth, she only vaguely realized, that lingered long after she'd swallowed the brew down. It settled happily in the pit of her stomach and pulsed there.

She looked at Miss Aggie, who smiled.

"Oh, 'tis just a dash of the whiskey. Just a wee one, mind you." She winked. "'Twill help you to sleep this night."

Libby didn't think she'd need any help to sleep. She was so exhausted she felt as if she'd just lived a full week's time in a day. Her hair was flat and drooping over her eyes. Every muscle had constricted, and her body felt as if it might actually mutiny if she dared even think of getting out of the chair. Even her head seemed suddenly too heavy to lift. But her luggage still needed retrieving from the trunk of the Vauxhall Astra. And, oh, how she would dearly love a hot shower. Still, the whiskey was bringing a not-unpleasant glow to her very frazzled nerves.

Maybe just a few more minutes . . .

She took another, healthier sip, and closed her eyes,
letting the whiskey's warmth ooze through her as the
two sisters bustled about the room, plumping a pillow
beneath her feet and draping a blanket over her. When
Libby had arrived on their doorstep, wet from the rain
and nearly numb from exhaustion, the sisters hadn't
once complained that she'd woken them at such a late
hour. The cottage had been dark when she'd rolled into
the drive, and she had sat there, with the rain dribbling
down the windshield, reluctant to wake whoever awaited
inside. But then a light had clicked on in an upstairs window, and a curtain had parted just slightly. A second
later, every window in the cottage, it seemed, was awash
with light, and the door was swinging open to show the
two tiny figures waving her inside.

Within a quarter hour they had a fire rolling in the
grate beside her, *tsk*ing over her tale of having gotten so
utterly lost and shaking their heads in dismay over the
unqualified Neanderthal who had threatened her with the
shotgun.

"I cannot think of who it could have been," wondered
Aggie aloud. "They're a simple folk in this village, fish-
erfolk and farmers mostly, but gentlemen the lot of them.
There's none would dare point a shotgun at a lady any
more than he'd dare point it at himself. And to refuse to
help you when you were so obviously lost—"

"Unless—" Maggie spoke up, her pin-curled head
cocking to one side.

Aggie stared at her, reading her thoughts as twins
often do.

"Aye, you're right, Maggie, dear. Could be that Angus
MacBean has been distilling that nasty brew of his
again. Remember that time he got himself so drunk, he
convinced himself he was a Jacobite back at Culloden?
Ran around the hills in naught but his nightshirt ranting

about Bonnie Prince Charlie and unrequited glory. Nearly got himself killed when he jumped into the loch."

"Oh, 'tis true, 'tis true," Maggie agreed. "Tell me, dear, what did the man look like?"

Libby tried, but for the life of her she couldn't think of a single feature, until—

An image, gray eyes the color of storm, flashed through her mind.

"I—I don't remember," she mumbled.

"Was he tall or short?"

Tall . . . very tall.

"Tall, I think. I don't really remember."

"Dark or light?"

"I didn't notice . . ."

"Old or young? Fat or thin? Clothed or wearing his nightshirt?"

Libby simply shook her head, closed her weary eyes. The whiskey was having a wonderful effect on her, making her feel as if every limb were happily aglow.

"Well, no matter," Aggie said. "You're here now with us, safe and well. 'Tis been some time since we've had an American come to stay, off the beaten path as we are up here in this village. Tell me, what is it that brings you to us, dear? Dear . . . ?"

"Oh, the poor sweet lamb," said Maggie to her sister. "She's fallen off to sleep. We should wake her, so she can sleep in a proper bed."

"No, let us leave her 'til the morn. I daresay she'll be too tired to notice, and that couch is soft enough. We can talk with her again in the morning. Her story, whatever it is, will certainly keep till then."

When Libby next awoke, the sun was shining on a new day.

She closed her eyes, blinked, filling her lungs with a long, deep breath that smelled of potpourri and baking, then reached for her eyeglasses. But they weren't there, where she usually left them, tucked in her bedside tissue box. A moment later, it hit her.

Scotland.

It hadn't been some crazy, terrible dream after all.

Libby sat up, looked around. Through the haze that was her myopic vision, she spied what appeared to be the rounded figure of a clock sitting on the table beside her head. Its face was a blur, but her glasses, which she didn't even recall having removed the night before, were set beside it. She pushed them onto her nose and then picked up the clock, an older, windup model. She put it to her ear. Surely it couldn't be ticking. It couldn't really be noon.

Could it?

"Ah, good morning, child. Or should I say good afternoon?"

It was Miss Aggie, Libby remembered, coming that moment into the parlor, almost as if she'd been watching for Libby to wake. She was wearing a frock of pale yellow almost as sunny as the light coming through the curtained front window, her hair curling like a soft halo around her face. She looked fresh and cheery and endearingly lovely.

Libby, however, was still wearing the clothes she had worn the day before, and her hair was in an utter muddle around her utterly muddled head.

She pushed it back and out of her eyes.

"I'm so sorry," she said, squinting her eyes, which still rebelled against the glare of the sunlight. "I seem to have fallen asleep in your parlor. I don't usually sleep this late."

"Oh, 'tis just the jet lag, dear. You've got to acclimate yourself to our time, you know. 'Twill take a few days, to be sure."

"Tea, dear?"

The other sister, Miss Maggie, came into the room then, a vision of smiling pale green, tea tray securely in hand. A linen-wrapped basket of scones sat atop it with little accompanying pots of marmalade and jam. Just the sight of the tray made Libby's stomach clench. She hadn't eaten anything since the small snack she'd been given during the flight from London the afternoon before, and the granola bar she'd munched on while registering for the rental car. She took a scone from the basket. It was still warm. She didn't even pause for jam but bit into it, and closed her eyes.

It was delicious, just as wonderful as the scones her mother had made all her childhood. Never, in all the places she'd traveled, had she ever found a scone that tasted quite like her mother's. Until now.

Already she felt the tears threatening.

"Oh, dear. You don't like the scones?"

"No." Libby shook her head. "They are very good. It's just that . . ." She took a deep breath. "They remind me of my mother's scones."

At this, her tears won the fight. In fact, she couldn't seem to stop them. First, the night before in front of a total stranger, and now this. Good God, what was wrong with her?

"Oh," Aggie brightened. "Well, then, your mother must be a very good cook. Maggie's scones are quite a prize, indeed."

"My mother *was* a wonderful cook." Libby struggled to take hold of her emotions. She sniffed loudly. "She passed away two weeks ago."

"Oh, you poor sweet child."

The two women surrounded her, enfolded her, alternately patting her on the hand, *tsk*ing, and passing her fresh tissues.

"I'm sorry," Libby said, shaking her head. "I don't know what's wrong with me. I'm not usually this weepy."

"'Tis obvious, dear," Aggie said. "You're overwrought. But you've come to the perfect place to recuperate. You'll find this village is just lovely for that sort of thing."

Libby nodded, collected her emotions. "It's not the only reason I've come here, to this place. I believe my mother might have been born in this village."

"Was she?"

"In this house?" Maggie added.

Libby shook her head. "I do not know where she lived. I'm not even sure she was from the village at all."

She spent a quarter hour telling them her story, of the stone and the mysterious photograph. "So I have come here to try to find out if this man in the photo could be her family."

"Oh! How exciting. What was her name, dear? We know everyone from the village. Perhaps we have heard of her family."

"Her name was Matilde. Matilde Mackay."

"Hmm . . . well, there are certainly a number of Mackays."

Aggie went to a desk and removed something from the top drawer. She handed a booklet to Libby, a directory, it seemed, of the village, its services, and its residents.

"I'm afraid you've your work cut out for you, love. Most every family in the village is a Mackay, married to a Mackay, or a cousin of a Mackay."

And indeed they were. Libby paged through the booklet, scanning the columns of names. There were three Angus Mackays, five Donald Mackays, and nearly a dozen Robert Mackays among numerous others. "Surely they're not all related?"

"Oh, goodness, no," Maggie chuckled. "We're not as backward as all that up here. As I understand it, there is the Mackay family, and then there is the Mackay clan. Back in history, those who were a part of the clan, that is, under the protection and rule of the chief, often took his name. Surnames are a relatively modern invention in

Scotland, considering how far back the history of this country stretches. It all stems from affiliation to the clan, and the major clan about these parts was the Mackay. Smaller clans that joined forces with the greater clan over the centuries often changed their names, too, as a pledge of allegiance to the chief, so to speak, which is the reason some of the smaller clans vanished. The people themselves did not 'vanish,' they just changed their affiliation."

"'Tis why at clan gatherings you'll find thousands of MacDonalds or Fergussons or Campbells," added Aggie. "Strength in numbers, you know."

Libby found herself very grateful that her mother hadn't come from a city the size of Inverness or Edinburgh. It would have taken her probably twenty years to get through all the Mackays there. Here, in this small village, the task would, she hoped, be much easier. "Well, then, it would seem I'd better start at A. Mackay and work my way through to Z."

Little more than an hour later, fed, bathed, changed, and suitably dressed for visiting, Libby made her way into the village.

From her Web research, Libby had learned that the village of Wrath had a population of approximately three hundred and fifty, twenty-seven of whom composed the one school's student body. The village's biggest claim to fame was its location; it was the most northwesterly village on the Scottish mainland, was the site of a nineteenth-century Stevenson lighthouse, and a far more ancient privately owned castle.

The rest of the population was fairly evenly divided in age, with slightly more than a third in the "over-fifties." It was that age group in which Libby had the most interest, for any cousins or acquaintances of her mother would more than likely be found there. And even if there weren't any direct family, it would be the older generation who would best be able to tell her if they recognized the man in the photograph.

Libby drove slowly along the village high street, taking in the small whitewashed cottages that lined the narrow roadway on either side. There was the post office she'd passed the night before, a petrol station and garage, a grocer and general store, a hardware store, the pub, and a smattering of other gift and craft shops. There was also a "chip shop" for takeaway meals and a quaint little café.

It was Saturday, and blessedly the weather was mild, the sun bright against a blue sky, with only the slightest chill in the air. The sweater and turtleneck she wore were more than adequate to keep her warm. She pulled the car into the small parking lot of the post office, which was attached to the grocer and general store. She had to smile at the sign that hung above the front window. It said simply THE STORE, quite obviously needing no further distinction. What better place, she decided, to begin acquainting herself with the local residents?

A small bell tinked above her head when she pushed open the door. Behind the counter, a woman of perhaps sixty looked up, peered at her with that sort of curious look reserved for strangers, then offered a soft smile.

Libby returned the smile and closed the door behind her. A rack of tourists' pamphlets lined the wall, and Libby made at browsing them while the woman behind the counter accepted payment from her other customer, thanked her, and wished her well. When she'd gone, the proprietress looked back to Libby, who had turned her attention to a shelf of homemade preserves.

"Good day to you t'day, miss. It is a fine one, aye?"

Her voice was melodious and immediately reminded Libby of her mother.

She nodded. "Yes, it is."

"A fair sight better than that spitting bit o' rain we had yes'treen." She nodded in agreement with her own comment, looking Libby's way more closely. "Anything in particular you're after looking for? Postage stamps, perhaps? Postcards? We've a rack of them here by the counter."

Libby took this as an opportunity to engage the woman in closer conversation. She approached the postcards and started looking through them, noting images of standing stones and castles and brilliant sunsets over glittering lochs. She chose one, an image of a herd of sheep crowding a single-track road. The caption beneath it said, "Rush Hour in Scotland." She would send it to Rosalia at the shop.

"You'll be wanting postage for the card, then?"

Libby smiled, nodded.

"Where will you be posting to, then? 'Twill determine the amount of postage you'll be needin'."

"The United States," Libby answered.

"Oh, I thought you might be American. From what part?"

"New York," Libby answered, and then added, "But I was born in Boston."

"Ah, New York," the woman nodded. "I've always wanted to go there, just once, to see it. It must be so exciting to live there, so many people and things to see."

"Yes, it can be."

"Is it true when they say you can stand on top of the Empire State Building and see some eighty miles away?"

"I have heard that is true."

"Can you imagine that? Why, that's nearly from here to Inverness!" She shook her head incredulously. "Will you be staying long in the village, then, or are you just passing through?"

"I'll be staying at least a little while."

"Isn't that lovely? Where are you staying, then?"

"At the Crofter's Cottage."

"Ah, the sweet *Sassunach* sisters' place. Yes, they run

a nice house there, they do. They'll take care of you right well. Well, 'tis glad I am you're staying even for a little while. Most pass through the village on the way to someplace else. But there's much to see here, too. Well, I certainly hope you'll enjoy your stay here in the village. We're not nearly as foreboding as the name implies. In fact, quite the opposite. I'm Ellie Mackay, by the way."

The woman held out her hand, and Libby shook it. "Nice to meet you, Mrs. Mackay. I'm Libby Hutchinson."

"Welcome, Libby Hutchinson. If there's anything I can do for you, all you need do is ask."

Libby nodded. "Actually, I've come to the village on a bit of family research."

"Have you now? Well, I've lived in this village all my life. Perhaps I could be of help, although I'm afraid I dinna recall any family named Hutchinson ever having lived here."

"It is my mother's family I'm looking for. She was born here, before she emigrated to America over thirty years ago. Her name was Matilde. Matilde Mackay."

Though she tried hard to mask it, the change in Ellie Mackay's expression was almost instantaneous. The sunny smile faded to a look of cautious speculation. "Indeed," she said, her voice trembling a little. "Matilde Mackay, you say? And you're her daughter . . ."

"Yes. She would have been about thirty years of age when she left the village."

She stared at Libby, chewed her bottom lip, then shook her head slowly. "I'm afraid I cannot say I ever knew of any Matilde Mackay."

"You're certain?"

She looked away, making a pretense of neatening an already neat display of candy bars. "Yes, quite. Will the postcard and postage be all, then?"

Libby simply nodded.

Ellie rang up the purchases quickly, accepted the

pound note in payment, and returned the change. "Perhaps you've got the name of the village wrong. If you asked your mum again . . ."

Libby shook her head, her voice dropping to a near whisper. "I cannot do that. My mother has passed away."

"She's . . . ?" Ellie looked genuinely saddened by the news. Too saddened for having heard the news about the passing of a total stranger. "Oh, I'm so sorry, child."

Libby wanted to press her, but she sensed she wouldn't get very far. The woman almost seemed afraid to talk to Libby all of a sudden. So instead Libby thanked her, and turned to leave. As she closed the door and stepped back out onto the footpath, Libby couldn't shake the feeling that there was something there, something she wasn't being told.

Chapter Four

Libby was met with the same response all along the village's high street, at the hardware store, the petrol station, and even at the pub. No one, it seemed, could ever recall anyone named Matilde Mackay. Or was it that no one seemed willing to admit that they did? She'd even put in a call to the Register Office in Edinburgh, which told her that they could locate no record of her mother's birth—not in Wrath Village . . . not anywhere in Scotland.

But there was still the underlying sense that something was there.

By the time Libby had reached the end of the village's main street, the sky was darkening with the coming of dusk and the wind was blowing in hard off the sea, tugging at her hair. Lights had begun to glow from cottage windows, while quiet laughter and the blare of a television spilled out from the pub's open door.

Libby had nearly decided to give up for the day when she noticed a little church up the hill overlooking the village. Built of stone, harled and whitewashed, it had a small steepled bell that was apparently still used to summon the villagers to Sunday service by way of a rope that trailed down to the painted blue door. Headstones and crosses tilting at odd angles littered the grassy yard inside the simple stone fence that encircled the sanctuary. Many of the stones were bleached white from the salty sea spray that blew in from the bay.

The gate gave a mournful squeak as Libby entered the churchyard and walked along the narrow pathway. There was a calmness to the little enclosure despite the sea wind and she lingered amidst the headstones, reading the names, the dates, the thoughtfully composed inscriptions. Some of the stones were so weathered, she could no longer read the names, others had toppled from the effects of time, lying where they'd fallen. She noticed a number of Mackays amongst those buried and found herself wondering whether any of them could be her mother's family.

Her family.

Libby walked to the church door, trailing her fingers along the rough end of the rope bell pull. She grabbed the door handle, even though she expected it would be locked, and was surprised when the door swung open easily.

Inside, the church was small, with a beamed ceiling and rows of wooden benches spaced evenly beneath the arched windows. Though dusk's shadow had darkened the light inside, Libby could easily imagine the sunrise beaming brilliantly through the windows as the minister stood in his pulpit preaching to his congregation.

There was a plaque on the wall that stated the church had been built in 1750, replacing an earlier church that had been located further outside the village. Libby walked along the flagstoned center aisle, stopping at the first row of benches. She rested a hand against the bench, the wood polished smooth by generations of parishioners who had sat through Sunday services. She could picture them, the men dressed in their Sunday best, mothers cradling babies in their arms while the older children sat alongside, fidgeting in their places. Every footstep she took seemed to echo with whispers of

the weddings, christenings, and funerals that had taken
place in this small sacred place.

She spied the baptismal font carved out of stone.
Could her mother have been christened at that same font
while the villagers looked on? Would she ever truly
know?

The frustration had tears welling in her eyes and
Libby let go a slow, unhappy sigh. Perhaps she should
just go back to the States, back to her studio walk-up on
West Seventy-sixth Street, with its view of the corner
Chinese take-out whose menu she knew by entrée number. Whatever it was, whoever was pictured in the photograph, had been unknown to her all her life. Perhaps this
legacy that her mother had left her was simply meant to
remain a mystery forever.

"Hallo?"

Libby turned. A figure stood framed in the doorway
behind her.

"Sorry to disturb. I was just checking things for the
night. I didn't think anyone was here."

Libby got up, wiping her eyes. "I'm sorry. I was just
leaving . . ."

He stepped forward to meet her, an older man, with
graying hair and soft, kindly eyes. "I'm Sean MacNally,
the minister here. Was there"—he peered at her—"something you were looking for?"

"I thought so." She stopped, shook her head. "But apparently it doesn't wish to be found."

"And are you certain you've looked everywhere,
Miss . . . ?"

"Hutchinson. Libby Hutchinson."

"Pleasure to meet you, Miss Hutchinson." He motioned toward the door. "Come, it's getting dark in here.
Let us have a wee walk, and perhaps you can give it one
last try."

Libby spent the next hour with the minister, telling
him her story over a pot of tea and a tuna sandwich in

his cozy kitchen. Like any good clergyman, he simply listened while she talked, offering a nod here, a smile of encouragement there. He was easy to talk to, asking her to call him by his first name, and Libby soon found herself talking about more than just the photograph and the odd crystal stone. For the first time, she talked about her mother's passing, and the feelings she had fought hard to keep locked away.

"It just doesn't make any sense," she finished, shaking her head. "It is as if my mother never existed, but I know there must be some connection to this village. She had to have left me that photograph and that stone for a reason. I've come all this way and I just feel as if I've failed her . . . again."

Sean looked at her. "Why don't you come back to the church in the morning? Although the Register Office should certainly have had record of your mother's birth, there could be any number of reasons why they couldn't locate it. Being so remote, our parish has retained many traditions of the past, particularly in continuing to keep the records for the parish as they have been kept throughout history, handwritten in register books. Every birth, marriage, and death since the church was built has been recorded and is archived there. If your mother was born anywhere in this parish, she'll be there. And we will find her."

The phone rang only a second before the fax machine clicked on.

Graeme grabbed the cordless, hitting the TALK button as he put it to his ear. The fax on the desk beside him began whirring a page through.

A moment later he was greeted by his mother's cheery voice.

"Hello, darling. Just thought I'd call to see how things were going . . ."

Graeme watched for the page emerging from the machine. "Shall I assume this fax is from you, then?"

"Ehm . . ." She hesitated, her voice becoming decidedly less cheery. "I thought I might give you fair warning rather than having it sprung on you unexpected."

Brilliant. He couldn't bloody wait.

Even as he said this to himself, Graeme could see the familiar wasplike logo of *The Buzz* newspaper slowly spitting out of the bottom of the fax machine.

Immediately beneath it, he saw the headline.

NEW FEATURE! THE "WHERE'S WALTHAM?" REPORT

A grainy photograph of him, attempting unsuccessfully to hide behind a pair of dark sunglasses and a baseball cap, came into view. He remembered the day the photo had been taken. It had been early spring, barely a week after they'd buried his father. He'd been walking Murphy in Green Park, hoping for a bit of peace and quiet reflection.

It was the last time he'd ever done that.

As soon as the page was through, Graeme took up the sheet and read it.

Devoted Buzz *readers have responded overwhelmingly, e-mailing, faxing, and otherwise sending in "Waltham Sightings" from in and around the U.K. Where is this most eligible bachelor and reclusive future heir to both the Dukedom of Gransborough and the Earldom of Abermuir hiding himself these days? More importantly, with whom is he hiding? Find him, provide us with a snapshot, and you could win the £1000 prize . . . and ladies, if you should succeed in getting a date with this enigmatic aristocrat, the prize is increased to £5000!*

The fax beeped, having just finished spewing through another page.

Graeme picked up what looked like another *Buzz* page. It appeared to be a map, marking each place he had supposedly been spotted, crisscrossing a route across the United Kingdom and the Continent, even the United States. Beneath it were thumbnail photographs of "possible" Waltham snapshots, a dozen or more of them, none of them clearly him—in fact none of them him at all. Most were nothing more than caricature, staged poses. "Waltham in a Mexican sombrero." "Waltham in a beret atop the Eiffel Tower." Bloody hell, there was even one of "him" standing with Elvis!

Graeme crumpled the fax into a ball and flung it into the hearth.

"Graeme?"

He'd forgotten his mother was still on the phone. "Yes?"

"Dear, why don't you just end this silly game and come out of hiding? It only adds to the feeding frenzy, you know, this reclusiveness on your part. It's a challenge I'm afraid they cannot deny themselves."

"I'm not hiding, Mother. And this isn't any *challenge*. I'm attempting to live a quiet and peaceful life. This is harassment, invasion of privacy, even stalking. A man should be free to live wherever and however he chooses without having to fear that the lens of some photographer's Nikon is going to be shoved up his—"

"Unfortunately, Graeme," his mother cut in, "you're not just any man. You're handsome beyond belief, wealthy with the absolute certainty of becoming even more wealthy, and unmarried. Remember those horrible, indelicate photos they took of Princess Diana working out at the gym? And then, afterward, all the papers could print for a week was the debate of whether or not she had evidence of cellulite on her thighs. They didn't care if she had visited three hundred AIDs patients that day, or had single-handedly ended world hunger. The poor thing had to be afraid to go to the loo lest some photog-

rapher's lens might be trained upon her bum. And much
as they'd like to, they can't hound her boys without in-
curring the anger of the free world. After what happened
to their mother, the press have to tread very lightly. Al-
ternate choices have been quite slim for the paparazzi—
until you came along, that is. For whatever reason, Fate
has made you heir to two very considerable legacies,
which, in turn, makes you considerably more than just
an average man. It makes you interesting. It makes you
extraordinary. And this reluctance to show yourself only
makes you that much more fascinating in their eyes."

"Bloody lucky me," Graeme muttered. He stared out
the window onto the grayness of the North Sea. He
would give anything to be able to board a ship down on
that same shore and disappear.

"What you need, dear, is to come out into the light of
their flashbulbs instead of hiding from them. Galas,
events, the queen's Christmas ball even. You need to be
everywhere, be seen with everyone, and eventually the
paparazzi will get bored with you."

Graeme chewed over his mother's words, weighing
them against his own introversive feelings.

"And don't even tell me you're considering plastic
surgery. I rather like your face the way it is. It shows
your most fortunate resemblance to me." She paused.
"Seriously, though, Graeme, there is one other thing you
can do to end all of this."

"What is that, Mother? Move to the North Pole and
frolic with the elves?"

She chuckled. "No. You could just get married and be
done with it."

Graeme frowned at the phone, even though he'd expected the suggestion. It was, after all, the surest way to
put an end to this madness, as well as fulfill his hereditary duty now that the continuity of two noble lines, one
English and one Scottish and both very ancient, de-
pended entirely upon him. Rather, on his ability to pro-

create. He thought of the many portraits of his ancestors that hung in the various family properties. For centuries his ancestors had managed to hold fast to their wealth and reproduce sufficiently to continue their noble lines into the modern age. So it wasn't just his mother, or his uncle, whose hopes he had riding on his shoulders. It was the hopes and determination of every one of those periwigged, regal-looking faces that lined the venerable halls of his legacy.

Perhaps his mother was right. With circumstances the way they were, he would never be able to just meet a girl, get to know her, fall in love. Every time he encountered a woman, he would always have to wonder whether her interest was truly in him or in the prestige and wealth of his titles.

So, then, why put it off any longer?

"Draw up a list. Indicate who you think is the best candidate," he said, his voice heavy with acceptance. "Talk to His Grace, my uncle. I'll be coming down to London in the next week or so for work. We can meet and finalize the details then."

Contrary to the morning before, Libby was up with the dawn the next day. She had hardly slept a wink throughout the night, so anxious about what she might find in the parish record books.

Miss Aggie and Miss Maggie were in the kitchen when she emerged from her bedroom, showered, dressed, and ready for the day.

"Goodness, child, but you're up early. Even the cockerel has yet to crow!"

Though Libby wanted to waste no time in getting to the church, she knew it was probably too early for Sean MacNally to have awoken. So she had a simple breakfast of porridge and tea with the sisters, listening to their birdlike chatter, all the while watching the clock as it moved maddeningly slowly toward the eighth hour.

She was sitting in the churchyard, pulling the weeds that had begun to overgrow one of the older graves, when Sean MacNally came through the iron gate around nine.

It was a beautiful morning, blessed with clear skies so blue and so full of fat white clouds that they seemed to have been painted by an artist's brush. The sea was mild, and she'd even taken a stroll down to the water's edge, where she'd been greeted by the gulls swooping low over the shore. The pocket of her jacket was now full of the seashells she'd quietly gathered. Libby smiled at the minister and stood up, brushing the dirt and grass from her hands. "Good morning, Sean."

"Good morning to you, Libby. You're here bright and early, I see. I try to do that myself sometimes. So many of these graves are forgotten. I won't keep you waiting with chitchat. I'm sure you're anxious to see those record books."

The minister led her inside the church, past the altar to a small room off the main nave. Once there, he fitted a rather ancient-looking key into the rather ancient-looking lock and shoved the door open to allow her inside. The room on the other side reminded her of a monk's cell, with a small single lamp at the center table. The walls, she saw as she stepped into the shadowed room, were lined with shelves of register books, and there was an antiquated, musty sort of smell that fittingly marked the room as an archive.

"I keep thinking one of these days I'll find the time to computerize these records." Sean smiled. "Of course, that would require a computer, which we don't have. We're still a bit nineteenth century here, I'm afraid. The school's headmaster offered to let me use the school's computer at night, but I just haven't gotten to the point of lugging all these books over there. It's difficult when you're the only minister for a region this size. I service this village and all the outlying settlements. So, we continue to write the records all by hand, in the way they have been done since . . . well, since time began, I suppose, more out of tradition than anything else."

He turned toward the shelves. "Now, let's start with the year your mother was born."

He removed a large folio-sized book that looked quite like a ledger, with pages of columns and boxes scribbled with notations. "The books are broken down into three sections," he told her. "Christenings, marriages, and then deaths. When one of these events occurs, the details are recorded as they happen. We send a form in to the Registry Office in Edinburgh and keep the original record book here. Then, at the end of the year, the books here are indexed in the back of the ledger by family surname, with a notation of the entry number and page number." He turned to the back of the book. "Would you know your mother's parents' names?"

"Hugh and Catherine Mackay."

"Well, the records are indexed by father's name, and there are likely to be several 'Hughs,' so it looks as if all you'll need to do is go through the Mackay births for the year. I've a few phone calls to make, so if you don't mind I'll leave you to it. Can I bring you some tea when I come back?"

Libby nodded and thanked him. As soon as he was gone, she read and then reread every Hugh Mackay birth record, but none of them indicated a daughter named Matilde having been born. She even went back and read every Mackay birth record, Hugh or not. Still there was nothing.

"I just don't understand it," she said a couple of hours later when Sean came back to check on her.

"Hmm . . ." He sipped his tea. "Are you certain your mother was born here in Wrath Village?"

"No, not exactly certain," she admitted. "But I have to believe there is some connection for her to the village."

Libby looked at him. "Why else would she have left me the photograph?"

Sean took up the photograph of the young man that Libby had found in her mother's things, giving it another, closer look. "I wish I could say I recognize the man, but I don't. There's a familiarity there, but nothing I can point a finger to. But then, I've only been here in the village the past seven years." He gave her the photo back. "And you're certain your mother's birth name was Mackay?"

All it had taken was his asking that question. It was as if a light suddenly switched on. "Wait a minute." Libby took up the record book again. "You said these entries were written as they occurred."

"Yes . . ."

"Well, one thing I do know for certain is that my mother's birthday was August twenty-fourth . . ."

She was already flipping through the pages, scanning the month column, and she began reading all the passages on or about August 24.

"These are christenings," Sean added over her shoulder, getting caught up in the search. "It could have been recorded days or even weeks after she was born, depending on the time of year, and if the family were farmers, depending on what was being done about the farm. People sometimes had to wait until after the harvest was brought in, or sometimes, if they lived outside the village, they just waited until when next they came to church services."

Libby started reading every christening record, starting with August 1, no matter the surname. And then, finally, she stopped.

"Listen to this, Sean. 'Christened this day, the thirtieth of August in the year of our Lord Nineteen Hundred and Forty-two, a daughter born to Hugh Donn, a crofter, and his lawful wife, Catherine née M'Leod, on Monday, the twenty-fourth of August. The christening was witnessed by Euan MacNeish and James Mackay, crofters, and the daughter was given the name of Matilde.'"

"Well, the first names certainly match," Sean said.

"And the date of birth, but what I don't understand is why she went by the name of Mackay. She even included it on my birth certificate, registering my name as Isabella Elizabeth Mackay Hutchinson."

Sean sat down beside her. "Libby, is it possible your mother had been married before she married your father? You said she was thirty years old when she married your father, aye? Is it possible that she had already been married once before, when she was younger, and was perhaps divorced or even widowed?"

Libby picked up the photograph of the unknown man. She'd just assumed it was a cousin or a friend. Could it be instead . . .

A husband?

Libby decided to take a short break before setting out on her next task, that of studying the parish marriage records, which would take much longer, since she would be searching a number of years, rather than just one. The musty air and low light inside the records room had given her a headache, so she'd decided on a short walk and some fresh air, escaping to the village's fish and chip shop—called simply the Chip Shop—down the street for lunch.

As she'd handed over her two pounds fifty to pay, Sean stopped by to tell her he had to leave the village for an outlying settlement that was in unexpected need of his services. He explained that he would have left her on her own but he wasn't at all certain when he'd be coming back that night. Would she mind very much if any further search through the record books had to wait until the morning?

Since she wasn't on any timetable, Libby bid him good-bye, picked up her newspaper-wrapped fish and the accompanying bag of chips, and took the short stroll to the village green.

There was a small garden there that in summer would be replete with native flowers, but now, in the chill harshness of autumn, the blossoms had long gone. It was still a lovely spot, with the small harbor with its fishing boats lined along the dock and the bay stretching out in the distance. Libby took a seat on a stone bench and quietly had her lunch. She thought of her mother growing up in the village and wondered if she'd ever sat at that same spot, on that same bench. She was so deep in thought that she didn't hear the footsteps approaching on the gravel walkway behind her.

"A fine day, is it no'?"

He was tall, dark, and definitely handsome, made all the more so by the smart constable's uniform he wore.

Libby smiled. "Yes, it is."

His hair was a rich red-brown, his eyes warm and hazel, and he took her smile as invitation to linger. He lowered onto the bench beside her, taking out his own newspaper-wrapped fish and bag of chips, then offered his hand in greeting.

"Angus MacLeith."

She took his hand, shook it. "Libby Hutchinson."

"American, aye?"

Libby nodded. "New York," she said, already answering what she knew would be the next question.

"East or West Side?"

Now that she hadn't expected. "West."

"Upper?"

She nodded. "Seventy-sixth and Amsterdam."

He smiled. "Ah, yes. Zabar's. H&H Bagels. And Gray's Papaya."

"Best hot dogs in the city," she agreed.

He took a bite of his fish, swallowed it down with a drink of his soda. She did the same, eating in companionable silence.

"So what's a New Yorker doing here of all places?"

"I might ask the same of a Highlander who so obviously knows his way around New York."

He nodded, grinned. "Trained with the NYPD. Left a few months after 9/11."

She nodded, thinking she understood. But she didn't.

"Great blokes, the NYPD. Would still be there today, but my sister lost her husband, accident on the North Sea oil rig where he worked. She needed someone to help her meet the rent, raise her three kids. And the village I had always known as home suddenly found itself in need of a constable. So I came back, and here I am. PC Angus MacLeith. Keeper of the village of Wrath's peace."

Libby nodded, munching on a chip. It was an amazingly small world sometimes.

"You haven't answered my question yet," he said a moment later.

Libby looked at him. "Oh. You mean why I'm here? My mother was born in the village."

He nodded, understanding completely. "Come to see the homeland, then?"

"Yes, I—"

Libby was just about to tell him the rest of her story when she spotted a black Land Rover driving slowly by. It wasn't the vehicle, which she'd never seen before, but the driver, whom she'd *definitely* seen before, that had caught her attention.

It was the man she'd been confronted with that first night, who had threatened her with the gun in the rain.

Angus noticed her staring. "Is something wrong, Miss Hutchinson?"

"Who is that?"

"That would be Mr. Mackenzie. The village's latest incomer."

Libby watched as he turned the Land Rover to park in front of the hardware store and got out. He was taller than she remembered, six-foot-three-at-least tall, and lanky in build as he unfolded himself from the driver's seat. Dark hair, in need of a cut, curled loosely at the collar of his canvas outdoor coat. He wore jeans that were well lived in, and a black sweater under his coat that fit loosely over his body.

And then he looked at her, as if sensing her stare. And he frowned.

Libby felt a flush rise to her cheeks despite the chill air. She couldn't look away.

It was he who broke the stare first, as he turned and disappeared inside the hardware store.

Libby sat staring for several moments afterward, until out of the corner of her eye she noticed Angus getting up from the bench to leave. She realized then how incredibly rude it had been of her to sit there gawking at the other man while the constable had been sharing a lunch with her.

"It was nice to meet you, Mr. MacLeith."

"And you, Miss Hutchinson."

"Please," she said, smiling in apology for her behavior, "just call me Libby."

He smiled, nodded. "Well, Libby, if there is anything I can do to make your stay in the village more pleasant . . ."

"Thank you."

She got up and watched as PC MacLeith headed down the street in the opposite direction.

Tossing the remnants of her lunch into the waste bin, Libby turned and cut a path toward where the black Land Rover was still parked.

Chapter Five

Libby decided she had every reason to want to check the mysterious Mr. Mackenzie out further. He had, after all, threatened her with a gun. Well, he hadn't actually *threatened* her. But he certainly could have.

She completely ignored the fact that if she had been so inclined, she could have just reported the incident to the constable and been done with it.

The bell above the door of the M'Cuick's Hardware and Everything store gave off a tinkly sound as she pushed her way into the store. Mops and brooms and tall, narrow shovels stood like the queen's guard just inside the door beside bins of screws, nuts, bolts, and nails. There was a paint mixer with splashes and drips of color, and shiny metal buckets, the sort you rarely saw anymore except perhaps outside antique stores with bunches of petunias growing in them. Libby stopped just inside the door when she saw the man, Mackenzie, standing at the counter, obviously paying for whatever he'd come for.

He turned to leave—and came face-to-face with her.

"Excuse me," she said quietly.

He stared at her. He looked like he wanted to say something, but he didn't.

She blinked at him.

The hardware store owner interrupted. "Is there something I can help you with, miss?"

Libby stepped around him and realized that her heart was pounding. "Yes. Hello. I was looking for a voltage converter."

She'd decided while she had been going through the church records that she could help Sean MacNally by recording the parish data while she went through it into an easily indexed and searchable database, similar to the one she used for her book searches. She didn't actually expect that such a small, remote shop would have something as sophisticated as a voltage converter for her laptop. In fact, she'd only used the errand as an excuse to come into the shop.

"U.S. to U.K.?" the store owner asked.

"Yes."

"What's it for then? Hair dryer? Curling iron?"

"No," Libby replied. "A laptop computer. I suspect it wouldn't be something you normally carry—"

"Got one right here. Just let me see . . ."

She heard the bell tinkle behind her, indicating that Mackenzie had left. She chanced a glance just as he was ducking into the Land Rover. Moments later, he was pulling away.

Libby stood and watched as the shopkeeper started tugging a succession of drawers on the wall behind him, sorting through gadgetry of every type imaginable.

He was an older man, perhaps seventy, with a balding head and wisps of wiry, grizzled hair. A natty cardigan sweater and trousers covered his narrow frame, and he wore thick-lensed eyeglasses on a nose that was both short and veined. His dark eyes, however, had a twinkle about them that came just as easily as his warm smile. He reminded Libby of the spry terrier, Robbie, she'd had as a child, who till his fifteenth year had still trotted about the beach like a puppy.

"Is this it?" The shopkeeper lifted the item up to see it

through his bifocals better. "Nae, that's for a French connection." And then he chuckled at his own joke. "French connection—funny that."

He continued yanking out drawers, muttering things like "German" or "Japanese" as he went. And then . . .

"Ha! I knew I had it. One U.S.-to-U.K. voltage converter." He showed it to her proudly. "Now mind this switch here. For the laptop it doesn't matter, because most laptops are built to handle voltage variances, but check the settings if you're planning to use this for your hair dryer or that sort. If you have the setting too high, you'll burn the wee thing clear out."

Libby nodded. "Thank you, Mr . . . ?"

"M'Cuick," he answered. "Ian M'Cuick of M'Cuick's Hardware and Everything."

Libby smiled. "Well, you've certainly lived up to that name."

He shoved his hand toward her. "Pleasure to meet you, Miss . . . ?"

"Libby Hutchinson."

"Welcome to our wee village, Miss Hutchinson." The shopkeeper smiled, leaning on the counter. "I hope you'll enjoy your visit. Anything else I can get for you?"

"No, I think that's all for now." And then she paused.

He hadn't been at the shop the day before when she'd come asking if anyone could tell her about her mother. It had been a woman, older, most likely his wife.

"Then again, I wonder if I might ask you a question?"

"*Cairr*-tainly," he replied, stuffing some of the gadgets he'd taken out back into their drawers.

"Have you lived in the village for very long?"

"All my life. Born in this very house, above this very shop, one blizzard-stricken December night." He turned, grinning. "Or so my mother liked to tell me."

"I wonder if you would remember a girl who once lived here."

"I should think so. What was her name?"

"Matilde Donn."

This time Libby gave the surname she'd found in the church records, not Mackay. Even so, she'd expected the same frown and shake of denial she'd received the previous day. Instead, the shopkeeper got a look of obvious recognition on his face, just as he had when he'd been searching for the converter.

"Matilde Donn. Now that's a name I havena heard in a long time. Oh, she was a fine, bonny lass, she was. Went off to America I heard, some thirty or more years ago. Aye, I knew her. But I'm afraid I canna tell you where to find her now. She's ne'er come back nor written since she left us, I'm sorry to say. Do you know her?"

Libby looked at him. "She . . . she was my mother."

He stopped what he was doing and looked at her curiously. "You're Matilde's girl?"

"I am—at least I believe I am. You see, my mother always told me her name had been Mackay, Matilde Mackay. But according to the church records I found, her surname would have been Donn."

Ian simply nodded. "Aye . . ."

"Would you know why? Would you know if perhaps she had married once before?"

Where his face had been open and willing moments earlier, it now took on that same expression Libby had seen the day before. It was a look of hesitant withdrawal. His voice dropped to nearly a whisper. "I'm afraid I cannot answer that for you, lass."

Libby stared at him, frustrated. Why did it seem that every person in this village was trying to hide something from her?

"Please, Mr. M'Cuick. Won't you help me? My mother has passed away just recently. I just want to know who she was and where she came from."

At the news of her mother's death, his face genuinely saddened. Libby spoke to that emotion.

"All my life my mother told me there was nothing to

tell of her childhood in Scotland. She led me to believe that there was no one and nothing about her life before she came to America that she could share. But then she left me something." Libby fished in her pocket and pulled out the photograph. "She left me this photograph. I do not know who the man is, but obviously he meant something to my mother. I must find him. I must tell him about her. Can you tell me who he is?"

The shopkeeper looked at the photograph scarcely more than a moment and then repeated the words he'd spoken before. "I'm afraid I cannot answer that for you, lass."

She stared at him and felt her eyes begin to well in frustration. "You cannot, or will not?"

Something was preventing him from talking to her. He wanted to, she could tell, but something was holding him back. She saw him glance behind her quickly, then he looked back at her. His eyes almost seemed to be trying to tell her something. Libby glanced back and saw a woman standing by a display of lightbulbs, very obviously listening to their conversation.

Finally he said, as if he were answering a tourist's question, "The Mackays have been a part of this land since nearly the beginning of time. In fact their clan castle, Castle Wrath, yet stands just outside the village. Much of the history of the clan surrounds that castle." He took an ordnance survey map from a rack that stood near the cash register. "This will certainly help you in your explorations."

Libby looked at him, knowing it was all she was going to get from him, at least for the moment. She fished in her jacket pocket for some change.

"Nae, lass. The map is my treat. 'Tis the least I can do," he whispered, adding, "for your ma."

Libby understood. She took the map, squeezed his hand. "Thank you."

Outside the shop the sky was darkening. Gone was the

artist's-palette blue, the puffy clouds. Heavy storm-clouds were moving in swiftly off the sea, swollen with the rain that would soon fall. Libby walked the short way back to the Crofter's Cottage, arriving just in time for tea with the sisters.

"Hallo, dear! We were hoping you'd be back for tea. Aggie baked you some of her shortbread, don't you know?"

Libby didn't have the heart to decline, even though she was anxious to get in the car and head out to that castle.

As she sat with the sisters, she decided to keep her discoveries from that morning to herself. Whatever it was that was preventing most every person in the village from speaking to her, she certainly didn't want to implicate these two in it as well. They'd been so kind to her, welcoming her into their home and not looking on her as if she carried the plague, as had some of the other villagers she'd encountered. One in particular had even closed the window shutters as she approached and refused to answer her knock on the door.

When they'd finished with the tea, Libby made to leave. Miss Maggie asked what she was about.

"Just some sight-seeing," she said.

"Have you a map?"

"Yes. I picked one up at the hardware store."

Aggie smiled. "Ah, Ian M'Cuick's shop. Nice man, isn't he?"

"Yes, he is."

"You know, dear," Maggie went on, "it looks as if a storm might be blowing in. Perhaps it would be better if you were to wait till tomorrow for your sight-seeing. Aggie and I would be happy to have a third for whist."

Libby smiled. They so obviously longed for a newcomer's company. "I won't be gone too long. And I'd be happy to play when I return, if you don't mind teaching me. I'm afraid whist isn't one of the games I know."

Both ladies brightened at the notion of a willing pupil. "Wonderful. We'll have shepherd's pie for dinner, then. And a pudding for dessert."

With a brief stopover in her room to drop off the voltage converter and grab her handheld (for note taking) and camera (for picture taking), Libby headed for the car. As she pulled out of the driveway, she realized she'd forgotten her umbrella, but figured she'd be back long before the rain hit.

Once she was outside of the village, she pulled into a passing place and took out the map for a quick study.

The map was incredibly detailed, illustrating every cairn, stone circle, and ancient broch that spotted the area. It also showed all roads and paths, marked or unmarked, and even some of the homesteads. It would have been a great help to her that first night she'd arrived.

She refolded the map and pulled out of the passing place, heading along a landscape filled with rises and falls and hills that were green with twisting, turning burns, some no wider than a ditch. Awesome mountains, green and ridged from the winter snowmelt that trickled down into rippling lochs, stood swept with heather and gorse, now brown with the approaching winter. According to her travel book, in the spring they would be bright with brilliant purple and yellow blooms. Trees were sparse, growing most often together in a copse. Every so often, she passed a house or a cottage surrounded by acres and acres of pastureland.

One of these pastures seemed to fall at the same spot on the map where one of the stone circles was supposed to be located. Libby slowed the car to a crawl, peering over the landscape, expecting to see something similar to Stonehenge. All she saw was grazing sheep—acres and acres, it seemed, of grazing sheep.

She stopped, pulled into a lay-by. She'd grown up in one of the most historic regions of the United States, but even there, stone circles weren't something one ever came across. She might never get the opportunity to see one again.

She got out of the car and stood at the side of the road, shading her eyes, as if that might help her to spot it. She was so caught up with looking that she didn't even hear the footsteps approaching from behind.

"Lookin' fer somethin', are you?"

"Oh!" Libby almost jumped. "I didn't hear you. I was just . . ."

He was an older man, probably early seventies, substantially built, with thick arms and a barrellike chest. He had a cap fixed firmly on his brilliantly white-haired head, his face was careworn, and his eyes, pale blue, sparkled with lively warmth.

"The map indicated there was a stone circle somewhere near here, but I can't seem to find it."

"Oh, aye," he said. "'Tis just over that rise. Would you like I can take you to it?"

"Thank you." Libby smiled. "That would be lovely." She held out her hand. "I'm Libby Hutchinson."

"Hallo to you, Libby Hutchinson. I'd be Gil." It was all the name he offered in reply. Just Gil.

He'd lived on the estate (as he called it) all his life and spent his days working as something he called a "ghillie," which Libby came to understand was someone who looked after the landscape, watching out for poachers, protecting the village from rabid wildlife. With him he had a small brindle-colored terrier whom he called simply Lad and who was presently nosing around the thick grass in search, no doubt, of something to chase.

"'Tis a marvelous place, this," Gil said. "We've ospreys that nest here, and a number of capercaillie. They're endangered elsewhere, don't you know?"

Libby hadn't known. Of course she didn't know what in the world a capercaillie was, either. She simply nodded.

" 'Tis usually hillwalkers and naturists who come lookin' fer the stones," he said, giving her a once-over. "You dinna look much like a naturist." And then he added on a chuckle, "For one thing, you obviously bathe."

Libby smiled. "No, just a curious tourist, I'm afraid."

"Well, then, this way. Oh, and mind the sheep as you go."

They chatted together as they crossed the field, the sheep hopping away whenever they drew too near and Lad barking excitedly after them. Libby was grateful for the rubber soles of her duck shoes because the ground was boggy and wet beneath her feet. The wind had also picked up and was pulling at her hair, sweeping it into her eyes as they walked.

"So here they are now," Gil said, motioning toward fifty or more stones, none of them more than two feet in height, fanning out across the hillside. They were moss-splotched, weathered, each differently shaped from the other. They were nearly so obscure, so overgrown, she could have easily walked past them without even noticing them, without noticing the exact placement of one to the other in a perfectly circular formation. But just to stand among them, with the wind sighing through the tall grass, surrounded by the earthy smell of the peaty ground, gave one a sudden sense of peculiar timelessness.

"What are they?" she asked.

"Naebody can say for certain. Some are of the opinion that they are megalithic, some sort of ancient astronomical gauge. But I much prefer the local legend of the stones."

"Which is?"

"Well, tradition claims that the circle marks the site of a battle that was waged between two rival clans, the Mackay and the Sinclair. The Mackay, they say, won the battle, thereby securing this land, and set up a memorial to the day by burying the dead of both clans in this circle, marking the head of each fallen warrior with a stone. Only fifty-three remain today, but there is evidence that at one time the stones numbered well over two hundred."

Just then Libby heard a sound, like a church bell, dinging three times.

Gil looked at her and grinned. "That would be my mobile ringing." He pointed in the distance to a small cottage tucked against the side of a steep hill. A welcoming spiral of smoke issued from its short chimney. As if on cue, the bell rang again.

"The Widow MacLeod is calling me to tea. I promised her I would tend to her ailing milch cow. Seems she's got a sour stomach—the cow, that is, not the Widow MacLeod. Won't give her any milk, so I guess I'd best see to the cow afore tea, aye? I'm partial to cream in my tea. Would you care to join us, then?"

Libby gave a glance to the sky, which was darkening fast. "I'd love to, but I'm afraid my time is short today. I would love to come back another time, though."

"Anytime you'd like, lass. The good widow loves visitors, especially lasses. She had six sons and her husband, Alec, afore he departed this life, so she's lived with naught but lads all her life." He turned to leave. "Stay with the stones long as you wish. They'll not be going anywhere anytime soon."

Libby thanked Gil and watched him go, whistling for his terrier, who fell obediently into step beside him. She liked him. He was the sort of man who made you feel as if you'd known him all your life, and she suspected he would have an endless repertoire of stories and legends that he could share. She realized only after he'd left that she'd forgotten to ask him whether he'd ever known her mother. Perhaps, she decided, she could seek him out the next day.

Libby didn't leave the stone-strewn field immediately,

but remained, lowering herself into the tall grass and flattening her hand against one cragged stone. She thought of Gil's story, of the local legend surrounding the stones, and tried to imagine the field centuries earlier, peopled not with sheep but with kilted Highland warriors, claymores drawn as they locked in fierce battle. If she closed her eyes, she could almost hear their war cries carrying on the wind.

Yes, she had to agree with Gil that was definitely the most inspired explanation for the stone circle.

A short time later, Libby returned to the car and continued down the road. The road narrowed, then fell unpaved, but this time she knew she was on the right course. She checked the map as she entered a wooded thicket, past a cottage and a tall iron gate. Then, as the drive turned toward the sea, she finally saw it.

It was a castle much like any fairy tale she'd ever read, and it stood framed almost perfectly in the break in the trees. Twin towers flanked it on either side, so pristinely whitewashed that it almost seemed to glow. In fact, just as she looked at it, the sun seemed to break through the clouds, bathing the keep in a misty, delicate light. The image of it stole Libby's breath, and she brought the car to a stop so she could fully appreciate the view.

It was quite simply the most beautiful place she'd ever seen.

The map indicated that the castle was privately owned, but Ian M'Cuick had sent her here for a reason. It was the Mackay castle, he'd said. Libby hoped that whoever lived in the castle wouldn't mind her stopping by to ask a few questions.

But as she guided the car through a second set of gates, she found herself hitting the brakes, coming to a sudden, skidding halt.

There, once emblazoned but now little more than chipped and patchy ironwork, was the silhouetted image of two thistles intertwined. It was the same emblem that had been carved into the box where she'd found the stone, the same emblem her mother had always stitched on her handkerchiefs. Libby's pulse began to race in anticipation.

She pulled the car into a space off the main drive and cut the engine. As she got out, she could see that the castle had been built atop a sea cliff, high above the North Sea. The wind was stronger here, buffeting the castle, pulling relentlessly at the map she carried. The view from the castle's seawall seemed to stretch to the very end of the world.

It was as she walked to the arched front door that Libby noticed the mud on her shoes. Not the first impression she wanted to make. She spotted a boot brush in the shape of a hedgehog waiting to the side of the door and was bent over making good use of it when the front door suddenly, unexpectedly swung open.

"I hope you won't mind my using your boot brush. I was just—"

Libby looked up into a familiar and utterly unexpected face.

"Oh," was all she managed.

"You," was all he said in response as he wore that same scowl she'd now seen twice before.

Chapter Six

Libby stared up at Graeme Mackenzie's frowning face in mute disbelief.

"You . . . you live *here*?"

"I believe you already knew that."

He was wearing the same black sweater and jeans she'd seen him in earlier at the hardware store, only this time his feet were bare—and he had a pencil stuck behind his left ear. His accent, she noticed, sounded more English than Scottish.

"How could I possibly know that?"

His frown deepened. He crossed his arms over his chest, one brow lifting incredulously. "I hope you don't expect me to believe you've gotten yourself lost again."

Gotten herself lost? Libby stared at him, trying to decipher his words.

And then she realized.

That first night. The gun. The *man*.

She had been here?

It had all looked so different in the dark, and she'd been so tired, the memory of that night was really just a blur. Still, exhausted or not, she certainly would have remembered seeing a castle.

"I'm sorry. Truly. I had no idea."

"Right," he said skeptically. "So what am I to believe now? That you're here selling assurance policies?"

"No. I'm here because I was told this is the Mackay castle."

"It is—rather it *was*—the Mackay castle. It was recently taken over by new owners. But then you already knew that, didn't you?"

What on earth was he talking about?

"Look, Mr. Mackenzie, I don't know what you're thinking, but I really did just come here to do some research."

"Research? Is that what you call it?" His face hardened. "Well, I'm afraid you've come to the wrong place."

And with that he slammed the door soundly in her face.

Libby stood with her mouth open, staring at the weathered door, a mixture of outrage and disbelief clouding her vision.

"I see," she said to the iron door knocker. "Well, then, I won't trouble you a moment longer."

She trudged back to the car and got in, muttering every word she could think of to describe him along the way.

"Rude . . ."

"Unrefined . . ."

"Ill-mannered . . ."

"Insufferable . . ."

"Handsome . . ."

What?!

Ignoring that last thought, she jammed the key into the ignition and cranked it.

The car coughed, actually coughed, in response.

And then it went absolutely silent.

Libby turned the key again.

Nothing.

Again.

Nothing.

Damn!

"No! No! No!" she said out loud to the steering wheel.

She tried pushing the NAV button. It had been useless since that first day, but she tried it anyway. It didn't make a sound.

"What next?" she asked aloud.

She got her answer a second later.

The skies above her suddenly split in two with a re-sounding clap, and the rain that had been threatening came down in a sudden, roaring barrage.

It was the most unbelievable thing Libby had ever seen. The rain was pounding the car as she sat there with the windows steaming from her frustration. She counted off five minutes, three hundred seconds exactly, and then tried the engine again.

Nothing. Not a cough. Not even a click.

She counted off three hundred seconds more, and tried it again, tried it another seven times, all with no success.

In that time, the rain had only gone on to fall harder, pelting the car with a pebbly staccato.

Libby looked outside. Night was falling. She was miles from the village, too far to walk even back to the kindly Widow MacLeod's. Oh, how she wished she'd taken Gil up on his offer for tea. She could be sitting snug in a warm kitchen at that very moment, enjoying a bite of shortbread, her mood all the better for not having had a door slammed in her face by that utter boor.

A roll of thunder rumbled across the courtyard, shud-dering through the car, taunting her for her bad decision making.

She certainly couldn't sit in the car all night. For one thing, she needed almost desperately to use the bath-room. And she needed to call the car rental agency for assistance. She peered across the courtyard, through the haze of pouring rain, at the very door that had minutes ago been slammed in her face.

She had no other choice.

Libby pulled her coat up over her head and made a dash for it, splashing across the courtyard to the door once again. With a fist, she pounded on the wood, then used the door knocker for added measure.

He wasn't answering. She could feel the rain soaking through her light jacket, saturating the sweater she wore underneath it, weighing the wool of it down. A puddle had formed around her feet, soaking her shoes. She tried to press in as closely as she could to the castle wall, looking for some small bit of shelter. After another round of unanswered pounding, she tossed politeness to the wind and tried the latch.

It was locked.

"Please!" she shouted against the roar of the storm. "It's an emergency!"

Finally, after what seemed like a lifetime, she heard the latch click, and the door opened, allowing just a sliver of light from inside. It was enough to afford her a glimpse of one very disapproving eye.

"I know you have made your feelings about outside company abundantly clear, but my car will not start. I cannot leave. Please, I just need to use your phone."

He just stared at her while the rain continued to drown her.

"Please," she said, desperate now, "here are the keys. You can go and try it yourself if you don't believe me. Please!"

Frowning deeply, he pulled the door open only wide enough for her to squeeze inside.

Libby found herself standing in a shadowed entrance hall whose only light was a small lamp set on a table against the wall. It threw tall shadows all the way up the bare stone walls to a beamed ceiling, which echoed with the sound of the closing door. She stood dripping on the flagstoned floor, staring up at him, wishing she were anywhere—anywhere—but there.

"I just need to call the rental car agency so they can bring me another car."

Outside, a clap of thunder gave a sudden, jarring boom, rattling the castle windows.

And then, as if to seal her wretched fate, the lights went out. Everything went black.

Libby froze, waiting in the silence.

A moment later she heard a drawer open, a match struck, and she watched as he lit a candle. He looked at her in the flickering, ghostly light. "Leave your coat to dry on the hook there and your shoes on the mat."

Libby shucked off the saturated jacket. Her shoes sloshed when she yanked them off her feet, and her socks were soaked to the toes.

"Follow me."

He was so tall, and his expression was so austere, he made her think of the eerie butler from *The Addams Family*. What was his name?

Lurch.

Perfect.

He led her through the hall and up a short flight of stairs, crossing first one room and then another as they moved further into the house. Libby couldn't see anything except the flickering of his candle and his frowning profile illuminated in its hazy light. They turned a corner, and Libby spotted firelight spilling from an open doorway ahead. He stopped there, showing her into a den of sorts with overstuffed sofas and armchairs set before a stone hearth with a roaring fire.

The room was rather medieval-looking, with a low, beamed ceiling and narrow windows cut into the thickness of the castle walls. Libby crossed to the hearth, but even the warmth of the fire couldn't penetrate her drenched clothes. She felt her teeth begin to chatter.

"You should remove your socks and set them to dry by the fire. I'll go and see if I can find something for you to wear."

"No, really. That isn't necessary. If you'll just show me where your phone is . . ."

He picked up a cordless from a table. "No electricity."

"Is that the only phone?"

"Other than the fax machine, yes."

"I knew I should have gotten a mobile . . ."

"Wouldn't do you any good. We're too remote for any services."

She nodded. "Well, surely the power will be restored momentarily."

He looked at her with as much incredulity as if she had just stated she still believed in Santa Claus. "Likely not before the morning, I'm afraid."

"The morning?"

"If it's an area outage, yes. If it's a problem just here at the house, it could take longer. In any case, I can't even notify them of the problem till tomorrow when I drive into the village."

That's right, Libby remembered. He had a Land Rover.

"Perhaps you could just give me a lift back to the village now? I know the weather is dreadful, but you could use the phone at the B and B where I'm staying to call the power company and—"

"I gave my vehicle to the housekeeper. She has gone down to Inverness for shopping. She won't be back till tomorrow."

Libby had run out of suggestions. She didn't know what else she could say. So she just stared at him, her hair dripping onto her nose.

"I'll just go and find you something to wear, then."

Libby stood in front of the fire and waited for him to return.

The room, she noticed, giving it a closer look, was well lived in, not pristine and perfect as one would expect of such a dramatic castle but quite homey, with pillows of varying sizes and colors scattered across the two sofas, and various books and odd bits littering the table-tops. The inner walls were warmly paneled in rich golden oak that glowed in the light of the fire. In the corner, a pair of shoes were drying by the hearth and Libby noticed a dog lying on the well-trodden carpet by the heating register.

"Hello there," she said softly, hunkering down and extending a hand in greeting.

He was a black-and-white collie with floppy ears. When he lifted his head to give her fingers a sniff, she noticed he had one blue eye and one brown.

She was scratching the dog behind his ears when Graeme came back into the room. He handed her a gray cable-knit sweater and a pair of sweatpants with a drawstring waist.

"What's his name?" she asked.

"Murphy." He held out the clothes. "I'm afraid this is all I could find that would suffice. You'll have to roll back the pant legs a bit."

Libby stood there, staring at him.

He stood staring back.

Finally she asked, "Bathroom?"

"Oh. Of course. My apologies. It's just down the corridor to the right. You can take the candle to help you find your way."

Libby tucked the clothes under one arm, took up the candlestick, and headed down the hall. She found the bathroom moments later, little more than a closet really, with a sink and a toilet and nothing much more. She wondered if the room had previously been a broom closet, before the addition of modern indoor plumbing.

She closed the door behind her, looked in the mirror, and groaned. Dear God, she looked a fright. Her hair was plastered to her head like a soggy black mop, and her mascara had run where the rain had pelted her face. She looked like a sad, drowned raccoon.

She quickly peeled off her wet clothing, giving her

socks a squeeze over the sink. She washed her face and fluffed her hair dry with the hand towel she found in the cupboard, then slid his sweater over her head. As he was a great deal taller than her, it fell nearly to her knees, completely enveloping her. The wool smelled pleasantly of detergent and cedar and was soft, not at all scratchy. She pulled the sweatpants over her legs, and pulled, and pulled some more until her feet finally poked out the bottoms. Tying the drawstring waist, she rolled the cuffs over four times so she wouldn't trip on them. Then she headed back to the den.

She found him sitting on a sofa, staring into the fire. The lines of his face were pronounced in the firelight, his dark hair burnished a rich bronze. His eyes, she noticed, had long lashes.

Any thought of Lurch was immediately quashed.

He didn't say a word as Libby carefully draped her jeans and sweater over a wooden drying stand near the hearth. She turned to face him.

The moment she turned, Graeme was struck by the sight of her standing there wearing his clothes. Though the sweater swam on her and the sweatpants looked as if they could easily accommodate two of her, somehow she still looked incredibly, undeniably feminine.

He blinked, and then quickly reined in his senses. "I took the liberty of pouring you a whiskey to help chase away the chill. Without any power, I'm afraid I couldn't boil water for tea."

"Thank you, Mr. Mackenzie."

He frowned as she used his name, this a second time. He knew perfectly well he hadn't revealed it to her. But what else should he expect? Of course she knew his name. Thanks to that rag of a tabloid and its bloody contest, everybody in bloody Britain knew his name.

He watched as she took up the whiskey glass and folded her legs into the soft cushions of the opposite sofa. Her hair curled wildly around her face, making her appear vulnerable somehow. She took a small sip of the whiskey, a drink she was apparently not much accustomed to if the telltale grimace that followed was any evidence.

"I feel at quite a disadvantage," he said. "You seem to know my name, but I do not have any idea of yours."

She looked at him. "Libby Hutchinson."

"And judging by the accent, I'd warrant you're from America. East Coast. New England. Not quite Boston, but close."

She nodded. "Impressive, although for the past several years it's been New York I've called home."

They chatted on, and Graeme found her easy to talk to as well as being very easy to look at, sitting there in her bare feet, snuggled in his wool jumper, appearing so without any agenda, so charming that he had to keep reminding himself that she was just another one of *them*.

No matter how much he hadn't wanted to allow her in, he wasn't so heartless as to leave her stranded in his driveway in the middle of such a terrible storm. He hadn't seen any sign of a camera yet. In fact, she hadn't come in with so much as a purse. Still, to be safe, he knew he'd better keep as much distance between them as possible and have her out of there at the earliest opportunity.

Graeme stood up.

"I'm afraid none of the bedrooms are in readiness for guests, so I hope you won't mind doing with a blanket on the sofa. You'll be warmer in here with the fire anyway."

"Oh," she said, clearly surprised at his abrupt leavetaking. It had barely gone seven o'clock, rather early yet for retiring. "Yes, the sofa will be more than fine. Thank you."

He realized he probably should have offered her supper, even if only a cold sandwich.

"The kitchen is just down the hall, past the bathroom,

if you'd like something to eat or drink. There's sliced ham in the refrigerator." He almost told her to make herself at home, but thought the better of it. "And if you look in the cupboard, you might even manage to find a package of Hob Nobs."

"Thank you," she said. Then after an awkward stretch of responding silence, "Good night, then."

He gave a single nod. "Good night, Miss Hutchinson."

An hour later, Libby couldn't stand it anymore.

She simply had to know what a Hob Nob was.

Despite the warmth of the fire, the floor was cold beneath her feet when she stood up from the sofa. She checked her socks, but they were still quite damp. She happened to notice a pair of slippers set beside the hearth and slid her feet into them before she headed for the door. They were quite big, so she ended up scuffing her feet against the wooden floor as she shuffled, candle in hand, down the hall toward the kitchen.

In contrast to the bathroom, the kitchen was huge, and modernly appointed, with a high, raftered ceiling that echoed with her footsteps. She set the candle on the far countertop and took a look around, noting the stove, a small washing machine, and a stainless-steel wall oven. She spotted the fridge in the corner and went to it, removing the platter of ham, a bottle of mineral water, and in a last-minute change of heart, the pint of Häagen-Dazs Coffee Mocha Chip she found tucked in the freezer.

She found a spoon in a drawer and searched for a bowl. When she couldn't find one, she stuck the spoon straight into the container. It was only half full anyway. Why bother to dirty a bowl?

The first spoonful of ice cream melted smoothly in her mouth, the perfect mixture of coffeehouse mocha and bittersweet chocolate chips. What was it about chocolate that made even the worst situation fade away? She eyed the ham platter, but decided against it and simply stood against the counter, ice cream carton in hand, watching the rain outside spilling down the window in sheets.

As she stood there, she thought about Miss Aggie and Miss Maggie, who were no doubt fretting over her absence. They would be keeping her plate of shepherd's pie warm in the oven while they waited for her to arrive for their promised card game. She could only hope they wouldn't spend the night watching the front window for her, even as she knew that they would.

In no time at all the ice cream had vanished. Libby tossed the empty carton into the trash bin and washed the spoon at the sink, setting it in the drying rack. She put the ham back in the fridge untouched, took up the water bottle as she turned to leave. She realized then she'd never found anything called Hob Nobs.

But as she reached for the candle to leave, she spotted something else, something that seemed to be scratched into the far corner window. It looked like some sort of writing.

Libby took up the candle, brought its light closer. There was an etching of some sort on the windowpane. As she looked closely, she saw that it read, "Malcolm and Kettie M'Cuick, 1753."

There were etchings on other panes, too, all names and dates, spanning some two hundred years. Libby stood and read through them all, captivated by this remarkable piece of history. Some had etched just their names, others had etched lines of poetry. But it was one pane in particular, high above the others, that had her stopping and catching her breath.

Matilde Donn, 1959.

Libby touched a fingertip to the glass where her mother's name had been scribbled as the swell of tears filled her eyes.

Matilde had been there after all.

Libby turned, seized with a feeling of gleeful validation. Other than that birth record, this was the first tangible proof that her mother had lived in the village, grown up there. Libby wanted to shout out loud—*Yes!* She wanted to high-five something. She wanted to tell someone this incredibly good news. Instead, all she found was an empty room.

And the only person she could possibly talk to quite obviously wanted nothing to do with her.

Back in the den, she was too keyed up to even think about going to sleep. She couldn't watch television or listen to the radio, so instead she headed for the shelf of books she'd spotted earlier, partly out of occupational curiosity, but also from a sheer desire for something to read.

She wasn't disappointed. Mr. Mackenzie, in fact, had impeccable taste in reading material, from both a substance and an investment standpoint. And his library revealed a lot about him.

He liked poetry, and historical literature, and also had a thing for contemporary thrillers. The *Culpeper's Herbal* was a bit unexpected, especially such an early edition, professionally rebound in tooled and gilt leather with some of the pages closely trimmed to the text. The book looked as if it had been well utilized, with some pages containing handwritten notations. On the market it would fetch easily into the thousands. A rare find, indeed.

As she scanned the other titles, her gaze fell on one book in particular. The gilt lettering on its spine read simply *The Book of the Mackay.* Libby removed it from its place on the shelf, turning it in her hands as she quickly assessed it with the eye of a collector.

Leather-covered boards. Raised bands on the spine. She opened the book and held one page up to the light. Laid paper. Late eighteenth century, she suspected. She turned to the title page, did a quick translation of the line of Roman numerals printed at the bottom: 1774. It was a rare edition, but what made it unique was the realization that it had been written by a woman.

Libby stared at the name printed in blocked letters across the title page.

"Lady Isabella Mackay of Wrath."

Had she been lady of this same castle? Women had rarely achieved publication at that time in history, and if they did, it was typically in poetry, more seldom in fiction, but rarely, if ever, in nonfiction.

Libby turned to the first page, and began to read:

> *What follows on these pages is an account of great history about a clan of profound importance in the annals of Scotland. In chronicling the generations, this author humbly hopes to impart not only the events of the past, but the lives of those who witnessed them. It is my hope that perhaps, God willing, my own descendant might one day continue this endeavor in a subsequent volume, setting down the lives and history of those who will follow after me.*

The heartfelt message, so beautifully written, immediately captivated her. Libby took the blanket and curled up on one end of the sofa where the light of the candle burned brightest.

Snuggling in, she began to read.

Chapter Seven

It was near two in the morning when the storm finally slackened, moving off to sea. Graeme knew, because he'd been lying in his bed, listening to the ebbing sound of it for the past several hours.

He hadn't slept at all.

All the while he'd been lying there, he'd been thinking about, picking apart, and troubling over the woman who lay just a room and a floor away. He wanted to know who she was. Then again, he didn't. Libby Hutchinson, she'd said. If that was her true name. What did he care if it wasn't? He didn't want to know her, didn't want to wonder about her, didn't want to imagine what she might look like without his sweater falling to her knees even as he knew he would never be able to wear that sweater again without remembering the way it had looked on her.

He'd tried everything he could think of to put her off—threatening her, glaring at her, being unforgivably rude. Still, there was something about her, some odd vulnerability that just didn't seem to fit with the image of the fortune-hunting coquette he usually found himself faced with. He'd come to recognize the signs rather easily in the past eight months. And this wayward American just didn't have that hungry spark in her eyes. Perhaps that was just her game, a subtle charade to try to take him off his guard. Perhaps she was just better than most at hiding her true intentions.

Graeme gave up on sleep when he heard the clock ring two. He got up from the bed, crossed to the window. Standing there, leaning one arm against the wall, wearing only a pair of pajama bottoms, he looked out on the expanse of depthless, endless black that was the moonless Highland night. The only light that could breach it came from the distant lighthouse that stood farther north along the coast.

As usually happened whenever he was left alone with only his thoughts for company, memories of Teddy and Wins began to surface. Teddy would have turned forty that year. And Wins probably would have taken the cup in polo. One had been his brother, the other his cousin, although for all their short lives, they'd been more like the Three Musketeers. They had grown up together, spending summers at the Gransborough ducal estate, going to Eton within years of one another, even attending university at Trinity Hall at Cambridge.

It never should have happened the way it had. They'd both been expert skiers, had skied the slopes of Klosters since they'd been lads. But the slope they'd chosen to race each other down that day had been clearly marked *off-piste*. Dangerous—forbidden. Graeme had tried to dissuade them, but in the end, not wanting to appear gutless, he had reluctantly gone along. He hadn't even tried to keep up. He'd never been as reckless, as fearless, as the other two, had never felt the need to win so deeply as to risk his life.

He remembered seeing them tearing down the slope, side to side as they took the first turn. Graeme had barely caught a glimpse of them before they'd hit the patch of ice, missing the second turn and colliding straight on with a wall of sheer, unmoving cliff.

It had happened so quickly, so suddenly. And had been so horribly irrevocable.

Turning from the window, Graeme ran a hand back through his hair, then over the rasp of his unshaven jaw. He pulled a robe on over his lounging pants but didn't bother to belt it, looked for his slippers but didn't see them. He'd probably left them in the drawing room.

His bedroom was the first off the upstairs landing. He'd chosen it both for ease in getting to it, situated as it was just across the hall from his office, and also because it was directly above the drawing room and thus drew some of the warmth from the hearth below. It wasn't the largest of the upstairs chambers, but it suited him adequately. It wouldn't have made sense to open one of the master chambers on the floors above just so he could sleep alone in a bed made for two.

As it was, he'd been living at the castle only a few weeks and hadn't had the time to give the other rooms more than a cursory glance. But he'd paced the hallways enough at night to know each step on the stairwell, each turn of the hall without benefit of any light.

He took the back stairs and emerged into the kitchen, lighting a kerosene lantern kept on the counter there. Power outages were common, and he'd yet to look into getting a generator. He wanted tea, but since there was no power to heat the water, he went to the deep freeze instead. The ice cream he'd been going for, however, wasn't there.

He glanced in the rubbish bin, saw the empty carton, and realized she'd beaten him to it. He smiled to himself as he took the container of Hob Nobs from the cabinet, poured himself a glass of milk, and dipped the biscuit before taking a bite.

When he'd finished his early-morning snack and rinsed out his glass, he started for the back stairs. But he stopped, hesitating on the first step. A moment later, he turned for the opposite hall.

The fire in the drawing room had died down to a barely burning glow. Graeme took a fresh peat brick from the sledge near the hearth and set it atop the embers, stirring them with the fire tongs until the brick took flame. He added a couple of logs to keep it burning, noticing the chill in the room. Then he stood and turned toward the sofa.

She was asleep, snuggled tightly into the corner of the sofa with a book barely clinging to her fingertips and a pair of wire-rimmed eyeglasses barely clinging to her nose. He remembered the glasses from the first night, when she'd driven down the drive so apparently lost. He remembered, too, how she'd burst into tears and how he'd felt like the biggest cad in the world.

Graeme bent, took the book and set it on the table, took the glasses and set them on top of the book. But he didn't leave. Instead he lowered himself into the armchair and studied her in the light of the fire.

She really was quite lovely. The rain had brought out the natural curl in her dark hair, softly framing her face, and her lashes, long and dark, curled against her cheek. He knew from the first time he'd seen her that her eyes were blue, but not just any blue. They were the color of the North Sea, and when she'd been standing there, out in that rain, practically demanding that he let her inside, they'd been just as stormy as the sky.

She had one arm raised, supporting her head, and her mouth was curved just slightly, as if in sleep she knew some delicious secret. It was a full mouth, a mouth made for kissing, and he knew a sudden almost undeniable desire to do just that.

But he didn't.

Graeme rose from his chair and reached for the blanket that covered her, tugging it back from where it had slipped off her shoulders. He watched as she stirred, the sleepy smile fading from her lips as she let go a heavy sigh.

Had it been another time, another place, had he lived another *life,* Graeme wondered . . . perhaps things could have been different.

Unfortunately, wondering was all he could allow himself to do. He was, after all, Graeme Mackenzie, the most hunted bachelor in all Britain.

"Bloody hell!"

The sound of the muffled curse stirred Libby from her sleep, had her opening her eyes and scanning the room around her.

She was alone, a fire burning in the hearth, fueled by a fresh supply of peat that was infusing the room with its earthy sweet scent. Outside, the day had broken, beaming through the scattered clouds and splashing its light across the room. The window was open, just barely, and she could hear the birds outside, chattering to one another in a symphony of chirps, tweets, and chitters.

Until a pot went crashing against the stone floor.

An even more colorful curse followed.

Libby retrieved her eyeglasses from the table beside her and ran a hand through her disheveled hair. She must look a fright. How she wished she'd thought to grab a hairbrush the night before when she'd ducked out to the car, sheltering beneath the cover of an umbrella she'd found near the door, to retrieve her glasses so she could remove her contact lenses for the night and not wake to find them glued to her eyeballs.

Standing up from the sofa, Libby followed the sound of crockery to the kitchen, where she found Graeme Mackenzie in front of a conspicuously smoking frying pan. She watched as he shoved the sleeves of his sweater up over his elbows, appreciating the view of his rather well-fitting Levi's.

"Good morning," she said after a few stolen moments.

He turned, his expression visibly flustered. "Oh. Good morning, Miss Hutchinson."

"Libby," she corrected.

"Libby. Sorry if I woke you. I—" He glanced nervously at the stove. "I seem to be having a bit of trouble with the hob this morning. I trust you slept well?"

She started to answer that she had, that she'd slept better than she had in a long time, but there came a loud sizzling sound from the stovetop. Graeme turned to where a pot of something milky was currently frothing over.

"Ballocks!"

He pulled the pan off the burner and swung it, dripping and steaming, to the butcher block to cool. He really did look as if he were in over his head.

"My apologies for the outburst. Apparently the rigors of preparing a pot of porridge are beyond my very limited culinary capabilities."

"Well, at least the power is back on." Libby came into the room. "I'm no gourmet chef, but my guess is you've just got the fire a little too hot on the burner," she said, taking up a spoon and stirring the porridge pot. She added a dash of water from the tap to the fast-thickening mixture, stirred it some more. "It's all right, though. It'll finish cooking and cooling fine enough there." She looked at the frying pan and the blackened pieces of bacon curling inside of it. "Those, I'm afraid, cannot be salvaged."

She spotted Murphy sitting, watching them both from the far corner of the kitchen, no doubt having fled from the ruckus. "Although he'd likely appreciate them," she said, plucking the bacon from the pan and into Murphy's dish before she set about scrubbing out the frying pan for a fresh try. "Have you any eggs?"

A half hour later, Libby followed Graeme into a dining room, carrying plates of freshly scrambled eggs, some much less blackened bacon, and two small bowls of porridge on a tray.

In contrast to the den where she'd spent the night, the

ceiling in this room was quite high and fretted in decorative plasterwork. A wall of tall, elegantly draped windows faced out onto the sea, and an elaborate marble-framed hearth highlighted one wall with a huge mirror framed in gilt above it. A glittering crystal chandelier hung over the center rosewood table, reminding her of the mansions she'd toured on a school field trip as a child in Newport, Rhode Island.

They took the two seats at one end of the long, stretching table, closest to the windows. They sat together and shared a pleasant breakfast with the sun beaming in through the windows.

"The view is stunning," Libby said over a small bite of toast.

And it truly was.

The restless sea stretched in all directions, capped in white, bold and deeply blue, with fat, billowing clouds scattered across the morning sky. Gulls dipped and soared on the current of the wind.

Graeme nodded over a sip of his coffee. "Whoever it was who chose this site to build a castle, he certainly knew what he was doing."

"Actually, his name was Angus Du Mackay. I read a little about the castle last night before I fell asleep. Did you know a fortress has been standing on this site for nearly six hundred years? It fell to ruin during the seventeenth century and was restored in the eighteenth century by a Mackay chieftain and his wife. In fact it was she who wrote the book I was reading."

"I had no idea the castle was quite that old."

"I would have thought your real estate agent would have told you that when you bought the place."

Graeme looked at her. "Actually, I'm the caretaker here. The castle was purchased by another party."

It wasn't exactly a lie.

The castle had been purchased and put into a trust for the earldom of Abermuir, a title currently held by his mother, the Countess of Abermuir, to be inherited by Graeme.

A tall case clock standing by the door struck ten as they finished the last of their breakfast.

Libby stood, started to clear the table; Graeme got up to help her. In the kitchen, she flipped on the tap, filling the sink to wash. She tossed a dry towel to him. "I'll wash. You dry."

And he did. Graeme had never dreamed that he could find pleasure in such a thoroughly domestic enterprise. More than once their hands brushed as she handed him the dishes to dry. Each time they did, the kitchen seemed to grow that much warmer.

When they were finished, she turned toward him, standing at the sink with the sun playing on her dark hair, her eyes bright, her mouth so very near.

"I probably should call the rental car company," she said.

Graeme tore his eyes from her mouth. "Right. The phone is in the front hall."

Libby nodded, started for the hall, passing the den where she'd slept the night before. She took up the phone to dial, then realized she had left the rental agreement with all the information she would need in the car. She headed for the front door to retrieve it—

—and froze.

High on the wall above the main stairwell stood a portrait, a huge, full-length image of a woman. She wore an antique-looking gown with wide, elegantly draped skirts and full, lacy sleeves. She was standing on the very staircase she graced, and she was beautiful, her dark hair strung with pearls as pale as her milky skin. But it wasn't the rich satin of her gown, or the brilliant blue of her eyes that captured Libby's attention.

It was the stone hanging around her slender neck.

The same stone Libby had found hidden away in her mother's secret chest.

"She's beautiful, isn't she?"

Libby was so overwhelmed by the portrait, she hadn't heard Graeme come up behind her. She turned to look at him, speechless.

"Is something wrong? You look as if you've just seen a ghost."

"Who is she?"

He shrugged. "I'm afraid I do not know. The portrait was hanging there when I arrived. The sale of the castle must have included all the furnishings." He looked at her. "Why do you ask?"

Libby reached toward her neck, to show him the chain and the stone that she wore beneath his borrowed sweater.

But down the hall there came a sudden knocking on the front door.

Libby stilled as Graeme turned and headed for the door.

She heard PC Angus MacLeith's voice a moment later.

"Good morning, Mr. Mackenzie. I, ehm, noticed Miss Hutchinson's vehicle in your drive. I assume she is here?"

Graeme stepped back and allowed the constable inside.

"Hello, Angus," Libby said, waving beneath a sweater that was so obviously not hers. She could only imagine how this must look.

"Good morning to you. We were worried in the village that you'd run into a bit of trouble last night."

She nodded. "The rental car. It has apparently decided to go on a vacation of its own. It wouldn't start. Mr. Mackenzie was kind enough to offer me shelter for the night." She looked down at the oversized sweater and pants. "And clothing, after I got drenched in the storm."

Angus looked at her, weighing her words, then nodded. "The sisters o'er at the Crofter's Cottage have been calling me every hour since nightfall last night. They're worried sick over you."

"I knew they would be. I couldn't call. The castle lost power in the storm."

He nodded. "Have you phoned the car hire this morning?"

"I was actually just about to when you arrived."

"Why don't I have a look at it first? Perhaps it's something I can tend to. Might save you the trouble."

She nodded. "I'll just get the key."

Libby met Angus and Graeme out on the drive after quickly shoving her feet into her still-damp shoes. Angus had the hood of the car open and was bent over it, doing whatever it was that men did beneath the hood of a car.

Libby got in, tried the key when Angus called for her to. The engine clicked, then nothing more. Angus fiddled with it some more, called to her to try it again. Nothing. On the third try, the engine turned easily.

"Thank you," she said. She left the engine to idle and got out of the car.

"It's got a loose spark plug fitting. I was able to tighten it enough for now, but you'd better take it by MacNeish's garage in the village and have it looked at it."

"Thanks. I will."

They stood there a moment, all three of them, saying nothing.

"If you'd like," Angus finally said, "I can follow you back to town, just to make sure that plug doesn't come loose again."

"Oh." Libby looked at Graeme, who was looking down at the driveway. "Yes, that would be great. Thank you, Angus. I'll just . . ." She caught Graeme's eyes as she turned. His face had changed from earlier that morning at breakfast when he'd been chatting with her. Then he'd been easy, relaxed in her company. Now he looked withdrawn, even guarded. "I'll just get my things from inside."

He nodded silently.

Libby ran inside the castle, grabbing her jeans and socks and sweater from the rack where they'd dried overnight. She paused a moment, thinking she would change into them, but thought better of it. She would wash the sweater and pants she'd borrowed and return them in a day or two. It would give her an excuse to come back and look more closely at that portrait.

"Thank you so much for—everything, Mr. Mackenzie," she said to Graeme out on the drive. "I'll . . ." She looked at him. "I'll be sure to wash your things and bring them back as soon as I can. I appreciate the loan."

"My pleasure, Miss Hutchinson," he replied. Even in his voice there was a noticeable aloofness.

Libby tossed her things into the backseat, then got into the still-idling Vauxhall Astra. She saw Angus nod in parting to Graeme, then head for his patrol car. She gave Graeme one last look before easing the car into reverse.

Chapter Eight

The two spinster sisters descended upon Libby the moment she stepped through the door of the B and B.

"Oh, thank goodness you are safe!"

"Whatever happened to you?"

"We were worried half to death!"

Libby allowed them to lead her—as if she had any other choice—into the kitchen, where she spent the next forty minutes relating the events of the previous night over a hastily brewed pot of tea.

"Well, it certainly was a lucky thing that you were at the castle when the car quit like that."

Lucky, Libby agreed. Perhaps, having discovered the things she had—the thistle emblem on the gate, her mother's name etched in the window, the portrait and the woman wearing the stone—perhaps just a little fated, too?

"So tell us," Aggie said, topping off Libby's tea, "what of this Mr. Graeme Mackenzie? He's quite the village mystery, you know. Rarely comes to town or talks to anyone. Stays up there all alone, except for Flora, the police constable's sister, who works as his housekeeper. But she won't tell us a thing about him, and we've yet to even see the man ourselves."

"He's . . ." Libby paused to choose her words carefully. "He's cordial."

"And handsome, too, they say."

Libby avoided their eyes, adding cream to her tea. "Hmm? Yes, I guess you could say he's handsome."

He certainly had done that pair of Levi's justice.

"And no one knows who he is or where he comes from."

They were staring at her, obviously hoping she would reveal some juicy tidbit they could then repeat throughout the village.

But there was nothing to reveal.

Libby realized then that while they had chatted together over breakfast that morning, he had told her virtually nothing of himself.

Libby made to rise from the table.

"You're leaving?" they asked in nearly perfect unison. "But you've just gotten back."

"I think I'll have a quick bath, change, and then I've a stop to make at M'Cuick's store. Need to ask about a gadget for my computer. Can I get anything for either of you while I'm in the village?"

An hour later Libby was walking down the high street, the sisters' market list tucked in her jacket pocket.

The day had held fair, brushed with a soft, salty breeze that whispered in off the sea. As she walked, she noticed that many of the villagers were out, giving her curious glances. Undeterred by their unwillingness to talk to her the days before, Libby waved and smiled, calling out pleasant greetings to them. They returned the greetings, all the while keeping a safe distance from her, the village's newest "incomer."

Ian M'Cuick poked his head up from behind the counter, where he was sorting through boxes of screws as Libby entered the store.

"Ah, Miss Hutchinson," he said, genuinely happy to see her. " 'Tis relieved I am to see you came to no harm in the storm yestreen. 'Twas quite a fierce one, it was."

Libby smiled, nodded. "No, no harm, just a thorough

soaking from the rain—and a loose spark plug fitting. I left the car at MacNeish and Sons' garage."

"Ah, Sean MacNeish will take care of that for you straightaway." Ian looked at her over the top of his inventory sheet. "I understand you spent the night at the castle."

"Well, news certainly travels quickly."

"Och, 'tis a small village, lass. The setting of the sun is newsworthy here."

Libby picked up a small flashlight from the counter rack, the sort that attached to a keychain. Remembering the night before, she decided to buy it. "It is a beautiful place, the castle," she said, as nonchalantly as if she were discussing the weather. "Have you ever been to it?"

"Oh, aye," Ian answered. "When I was a lad, there was a ball held at the castle each winter. 'Twas tradition that the laird would host the ball and all the village would turn out. It was quite the event, looked forward to by everyone each year." He sighed. "But when the last laird died, so did the tradition of the winter ball. He was a good man, the laird. Our last Mackay laird of Wrath."

"Did you know the family, Ian?"

"Oh, aye. The Mackay and the M'Cuicks have a close tie that goes back to the eighteenth century when my ancestors worked at the castle."

"Would they be Malcolm and Kettie M'Cuick?" Libby asked. "I saw their names etched into a pane of glass in the kitchen."

Ian smiled. "My great-grandparents four times over. I'm told they met and fell in love at the castle, that he saved her life when she'd been left for dead. I remember when I was a wee laddie, I would always slip away from the laird's ball and steal to the kitchen. I could sit there and stare at that window for hours, just reading every name."

"So you must know quite a bit about the castle's history."

"Oh, aye. A bit."

He seemed willing talk to her that morning, so Libby pressed on.

"There is a portrait in the castle, Ian, that hangs just above the hall. It's of a lady"—Libby reached for the chain around her neck—"and she was wearing this."

Libby slipped the chain from beneath the collar of her sweater, pulling until the crystal emerged.

Ian blinked as his eyes locked on the stone. The surprise in his expression was genuine.

"You know this stone," she said.

"Aye, lass. I do. 'Tis Lady Isabella's stone."

"Lady Isabella Mackay?"

"Aye. She was the wife of a Mackay chieftain. 'Twas her you saw pictured in the portrait."

"Isabella is my name, too. Libby is sort of a nickname."

Ian simply looked at her. "Is it now? Hmm . . . and you're wearing Lady Isabella's stone—"

"Ian M'Cuick!"

The sudden blast of a woman's voice coming from behind her startled Libby. She turned and recognized the woman who had been at the store the first day she'd come, the same woman who'd denied knowing who her mother had been. Only this time the woman's unfriendly smile was turned upon Ian.

"Miss Hutchinson," Ian said, as if she'd just interrupted nothing more than a discussion of the weather, "have you met my dear wife of forty-seven years, Betty M'Cuick?"

The woman wore an expression that was anything but welcoming. "Hello," she said somewhat gruffly.

"Mrs. M'Cuick, it is a pleasure to see you again."

"I already told you, lass, we canna help you."

"Now, Betty—"

"But, Ian, what about—"

"*Wheesht,* woman! The lass has the stone. D'you ken

what that means? It's come back again. The stone is returned." His voice dropped softly. "She has a right to
know, Betty."

Betty looked at her husband. Her face, severe to begin
with, was pinched with worry as she beseeched her husband with her eyes.

"She has a right to know the truth," he repeated.

Finally, slowly, Betty nodded.

Ian glanced quickly at his wristwatch. " 'Tis nearly
time to close up the shop for tea. Why don't you take the
lass upstairs whilst I hang the sign and lock the door. I'll
be up directly."

Libby followed Betty up a narrow flight of back stairs
to a small parlor that was decorated in tartan woolens
and quaint little knickknacks. A fire burned sluggishly in
the hearth, and Libby took a seat on the small sofa while
Betty tossed a peat brick on the grate, poking at the embers to stoke a flame. Libby watched as she straightened,
tucking a graying strand of hair behind her kerchief.

"I'll just go and boil the water for tea."

"Can I help you?" Libby asked, but was answered
with a simple dismissive wave of Betty's hand, leaving
her to sit alone, staring at the modest walls.

Ian came into the room some five minutes later, at almost precisely the same moment that Betty returned
with the tea tray.

"Now," Ian said, his eyes lighting on the basket of
scones Betty had brought, "first, I must apologize to you
for the less-than-neighborly reception you've received
from some of the villagers." He eyed his wife. "We're
not at all an unfriendly sort. Quite the contrary. Under
other circumstances, you would have been welcomed
with open arms and the best of Scottish hospitality. Perhaps after I've said my piece, you'll understand more the
reasons why."

Libby found herself holding her breath as she waited
for him to go on.

"The stone you wear is very old," Ian began. "Older than any recordable history can be traced. 'Tis legend which tells us the stone was given to the first Mackay chief by a mermaid."

"A mermaid?" Libby said.

"Aye. She lives, they say, in *Loch na Maighdean Mhara,* across the moor from the village. Many claim to have seen her, even in recent days, sunning herself on the rocks. She is the Mackay guardian spirit, and her stone became the guardian stone of the Mackay clan. It was passed chief to son for hundreds of years. Over the ages, it has been used at various times and in various ways, for healing, as prophecy, all in preservation of the clan. There was one such occasion no less than some two hundred and sixty years ago, when a clan chieftain was mortally wounded in battle. He was on the very brink of death, they say, and the stone was dipped into the water that was used to wash the man's injuries. Miraculously, he recovered. 'Tis said he lived long enough to see his great-grandchildren running across these very hills."

Ian had the true voice of a storyteller, and Libby found herself completely caught up.

"You must have noticed sometimes that the stone seems to change, coloring like an ember or a piece of ice."

"Yes," Libby nodded, fascinated. "I thought it was my imagination."

"Well, some, mostly those skeptical of its powers, insist it is merely some sort of natural reaction of the stone. Others believe that it portends events of importance to the clan—births, times of danger, even deaths. Obviously such an instrument, if it were true, would be of great value to a Mackay enemy, and there are those who have tried to steal the stone for their own. But always the stone would return, usually following the mysterious death of its captor. But whenever it returned, it brought with it a period of great prosperity to the clan. Only once before did the stone completely vanish. The chief's heir had carried it into battle and was thought lost, the stone lost with him. The clan fell into dark times, with much strife and tragedy. Until the day a beautiful lady came to this place, carrying the missing stone with her. From then on, the stone no longer was known as the Mermaid's Stone, or even the Mackay Stone. It became known as Lady Isabella's Stone, for 'twas she who returned it. With her, the stone was no longer passed father to son"—he looked at her closely— "but was kept safe by each laird's wife."

Libby looked at him. "So you are saying the stone was missing before I brought it here with me now?"

Ian merely smiled, he didn't answer her, just then went on with the telling of his tale. "Now, Matilde Donn was a crofter's daughter, and when she came of a certain age, she took a position of employment at the Castle Wrath, working about the house, in the kitchen, above-stairs. Her favorite place, however, was the library, and she'd sneak away whenever she could to read."

Libby nodded. "My mother always loved to read."

"It would stand to reason. She had an ancestor who was a great Gaelic bard. He's buried in the old church, you know."

Libby looked at him. "Ian, who is the man in the photograph I showed to you?"

He smiled. "He is Fraser Mackay. He was the last Mackay laird's only son and heir."

"So then how did my mother come to—?" Libby looked at them both, suddenly remembering Ian's words: *no longer passed father to son . . . but was kept safely by each laird's wife.*

The laird's wife.

"Are you saying that my mother was, that she was married to this Fraser Mackay?"

Ian breathed deeply. "Matilde told me, told everyone,

they had been married. One thing is for certain. There was no doubt she had a bairn growing in her belly when she left the village some thirty years ago."

"What?" Libby looked from Ian to Betty. The woman's expression had softened, her eyes dark with compassion. She nodded slowly.

"You're saying—?"

"Aye, lass. You're the child your mother was carrying. You are the Mackay heir."

Libby went short of breath. Her chest felt tight and she blinked, trying to focus her thoughts. "But this cannot be. My father was Charles Hutchinson. I have a birth certificate with his name on it."

And then Libby remembered something, something that had seemed insignificant at the time but that now was ominously noteworthy.

Shortly after Libby had taken the position at Belvedere Books, she'd had to apply for a passport for her work, in case she might ever have to travel out of North America for a sale. She remembered she'd had to call her mother to ask her for a copy of her birth certificate, and her mother had seemed almost reluctant to send it. In the end, she'd finally said she would check with John Dugan, the family lawyer, for a copy.

Remembering that now, Libby looked down at the image of the man who smiled out from the photograph, looked at him as if it was the first time she'd ever seen him. And suddenly she knew why he'd looked so familiar to her.

It was his eyes.

They were the same eyes she had seen staring back in the mirror all her life.

She looked at Ian. "Where can I find him? Where can I find this Fraser Mackay?"

"I'm afraid you cannot, lass. Young Fraser's parents, the old laird and lady, were unaware of their son's relationship with Matilde. Given the fact that she was one of their housemaids, they wouldna likely have welcomed the news. Most certainly Fraser's mother, Lady Venetia, wouldna have welcomed it. Lady Venetia was a proud woman. The laird had met her while on the Continent, and her father was some sort of Dutch count. She had very definite ideas about bringing the Mackay lineage to a distinction that would rival that of the other great Scottish families. Knowing this, Fraser convinced your mother to marry him without first telling either of their families. I'm sure he thought that once the deed was done, his parents would have to welcome their new daughter-in-law and their expected grandchild. But in the end, it didn't matter. Lady Venetia simply refused to acknowledge the marriage.

"According to another of the housemaids"—Ian glanced at his wife—"in fact it was my Betty here, it was a most terrible scene. Fraser suggested Matilde return to her parents to allow him to talk to his family alone. He hoped he could convince them to accept her. It was the last time anyone ever saw him."

"What do you mean?" Libby blinked, trying to understand. "What happened to him?"

"It was reported that they'd apparently gone sailing out by one of the isles off the kyle. There was a storm. The boat capsized. The laird and Lady Venetia, they were rescued from the sea by a pair of passing fishermen. Young Fraser, however . . ."

"He drowned?"

"It is a powerful stretch of sea, and many a sailing craft has met her demise upon its unforgiving current. His body was recovered over a fortnight later, washed up on one of the nearby beaches. In any case, it left your mother, and her family, in a terrible predicament. They were tenants of the Wrath estate, as we all are here in the village. Out of anger for their loss, the laird and Lady Mackay evicted your mother's family from their farm and then burned the place to the very ground so they could never return. Anyone who was found to help them, even if they so much as sheltered them for a night, they, too, would be evicted from their homes. Your mother and her family, they had no choice but to leave. That is why no one in the village would speak to you of your mother, lass. Because those who were here then remember well those dark times, and even now, some three decades later, there is still the terrible fear."

The fear of Lady Venetia Mackay's wrath.

Because of the five-hour time difference between the United Kingdom and the States, Libby had to wait until later that afternoon to place a call to John Dugan.

Lunch had been ready and waiting at the Crofter's Cottage when Libby had returned from the village. Libby had tried to remind the two sisters that they ran a bed-and-breakfast, not a bed-and-breakfast-lunch-and-dinner, but they just couldn't seem to help themselves. They set out a place for her at every meal, inquired as to whether she liked various dishes, planned their meals around her. And the baking! Fresh batches of shortbreads, scones, and biscuits appeared daily. It was like having two identical doting grandmothers at once.

As she sat there surrounded by a spread of cold-cut sandwiches, salad, crisps, sliced peaches, and shortbread still warm from the oven, the two sisters must have sensed that Libby's thoughts were elsewhere. They didn't pry, just offered her a dish piled high with portions of each of the aforementioned items and a seemingly bottomless pot of tea as they chatted about the latest village gossip—the upcoming whist tournament at the Village Hall and old Hugh Mackay's goat, who had apparently roamed over to the neighboring croft and eaten Farmer Bain's wife's knickers, which had been out drying on a clothesline.

"Well, at least the beast got a substantial meal out of

them," Maggie chirped. "He'd have starved if he'd tried that over at Bessie MacNeil's cottage."

"That skinny thing? She's a walking stick, she is!" Aggie dissolved into a spell of giggling so girlish it belied her graying hair. "'Tis like comparing a smorgasbord to little more than a dry biscuit!"

Normally Libby would have enjoyed listening to them, the cadence of their voices and their wry, lyric mirth. But her attention kept drifting to the clock on the wall and the absolute slothfulness with which it was ticking.

Finally, at precisely two o'clock, Libby stood and took her dishes to the kitchen.

"Would you mind if I used the phone?" she asked as the sisters set to work at the kitchen sink.

"Of course not, dear. Calling the car hire company again?"

"No. I need to make a call to the States."

"Oh, no trouble. It is just there, on the wall."

"Actually," Libby said, eying the phone, "it's sort of a private call."

"Oh." Aggie looked at her as if she just couldn't fathom such a thing as a need for privacy.

Maggie, who wore a mint-green apron to protect her mint-green dress from the dishwashing suds, jumped to attention. "There's another phone, in the office where we keep all the business records. You can close the door so the kitchen noise won't disturb you."

Libby nodded and smiled in appreciation. "Thank you."

The "office" was little more than a closet, large enough to just fit the antique writing desk and chair she found inside with the shelves of papers, books, and supplies that hung above it. There was no window, and in fact, she had to lean back against the desk in order just to close the door. Dropping into the seat, Libby took up the phone and started punching in the overseas exchange.

After a slight delay, she heard the phone on the other end of the line begin to ring.

"Good morning. John Dugan's office, Kathleen Spencer-Brown speaking. May I assist you?"

Kathleen Spencer? Libby had gone to school with her, although they'd moved in completely different social circles. Kathleen had been with the teased-hair, Madonna-ite navel-showing, Daddy-bought-a-brand-new-car-on-her-sixteenth-birthday set. She'd spent the whole of their high school years lip-locked to Jimmy Brown, team quarterback and unquestionable hunk. Obviously, from the name she'd just given, she had managed to keep him lip-locked long enough to get him to the altar.

"John Dugan, please," Libby asked, in no mood for revisiting high school memories.

"May I ask who's calling, please?"

Damn.

"Isabella Hutchinson," she replied, purposely trying to disguise herself with the first name she'd never used in school.

"I'm sorry, Miss . . . Libby? Libby Hutchinson? Is that you?"

Damn, damn, damn.

"Yes. Hi, Kathleen. I wondered if that was you. How are you?"

"Oh, fine. Busy, busy, busy. I'm working part-time here now that the kids are in school. Mr. Dugan was willing to let me off at three each day so I could be home in time to meet the school bus. You know how that is . . ."

Libby could almost hear the thoughts cranking through Kathleen's brain as she realized that Libby, after the very public wedding fiasco of six months ago, and still obviously using her maiden name, probably didn't know how it was to have to meet the local school bus at all. "Yes, well, may I speak with Mr. Dugan, please?"

"I'm sorry, Lib. He's not in at the moment."

Lib?

She tightened her jaw. She could not wait for him to call her back.

"Look, Kathleen, I had that same job the summer after high school, so I know perfectly well that he is in. In fact he's sitting in his office, at his desk, with his cup of coffee on a coaster to his right, a half-eaten jelly donut on his left, and the morning edition of the *Globe* open before him. Isn't he?"

There was a pause. Kathleen obviously didn't know what to say.

"I am out of the country, and I only have a very small window of opportunity where our time zones are compatible. This is that window, Kathleen. Right now. I need to speak with him urgently."

A heavy sigh. "Hold on."

Kathleen, she could tell, was not pleased, but she left Libby to listen to the strains of Elvis's "Heartbreak Hotel" on Muzak as she waited. Dugan always had loved the oldies. She even found herself softly humming along when, a moment later, she heard the line pick up again.

"Hello, Isabella."

John Dugan, Ipswich-by-the-Sea's most notable attorney-at-law was the only one, other than her mother, who had ever called her by her full first name. Even sitting as she was an ocean away, Libby could picture him clearly, in his dusty office with stacks of paperwork and lawbooks piled fort-like around him. His thin, graying hair would be combed over the balding spot he tried so hard to hide, and his tie would be crooked even though he'd only just started the day. There would be a dusting of powdered sugar on his lapel from the donut he was having for breakfast, and his fingers would be smudged from the ink of his morning paper. When she'd worked for him, Libby had spent most of her workday fighting a never-ending battle to tidy up behind him. She rather doubted that Kathleen Spencer-Brown would demean herself to follow suit.

"Hello, Mr. Dugan."

"Kathleen said you were calling from overseas. Still in the U.K.?"

All the words she'd prepared to say to him suddenly took flight, leaving her mind as blank as a plank.

"Isabella? Is something wrong?"

She closed her eyes and said merely, "I know the truth."

His responding silence confirmed for her that he, too, knew.

She heard him say, "Kathleen, would you please close the door?" He said to her a moment later, "I wondered when you'd call."

She didn't answer him. Instead she tightened her fingers around the receiver and said in a voice that betrayed her tumbling emotions, "Why didn't you tell me?"

Chapter Nine

"Why didn't you tell me?"

With those words, the tears that Libby had spent the past several hours holding in check came flooding forward. She bit her bottom lip, squeezing her eyes to try to stop them from coming. Her breathing hitched. She swallowed hard.

"I couldn't tell you, Libby. It was your mother's wish. She wanted you to go to Scotland, to learn everything for yourself."

"But I don't understand. What am I supposed to be learning? My father is Charles Hutchinson. It says so on my birth certificate. I have a copy of it with me right here."

"That is an amended birth certificate. It was changed after you were legally adopted by him when you were an infant." He paused. "I do not know everything, only what Matilde told me when she and your father first came to my office to seek the adoption. But one thing I do know, Libby, is that Charles Hutchinson was your father in most every possible way. He provided for you and your mother. He raised you. He watched over you. He loved you for nearly the whole of your life. The only thing he didn't do was play a part in your conception."

Libby sniffed, struggling to gather her emotions. He gave her a moment.

"Libby, what have you learned about your mother's life in Scotland?"

"I know that she worked at the Mackay castle. She met and fell in love with the son of the laird. His name was Fraser Mackay. Presumably she found herself pregnant, and they married secretly. But his family wouldn't accept her. They didn't think that she, a housemaid, was good enough to be the wife of the laird. Fraser thought to convince them, but then something happened. There was an accident. He drowned. My mother and her family were evicted from their home by the laird. That is all I know. I don't know where they went, or how my mother came to live in America."

Dugan supplied the rest. "Your mother was a widow, pregnant, and penniless when she left the village. She went with her parents to Glasgow, where she met Charles Hutchinson. He was an American professor working at university there for the summer and she had gotten work at the library. He'd asked her to help him with some research. By the end of that summer, he'd convinced her to marry him and return with him to the States so he could provide for her, and be a father to you."

"But she left her parents, her family, behind. Why did she never come back, even once, to visit them?"

"She was frightened, Libby. Frightened for you."

"For me? Why?"

"The Mackays were a powerful family then. She was afraid if the laird and Lady Mackay discovered where she was, who you were, they would come after you, claim custody in Fraser's name, and she would never see you again. Without Fraser, they had no heir. Matilde asked me to make inquiries every so often after the welfare of her family. Her parents, having lived all their lives in the Highland air, didn't fare well in the city tenements in Glasgow. They didn't last very long after she left." Dugan exhaled slowly. "I'm sorry, Isabella. I couldn't tell you this earlier. Your mother would permit me to reveal it to you only after you had gone there—and after she had passed away."

Libby dropped her head, leaning against the receiver she held to her ear. "I just don't understand why she never told me. We shared everything. At least I thought it was everything."

She fell silent as she fought to absorb it all.

So much. So very much. It overwhelmed her to the point that she wondered if she could still breathe. It seemed as if everything she had ever known in her life was gone, swept away like images on a chalkboard, leaving her now with an empty, dusty slate.

And then Ian M'Cuick's words echoed through her thoughts.

You're the Mackay heir . . .

The heir.

"Libby, what will you do now? Will you come home?"

She lifted her head, taking a deep breath. "I'm not certain just yet."

"Well, be sure to stop by the office when you get back. We've some things to discuss, about the house—"

"Dugan?"

"Hmm?"

"I wonder if you would help me with something."

A half hour later, Libby hung up the phone feeling slightly better than she had upon picking it up.

By the end of that phone call she had managed to come to some semblance of acceptance with the truth of her paternity. It didn't change anything she felt about the father she had known, about the memory of the childhood he'd given her. Charles Hutchinson would al-ways—*always*—be her father. And she could almost come to terms with her mother's reasons for keeping it from her, although it made her feel as if she hadn't really known her mother at all.

But she was here, in Scotland, in the village. And so, she would get to know her. She would get to know her mother, and the man who had been her father, through the place, the village where they had been born, where they'd grown up.

And where they had fallen in love.

"Excuse me, sir?"

Graeme looked up from the drawing table he'd been bent over for most of the day. He blinked, pressing his fingers against his tired eyes as he turned. The house-keeper, Flora Something, he could never seem to re-member her last name, stood hovering in his office doorway.

"I've left your supper on the stove, and I've finished up all the other things needed done, so I'm goin' to head home for the e'ening, aye?"

Graeme glanced at the clock. Five o'clock. He knew she had a family of her own to see to in the village, chil-dren who were no doubt waiting for their supper and missing their mother. "Yes, that's fine, Flora. Thank you."

"The stew is simmering, so you can hae it whene'er you're ready to eat. There's fresh scones in the warmer, too."

"Thank you. I'll see you in the morning, then."

The woman nodded as she backed out of the room.

Graeme remained in the office until he'd heard her close the front door behind her, watching out the win-dow as she disappeared down the footpath that led to her cottage on the outskirts of the village.

He'd hired Flora for just that reason. She lived close enough to walk to her home, and she had a family of her own to tend to, thereby doing away with any notion that she would live at the castle. She was also the sister of

Angus MacLeith, the village constable, a widow who could use the money he paid her and who wouldn't be prone to gossiping. The arrangement had worked out perfectly. Most of the time Graeme could fend for himself. He needed someone only to help out with the housekeeping, the laundry, and cooking. Breakfast the other morning had proved he was pretty hopeless when it came to the kitchen.

As had happened more than once in the past couple of days, thoughts of that breakfast brought thoughts of the young woman who had spent the night curled up on his sofa. Much as he didn't care to admit it, he'd been disappointed to see her leave so early that day. He'd enjoyed having her company that morning, the lively and interesting conversation. And the sight of her wearing his sweater, her dark hair tousled from sleep around a particularly fresh and lovely face, certainly hadn't been any hardship either.

He just didn't know what to make of her.

Having spent months as the Most Hunted Bachelor on British Soil, Graeme had become adept at recognizing the usual indicators—the coy smiles and knowing glances, the calculated attempts at seduction. Libby Hutchinson, however, had shown none of these signs even though she'd had plenty of opportunity.

When they had been alone, she hadn't so much as tried to charm him, flirt with him, or climb into bed with him. Instead she'd preferred curling up with an old book on the sofa after raiding his freezer for the Häagen-Dazs.

Graeme turned from his drawing table and walked the hallway to the back stairs. When he reached the bottom, the kitchen yawned before him, empty and silent. A single plate, a fork, and a knife sat upon the butcher's block waiting for him.

For him alone.

The idea of sitting in that vast dining room, alone at one end of that vast, elegant table, held no particular appeal, so instead Graeme clicked on the television that sat on the kitchen counter just as the BBC News came on.

He put on the kettle for tea, listening with half an ear to the day's top stories. He was hunched before a cupboard looking through the tea rack when the familiar sound of his mother's voice came trilling from the television set.

He looked up, not at all surprised to see her standing before Westminster Hall, graciously debating the most recent round of reforms in the House of Lords. She was, after all, one of the only ninety-two hereditary peers who had managed to keep their seats in the recently reformed House and one of the sparse few women who populated that great hall. A peeress in her own right and an indefatigable campaigner against such things as genetically modified crops and inequities in the public health service, Gemma Mackenzie, Countess of Abermuir, took her place in the churning machine of British politics very seriously.

It was a role he would one day find himself playing as well, for despite the fact that his love had always been— would always be—architecture, politics were a tradition on both sides of his family, and a tradition that must endure at all costs.

Graeme stood for a moment and watched his mother. It was impossible not to be impressed by her. Despite the fact that she'd exceeded her sixtieth birthday, she possessed a timeless beauty and elegance that only grew more perceptible the older she got. A creamy set of pearls draped a graceful neck that in her younger days had been likened to that of a swan. Dark hair, modestly touched with gray, was perfectly coiffed in a neat French twist.

She'd married his father, a younger son of the Duke of Gransborough, after a long and steady courtship that had played out in the society pages. It was a brilliant match, a mix of his prestigious lineage and her unfettered political aspirations. Gemma Mackenzie was the only child and heir of the Earl of Abermuir, a title that quite fortunately could be passed through the female line in absence of a male heir. The only stipulation was that whoever the future countess married would need to take the Mackenzie name.

It hadn't been any issue for Graeme's father, Maxwell Gransworth. As the youngest of three sons to his father, the duke, his chances of inheriting were next to nil. When asked, he admitted he rather liked the sound of "Maxwell Mackenzie"—made him sound rather like a Scottish James Bond, he'd say. They'd married in London's St. Paul's Cathedral in a ceremony that had been attended by the queen. A year later, they'd heralded the arrival of his brother, Thaddeus, or Teddy for short.

Three years after that, they'd had Graeme.

Graeme had been nine years old when his mother's father, the Old Earl, as they'd called him, had died. She'd become a countess and had dived into the political pool seemingly overnight. She'd been at it nonstop ever since.

"So, Lady Abermuir, on a lighter note . . ." asked the reporter, "how about answering the question currently pressing on the minds of countless hopeful young single women all across Britain? Just where is your son, Lord Waltham, hiding himself these days?"

Graeme frowned at the smirking reporter on the screen, awaiting his mother's response.

Consummate professional that she was, she scarcely batted an eye. "He is in hiding, you say?" She laughed. "How can that be, sir, when I speak to my son nearly every day?"

And with that, she nodded her head, smiled, and said a parting thank-you, leaving the interviewer little opportunity to pursue the line of questioning any further.

Brava, Mother.

Graeme switched off the television. It was then that he

heard a distant knocking coming from the front of the house.

Now what?

Still stung by the television reporter's snooping, he yanked the front door open and, without even looking to see who awaited on the other side, barked, "What?"

Libby Hutchinson stood there, looking at him uncertainly. "I, uh . . . I was just bringing back your things."

She held out the sweater and pants he had loaned her.

He simply stared at her.

"They're—" She hesitated, blinked. "They're freshly washed."

"Yes, well, thank you," he managed. At her wounded expression, he shook off the dark mood that the television news had given him. "My apologies. That was unforgivably rude. It's been—" He shook his head. "It's been rather a long day."

She looked at him.

There came a whistling noise from the back of the house.

The tea kettle.

Graeme turned, looked back. "Say, I have a pot of stew and some fresh scones for supper. Would you . . ." He hesitated just a moment, and then threw caution to the wind. "Would you like to stay for dinner?"

She smiled, nodded. "Yes, sure. That would be nice."

Libby closed the front door and hung her jacket on the hook as Graeme hurried back to the kitchen to check the insistent whistling. She came in just as he was grabbing the wheezing kettle and shutting off the fire. She noticed the lone plate sitting on the butcher block, the single set of utensils. It was a sight she'd seen so many times in her own apartment back in New York.

She'd spent the day wandering around the village, and then had asked Ian if he could direct her to the place where her mother's family had once lived and farmed. He'd shown it to her on the map, and she'd gone, although all that remained was the blackened rubble of what had once been a family's home. It had left her feeling more miserable than she could have ever imagined. Without even realizing it, she'd found herself taking the turn toward the castle, having no real reason for doing so.

"Have any wine?" she asked.

He looked at her. "With stew?"

"Sure." She went to the wine rack. "It's a versatile dish. Goes with either red or white."

She wasn't much of a wine connoisseur, but her employer, Mr. Belvedere, certainly was. She recognized one of his particular favorites among the bottles in the rack, an Australian Shiraz. She grabbed it and two of the wine goblets hanging from the cabinet above her head.

"If you'll do the honors with the wine, I'll dish out the stew."

Graham took the bottle and glasses and headed for the dining room.

When Libby came in a few minutes later, he had opened the wine and poured them each a glass. The lighting in the room was low, intimate, provided by the dimmed chandelier that hung glittering above the table. Libby set a plate near each glass, then quickly went back to the kitchen to retrieve the basket of scones.

She smiled at Graeme as she took the seat beside him and picked up her goblet. "Here's to . . ." She searched for an appropriate or witty toast to make, but could think of nothing either appropriate or witty. So she shrugged. "Here's to stew and scones."

"Indeed," Graeme agreed, and raised his glass before taking a sip.

"Good choice," he said, setting his goblet on the table.

Libby stirred her stew with her fork, took a bite. "You certainly make a fine stew, Mr. Mackenzie."

"I'm afraid I can't take the credit for it. It is my

housekeeper's doing. As you saw from breakfast, I'm pretty hopeless in the kitchen."

They passed the first few minutes of the meal exchanging pleasantries and casual conversation about the weather and the current state of affairs in the world. She asked him which team he supported in soccer (football, he'd corrected), Scotland or England. He asked her whether she went for the Yankees or the Mets.

"The Yankees!" she said, as if the answer should be obvious. "Although I probably shouldn't admit that, coming as I do from Boston."

He poured her another glass of wine.

"So," he said, "what do you do for a living back in the States?"

The wine had melted away much of the tension of his day, and the ease with which he found he could talk to her had Graeme delving into more personal, previously avoided conversation.

"I acquire books for an antiquarian bookseller in Manhattan."

"Indeed?" He didn't know why he should be surprised. The occupation suited her perfectly. "Is that what brings you to Scotland? A rare-book-buying mission?"

She smiled. "No. Actually, I'm here for more personal reasons."

He sipped his wine, waited for her to go on.

"My mother was born and raised here in the village."

"Oh, did she come along with you?"

Libby shook her head, dropping her gaze to her hands. "She passed away last month."

Having suffered the loss of his own family so recently, Graeme recognized the rawness of her grief.

"I'm very sorry." He shook his head. "It's never easy. I lost both my brother and my father in the past year, as well as a cousin."

Why had he just told her that?

She reached a hand to his, covered it. That simple gesture touched him more deeply than he'd been touched in a long, long time. Graeme soon found himself telling her the story of it, needing to tell her, needing to purge himself of the sheer weight of it. All the while he spoke, she kept her fingers wrapped closely around his.

"I just wish I could have had one last chance to talk to my mother, you know?" she said later. "To ask her the questions I was always too busy or too afraid to ask her, to tell her the things I always thought I'd have time to say."

Graeme knew exactly what she meant.

After the meal, Graeme steamed a couple of lattés, and they took them into the drawing room by the fire. Night had fallen, and the room was awash in the hearth's glow, inviting, enticing.

"So this is a Hob Nob," Libby said as she sampled the chocolate-dipped cookie. "These are almost as good as the Girl Scouts' Thin Mints back home in the States. I defy anyone to eat less than a full sleeve of them in one sitting."

"Well, I'll have to try them sometime."

They were sitting on the floor by the fire, Graeme leaning back against the sofa and she sitting cross-legged on the rug. Murphy had his head resting lazily on her lap, and for a brief moment, as he watched her softly stroking her fingers over him, Graeme was envious of the dog.

The firelight was dancing across her face, shimmering in her dark hair. He watched her take a sip of her coffee, close her eyes, and let go a soft breath. When she opened her eyes again, they met his, and locked there.

Opportunity had presented itself. All he had to do was lean toward her, and kiss her. He knew she would let him. He knew she wanted him to kiss her as much as he wanted to kiss her himself. All he had to do was make one move, one gesture . . .

But the instincts of suspicion and distrust he'd perfected so well won out so he got up instead and picked up the empty coffee cups for the kitchen.

"Well, it's getting late . . ."

The shadow of disappointment that came over her face wasn't lost on him. "Oh . . ."

As Graeme walked to the door, he'd never before felt so conflicted. For so many months, everyone he'd encountered, most assuredly every woman he'd encountered, had been out for only one thing. He'd been distrusting for so long, he wondered if he even knew any more what it was to trust at all.

Chapter Ten

Libby spent the next few days out walking the village proper, taking photographs, visiting historical sites, stopping to talk to most everyone she encountered, while in the evenings, she continued her work of cataloging the parish archives on her laptop.

She still hadn't found a record of her mother's marriage to Fraser Mackay, but now that she knew the truth, she didn't press any of the villagers who might have known them further. Lady Venetia Mackay was still their landlord, and knowing the difficulty of their position, Libby kept her conversations with them focused on the village, its history and its daily life. The change in the villagers was remarkable. As Ian had assured her, once they realized she wouldn't put them at risk, they quickly began to open up and show her the kindliness and hospitality that had been the trademark of the Highlands for centuries.

No one had done a more notable turnabout than Betty M'Cuick.

"Och, your mother had a wicked sense of humor, she did," Betty said to Libby as they sat together in the M'Cuicks's parlor one afternoon. Ever since that first day when Ian had revealed the truth to her, Betty had been regaling Libby with memories of Matilde. She even seemed relieved to be able to talk about her friend after holding her silence for so many years.

"When I'd be cleaning the loos at the castle, she'd leave a toy mouse behind the toilet. Once she even put a rubber snake in the bowl! Always getting me into trouble, that one. And she knew I'm terrible frighted of the ghaists—"

"Ghaists?"

"Spirits . . . presences . . ."

"Oh, ghosts . . ."

"Aye, ghaists. That castle is full of them, you know. Your mother'd sometimes slip herself underneath the beds and when I was tucking in the sheets, she'd push the mattresses from underneath and scare me half to death."

It was a side of Matilde that Libby had never even glimpsed—playful, a young, gregarious, carefree girl.

"Then there were the times she and Fraser would want to sneak off to be alone. Once they were"—Betty looked at Libby, her face reddening—"ehm, they were *together* in the stables, and Lady Venetia took it into her head to have an afternoon ride about the estate. I was out hanging up the wash and spotted her just as she was entering the stables. She must've thought me a lunatic, the Lady Mackay. There I was hollerin' and wavin' my arms with the bedsheet flappin' like a ghaist m'self. The lady came running to see what the clamor was about, and all I could think to say was that I'd been frighted by a wasp. Lady Venetia wasna too happy wit' me, but your mother and Fraser, they managed to slip out of the stables afore she could discover them."

Libby didn't know what shocked her more, that her mother had been so daring and reckless or that she herself had possibly been conceived in a stable loft.

"I wish I had known her then," she said wistfully. "She must have been beautiful."

"Aye, she was a bonny lass, all that blond hair.

Looked like Grace Kelly we used to say . . . Och!" Betty sat up suddenly. "Why dinna I think of it sooner?"

She went to a standing cabinet in the corner of the room, fished through a drawer, and came back a few moments later with a small black-and-white photograph.

She handed it to Libby. "This was taken by the young laird that last summer afore . . ."

Before her mother had been banished from the village, and the only home she'd ever known, Libby couldn't help but think.

But the photograph showed a happier time. There were two women pictured, dressed in starched black-and-white maids' uniforms, arms linked, standing barefoot on a beach. Matilde and the other woman, obviously Betty, were hiking up their skirts above their knees, striking a chorus-girl pose for the camera. Libby knew her mother immediately. Though she was thinner, and her hair was bound behind a white head scarf, her eyes and her subtle smile were virtually the same. But there was a difference. This Matilde was young. She was bold and she was sassy. And from the way she was glancing at the person taking the photo, she was quite obviously head over heels in love.

Libby made to hand the photo back to Betty.

"Nae, 'tis yours to keep, lass," she said softly, reading the emotions that brimmed in Libby's eyes. "'Tis the least I can do."

"Thank you," Libby said, and hugged the woman who had been her mother's friend. "Thank you for everything."

From Betty, Libby was slowly coming to know Matilde in a time that had almost been lost to history. From her visits with the other villagers, she began to learn more about the village itself.

Over tea with Elspeth MacNeish (whose husband, Sean, had repaired the loose spark plug in her car), Libby learned that the village was a relatively new one—new in that it had been founded around 1750 instead of centuries earlier like many of the surrounding settlements. It had been Lady Isabella Mackay and her clan chieftain husband, Calum, who had encouraged the settlement of Wrath, providing land for those who had worked on the refurbishment of the castle, encouraging them to farm and fish and set down roots at a time when many of the other Highland estate owners were pulling out their people and discarding them like weeds.

Another villager, Alexander "Sandy" Mackay, told Libby of Calum and Isabella's marriage—and the twelve resultant children. Amazingly for that time in history, all twelve survived into adulthood, and most of them settled at various places about the vast Mackay estate. Sandy knew the complete lineages of every one of them, as well as those of their many descendants who still lived in the area. Though she may have been an only child all her life, Libby suddenly found she had Mackay cousins aplenty, Sandy himself among them.

It was a wet and rainy late October evening when the call from James Dugan rang in at the Crofter's Cottage. Libby took the call in the office, leaving Aggie and Maggie in the midst of a rather heated hand of whist.

"Isabella, I've checked into the things you asked me about. And I have some news."

Libby took a breath, waiting. "Yes?"

"Okay, it seems the Mackay estate, like many of the other Highland estates, was put into a trust thirty years ago to protect it from what would be a crippling battery of taxes on the death of the old laird. It was a formality, really, as there was no known heir, but because the laird and Lady Venetia never had Fraser officially declared dead, it was all quite legal. The way in which the trust was written, however, is particularly interesting."

"Oh?"

"I don't quite know how to tell you this, but if your

mother truly married Fraser Mackay, and you can prove it, then you, not Lady Venetia, are the rightful landlord of the estate."

Libby blinked. "You're sure?"

"It certainly seems so. It is because you were born to the estate, and not married into it, that you would take precedence."

Libby was quickly getting confused in the flood of legalities. "So what does this all mean, Dugan?"

"I'm not sure exactly—" She heard him shuffling through some papers. "Libby, I have a colleague, a solicitor in Edinburgh, who would know far more about the Scottish property and inheritance laws than I do. I think you should contact him. It was he who researched all this information for me. I told him your situation, and he seemed very interested in speaking with you directly."

Libby quickly scribbled down the solicitor's direction before thanking Dugan and bidding him good-bye.

She sat for a moment, trying to gather her thoughts. She'd asked Dugan to check into the details of the Wrath estate only for research, to confirm what Ian M'Cuick had implied when he'd told her she was the Mackay heir and to find out what that might mean once Lady Venetia passed on.

But this? She stared at the scrap of paper with the solicitor's name scribbled across it, trying to decide. The hour was late. The man probably wasn't in his office. She wasn't even certain she wanted to pursue this any further. Perhaps she could just leave a message on an answering machine and let the rest be decided by fate.

She picked up the receiver and punched the numbers before she could talk herself out of it.

The line picked up on the second ring.

"Hamish Brodie."

Libby opened her mouth, but no sound came out. She

had been so certain he wouldn't be there, she hadn't even thought of what she would say if he were.

"Hallo? Is anybody there?"

"Yes," she managed. "Hello. Mr. Brodie. My name is Li—, my name is Isabella Hutchinson. James Dugan said I should contact you."

His voice boomed a welcome from the phone. "Good evening, Miss Hutchinson! Jimmy said you might be calling. I'm so pleased that you did."

"I don't quite know why I have, sir. I'm not at all certain what any of this means. I guess I'm just hoping to find out the truth."

"I understand. Say, this is quite a bundle of biscuits to go over by phone. By odd coincidence, I happen to be traveling to Inverness tomorrow on another case. I'll be in court up there most of the day, but is there any possibility you might be willing to meet with me for dinner? I know this brilliant little Italian place right by the river . . ."

Sounded harmless enough. "What time?"

"Say, about seven?"

Libby quickly jotted the time across the Post-it note on which she'd written his name and number. "What is the name of the restaurant?"

"Oh, right," he chuckled. "Might help for me to tell you that, aye? It's Antonio's on Church Street just across from the river. You can't miss it."

The pen hovered just above the note as a shiver chased along Libby's shoulders. Antonio's had been the name of her and her mother's favorite restaurant in Boston. It was the only place they ever went for dinner when they went into the city. Of course, some would say there must be thousands of Italian restaurants called Antonio's scattered across the globe. Still Libby couldn't help but wonder if this odd coincidence was no coincidence at all, but instead some sort of indication from her mother telling her she was doing the right thing.

"Seven it is, Mr. Brodie. I'll see you then."

When she came back into the parlor, Libby found Aggie and Maggie still sitting in the parlor, their cards fanned out in front of them, twin sets of eyes trained inquisitively upon her. The theme song for their favorite television show, *The East Enders,* was just chiming in from the small set that stood in the corner of the room.

"I'll be going to Inverness tomorrow," she announced.

"Indeed?" Aggie said, hoping to inquire without having it seem she was inquiring. "Ehm . . . to do with the car hire company, dear?"

"No. Everything seems to be fine with the car since Sean MacNeish looked at it. I'm just going for some sight-seeing and dinner with the friend of a friend."

"Oh, how lovely, dear," said Maggie. Libby could see Aggie trying to get a peek at her sister's cards. Maggie noticed it and lifted her hand out of eyeshot, shooting her twin a warning glare.

"I was thinking I'd go down early in the morning, take in some of the city's sights, perhaps do a little shopping. I don't seem to have brought a sufficient number of warm clothes for the climate here. Is there anything I can pick up for either of you while I'm there?"

Within twenty minutes, Libby had an itemized list with everything from artichokes to a seven-inch zipper, preferably mint green.

At dawn, Libby got up from her bed, dressed quietly in the near darkness, and slipped out before either of the sisters was awake. She took a scone from the basket and quickly brewed a thermos of tea, and was on the road for Inverness before seven.

The drive across the Highlands this time was comparatively more pleasant than that first, middle-of-the-night jaunt she'd taken upon arriving. The dawn crept slowly

across the morning sky, shining on a clear day blessed
with brilliant, glorious sunshine.

The Highlands in this, the far north, were the wildest,
most beautiful, and most unspoiled landscape Libby had
ever seen. Stark, staggering mountain faces, touched
white with snow at the peaks, loomed like ancient
guardians above dark lochs and peaceful rolling glens.
She passed the ruins of ancient brochs where prehistoric
man had once lived and crumbling castles where herds
of red deer roamed as free and as wild as the clansmen
who had once roamed there. Eagles soared overhead,
swooping low over the high pine tops in search of their
prey. Shaggy orange cattle and wooly sheep grazed
lazily on rolling pastures until the farmer's collie came
barking and leaping to direct them to another field.

Libby was glad to have the day away from the village,
for it gave her the chance to think, to think about the
thing she'd been avoiding the past few days.

Graeme Mackenzie.

More than once since that night she'd shared the stew
dinner with him, she'd almost taken the left instead of
the right turn on the road from the Crofter's Cottage,
heading to the castle. She'd invented a handful of ex-
cuses—she'd left her favorite pen there, she thought he
might like some of the sisters' shortbread—all of them
devised to hide the true reason, which was, quite simply
that she wanted to see him again.

It was the first time in a long time that she had wanted
to see anyone. Though she'd gone out with casual acquaintances, Libby really hadn't allowed herself to
"date" anyone since Jeff. She'd sworn she would never
risk her heart again. It hadn't been a difficult promise to
keep. While most of the men she'd met had been perfectly interesting, none of them had sparked even the
slightest feeling that would have led Libby to pursuing a
further relationship. In fact she'd become so skilled at

closing off her heart, she'd begun to think she'd locked it permanently.

Until Graeme.

When they'd been sitting before the fire that night sharing latté and conversation, Libby had thought that he might actually kiss her. God knows she'd wanted him to. She'd wanted him to kiss her so badly her blood had practically sung with it. Even as she'd been sitting there, staring at him in the firelight, she'd imagined him leaning toward her, could almost feel the heat of his hands as he took her shoulders and pulled her toward him.

Just the thought of it had left her pulse pounding and her insides twitching with need. And she had sensed that he'd wanted it, too. It had shone in the dark of his eyes, in the deepness of his heated stare. But then he'd ended that moment, ending it so abruptly it had left her dazed.

Had she imagined it, that spark, that awareness between them that had been so tangible, so real, it had rivaled the heat of the fire? She had to believe that he'd felt it, too. Why, then, had he done such an about-face at the very moment when they could have been exploring the attraction between them?

And they said women were complicated creatures.

Libby had taken her time in driving and reached the bridge that spanned the firth outside Inverness just after ten that morning. Following her trusty road atlas, she directed the car through a series of roundabouts and turning, winding streets, as she headed for the center of the town.

Inverness, she'd read earlier in her guidebook, was known as the Capital of the Highlands, tucked as it was nearly perfectly between east and west, far north and south. The River Ness, which fed off of the same firth she'd crossed upon arriving, meandered through the city center all the way to the loch of the same name, the very one where the famous "Nessie" was reputed to live.

In the middle of the town, tall church spires pointed to the sky, and old stone buildings pressed in on the narrow streets like crowding parade bystanders. As she approached the city center, a proliferation of tiny shops and restaurants began to line the streets on either side. It was a pleasant day, and streams of pedestrians were strolling along the sidewalks, shopping bags in hand. She found a parking lot as close to the restaurant as possible, and pulled into the nearest space. Shopping list in hand, she set off for a walk through the town.

Her first stop was the woolen shop, where she bought three thick Aran-style sweaters in various colors, with turtlenecks to wear underneath them, and a tartan lamb's-wool wrap just because it had been cut from the Mackay tartan. At an outdoor shop, she exchanged her L.L.Bean duck shoes for a more comfortable pair of waterproof ankle boots, and bought a waterproof, insulated jacket called an anorak. Oh, and something the sales clerk assured her were a veritable necessity for the Highlands—a pair of knee-high rubber boots called Wellingtons. Anything waterproof, Libby quickly learned, was a true Highland necessity.

After leaving the shopping bags in the car, Libby set off to gather the items on the sisters' shopping list. There was the grocers', the chemists', and a shop they'd specifically requested that sold their favorite brand of knitting yarn. A tea shop, the picture framers', and then finally, the sewing shop. By the time she found the seven-inch mint-green zipper, it was nearly five o'clock. The daylight was waning, and most of the stores were closing for the day, but Libby still had two hours before she was to meet Mr. Brodie. She asked the shopkeeper at the sewing store if there was any place she might go to sit for a cup of coffee and some quiet time.

"Oh, that would be Leakey's," the lady replied with a

smile. "Just around the corner on Church Street. They've a café and those big overstuffed chairs, and as luck would have it, they have extended hours tonight, till eight."

Libby had expected a coffee bar, like the Starbucks back in New York. What she found, however, was a small billboard sign with the name Leakey's written in colored chalk, standing on the sidewalk outside what appeared to be an old church. The scent of brewing coffee lured her inside the arched doorway, where a plaque on the wall read GREYFRIARS HALL, FORMERLY ST. MARY'S GAELIC CHURCH.

What she found, however, was not a coffeehouse but Scotland's largest secondhand and antiquarian bookshop.

"I've died and gone to heaven," she whispered as she walked along a wooden floor that had previously been trod by generations of churchgoers. Inside, it was similar to Belvedere's back in Manhattan, with ladders set before shelf after shelf of old, out-of-print books, but without the glass cases and protective white gloves. Here the patrons were actually allowed to look through the books, touch them, smell them, browse through them for an hour or so over a cup of coffee, and all without having to commit their entire Visa credit limit. Libby took a book from the shelf, opened it to the inside cover. Mr. Belvedere, she decided, would have considered the low prices they charged a sin.

Soft Celtic music was playing in the background, and for the first time in weeks, Libby felt back in her element. She chatted with the shop owner, Mr. Leakey, sharing stories about the book business, and by the end of their conversation, she had committed to a partnership whereby they could work together, Leakey's and Belvedere's, on those special requests from customers looking for particular titles. It was a method Libby used to find so many of her customers' most desired "wants,"

and she had a network of shops and sources with whom
she kept in constant contact.

Libby spent the rest of her time just browsing the
shelves for her own personal interest, getting so lost
that she scarcely realized how much time had passed
until she heard the tall clock on the wall chiming seven
o'clock. She looked at her watch, confirming the time,
and realized she was late for her dinner appointment
with Mr. Brodie. She bid Mr. Leakey farewell, paid for
her coffee, and hurried down the street toward the river
and Antonio's.

The restaurant was dark and candlelit inside with
strains of Dean Martin singing about *amore* competing
with the sounds of dining chatter and clattering plates.
There was no maître d' at the front to greet her, so she
glanced around the dining room until she spotted an
older gentleman who looked to her very like a solicitor.
She approached his table quietly.

"Mr. Brodie?"

The man looked up from his lasagna. "No, I'm afraid
not."

"Oh."

"Miss Hutchinson?"

Libby turned to see a man of about fifty, wearing a
tweed jacket and crooked tie, with unkempt, wiry hair
and spectacles that drooped at the end of his bulbous
nose.

He looked so much like Dugan they could have been
twins separated at birth.

"Mr. Brodie?"

"Aye, I would be the one."

They shook hands, and he motioned to the chair
across from him at the table set for two. Libby shucked
off her jacket and draped it over the back of her chair as
he quickly poured her a glass of wine from the bottle he
had already ordered.

"I'm so sorry I'm late. I was at this bookshop down the street . . ."

"Oh, Leakey's? Brilliant place, isn't it? No need for apologies. Court went a bit late today. I only just got here myself. Why don't you have a look at the menu. We'll order first, and then get down to business."

Libby had been so busy shopping all day, she hadn't stopped for lunch. She suddenly realized she was starving. The wonderful smell coming from the restaurant's kitchen had set her stomach to rumbling the moment she'd come in the door. She ordered her favorite dish, linguine with white clam sauce, and a small salad. Mr. Brodie, who, judging from his round girth, was obviously accustomed to good food, settled on the veal piccata.

"So, Miss Hutchinson . . ."

"Please, sir, call me Libby."

"Libby, it is. Hamish here, then. So then, Libby, first I thought I would acquaint you with the property known as the Mackay Estate."

He handed her a map with the boundaries of the estate marked out in red ink. Libby read the small legend beneath it, and then read it again.

It was over fifty thousand acres.

Fifty thousand.

The five and four zeroes sort of fifty thousand.

Libby was dumbstruck.

"It had at one time been part of a much larger estate," Hamish explained, pointing to the map. "Over one hundred and fifty thousand acres, but over the centuries it's been broken up, smaller pieces of it sold off to pay debts or for upkeep on the rest of the estate. The fifty thousand remaining today consist of two separate plots. The larger portion, over forty thousand acres, includes the village of Wrath and much of the surrounding countryside. The other eight thousand acres are located some forty kilometers east of the village near the much larger village of

Tunga. The chief of the Mackay received that part of the property back in the late seventeenth century from the British Crown. It is the reason why it isn't part of the original estate. That bit is where Lady Venetia lives today, at a place called Tunga House."

The way Ian had spoke of Lady Venetia as an absentee landlord, Libby had expected she lived someplace far, far away, like London, or even her native Holland.

"I knew she was alive, but I didn't realize she still lived in the Highlands, and so close to the village, too."

They finished their dinner while Hamish explained the rest of the particulars about the estate, the annual income from rents, the costs, the potential improvements. They were sharing a slice of cheesecake over cups of cappuccino when Hamish leaned back in his chair, patted his satisfied belly, and asked, "So what will you do now that you've discovered all you have, Libby Hutchinson?"

She shrugged. "I'm not quite sure. I'll probably spend a little more time in the village, finish up my research on my family, and then return to the States, I guess."

"Or . . ."

She looked at him. "Or what?"

"Or, you can file paperwork claiming your rightful inheritance."

"Why would I want to do that? I have no interest in revenge against Lady Venetia. I don't even know her."

"Perhaps not revenge, but what about preservation?"

"Preservation? What do you mean?"

"Libby, when I was doing this research, I came across some rather disturbing information." He took a quick shuffle through his sheaf of papers. "Apparently Lady Venetia intends on selling the entirety of the estate to a Dutch mineral drilling company—everything, that is, with the exception of the castle, which, as you know, she has already sold. She did that because she apparently promised her husband, your grandfather, the old laird, that she would never sell the castle his ancestors had worked so hard to preserve to anyone who might seek to tear it down. The land, however, is another issue, and if she does sell the land, it will include the whole of the village."

Libby already didn't like the direction the conversation was heading. "And if she does that, then what will become of the villagers?"

"Well, you've been to the village. You can see that a good deal of their livelihood comes from tourism, particularly in the summer months. People flee to the remote points of the Highlands to escape the things that blemish the landscape in the south, like factories and"—he looked at her closely—"*mineral drilling plants.* If Lady Venetia succeeds in making the sale, it will have a definite and adverse effect on the tourism industry in the village of Wrath. Vacationers and hillwalkers don't want to come all that way just to see an eyesore of a drilling plant. They come for the unspoilt landscape, the wildlife, the peace and quiet."

And the charm of living, just for a little while, in a place where people greet you on the street as if you were an old friend.

Libby thought of the sisters, Aggie and Maggie, and their beloved B and B. She thought of the picture postcards in Ellie Mackay's store, the fishing rods and the walking sticks stacked in the corner, waiting for the next influx of tourists. She thought of the craft center and the nimble fingers that spent the winter weaving and knitting the local wool into sweaters, wraps, caps, and blankets to sell. She thought of the boaters who she'd learned spent much of the summer months ferrying passengers back and forth from the mainland to the many islands off the mainland. She thought of the perfectly unblemished landscape she had just enjoyed that very morning, the ancient ruins, the place that her ancestor and namesake, Lady Isabella, had created, where her great-grandchildren's great-grandchildren still lived and flourished.

"But how? How could I possibly stop her?"

Hamish got an eager light in his eye. "First, we would file an injunction to block the sale, challenging Lady Venetia's right to sell any part of the Mackay estate. As I see it, what it's going to come down to is your ability to prove your parents' marriage. With verifiable proof of your legitimacy, Lady Venetia will be unable to do a thing to the estate, and she will be forced to acknowledge you as the Mackay heir, as we both know you rightfully are."

"And in the process, I'll be picking a rather big fight with one very angry and, if the stories are to be believed, formidable, grandmother. I really don't have any wish to *own* an entire village, Hamish. I have a life in America, a job to return to . . ."

And nothing else.

Libby shook the thought off.

"But this is where you can really make a difference, Libby. Land ownership in Scotland is currently under radical reform. You see, up until now Scotland has been the last civilized country in the world that still adheres to feudal law."

"Please tell me you're going to explain what that means," she said. "Right now I have visions of ermine-robed kings and jousting tournaments."

He grinned. "Basically it gives the landlord supreme rights over the people who live on the land. For instance, if the villagers decided they wanted to, oh, I don't know, build a swimming pool for the community, where they could teach their children how to swim properly, dramatically reducing the number of drownings that are an unfortunate circumstance of living so close to the sea, they would have to apply to Lady Venetia for the permission to do so. And Lady Venetia could deny them this right. She, after all, owns the land."

Libby was stunned. "But that's terrible."

"True, but it is happening all across the Highlands.

The large estate owners of today—well, a good many of them, unfortunately—don't take much of an interest in the lives of the people who actually have to live on their land. They come once, maybe twice a year, usually to collect the rents and do a bit of stag hunting, to *feel* what it's like to be a Highland laird, but they want to keep their estates as their own private playgrounds, available for their own benefit. They don't want to see growth and improvements in the villages that pepper their land, because it will mean more issues they will have to deal with, which will mean less leisure time for themselves."

"Is there nothing we can do?"

Hamish nodded. "Some communities have successfully managed to buy out their landlords in lieu of other absentee landlords and have taken the control of the land into their own hands. It is a rare thing. As you can imagine, very few landlords are willing to sell their land at an affordable price to the community when they can ask millions more from American movie stars—or Dutch mineral drilling companies. But through mortgages and grants, you could turn the bulk of the land back to the people who have lived there all their lives and who have the biggest stake in its preservation and protection."

Libby remembered then the fear she had seen in the eyes of every one of the villagers when she had made inquiries about her mother. It was terrible enough that they should have to live with such fear, fear that their very homes would be taken away from them. But now this? How long would it be before this mineral drilling company decided it wanted to vacate the village for its own use?

She thought of the garden that sat in the village square, the handprints of the schoolchildren that had been pressed in the new concrete walkway the day it had been poured. She thought of the churchyard filled with the generations who had lived in the village, people who had worked, raised their children, passing on a way of life that in other parts of the world had simply ceased to exist. In the short time she'd been there, the village and its people had wound their way deep into her heart.

"File whatever paperwork is necessary to stop this proposed sale, Hamish. I will do what I can to find the proof of my parents' marriage."

"Brilliant!" His eyes were positively alight with the challenge. "Now, before you go, just a few preliminary questions for the paperwork. Your age? Oh, wait, I've got your birth certificate here somewhere . . ."

"My birth certificate? How did you get that?"

"Oh, just a simple call to the Scottish Registry Office. They have the records for all Scottish births and—"

"But I'm American, Hamish."

"Your *citizenship* is American, my dear. But I can assure you that you were indeed born on Scottish soil. I have with me a faxed copy of your original Certificate of Birth. Here. Have a look. A certified copy is on its way to me by post."

Libby took the document and read each detail.

She'd been born in the Glasgow Royal Maternity Hospital at 7:24 p.m. on March 23, 1972. She'd weighed seven pounds, two ounces, and had been eighteen inches long. Her mother, Matilde Mackay, was age thirty-three; her father, Fraser Mackay, was listed as deceased.

As Libby stared at the document, Hamish went on with his questions. "So, then, are you married?"

Libby blinked, felt a familiar sting at the question.

Would "almost" qualify as an answer?

"No. I'm not married."

"All right, so then I assume no children of your own?"

"No."

"Well, that will keep things neat and simple."

Libby, however, didn't quite see it that way.

"Hamish, how long do you think all this will take? As

I said, I have a job back in New York, which isn't that much of an issue. I think I can convince my employer to grant me field work here, but my passport only allows me to stay for up to three months."

"Right. But you are, by birth, a Scottish citizen. I don't expect any trouble, though it will require the filing of some paperwork to extend your visiting privileges. I'll get in contact with the Home Office to see what we need to do. Then I'll give you a ring once I have the court date scheduled. I'll do my best to hurry things along."

Chapter Eleven

Graeme balanced the point of his walking stick on the toe of his left Wellington as he stood atop the cliff, at the very edge where the land gave over onto unrelenting sea. Two hundred and fifty feet below him, waves pummeled the rocky coastline, the sound of them roaring up to meet him like a storm even on this calm autumn day. Seabirds cried, soaring on the tumbling current of the crosswind, and the air was spiced with a mixture of salt, the sea, and the fading heather that blanketed the landscape around him.

It was a view that would offer unending inspiration for poet, artist, and author alike. It was timeless. It was overwhelming, and it was the perfect place to be alone.

He'd come to Castle Wrath for its solitude, for its remoteness and its effectiveness for hiding out. He had intended to remain only long enough for the press furor to die down and to finish the project he was currently at work on. It was an agreement he'd made with both his mother and his uncle. He'd been hounded for weeks straight, had found a photographer hiding in his garbage Dumpster one morning, and a leggy blonde waiting in the men's washroom at his firm the same afternoon. He'd informed his mother and his uncle that night that he was changing his name and moving to Siberia.

"Graeme, dear," the countess had said, "you don't mean that."

But he did. And he told her so.

"I am working on the most important project of my career." He looked at the duke, already anticipating what he would say. "Yes, I know. A career as an architect would be too much of a demand on the time I need to devote to my place in the nobility. And I have agreed to give up my career, even before I assume the titles. But you agreed I would finish this project, and now this, this *life* is preventing me from doing that."

It wasn't only the press Graeme had been running from when he'd come to Castle Wrath. He'd been running from his life.

Something in his voice must have given his mother pause, because the countess had looked at the duke and had merely said, "We must do something."

The duke had thought about it.

"Find a place. Not Siberia—someplace preferably on the U.K. mainland where you can continue your work and finish up this project."

And so he had found Castle Wrath.

Graeme had always known the day would come when he would have to leave the castle. The very nature of his agreement with the duke had guaranteed that, but in the weeks he'd been there, something had happened. Something completely unexpected.

This place—not just the castle but the whole of this part of the country—had come to mean something to Graeme. When he was here, he could choose to *not be* that heir, *not be* that title. He could be something as simple as a castle caretaker. He could allow himself to enjoy the company of a woman.

When he was here, at this place, he felt he could finally *breathe*.

Graeme knew he would never find another place like it.

And the truth was, he didn't want to.

Now all he had to do was figure out a way to break the news to his uncle, the duke.

All along the drive back from Inverness, Libby went over the details of her conversation with Hamish.

She was having no second thoughts about her decision to pursue her inheritance. In fact, just the opposite. The more she thought about the lives that would be forever altered by Lady Venetia's plans for selling the estate, the more determined she was to do whatever she could to stop it. She would spend every free moment poring through the church records. But even if she was unable to prove that her parents' marriage had ever taken place, Hamish had suggested that at the very least, the litigation of it could delay the sale of the estate long enough for certain land reform provisions to allow the villagers more of a fighting chance on their own.

Hamish had advised her that she could tell no one of what she was doing. If one of the villagers, spurred by his own fear, happened to forewarn Lady Venetia, she could very easily set her own legal representatives to the task of trying to prevent their efforts. And that would spell disaster for the villagers.

"An unanticipated offensive is always the best strategy," Hamish had said, sounding quite like a military general, when she'd bid him farewell outside the restaurant.

He would be in touch with her by phone, he'd promised, until he could arrange to have the initial court session scheduled.

It was late afternoon the following day when Libby decided to stop in at the village's only café, a charming place called the White Heather. The weather was odd, overcast and still, as if even Mother Nature were waiting for something to happen.

Libby had been at the church all that day, searching

the records, but to no avail. She refused to feel the disappointment, just as she refused to believe there might not have been any marriage at all. There had to have been. She just had to keep on looking.

The café was housed in a pretty bright blue cottage that stood at one end of the village high street. Flower boxes hung below the windows, and the chimney smoked with a welcoming fire. Inside, small tables covered in red checkered linen were scattered beneath the exposed beams of the low-ceilinged dining room. A tabletop stereo played faint Celtic dancing music.

Janet Mackay, the proprietress herself, came out of the kitchen when Libby ducked inside. She was carrying a tray to her only other customers, a couple of touring backpackers who'd apparently decided to forgo the trail mix and granola that evening for Janet's more appetizing menu.

"Find yourself a seat, lass," Janet called as she flitted by. "Any table y' like."

Libby smiled, nodded in greeting to Janet and the backpackers, and went to a small, two-seat table in the corner by the front window. The day's offerings were scribbled on the café's chalkboard.

"Hav'na seen you 'round much, lass," Janet said as she came to meet her, bringing a steaming pot of tea.

Janet was about Libby's same age, and had the trademark Mackay dark hair and blue eyes, the first cropped short and moussed in a spiky 'do, the second heavily lined and mascaraed. She'd opened the café just a few years earlier, after returning to the village in which she'd been born. Before then, she'd lived in Edinburgh, where she'd been apprenticed with a restaurant and had learned all she needed to know about running her own place.

"I was to Inverness yesterday," Libby told her, "and have been doing a bit of sight-seeing as well." She glanced at the chalkboard. "I think I'll try the salmon. Grilled."

"Grand. Chips, peas, and salad with that?"

"That would be great. Thank you."

"Oh, and I've got a lovely wild berry crumble with a warm custard topping on the sweets menu tonight. You'll not want to miss it."

Libby took the local newspaper, the *Northern Times,* from the front counter while she waited for her supper. Sipping her tea, she started reading through the local stories, country commentary, and community news bits. The features were sorted by village, consisting mostly of farming items and whist game results. On the cooking pages, an Isobel MacRae from the village of Thurso shared her award-winning recipe for something called Clootie Dumplin's, while Mr. Arthur MacArthur of Durness had advertised in the classifieds, hoping someone might buy his "round table." "Knights," he'd added wryly, "are not included."

On the next page, a notice of an estate sale being held the following day caught Libby's eye, particularly when she saw that "a full library of books" was among the many items listed on offer. Just that morning, she'd phoned Mr. Belvedere in New York to let him know that her leave of absence was going to be quite a bit longer than she'd expected. It hadn't been the sort of news he'd hoped to hear, but she'd appeased him with the promise that she would be combing the attics of the Highlands for long-hidden rare editions to decorate his shelves while she was away.

After jotting the details of the sale into her handheld, Libby turned to the newspaper's Community News section. As she read through the columns, her gaze fixed on a photograph printed at the top of the page. A moment later, her breath stuck in her throat.

Pictured was an elderly woman, flanked on either side by smiling, suited men. A wide tartan ribbon was stretched before them, which the lady was in the process of cutting with a huge claymore sword. The photo's caption read:

> *Lady Venetia Mackay appears for the honorary ribbon-cutting ceremony at the newly christened Clan Mackay Centre in the village of Tunga.*

Libby stared for the first time at the image of the grandmother who'd never wanted her.

She certainly didn't look menacing. In her early eighties, Libby guessed, tidily dressed in a blouse and jacket with a brooch on one lapel. A handsome woman. Her hair, which appeared to be stark white, was arranged in the sort of unassuming bouffant so often preferred by the older generation. Some might say her high forehead and aquiline nose were signs of an imperious temper, her close-set dark eyes a narrow point of view. Her mouth was a shape that hinted at a predisposition toward frowning. Libby studied the image closely, searching for some sign of a resemblance between them. She could see nothing, nothing at all, that would indicate this woman was anything other than a complete and utter stranger to her. The truth was, as she looked on the photograph, Libby felt nothing as well. Not so much as the faintest emotion.

"Fine evening to you, Libby."

She looked up. "PC MacLeith. I didn't hear you come in. Nice to see you."

"And you likewise. Just picking up some takeaway for my sister and the kids. Two of the bairns are in bed with chest colds. The other has a heaving stomach. She's had her hands full all the day." He glanced at the newspaper that was still open in front of Libby. "Reading about the new Mackay Centre, are you? I hear 'tis a fine facility. Have you been to it yet?"

"No. I only just now read of it."

"We almost managed to land the facility here in the

village, at the castle, actually, afore it was sold. Most thought it the more sensible choice, given that the clan has such deep roots at the place and the castle had been standing empty for so many years. We even had financial assistance being provided by the Highland Council, but Lady Mackay, she just wouldn't see her way to providing the property for it. Gave a spot of land in Tunga for the centre instead, and then even provided the funds herself to have a brand-new facility built. I would have thought the Mackay castle a more fitting site for the clan center, 'specially since we hold the Mackay games here in the village each year. But there you have it. More's the pity, too. Would have provided some much-needed local jobs and a boost to the tourism in the area. Every Mackay coming through would stop at our little village. But now, they'll be going to Tunga instead."

Libby frowned, glancing at the photograph once again. "Yes, that is a pity."

She folded the newspaper and tucked it under her purse. "So, no high crime to fight tonight, PC MacLeith?"

Angus crossed his arms. "Well, nae, unless you'd consider the Bain lads to be hardened criminals for stringing the headmaster's breeks up the village flagpole."

"They didn't!"

"Oh, aye, they did." Angus nodded. "Wouldn't have been so bad either, but with the weather having been so fine, the headmaster had taken it into his head for a dip in the loch and, well . . ."

Libby tried to hide her grin behind her hand.

"Frichted the poor Widow MacNamara nearly straight to her grave, him tumbling over her garden wall, arse-over-head, then snatchin' her best Sunday kirtle off the line to cover himself. She thrashed him all the way down the high street with her cane, demandin' that he give the kirtle back."

Libby gave in to her laughter as an image flashed

through her mind of the rather large, rather hairy head-master, Hector MacNeil, wearing the widow's kirtle like a hula skirt. "That's what I get for taking a day to go to Inverness. Looks like I missed all the excitement."

Janet appeared then, bringing Libby's dinner and a takeaway sack for Angus.

"I'll just get your change," she said after Angus had paid her.

"Nae, keep it, Janet. You've given me enough free cups of tea on cold winter nights t' more than make up for it."

"Well, then, thank you, dear." She looked at Libby. "You know, this one's a keeper. You should snatch him up, miss, afore someone else does."

Neither Libby or Angus could think of a response, and Janet said quickly, "Now, you let Miss Hutchinson to enjoy her dinner afore it goes cold, aye?"

And with that she was gone, humming her way into the kitchen.

The awkward moment that followed seemed to stretch into eternity. Finally Angus said, "Well, I won't keep you, then. A good e'en to you, then, Libby." He tipped his black-and-white checkered constable's hat in parting.

She nodded, watched him go, wishing she could have thought of something more to say. But what could she have? Yes, Angus was congenial, kind, and certainly handsome. And given the sacrifice he'd made to return to the village to help his widowed sister, he obviously held a high standard of commitment and loyalty. Any number of women would be falling over themselves for a chance with him. In fact, during the drive back from Inverness, Libby had been thinking what a pity it was Angus hadn't crossed paths with Rosalia while he'd been living in New York. They would have suited each other well. But Libby herself felt nothing more for him than warmth and friendship. She sensed from his reaction just then that he felt the same.

As she took up her fork to start on her supper, Libby heard the bell and noticed Graeme Mackenzie just coming in to the café. Spotting her, he smiled just slightly, removed his coat, and hung it on the coatrack by the door before he turned to scan the array of empty tables in the room.

Now *he* was another matter.

"No leftover stew tonight?" she asked as he headed across the room.

He shook his head. "Housekeeper's home with sick kids. Told her I'd fend for myself."

"Oh. Would you"—she motioned to the chair across from her at the table—"care to join me?"

She watched him think about it, then he nodded. "Thank you."

Janet came bustling out of the kitchen. "Ah, good evening, sir. Can I get you tea?"

"Please." Graeme glanced at the chalkboard. "And I think I'll just have the same as Miss Hutchinson for dinner."

"Very good, sir."

"Here." Libby pushed the plate into the center of the table. "Janet just brought this. Why don't you share it with me while you wait for yours? It's far too much for me to finish, and I wouldn't feel right eating while you're waiting for your dinner."

She thought he might refuse, but he picked up his fork and flaked off a bit of the salmon.

He looked tired, she thought, stealing a glance at him. And his face was shadowed with a beard, as if he hadn't taken the time to shave that morning.

"I was in the village yesterday," he said as casually as if he'd been discussing the weather. "Didn't see you."

He'd been looking for her?

Libby told herself not to let her imagination run wild.

"I went to Inverness yesterday. Some shopping and dinner with an acquaintance. I've also been busy doing some family research here in the village."

He nodded, caught a glimpse of the newspaper. "Any interesting local news bits?"

"If you're looking for the local whist results." She smiled. "And . . . there's an estate sale in one of the nearby villages tomorrow." She hesitated. "If you're not busy, perhaps you'd be interested in checking it out with me?"

Graeme swung the Land Rover into the narrow drive of the Crofter's Cottage early the next morning. He had told Libby he would be by to pick her up at nine. A quick glance at his watch told him he was fifteen minutes early, so he lingered behind the wheel, sipping his thermal cup of coffee and wondering what the devil he was doing as he waited for the clock to catch up with him.

He'd come up to the Highlands to get away from members of the opposite sex. And yet, in the past days, he'd found himself drawn to this particular one time and again, watching for her, wondering where she was, what she was doing, even creating an errand in the village just on the off chance that he would see her. What was it about her, he wondered, that was different from the scores of other women he could easily have had? Was it that fact alone—that she wasn't hiding in his shower stall or trailing him to the corner newsstand—that provided the attraction?

He should go, he knew. He should turn the car around and go back to his castle hideaway. But, he didn't.

His knock on the door at precisely nine o'clock was answered by an elderly lady wearing a pale yellow housedress. She peered at him from behind a pair of thick-lensed spectacles.

"Good morning to you, sir. How may I assist you?"

"Yes, good morning. I'm here for Miss Hutchinson."

"Ah, and who may I say is calling, please?"

"Graeme Mackenzie. I believe she is expecting me."

"Oh! A pleasure to meet you, Mr. Mackenzie. Yes, I am Miss Aggie. Libby is on the telephone at the moment, but I'm sure she won't be long. Do come in and wait in the parlor. Would you like tea?"

"No, thank you."

The woman nodded. "Well, I'll just go and tell her you're here, then."

Graeme took a seat in the modest parlor, stretching his long legs out in front of him as he lowered into one of the lace-covered chairs. He waited, listening to the muffled sounds coming from the other parts of the stone cottage.

He looked up when he heard someone, expecting Libby, only to find the same woman who had invited him in, returning now with the tea tray he'd declined, and this time wearing a green frock.

How had she changed *and* made a pot of tea so quickly?

"Oh, hello there," she said, as if seeing him for the first time. "I didn't know we were having a guest for tea."

Graeme opened his mouth to speak, but had absolutely no idea how to respond. Surely fewer than three minutes had passed since he'd spoken with her at the door, yet here she was, acting as if they'd just met. What was he supposed to say?

Thankfully he didn't have to say a thing, because Libby came into the room just a moment later.

"Sorry I kept you waiting."

It was perfectly okay.

She looked lovely. Her dark hair was down and loose, brushing her shoulders and curling in a charming flip under her chin. She wore a simple khaki skirt that fell to her ankles and a pale ivory sweater that clung alluringly to her breasts. Her slip-on canvas shoes had very little heel, bringing the top of her head to just above his shoulders. She had a tartan wrap folded over her arm. Silver earrings, he noticed, dangled from her ears, peeking out from underneath her hair.

"Graeme Mackenzie," she said, motioning toward the older woman, "allow me to introduce Miss Maggie."

"I believe we've already met."

"We have?"

Quite obviously the woman suffered from a failing memory. Graeme looked at Libby, decided against reminding the woman of their meeting only moments ago, and simply stuck out his hand in greeting. "My mistake. Pleasure to meet you, Miss Maggie."

When Graeme turned to help Libby on with her wrap, he found the woman again suddenly standing behind him, now wearing the yellow frock she'd greeted him in at the door.

"I see you found Libby," she said sunnily.

He turned, stared at the woman in green, then back to the woman in yellow. Then he looked at Libby, who was grinning, obviously enjoying his confusion.

"Let me give you a hint. Miss Aggie"—she pronounced the name slowly so he could hear the difference—"always wears the yellow. Miss Maggie, the green."

"Thank you for that rather useful piece of information."

Behind them, the sisters were tittering, having just realized their unintended charade.

"That wasn't very fair of us, was it, Mr. Mackenzie?" said Miss Maggie.

"Are you sure you won't stay for tea?" asked Miss Aggie.

"I think we'd best be off," Libby answered, coming to the rescue. "I'm not sure how long it will take us to get to the estate sale. I wouldn't want to miss out on any treasures by arriving too late."

Graeme couldn't have agreed more. Somehow he suspected if they stayed for tea, it would be well past noon by the time they managed to disentangle themselves for their outing.

Chapter Twelve

The drive to the estate sale took them a meandering route along the northernmost coast of the Scottish mainland.

They passed through several small villages and sparse settlements all separated by mountains and vast tracts of wild, untamed moor. The sea stretched far to the north beside them, and the day was mostly clear with a modest, teasing wind. A clump of dark clouds, however, was gathering low and to the north, threatening rain later that afternoon.

They made good time driving and so stopped once or twice along the way to watch the soaring path of a sea eagle or to explore the ruins of an ancient castle. The sale would open at noon, with a preview at eleven. With five minutes to spare, they rolled up the drive and swung in to park beside the other cars.

The former Victorian hunting lodge where the sale was being held was a huge Gothic-looking pile with a mishmash of narrow turreted towers and gargoyles peering out along the roofline. According to the newspaper, it had belonged to an elderly war veteran who had become quite a hermit in his later years, refusing to leave his house or admit anyone other than his trusted valet. A niece and nephew from London had been left with the task of sorting through his effects and had decided it would be far easier to dispose of the nearly three generations' worth of belongings at a local sale, instead of having to haul it all to the south to be sold through Sotheby's or Christie's in London.

A yellow-and-white canopy had been set up on a stretch of green lawn with signs that directed Graeme and Libby inside. Once there, Libby headed off for a quick peek at the books area while Graeme had a browse of some of the other items that would be offered for sale.

He was looking over a rather fine example of a seventeenth-century Flemish tapestry when he suddenly heard his name being called from across the room. The voice that called him, however, was not Libby's, but the very deep, very distinctive voice of Henry Cabotte, otherwise known as the Earl of Ashburnham.

"Graeme, m'boy! I thought that was you. I told Clarissa there, 'Say, isn't that the Mackenzie lad?' She told me I must be mistaken, that no one had seen you in weeks, so of course I had to come over here to prove it to her."

Graeme turned to where indeed Lady Ashburnham was standing, smiling under the brim of her wide straw hat. He offered a casual wave.

"So, what the devil are you doing all the way this far north, and at an estate sale of all things?"

Think, Graeme told himself. *Think fast.*

"Just decided to take advantage of this incredible weather before winter comes storming in, my lord. Saw the signboard on the main road and found myself wandering in."

"Yes, us, too. Alone, are you?" The man never had been one to mince words.

"Of course. Just flew up for the weekend. Get away from the city and all."

The earl chuckled. "Quite. We've a place over on the coast. Stunning sunrises. Unfortunately we can only get up here once or twice a year. You know"—he narrowed his gaze on Graeme—"you should come, stay the weekend with us. What are you, in some dreadful B and B someplace? Nothing much else up here but B and B's and country inns."

Graeme simply smiled.

"Might as well be camping, m'boy—positively primitive. Come, now! I'll not brook any refusals. Your mother would never forgive me. We're not far a'tall, and we've a couple thousand acres if you're of a mind for some stag hunting. Clarissa'd love it. The company of another, I mean. Not the hunting, of course."

Graeme glanced to where the countess had been standing, but saw Libby instead just making her way back from the books area.

Bloody hell.

He pivoted, giving her his back. "Thank you, my lord, for your kind invitation, but I'm afraid I'll have to decline. I've actually got plans to fly up to the Orkneys for a spot of bird-watching."

"Oh." The earl looked confused. "Wouldn't have put you as a bird-watcher."

"Indeed," Graeme said. "I find it is most meditative." He cut their chat short. "It was a pleasure to see you again, my lord. Please give my farewell to Lady Ashburnham. If you'll excuse me . . ."

Graeme quickly turned and headed out of the tent before Libby could spot him talking to the earl.

He was standing outside, leaning against the back of the Land Rover, when Libby came out of the tent some time later.

"There you are!" she said with obvious relief. "I was beginning to wonder if you'd abandoned me. I didn't know how I was going to get all the books I just bought home."

Graeme looked at her. "So you were successful?"

"Oh, yes!" Her excitement was alight in her eyes.

"What a trove! Some of these books don't appear as if they've ever been read, and they're over a century old. More than one of them are first editions, too."

Two of the sale workers had followed her out and started loading the books into the back of the Land Rover. There were at least twenty or thirty books that Libby had bought.

"I saw you talking with a man earlier," Libby said. "Someone you knew?"

"Hmm? Oh, no. He was just asking me about the tapestry I'd been looking at. I think he was afraid I was going to try to outbid him on it. Ready to go?"

To celebrate Libby's success in negotiating a good price for the books, they spent the rest of the afternoon sight-seeing. Most of the touristy attractions were either closed or just closing for the season, but Libby still managed to find a few souvenirs for her friends back home—postcards, tins of shortbread, and woolen lap blankets in colorful tartan patterns.

When she spotted the sign for the village of Tunga, she asked Graeme if they might stop in.

"I read in the newspaper about a Mackay clan center that was recently opened here. Perhaps I'll find something to help me with my research."

Minutes later, they were pulling into the newly paved drive.

Characterless and plain, the building itself was little more than a cottage-sized box with stark white walls and a slate roof. They were greeted by a huge portrait of Lady Venetia inside the door, while Graeme paid the three pounds each for admission.

The clerk who counted out their change noticed Libby staring at the portrait.

"She is a striking woman, isn't she, though?" she said proudly. "That's Lady Venetia Mackay, our benefactress. It was through her generous donations that we were able to open the center."

Libby merely nodded.

"If I can answer any questions for you, please don't hesitate to ask."

Inside, there was a collection of clan artifacts and mementoes hanging on the walls and encased in glass displays. The Mackay tartan was hung everywhere, and the clerk noticed Libby's wrap of the same design.

"Oh, are you a Mackay?"

Libby smiled and said simply, "I like to think so."

She noticed a wall of paintings and photographs of the various Mackay clan chieftains during the centuries. At the end of the portrait line was an oil painting of the last Mackay of Wrath—and his only son, Fraser.

Her father.

In the portrait, he was formally dressed in suit coat, kilt, and tie, standing behind his father's chair. Unsmiling, his eyes were vague and his expression was austere, very different from the laughing, carefree young man pictured in her mother's photograph. Libby decided she liked that image better.

She read the placard pinned to the wall beneath the portrait.

CHARLES MACKAY IV, THE LAST MACKAY LAIRD OF WRATH, AND HIS SON AND HEIR, FRASER MACKAY, WHO WAS TRAGICALLY LOST DURING A FAMILY FISHING TRIP. SADLY, HE DID NOT LEAVE BEHIND ANY ISSUE, BRINGING TO AN END THIS NOBLE AND PROUD MACKAY SEPT.

Libby blinked, frowning.

Graeme stood behind her, reading the placard.

"So that would explain why Lady Venetia sold the castle. The place must hold very sad memories for her after the loss of her son."

Libby could only nod silently.

"Did you see this?"

Graeme motioned Libby over to a small display that read:

THE LEGEND OF THE MACKAY STONE.

There were photographs and a brief history of the stone, relating its purported origins and the various "miracles" it had performed over the centuries.

"'Tis quite a tale," Graeme said after reading the information posted.

"Oh, 'tis no tale, sir." The clerk had come to check on them again. "The stone was once very real. In fact, there are those still living today who remember seeing it."

"So what happened to it?"

The clerk motioned toward the portrait of Fraser. "The most common belief is that the stone went down with the last laird's son, Fraser Mackay, when he was so tragically drowned. He was known to have been the last person to have it. Others believe it was stolen. 'Tis sad, it is, that such an important piece of Mackay history is lost to us forever."

Libby could do nothing more than stand, listening between them, while the very stone they were discussing hung hidden underneath her sweater.

"Does Lady Venetia still live in the area?" she finally asked, trying not to feel like she was a spy in an enemy camp. She just couldn't deny a certain curiosity about the woman whose actions had played such a large part in her life's direction.

"Oh, indeed. She lives right here in the village. In fact, if you look out this window, you can just see her house, Tunga House, over the treetops."

Libby took a glance at the distant pitched roof, just making out the smoking chimney. She found herself wondering what Lady Venetia could be doing at that moment and what she would do, what she would say if she knew that the granddaughter she had forsaken was so very close?

It had started to rain while they'd been in the center,

and the storm that had been building all that day was soon pouring down in buckets. It was a fitting backdrop to Libby's mood, which had been dampened by the visit to the center and her grandmother's home village. Daylight had vanished almost completely behind the clouds, and the driving was slow, the rain almost seeming to fall sideways at times.

They stopped for petrol in a small coastal village and decided to have dinner at the local pub while they waited to see if the storm would move on.

Soon after, they discovered that getting back to Wrath was going to be more of a challenge than they'd thought.

"Road's flooded," said the police constable who stopped them just as they were leaving the pub. "The burn's spilled over. Can't get through."

"Is the water so high that a four-by-four couldn't get through?"

"I shouldn't like to chance it, sir. The road dips quite low at the bottom of the hill. And we've already lost a tractor in it."

Graeme asked him if there was any other way around it.

"Aye, you'll have to go back and take the A897 south, then double back north."

He showed Graeme the route on the road atlas. It would take them more than half the way south to Inverness, and then at least another two hours' drive northwest from there to Wrath Village.

Graeme shook his head. "It would take us three, four hours to detour, at the very least."

"In this weather, probably longer," the constable said. "My suggestion would be that you take a room at Lily Middleditch's B and B. It's just down the road there, and I think she's got room for one more set of guests. I've sent a couple others her way, and I know she was just closing for the season, so things might be a bit stretched. But she'll do her best by you. This storm's s'posed to pass through o'er the night. By morn, I'd expect you'll be able to cross without any trouble."

Graeme looked at Libby. "What do you think? I'll make the drive south if you'd prefer to push on for the village."

She shook her head. "It's been a long day of driving already, Graeme, and right now a warm, dry B and B sounds far more appealing than driving all night and risking getting stranded in the middle of a moor somewhere."

Graeme thanked the constable, who gave them directions to the B and B and promised to radio Angus MacLeith in Wrath to let him know they'd been stranded so he could tell those who needed to know that they wouldn't be returning that night.

They found the B and B quite easily. The proprietress, Lily Middleditch, was waiting for them at the door, having been alerted to their arrival by the constable.

"Good e'en, m'dears." She was an older lady, with a fringe of silver curls and a floral housecoat. She ushered them into her front room. "Come in, come in. Get those wet things off of you and warm y'self by the fire whilst I see to getting your room. 'Tis a fearsome night, isn't it now?"

They soon discovered that the available accommodation actually consisted of one room . . .

. . . with one bed.

"Perhaps we should see if there are any other places nearby," Graeme said as Mrs. Middleditch set off to the kitchen to get the tea brewing.

Libby, however, wasn't much inclined to go back out into the storm. "Graeme, it's late, and for all we know every place else has already been taken up by other wayward travelers. We're both adults. I don't know about you, but I'm completely exhausted. I could curl up right here, right now."

And she did.

She kicked off her shoes, and lay back on the pillow, closing her eyes with a sigh. In seconds, it seemed, she had fallen asleep.

Graeme ducked out of the bedroom, closing the door softly behind him. He turned and very nearly collided with Mrs. Middleditch.

"Oh, sir! You gave me a fright!" She was carrying towels, other linens. "I was after bringing you and your wife some extra towels and blankets. Poor wee thing looked quite done in."

Your wife.

Graeme decided it would be best not to correct her. "Thank you. You're right, she is quite exhausted. In fact, I was just coming to tell you she wouldn't be coming down to tea after all. She's already fallen asleep."

"Has she now? The poor wee dear. Well, then, the tea's in the guests' lounge if you'd like a cup yourself. Otherwise, if you won't be needing anything else, I'll see you in the morning, then."

Graeme bid her good night and waited until she'd gone back down the hall. Then he turned back to the bedroom . . .

. . . and the bed he would be sharing that night.

When Graeme awakened, it was early morning, a single beam of sunshine stretching its light through the parted curtains. He could feel the softness of Libby's hair brushing against his face, could hear the whispered hush of her slumbered breathing, and he lay there, not daring to move.

He could think of many worse ways to have woken, but in that moment, he couldn't think of a single one that would have been more pleasurable.

During the night Libby had tucked her head against his shoulder and flung one arm loosely around his waist. Even now he could feel the warmth of her against him, the softness of her breasts nestled close to his side. In fact, he felt himself growing aroused just thinking about it, and realized it had been nearly six months since he'd been with a woman, and even longer than that since he'd woken with one beside him. For all his efforts to avoid just this same situation, he now found himself relishing it, reluctant to move so much as a muscle for fear he might wake her and spoil this wonderful, stolen moment.

Before his brother's death on that treacherous ski slope, Graeme had had what one might call a steady relationship in his life, although, in truth, it had been more of a "comfortable arrangement" than a relationship. They'd been "available" to each other when needed, both in and out of the bedroom. They would accompany each other to the necessary social functions and occasionally would find themselves accompanying one another into bed if ever the compulsion struck. But it seemed as soon as the news hit of Teddy's accident, she'd changed, virtually immediately. She'd suddenly suggested that they move in together, suggested, too, that he might take her home to meet his mother and his uncle.

And then Graeme had happened upon that scrap of paper in the desk drawer at her apartment, written in her familiar flowery script.

Lady Amanda.
The Marchioness of Waltham.
Her Grace, the Duchess of Gransborough.

Had it been anyone else, Graeme might have put it off as a flight of female fantasy. But he had "been with" Amanda for nearly five years. And though their relationship had been more casual than close, he liked to think he knew her, knew her probably better than even she realized. When she had wanted, desperately wanted, a promotion at her work, she'd written her name along with the new job title on scraps of paper and stuck them all over the place—on her refrigerator, in her Day-Timer, even making it her laptop monitor screensaver, in a belief that she could somehow make the promotion manifest itself.

And the funny thing was, it did. She'd gotten the promotion, almost as easily as if she'd written herself a prescription for it.

So she'd turned her determined sights in much the same way on him—rather, on his title, because none of those names he'd seen decorating the paper had been written as Mrs. Graeme Mackenzie.

And Graeme had ended their relationship that week, with a Post-it note stuck on her bedroom mirror.

It had seemed the most appropriate way of doing it.

When he allowed himself to fall in love, *if* he ever allowed it, it was going to be with a woman who wanted him for him, Graeme Mackenzie, not for the titles, the prestige, or even the social stature. And over the past eight months, as he'd been pursued across a good-sized stretch of the free world, he'd nearly convinced himself that such a woman didn't exist.

Nearly.

Lying there in the quiet solitude of that bed, Graeme allowed himself to consider for the first time that perhaps he'd been mistaken. He closed his eyes and pressed his face into Libby's hair, feeling her stir. Her lashes fluttered, and he watched her come awake.

"Good morning."

She didn't immediately notice that she was wound around him. He certainly wasn't about to point it out to her.

She blinked against the light. "The rain has stopped?"

Graeme nodded. "The sun has even decided to make an appearance."

She closed her eyes, breathed deeply. He looked at her, unspeaking, for several moments. It would be so very easy to kiss her. Just close his eyes and lower his mouth to hers and . . .

"Hallooo!"

The knocking on the door sent them both jerking upright.

"I'm so sorry to wake you," came a voice from the other side of the door, "but I'm afraid I must ask you to please move your vehicle. It's blocking the way for the sheep, you see."

Stifling the urge to groan, Graeme called that he'd be right out, and slung his legs over the side of the bed. Libby was already sitting on the bed's opposite side.

He opened the door onto the cheerfully waiting face of their proprietress, Mrs. Middleditch.

"Good morning to you," she said, glancing quickly at Libby behind him. "Oh, good. You're already dressed. I'm so sorry to disturb. Hiram's just got to get the sheep out when it's his turn on the common grazing ground, you see. Else he'll miss his turn, and the poor beasts won't have any grass to eat."

"That's all right," Graeme said.

"Would you be wanting the full breakfast this morning then?"

"Porridge would be fine, if you've got it," Libby answered quickly.

"Sir?"

"Yes, porridge is fine," Graeme said, and grabbed his keys, heading down the hall to move the Land Rover.

After a chatty breakfast of porridge and scones with the other guests in Mrs. Middleditch's dining room, Graeme and Libby were back on the road for Wrath Village. The dip in the road that had been washed out by the storm the night before was mostly clear, with just a couple of inches of water still covering the lowest point. As they drove, Libby found herself staring out the window at the coast, watching the sparkle of the sunlight on the water.

She'd slept well the night before, better than she had since her mother had passed away. At first she'd thought it must have been because she'd just been so tired the day before, but there was something else. That something else could only have been Graeme.

The ride back to the village went quickly, and before long Graeme was dropping her at the door of the Crofter's Cottage. He had some work to get to, he'd told her, a statement that Libby echoed. So she had a quick bath before heading for the church, laptop tucked under her arm. Sean MacNally was already there when she arrived.

"Good morning, Libby," he said as she walked into the churchyard. Several sheep went trotting away as she approached. They were brought inside the churchyard every couple of weeks to keep the overgrowth at bay, and they munched happily amongst the carved crosses and tilting headstones.

"How are you, Sean?"

"On this fine day, how could I be anything but?" He looked at her. "Did you have a pleasant day of sight-seeing yesterday?"

Libby spent a few minutes chatting about the estate sale and her success in finding a few truly remarkable editions. She ended with the tale of their getting caught in the storm and staying the night at Mrs. Middleditch's B and B.

"Well, sounds as if you had quite an adventure."

Indeed.

Libby passed the better part of the day going through the church records, transcribing the handwritten information into a fully searchable database similar to the one she kept for her work. At the same time, she had started compiling a family tree for herself, tracing her own ancestry back through time. The church records were a true treasure trove of information.

The most amazing thing to her was the realization that

for more than two hundred and fifty years, these people, *her* people, had endured in this same tiny corner of the world. While the Mackay side of her family was much more well documented, given the fact that they had been the lairds of this land, she was equally proud of her maternal line, hardworking, crofting people who had forged a life and had continued to flourish despite drought, famine, and even war.

Her mother, in fact, had been the first of her family to leave it, albeit unwillingly, and what a terrible decision it must have been for her. She'd been alone, expecting her first child, having just lost her husband, and she'd had to leave everything she had ever known to travel to a completely unknown corner of the world. And all of it had been because of the jealousy and resentment of Lady Venetia Mackay.

Libby left the church shortly before the supper hour with an aim to stop in at M'Cuick's store. When she walked in, two of the local ladies were standing at the corner display. They nodded to Libby in greeting as she walked by. But as she turned for the front counter, she caught a snippet of their conversation.

"I hear she's been out with the new laird."

"Aye, spent the night with him. More than once, too."

Libby felt a flush of color rise to her face, and strode across to the counter.

"Ah, good day to you, Libby."

It was Ian who came forward to greet her, and they shared a few moments of pleasant conversation.

"So," Ian said, "I'm sure you didn't come here just for conversation. Anything I can get for you?"

"Actually, yes. I was hoping you might have a telephone jack adapter in one of those mysterious drawers on the wall behind you, so that I might access the Internet with my laptop. I should have thought to ask you about it before, when I was in for the power convertor, but I hadn't thought of it."

"No trouble," he said. "U.S. to U.K., of course."

He poked through one of the drawers, then another, and another. "Hmm . . ." He rubbed his narrow chin. "Looks like I'm out of them. I could order one for you. Would take a week, maybe even a fortnight . . ."

Libby frowned. She had hoped to have access to her e-mail sooner than that. "Well, I suppose there's not much else I can do. So, yes, please, order it for me if you would."

"Does this mean you'll be staying on in the village for a while, then?"

"It would seem so."

She glanced at the two women who had been gossiping when she'd come in. She waited while they paid for their purchases, bid their farewells to Ian, then left the shop.

"I noticed there isn't any library in the village, Ian."

"Nae. Just the newsagent, but she doesn't carry much in the way of fiction. The mobile library comes through every other month. Always a wait list for the latest Ian Rankin mystery, of course."

"I was asking because I was hoping I might be able to access the Internet there."

"Och, no, lass. Afraid not."

"What about at the school? Do they have an Internet hookup?"

"Nae. They've been saving up for it. There was talk of having a whist night fund-raiser to help fund it, but I think it is more a training issue than anything else. Esme Macafie, the school administrator, is"—he looked at her—"well, she's getting on in years. The technological advances of the modern age are a bit beyond her, I'm afraid."

Libby tried to think of another solution. "I suppose I'll have to take another day and go to Inverness, then."

"Actually, I do know that shortly after Mr. Mackenzie took up residence at the castle, there was a British Telephone technician sent for. He was up there three days straight, told Janet Mackay o'er at the café that he was setting up a fully outfitted office—fax, computers, all state-of-the-art."

"Of course. I hadn't thought of that. Thank you for the information," she said. "You'll let me know when that adapter comes in?"

"Oh, aye."

Ian watched Libby turn for the door.

A moment later he heard his wife Betty come into the room behind him, poking about in the drawers.

"Ian M'Cuick!"

He turned to see her standing behind him. There was a small white adapter sitting in the palm of her hand.

"Isna this the adapter the lass was just after looking for?"

"Well, would you look at that? Hmm. Wonder how I missed it . . ." His eyes, however, were twinkling with mischief.

Betty gave him a stare. "You dinna learn from your last attempt at matchmaking?"

Ian frowned at her. He didn't much like being re-minded of that particular failure, especially since it had resulted in the loss of one of his closest friends, Fraser Mackay, and the subsequent banishment of another.

But he wasn't giving up just yet.

"All the more reason to make this one right, dear Betty."

Chapter Thirteen

Libby held up a bottle when Graeme answered the door.

"I'm afraid they didn't have much of a selection of wines at the local store, so I hope an ale will do."

"Ale is good," he said, smiling. "To what do I owe this unexpected surprise?"

"Well, I was hoping I might borrow some of your Internet time. I understand you're the only one for miles with a dial-up connection."

"Oh. Yes, of course."

Libby walked into the castle, set her coat on the hook. "I just have a few e-mails to send, and I need to check and see if there's anything earth-shattering I must attend to at work. I've never been away from e-mail this long before. I'm afraid I've grown to live by it."

Graeme showed her up to his office, where he was working before he heard her knock. The stereo was still playing his favorite Eric Clapton CD, his drawing pencil still lay atop the sheet.

"Oh, I'm sorry. I've interrupted your work."

Graeme turned down the music. "No, it's fine. I was due for a break. Been at it since we got back this morning."

Libby glanced at the drawing. "What is this?"

"Well, it's supposed to be a new government office in London."

"Oh, so you're an architect, as well as a castle caretaker?"

Graeme nodded. "I guess I'd hoped a stint in the country would help nurture some creative thought. God knows, this project could use all the help it can get."

"You don't sound very fond of it."

He shrugged. "It is a very *capable* building. It has everything it could need in the way of modern conveniences. Everything, that is, except for a soul." Graeme frowned. "These aren't my plans. They are the most recent attempt in a long line of other attempts on this project. Thus far, none of them have managed to garner approval from the project's main patron, the Prince of Wales."

"Prince, as in Prince Charles?" Libby blinked at him. "You're working for Prince Charles?"

"In a manner of speaking, yes. My firm has been retained to come up with a design that will satisfy him. I studied his architectural principles closely at university, so it was felt I might be able to resurrect what most have deemed a doomed project."

That and, given his family connections, it was thought that Graeme would have a better chance of passing muster with the notoriously high architectural standards of the prince. Graeme kept this last little bit to himself.

"That's quite a responsibility."

Graeme sighed. "Indeed. The thing is, I agree with the prince's opinions about the previous designs. None of them were up to the standard. The problem is I just can't seem to figure out how to break the pattern."

Libby was looking at photographs of the present site that Graeme had pasted up on the wall, as well as photographs from the early twentieth century and engravings from even earlier than that, when the building had had a much different purpose.

"It used to be a playhouse," he told her. "In its heyday

it saw the likes of Sarah Bernhardt and Lilly Langtry treading its boards."

"And now it's to be a government building?"

"Yes, after having stood empty for nearly a decade. It's got a fine location, but thus far none of the designs have been approved."

Libby was looking at the designs and the photographs alternately. "I don't know much of anything about architecture, but it looks like so far, all of the designs have sought to completely change the building's facade."

"That was the idea. It was just a matter of which change would best please the prince. Nothing too modern, or industrial. It must keep with the overall 'flavour' of London."

"Have you considered working with the facade instead? There's such a history there. It would be a shame to have it vanish behind some stark official-looking structure."

Graeme was peering at the drawing. "You think I should fashion a government facility after a playhouse?"

"Why not? You said the previous designs lacked a soul. The fact that this once was a playhouse *is* that building's soul."

Graeme considered her idea. It wasn't completely without merit. In fact, he had to admit, the more he thought about it, the more the notion of it truly intrigued him, even stoking a creative flame he'd begun to think was lost.

One of the biggest subjects for debate in the British capital city was that argument of modern architecture versus historical heritage. Throughout the twentieth century, the great noble mansions that had defined the city's squares two hundred years before had been torn down, demolished in the face of modern-day commercialism. After the damage of the Blitz of World War II, much of the rebuilding done in the city had been a matter of haste and cost-effectiveness against aesthetics. By comparison, after the Great Fire that had destroyed part of London in the seventeenth century, it had taken Christopher Wren thirty-five years to build St. Paul's Cathedral alone, and it was arguably one of the most distinctive features of the cityscape.

Perfection takes time. It was an idea that had been lost in the modern world's "do it now, do it fast" mentality. As such, modern architecture has been labeled, not without reason, as "sterile" and "uninspired."

This project could prove the exception to that rule.

"You mentioned the Internet . . ." Libby said, interrupting his thoughts.

"Oh, yes. The computer's just there." He waved across the room. "Just click on the browser's icon and it will connect automatically."

With Graeme obviously lost in his work, Libby took a seat behind the computer. Clicking the icon, she waited while the modem connected, watching Graeme out of the corner of her eye as she did. He was studying the drawings and photographs, and his expression was focused. Apparently her idea had struck a chord in him. In fact, he was so engrossed, she'd almost bet she could be standing there naked and he wouldn't notice.

Almost.

Once the computer had made the connection, she easily accessed her e-mail account. There were several messages from Rosalia, a couple more from other friends and acquaintances checking in or sending those interminable jokes that circulate continually throughout the World Wide Web. There were customers checking with titles they were looking for. There was also a message from Mr. Belvedere. Libby clicked on his message first.

Miss Hutchinson . . . (he never called her anything but)

> *I have considered your situation. I would truly hate to lose your knowledge and experience, but I*

*can't afford to keep you on salary if you're not see-
ing to your duties in the shop. I must admit that
your idea of continuing your scouting duties in the
U.K. does have its merits. And I want to give you
every opportunity to settle your family affairs as
needed. So, I will appoint Miss Mancuso (in other
words, Rosalia) as your stand-in here. You'll work
on commission. I'll give you forty percent on the
profit of anything you bring in. You will need to
communicate with Miss Mancuso regarding matters you were involved in here so that she will be
able to take care of anything that distance will prevent you from seeing to yourself. I hope this
arrangement will prove acceptable. In the meantime, you will still have your expense account to
cover the costs of purchasing and shipping. I have
received correspondence from three booksellers in
London whom you contacted, as well as a gentleman from an establishment called Leakey's in Inverness. You've obviously been keeping the shop's
interests in mind. When you return to the city, we
will discuss matters from that point on. And on a
more personal note, if you should come across any
rare editions of my own personal favorites, i.e.
Tolkien, Clarke, Wells, I would be most grateful for
your trained eye and expertise.*

Libby smiled. Mr. Belvedere was a closet sci-fi-
fantasy fanatic.

Forty percent was more than generous. In fact, given
the paltriness of her salary when compared to the cost of
living in New York, she'd just about been given a raise.

She closed the e-mail and typed a quick message back
to him, confirming her agreement with his arrangement
and thanking him for his consideration of her situation.
She gave him a listing of the books she'd bought at the
estate sale, indicating those that were already spoken for

by her customers, and then offered any of the others. She P.S.'d that she'd be sure to snatch up any of the afore-mentioned personal favorites for him first chance she got.

She clicked on Rosalia's messages next, which read just as the girl spoke, chatty, nonstop, with very little punctuation for breathing space. In them, she demanded to know everything about Scotland (mostly did the men really wear nothing under their kilts and were they all as good-looking as Mel Gibson in *Braveheart*). Libby e-mailed her back, expressing her excitement at their new working relationship. Then, with a glance at Graeme across the room, she added a P.S. assuring Rosalia that a good many Scotsmen were every bit as handsome as Mel Gibson in *Braveheart*, although she hadn't yet per-sonally discovered whether they really wore nothing under their kilts. "But," she added finally, "I have every hope to have an answer for you very soon. LOL!"

As she sat there, stealing glances at him over the com-puter monitor, Libby allowed herself the momentary pleasure of envisioning Graeme in a kilt, shirt open at the neck, hair ruffled from the wind. Somehow she knew he would look very, very good. For that matter, he would have looked good in the Widow MacNamara's Sunday kirtle.

She hadn't realized she hadn't yet clicked the SEND button when she suddenly noticed Graeme standing right behind her chair.

"Goodness!" She clicked the mouse button to close the message window and turned around.

"Sorry. Didn't mean to make you jump. I noticed you sitting with that rather intriguing smile on your face. I found myself curious as to what you were thinking about."

"Oh, just my work," she lied, and turned away from the computer.

He nodded. "I've some cold roast chicken in the refrigerator. Interested in a quick supper?"

"Sure."

They were just leaving the room when the phone suddenly started ringing.

Graeme went for it, and as he picked up the receiver, Libby motioned with her hands that she would meet him in the kitchen.

He nodded, took the call.

"Graeme Mackenzie."

"Darling!"

Graeme smiled. "How are you today, Mother?"

"Very well, dear. Had an invigorating day in the Lords."

"Take any prisoners?"

"That horrible Lord Faversham tried to sway the vote on my pesticides initiative."

"Tried, but I gather from your auspicious mood, he has failed?"

"Of course he did, darling boy. And I might say miserably at that. I rather doubt he has much in the way of an arse left to sit on. Not that there was much there to begin with."

Graeme chuckled. How he loved his mother's candid sense of humor. As he listened to her detailing the ins and outs of her political day, his gaze strayed to the computer monitor. He reached for the mouse and started clicking on various menus to shut the computer down. A beep issued from the hard drive, followed by the appearance of a small message box on the screen.

There are messages waiting to be sent. Send, then quit?

Graeme hovered the mouse pointer over the YES button, hesitating. As his mother's voice chattered on in his ear, he moved the pointer quickly to the e-mail outbox,

remembering Libby's jumpiness when he'd come upon
her earlier.

Though he'd begun to let down his guard with her, he
still couldn't quite put to rest the last niggling doubt that
she absolutely wasn't one of *them*. He wanted to believe
that she wasn't, wanted it more than he'd wanted anything in a long time. But there was always the pessimistic
suspicion itching at the back of his consciousness,
plaguing his most personal thoughts.

She'd been quite anxious to get to her e-mail. Could
she have been sending a message to the editor of *The
Buzz,* perhaps? Or some other scrounging paparazzi, revealing Graeme's whereabouts?

There was only one way he could be reasonably sure.
It wouldn't be the most gentlemanly thing to do, but perhaps just a quick peek at her e-mail could offer him the
last proof he needed to put any suspicions firmly to rest.

He clicked on the message, read it quickly.

She'd been telling the truth. She had been writing
about her work, after all.

His gaze paused on the P.S. of the message she'd sent
to someone called Rosalia. He felt the beginnings of a
smile tugging at the corner of his mouth.

So she wondered what a Scotsman wore underneath
the kilt . . . The image that came to mind warmed his
blood a good two degrees.

"Graeme? Are you there, dear?"

He clicked the button to send the message on its way.

"What? Oh, yes, Mother. Sorry. Was reading an e-
mail."

"How are things going with the project? Any inroads
on how to keep Prince Charles happy?"

"I've a notion of it. Need to work out some details."

"Splendid! Even though I miss your face, perhaps this
holing yourself up in the Highlands was a good thing
after all. Even that wretched tabloid has shown evidence

of moving on to greener pastures. I haven't seen your name mentioned in two whole days."

"Dare I hope?" He glanced at the office door. "Well, Mother, I'm rather in the middle of something right now, so I hate to . . ."

"No need to apologize, dear. I understand. I've a follow-up to prepare for Lord Faversham's faction. Do let me know when you'll be coming down to London so we can meet with His Grace to discuss things after you finish this project. Ta, darling!"

Half listening, Graeme hung up the receiver and headed for the kitchen.

But when he got there, Libby wasn't there.

"Libby?"

"In the study . . ." Her voice called from down the hall.

Graeme hesitated when he reached the doorway. She'd laid out a blanket before the fire with two plates of chicken, some sliced fruit, and a bottle of wine she'd snagged from his wine rack. Candles were lit around the room, and the sun was just setting through the windows. She was humming, kneeling to arrange things on the blanket, and affording him a rather lovely view of her backside.

She looked up when she noticed him standing there.

His pulse jumped. His stomach clenched.

"I thought a carpet picnic might be nice."

He swallowed hard, trying to tame his wild thoughts of stretching her out beneath him on that carpet. He came into the room and was greeted by the warmth of the fire, the warmth, too, of her eyes sparkling in the firelight. He lowered onto the floor beside her, and poured them each a glass of wine. The P.S. from her e-mail kept repeating itself through his thoughts. There was wine. There was firelight. For too long he'd denied himself the pleasure of the company of a beautiful woman.

Why the hell should he deny himself it any longer?

"Would you like—"

She never finished her question. Graeme reached for her, took her by the shoulders and pulled her against him as he captured his mouth with hers. He heard her suck in her breath in surprise, but a moment later she was kissing him back, splaying her fingers against his chest as he deepened the kiss, tasting her, knowing the soft caress of her tongue.

Her kiss was every bit as fiery as he had imagined.

He could taste the sip of wine she'd stolen before he'd arrived. He could smell the lavender soap she'd bathed in that morning. He could feel the soft, soft skin at the base of her neck, and he dragged his mouth to it, tasting it with his tongue.

He heard her moan, felt her body melt into his, and he pressed his hips against her, seeking to ease the roar of blood that was pulsing through his groin.

Slow down, he told himself. *Get hold of yourself.* But she smelled so incredibly good.

"Stay."

Graeme breathed out the word as his mouth kissed the tingling skin behind her ear.

"I'm not going anywhere," she whispered, and raked her fingers through his hair, dragging his mouth back to hers. She kissed him just as hungrily as he had her.

Graeme eased Libby down onto the blanket, all the while holding her in thrall with his kiss. Libby clung to him as he laid her back, sliding her tongue hotly over his. When she pressed her hips against him, seeking his hardness, Graeme couldn't keep from moaning out loud.

He thought certain he was going to explode.

He buried his face in her neck and slid his hands up, under her sweater, cupping her breasts. Libby gasped, arched her back against him. It had been so long, so very long. He watched as she closed her eyes, and saw the rapid rise and fall of every breath as he sat back and slowly, button by button, undid her sweater.

Libby blinked, her face aglow in the firelight as Graeme flicked open the last button and pushed back the folds of the sweater to feast on her with his eyes.

She was beautiful, her breasts full, inviting. He saw a chain that hung between them with a crystal-looking pendant that seemed to glow an unusual pink color. But it was the lacy scrap of bra, all that kept him from seeing her, from tasting her, that commanded all of his attention.

And fortunately for him, that lacy scrap of bra had a clasp in the front.

All he had to do was open it.

Graeme slid up beside her, lowered his mouth to hers, and slowly traced a finger down along her neck, between her breasts, moving the chain away as he took the clasp with his fingers and—

"Pardon, sir. I just forgot my—oh, dear God in heaven!"

Graeme and Libby shot up from the floor like two teenagers who'd just been caught under the high school bleachers.

A woman stood in the doorway, her eyes covered with one hand, her mouth covered with the other.

"Flora," Graeme said.

Libby yanked the front of her sweater closed over her breasts and tried to take a breath, feeling humiliated to her very toes.

"I'm so sorry. I had no idea. I—"

The woman shook her head, still refusing to uncover her eyes. "I'd forgotten my handbag and—oh, what the devil does it matter? Please, just pretend I was never here."

But that was just about to become impossible when Angus appeared in the hall behind her.

"Flora, did you find your . . . ?"

Libby hadn't thought she could be any further humiliated. But she'd been wrong. Even if her sweater hadn't been so obviously undone, the plates, the glasses, the bottle of wine. It was obvious they'd just intruded on a rather intimate setting.

Graeme saw Libby's mortification, and quickly shielded her as he led the other two from the room. "Perhaps we should check in the kitchen for your handbag, Flora . . ."

The missing bag was eventually found up in Graeme's office, where Flora had apparently set it before leaving for the day, inadvertently forgetting it there. Graeme let Flora and Angus out the back door, not saying a word about the scene they'd interrupted, and waited until he was certain they'd gone before heading back to the drawing room.

When he got there, the room was empty.

Libby had vanished.

Libby lay awake in her small single bed at the Crofter's Cottage, trying not to think about where she could be lying—and trying not to think about in whose arms she could be lying as well.

She curled up and closed her eyes, sighing deeply as she hugged her body tightly around the pillow. It had been so long since she'd felt this. The breathless anticipation. That giddy sense of carelessness. The slow, soft ache that seemed to pulse deep within her, melting through her every limb. It had been so long, she'd very nearly forgotten what it had felt like to want to be with a man.

It had taken her six months. Six months just to *feel* again. Six months to get over the emotional rubble of what she had come to refer to as "Hurricane Jeff."

Libby had known Jeff Webster nearly all of her life, growing up with him from primary school all the way through high school in Ipswich-by-the-Sea. His mother had been a friend of her mother, and even though they'd gone on to different colleges, they'd often crossed paths at town celebrations for the Fourth of July or Christmas. Libby had lost touch with Jeff after she'd moved to New York, and had thought of him only occasionally, usually when she would spend a Friday "Wine Night" with Rosalia and their small circle of friends, when conversation would inevitably turn to "The Guy You Had Most Wanted to Sleep with from High School But Never Had."

Until the day Jeff had suddenly, unexpectedly, shown up at the bookshop a little more than a year ago.

They'd shared a cup of coffee at the corner Starbucks, reminiscing and catching up over crumbling pieces of a blueberry muffin. After walking her back to the shop, Jeff had asked her out for dinner. It had seemed reasonable enough. He was looking for a job and was considering a relocation to New York. So of course he had called on an old friend, a familiar face in a strange and unknown city, someone who could tell him the best dry cleaners on the Upper West Side, or the quickest subway route to take to get to the financial district during rush hour. No doubt his mother had put him up to it.

But that one dinner had led to two. Two dinners had led to more. Eventually, several weeks and countless dinners later, they'd ended up sharing a breakfast in Libby's bed. Jeff had gone from "The Guy She Had Most Wanted to Sleep with from High School But Never Had" to the one who had her running like a schoolgirl to catch the ringing phone.

Though she'd always held a secret sort of crush for him, Libby had never done anything more than dream that fate might someday bring her and the sandy-blond, blue-eyed Jeff together.

That secret dream, however, had seemed to come true.

Jeff had moved into her apartment not long after, making it easier for him to conduct interviews and form

professional contacts. She'd be kidding herself if she
didn't admit that visions of her checkbook stating "Mrs.
Jeff Webster" hadn't danced through her fantasies fairly
early on. She had been, after all, thirty years of age, and
was more than ready to settle down into a stable, committed relationship.

But his proposal had been completely unexpected,
coming on a snowy Christmas Eve the year before while
ice skating beneath the stars in Central Park.

They'd set the date for late that April—a spring wedding in New England, when the daffodils and tulips
would be ablaze in the gardens. In late February, when
Jeff was finally offered a position with a Wall Street
firm, everything seemed to be falling into place.

If only she'd seen the signs, but she'd been too caught
up in wedding dress fittings, tablecloth color choices,
and whether to offer fish or beef at the reception. Jeff's
late nights at work hadn't seemed anything more than
the novice broker learning the ropes, and Libby had been
just too busy to notice his increasingly distant stares and
missed lunch dates. Too busy, or perhaps just a little too
afraid to admit to the truth, thinking that perhaps by pre-
tending it wasn't happening, she could somehow, magically, make it go away.

Everything would be better after the wedding, or so
she'd managed to convince herself.

In the end, it had been all so very clichéd. Nerves,
she'd told herself. Pre-wedding jitters. The bickering between them, the nights Jeff had spent on the couch, or
even later at the office. The plain truth was she'd been a
blind, naïve, utterly ridiculous fool.

But she wouldn't accept all the blame for it herself.
Even though he must have known days, even weeks earlier, Jeff chose to wait until the very weekend of their
wedding, their wedding eve, in fact, and just two hours
before the rehearsal and dinner being hosted by his own
parents. He hadn't even had the courage to tell her face-

to-face, but instead had sent her a text message on her cell phone.

M SORRY, LIB. CAN'T DO IT. HOPE U'LL B ABLE TO 4GIVE SOMEDAY.

Her responding frantic calls and messages had gone unanswered.

By the time she'd gotten back to the city, Jeff had already moved his things out, what little he'd had. He'd changed his cell phone number (the cell phone *she'd* gotten for him), and he hadn't so much as left a forwarding address. She'd found out a month later from her mother, who had heard it from his mother, that he'd moved his things out only to move them right into another apartment. Whose? A Park Avenue studio rented by her old high school friend, Fay Mills. Apparently, a leggy blond fashion model was more fascinating than a plain, ordinary antique-book seller.

Jeff's family had been devastated, and the "Webster boy's runner" had been the talk of Ipswich-by-the-Sea for months to follow. No doubt it still was. Such was the way of things in a small New England town. Events like that quickly became legend. Libby, however, had been spared having to hear it.

Though she hadn't wanted to admit it, it was the humiliation that had kept her from stopping in to see her mother as often as she previously had. She just couldn't face the stares, the pitying smiles, the knowing that every person in the town where she'd been born and had grown up knew she'd been summarily jilted at the altar.

So instead, Libby had thrown herself into her career. Working herself to exhaustion had been the only thing that seemed to help keep the heartache at bay. Eventually the sharp edge of her broken heart had dulled. She'd even gone out on a date or two, but never more than once with the same guy and never parting with anything more than a peck on the cheek. She simply used the excuse of work to discourage anyone who might have had more than a passing interest.

Always work.

Her mother had known it, had accepted it without a single word of complaint. Only now, after learning the truth of her mother's life in Scotland, did Libby even begin to realize just how much her mother had truly understood her daughter's need to run away.

But now, with Matilde gone, all of it—her embarrassment, her pride—seemed so utterly worthless.

Truth was, Libby hadn't had to attend quite that many estate sales, but it had been so much easier than facing her empty apartment night after night. Rosalia did get her to go out once, only by convincing her that it would be a group gathering and thus no pressure whatsoever for her to do anything more than sip her mineral water and listen to the conversation of others. Libby had gone, but had slipped away when the token "unaccompanied male" of the group had rested his hand a little too high on her leg under the table.

The touch of a man's hands on her skin hadn't produced anything in her except the bitter reminder that had things worked out differently, she could be sitting alone with Jeff somewhere just then, with his hand gripping her thigh possessively.

She'd sworn she would never long for the touch of a man's hands on her body again. And she hadn't.

Until she'd met Graeme Mackenzie.

When he'd kissed her so unexpectedly before that fire, Libby had wondered if she'd somehow dreamed it. The wine, the fire—it had been the perfect setting for such a fantasy, but there was no denying the touch of his hands on her, and the way her body had responded so completely, so utterly naturally to him.

It was the first time in a long time that she'd truly felt

alive, alive as a woman, a woman with physical needs and desires.

The intrusion of the housekeeper had been like a sudden jarring shower of ice-cold water. In fact, Libby remembered feeling quite numb for the first few seconds, as if it had been a dream after all. But then to have Angus appear as well? Her dream had quickly become the very worst nightmare. As soon as Graeme had ushered them out of the room, so obviously to spare her sensibilities, Libby had done the only thing she could think of.

She'd fled.

And now, as she lay there alone beneath a coverlet that had been knitted by two spinster sisters, she was left to do nothing more than stare at the ceiling, filled with regret, and think of what could have been.

Libby began to wonder if every significant moment for the rest of her life was destined to end up with her standing before a crowd of onlookers in complete humiliation.

Chapter Fourteen

The call from Hamish Brodie came early the next morning, just as Libby was entering the kitchen for breakfast.

"Checking in," he said abruptly no more than a half second after she'd put the receiver to her ear. "Just wanted to let you know I've filed the necessary paperwork with the necessary parties. I've requested a hearing with the Sheriff Court regarding Lady Venetia's right to manage the estate property, and have asked the Highland Council to sit in on the proceedings. They have an interest, you see, in seeing you succeed, and the community's future. I also wanted to tell you I have a copy of your parents' marriage record, which I received just yesterday afternoon from the Register Office."

Libby scarcely comprehended anything else he'd said before that. "You have?"

"Indeed. Let's see. It says here the marriage took place at a church called Balnakeil. It is up in your area, near to the village, I believe. Apparently it is a ruin, dating back quite some time, but it is still a listed church, though no one holds worship services there any longer. The minister of the village church at that time performed the ceremony there, no doubt to avoid the controversy of wedding them in the village without the blessing of the village's landlord, the Mackays. That also explains why you haven't been able to find any record of it in the parish records. The law only requires that the event be recorded with the General Register Office here in Edinburgh. Which it was. So, although it was a sort of secret ceremony, it is all very legal, I assure you."

Brodie ended the call with a promise to contact her just as soon as he had any further news.

After a quick breakfast of porridge and tea, Libby headed for the village church, bursting to tell Sean Mac-Nally, the one person she could tell, her good news.

"This is brilliant, Libby. Very clever of my predecessor to have performed their marriage there."

"Can you tell me where to find this Balnakeil Church? I would like to go there myself, to see it."

Sean showed Libby how to find the ruin on her Ordnance Survey map, where it was marked with a simple cross symbol, some three miles outside the village.

The Old Church, as it was called by the locals, was tucked away on a curving stretch of pure white sand that faced onto Wrath Bay. Libby stood on the headland above the beach and shaded her eyes, looking from the endless sea past the church, up to the stark white towers of Castle Wrath that stood high on the cliff above her.

It was the perfect place for the sanctuary. For though the roar of the open sea could be heard in the distance, here, somehow inexplicably, the shore was surrounded by a quiet calm, sheltered, it seemed, by heaven's own hand. Sean had told Libby that the church was indeed an ancient one, founded by a Saint Maelruhba in the eighth century. The present building, or what remained of it, dated from the late sixteenth century. It had fallen into disuse some two centuries later, around the time of the English Civil Wars, when the castle had been abandoned for a time, soon going to ruin itself. The weathered stone walls of the now roofless church ruin were clad in ivy, and its backdrop was the wild and unspoiled sea. Libby couldn't imagine a more peaceful resting place.

Among those buried in the churchyard were the ancient Mackay chiefs and their families, and others who had lived for hundreds of years in this place. There was a large stone marking the final resting place of a man called Rob Donn, the Gaelic bard who Ian had told her was related to Libby on her mother's side. Others were clansmen fallen in battle, the crew of a ship that sank off the treacherous waters of Cape Wrath in 1849, and even a notorious highwayman whose gravestone was complete with skull and crossbones. And there was another, now familiar name that was carved upon one of the more distinctive headstones.

Lady Isabella Mackay, wife of Calum Mackay, chieftain of the Mackays of Wrath, died this day, the 17th of January, 1800. A devoted wife to one, a loving mother of twelve, and doting grandmother to two and twenty. She loved this place in life, and so she reposes here in death, in the very shadow of the great castle she helped bring back to life. Ne'er afore a more noble lady . . . ne'er again a more beloved wife.

Libby found herself smiling softly at this most touching tribute. What would it be like, she wondered, to be loved so truly, so deeply?

This was her place, the one Libby had been named for, Lady Isabella, whose crystal Libby wore around her neck. She noticed that someone had placed a bouquet of wildflowers—heather, gorse, and a single white rose, now withered and dried—at the base of the granite stone.

Libby tugged at the chain and pulled the stone from beneath the heavy wool of her sweater, clasping it in her palm. The crystal felt warm against her skin even though the day was chill. Once again, the stone seemed to glow with its own inner fire.

Could it be it was trying to tell her something?

"Good day to you, lass. A fine day, is it no'?"

Libby turned to see the man, Gil, whom she'd met by the field of standing stones on that day that seemed now so long ago.

"Oh, hello, Gil. It is a fine day indeed."

She watched as he reached to sweep away the withered bouquet from Lady Isabella's gravestone, replacing it with a fresh one.

"Do you tend to the graves here?"

"Aye. Who else would be after doing it? I'm the ghillie of this estate, have been nearly all my life, though not many come any longer to this forgotten church. What brings you here, lass?"

Something about the man, something in his eyes, profound yet bright, seemed to whisper to Libby that she should trust him. Even the stone had changed to a soft, reassuring green. Libby decided to take a chance.

"My mother and father were married in this church."

"Indeed?" He blinked, clearly startled. "You're . . . you wouldna be . . . you're Matilde's daughter?"

She nodded, smiling. "You knew my mother?"

"Oh, aye. How could I no' when I've lived here all my life?" He doffed his tweed hat, scratched his graying head. "So tell me of your dear mother. She is well?"

Libby looked at him, shook her head. "I'm afraid she passed away. Last month."

The look on his face told her that he was truly, genuinely sorry to hear it. "I'd no idea . . ."

"I only discovered she was from the village when I was going through her things. She left me a photograph, and this crystal stone. I'm told it was once Lady Isabella's stone . . ."

Gil nodded, smiling softly. "Aye, and so it was. Now it is yours, as it should be."

"Gil, how did you know my mother was married here

at this church? No one else seemed to know of it in the village."

"Because, lass, I was here for the ceremony."

Libby felt a shiver take her. "You were?"

"Oh, aye, though none else knew of it. Your father asked me to stand up with him, and I was proud to do it. Ah, but it was a bonny, bonny wedding, too." He smiled, looking at the church ruin, his eyes turning a wistful, misty blue. "The bride, your mother, she wore a lovely gown, all pale ivory silk and light as a cloud. Her mother's gown, I believe, and she looked so lovely, just like a fairy maiden. It was held at dusk, just before the night, and they'd brought candles, so many candles, to light the sanctuary. Their wedding march was the sound of the sea, their congregation the birds who nest in these ruined walls. Ne'er have I seen a man more in love than your da wit' your mam. They thought, truly thought, that once they'd wed all would be well with the families." He shook his head. "But unfortunately, 'twas not to be."

Libby felt the cool sting of tears as she listened to him. She could see inside the church from where she stood, and clearly imagined the candles flickering in the wind, the soft rush of the sea breaking on the shore as her mother and father plighted their troth to one another in this ancient, beautiful place. They must have been so full of hope, so full of love for each other.

"I wish I'd known him."

Libby hadn't realized she'd spoken the words aloud.

"Ah, your father, he was a good lad. Back then, he was the sort who believed in things, believed he could change them, believed he could make a difference. He had great plans for this estate and the village, too. He loved this place almost as much as he loved your mother. Your mother and he, och, they were meant to fall in love. But some people, they just can't understand that love is a fated thing. You've no choice, no say in the matter whatsoever. Fate doesn't care what side of the silver spoon you come from."

He was speaking of Lady Venetia, Libby knew.

"The accident that took him, your father, it devastated this place. It has ne'er been the same since. But it will. Because you have the stone. Just as the legend says. You have brought the stone back and you will make it so because you are his daughter. You are the daughter of the Mackay. Look at the stone, lass. See how it glows against your hand. It speaks to you. Like Arthur's Excalibur, it tells that you are the one, the one who will save this place."

Libby saw that the stone had changed yet again, now glowing orange and pink like an ember in the fire. She felt a tingle that swept her from head to toe. It was as if this man could see, as if he knew everything, and listening to him, she truly began to believe.

"Do tell me, lass. Tell me of your mother's life in America. She was happy?"

"What?" Libby was still enthralled by the glowing stone. "Yes. I think she was happy. She had a good life, but she never forgot Scotland. She would sit on our front porch and stare out at the sea as if she was trying to look all the way to it. When I, or my fath—" Libby caught herself, explained. "I was adopted by a man named Charles Hutchinson, who married my mother after she left here. He brought us to America to live. Until my mother passed away, I never knew he wasn't my real father."

Gil's expression stilled. "Oh. Did she love him very much?"

"My fath—" She corrected again. "Charles?" Libby thought about it, thought about her childhood and thought about the woman her mother had been, the woman Libby was just coming to know. "In a way. I believe she did love him, but it wasn't a passionate love like the one she shared with Fraser Mackay. I would call it a 'comfortable' love, one that provided her with support, a home, a place to raise her daughter. It was a happy home. I can never remember words being raised in anger. But they never had any other children. It was always only me."

"Then he was a good man, this Charles Hutchinson, a good father to you, as well. I think Fraser would have been pleased to know that your mother found someone who so admirably took you and her into his heart."

Libby nodded. "Yes, I would like to think so. Perhaps he even had a hand in my mother meeting him." She looked at him. "Is he buried here?"

"Fraser? Aye." He pointed across to the corner of the graveyard. "Just there."

Libby walked in the direction he pointed, coming to a granite obelisk that looked more recent than most of the other stones in the cemetery.

IN MEMORY OF FRASER IAN CALUM MACKAY, LAST OF THE MACKAYS OF WRATH, A BELOVED SON WHO WAS TRAGICALLY TAKEN FROM THIS PLACE BY THE WRATHFUL SEA THIS STONE LOOKS UPON AND FOR WHICH THIS PLACE IS NAMED.

It was followed by a passage from the Bible. There was, Libby noticed, no mention made of his having left a widowed wife, or the child she had then carried.

Libby took a breath, spying a clump of still blooming heather just on the outside of the cemetery, fading violet against the coming dullness of winter. She knelt to break off a sprig of it and closed her eyes in silent tribute, laying it at the foot of her father's memorial, all the while wondering how different her life might have been had this man, her father, lived to make the difference he'd so wanted.

*   *   *

Libby spent quite a lot of time over the next several days with Sean MacNally, sitting at the small table in his kitchen, detailing a sort of preliminary list of improvements that could be made to the village if her case to regain the estate succeeded.

The capital to help fund the improvements would come mostly from the village itself, by way of the sale of certain properties to tenants who had lived on the land for generations. Those who couldn't afford to buy their properties outright could be helped with mortgages and grants arranged by the Highland Council by way of a special program that had been established and had, in the past, assisted other communities in buying out portions of other estates.

Libby's first priority was the school, and the purchase of an updated computer system, with capability for the Internet and a world of resources that this corner of the world had as yet no idea even existed. From the convenience of their computer monitors, the children could visit museums as far away as America, could read books from on-line libraries. There would be up-to-date textbooks and maps that showed the actual current layout of the globe. The ones they now had hanging on their walls showed East and West Germany as still separate.

After the school, there would be other improvements, and a planned effort to boost tourism in the area, with signposted historic walking trails, a village museum showing life through the centuries, and a bookshop that would carry guidebooks and other titles of interest to the village.

When they were finished, the list they'd compiled took up more than several neatly scripted pages. They forwarded it to Hamish Brodie's office so that it could be presented at the initial hearing before the Sheriff Court.

All that remained was for the news of the hearing to break.

And when it did, it broke in a big way.

Libby was sitting at the White Heather café with Angus MacLeith, sharing a lunch of lentil soup and ham sandwiches, when Graeme came in, striding straight across the dining room for their corner table. His face immediately betrayed that something was very, very wrong.

He slapped the letter with the instantly recognizable letterhead of Hamish Brodie on the table before her. "What in the bloody hell do you think you're about?"

"Oy!" Angus immediately stepped in. "You'd better just take a moment, Mr. Mackenzie, and calm yourself."

Graeme's outburst had drawn the attention of the other lunch patrons.

"Now why don't you take a seat and tell me what this is all about?"

"Apparently Miss Hutchinson thinks she has some claim to my home. She has filed an injunction in court attesting that she is some missing Mackay heir who suddenly, magically, discovered the legacy of the Wrath estate."

Angus had taken up the paperwork and was looking through it. "This is true, Libby?"

She nodded, looking at them both. "I didn't know of it when I came first here. I never knew it but my mother had been married to Fraser Mackay. I never knew that I was his daughter. I only found out about the legacy after I arrived in the village and started to uncover the truth."

Angus was still flipping through the pages. "These documents certainly seem to support that, Mr. Mackenzie."

"Graeme," Libby began, "I had no idea this would have anything to do with you. You're the castle caretaker. It's my father's mother, Lady Venetia Mackay, that I seek to stop. She has been acting as the trustee for the estate since the death of my grandfather, only what neither of you, what nobody in this village realizes, is that she means to sell the entire estate to a Dutch mineral drilling company that will come in and no doubt start evicting tenants to build a facility. She sold the rights to the castle only because she had to protect it. It is written as such in the Mackay trust. But the land of the estate is not protected and can be disposed of however she might wish."

Graeme was listening to her, thank God, but he still wasn't pleased. It was evident from the look on his face that he was still very upset.

"I couldn't tell you," she said, pleading with him with her eyes. "I couldn't tell anyone, because if Lady Venetia had somehow learned the truth, that I was here, that I even existed, she could have quickly closed the sale of the estate to the drilling company, which would only complicate the matter further, and might bring irreparable harm to the village. Don't you see? I have to do this. If I don't, there will be no village left. Your neighbors will no longer be the crofters and the countryside, but a mineral drilling factory. This landscape, everything special about this place, will be spoiled. The lives of the villagers will be ruined. I cannot allow that to happen. And I won't allow it to happen."

The news spread throughout the village and surrounding settlements as the day for the initial hearing in the Sheriff Court quickly approached. The hearing would be held in the town of Wick, at the district's Sheriff Court, and even though it was nearly two hours' drive east from the village, most everyone seemed intent on attending. Most everyone, that was, except Graeme. He had left the confrontation in the café that day clearly still feeling betrayed. Libby hadn't seen him since, although several times, she'd gotten into her car, even driving as far as the castle gate, only to turn around and leave without seeing him.

What could she possibly say to him?

Hamish Brodie had arrived two days before the hearing and had taken a room at the Crofter's Cottage to spend the time with Libby going over their legal strategy. The hearing, he explained, was really nothing more than a springboard. This sort of case was too substantial, and Hamish fully expected it would be moved up to the higher Court of Session in Edinburgh, perhaps even on to the House of Lords, which would ultimately decide the fate of the Wrath estate.

Meanwhile, the community was rallying around Libby. For too long the villagers had been kept from improving their way of life because of Lady Venetia's feudal rule over the village and surrounding lands. But now there was a chance for change. Those who had been too afraid to speak to Libby upon her arrival now greeted her openly in the street, inviting her in for tea. And everyone, it seemed, had a story to tell of her mother and father and the great love they had shared.

The day of the hearing dawned with rain, casting a fittingly somber mood on the proceedings. Libby walked into the courtroom with Hamish Brodie, who directed her toward two tables that had been set up before the bench. At the front of the room stood a high bench where the sheriff would sit to listen while the two sides presented their cases. From her one experience with jury duty, it seemed all very similar to the American court system.

Hamish and Libby took the table at the left. Libby sat while Hamish went to the other side of the room, shaking hands and exchanging greetings with the solicitors who represented the interests of the estate.

Lady Venetia, Libby noticed, was nowhere to be seen.

The judge came in, sweeping into the room in a flash of black robes and white curled periwig. He sat at the front of the room and faced the assembly, banging his gavel down as he called the hearing to order. Libby sat silently as Hamish outlined her complaint in its most legal terms, listening as the sterile details of her life were brought out for all to hear.

As expected, there were objections from Lady Venetia's solicitors, but Hamish performed à la Perry Mason, as if he had anticipated every one of their arguments, speaking clearly and with the confidence of the right and just. The sheriff asked a few questions, mostly dealing with Lady Venetia's handling of the estate thus far, and then, in the end, just as Hamish had told her to expect, the judge recommended that the case be moved to the next highest court, the Court of Session. Another hearing, this time in Edinburgh, would need to be scheduled.

"Is that all, gentlemen?"

The sheriff was preparing to call the hearing to a close.

Hamish spoke up. "One more point, if I may?"

Libby looked at him.

"I wish to address the issue of the Castle of Wrath. As was outlined in my complaint, the validity of the sale of this property is in question. It goes back to the same stipulation that Lady Venetia does not have the right to sell the estate in any part at all. I wish to suggest that until the matter has been decided by the higher court, Miss Hutchinson should have immediate occupancy."

What?!

Libby tried to get his attention, scribbling *No!* on the legal pad before her and underlining it three times. This wasn't what she wanted, no matter her legal right in the matter.

He ignored her and pressed on.

"Miss Hutchinson will have to extend her stay in Scotland, with the added expense of accommodation, while this matter is decided in the courts and the appeals that no doubt will follow. Since she was born in Scotland before emigrating to America, she holds dual citizenship in both countries, and so there is no impediment to her remaining in Scotland as long as she wishes. So, until the other party can prove their right to have sold the property at all, I see no reason why Miss Hutchinson shouldn't have access to the property to which we allege she is entitled, to allay the costs of her remaining in Scotland to see this process through."

The sheriff withdrew from the courtroom to consider the petition, no doubt to research any pertinent law. Murmurs from the villagers issued from behind. Everything suddenly felt so out of Libby's control.

"Hamish, this isn't what I wanted," she whispered to him.

"You must trust me in this, Libby. A good deal of our case hinges on your desire to assume responsibility for your birthright. Lady Venetia's advisors could argue that because you intend to return to America, and not even take possession of the property, you would be, in essence, just as much, if not more, of an absentee landlord as Lady Venetia, or the mineral drilling company, for that matter. Lady Venetia can claim she has no such plans to sell the estate, and can also argue her proximity to the estate. Absentee landlords are not well thought of in the Highlands. They have not been shown to have the best interests of the villagers at heart. I must establish a connection for you to the estate that will demonstrate your intention to stay the course. Having you renting a room at the Crofter's Cottage will not support this point."

The sheriff returned less than a quarter of an hour later.

"It is the judgment of this court, after much consideration, and given the size of the property known as Castle Wrath, that hereafter the castle shall be occupied by both Miss Hutchinson and the present tenant, until such time as a higher court determines who the rightful property holder should be."

The sheriff raised his gavel and brought it down with a resounding clap, closing the hearing until its continuance in the higher court in Edinburgh. It was only afterward, as she was driving back along the winding A836, that Libby realized exactly what had just taken place. And when she did, she hit the brakes, bringing the car to a sudden skidding halt.

Good God. They were going to be living together.

She and Graeme.

In that castle.

Alone.

Chapter Fifteen

Libby pulled the car slowly into the castle courtyard, the wheels crunching on the gravel drive as she parked alongside Graeme's freshly washed and gleaming Land Rover. The larger SUV dwarfed the mud-spattered semi-compact.

She cut the engine, but she didn't immediately get out of the car. Her nerve, not very strong to begin with, was slipping further still now that the moment was at hand. She'd waited two days after the hearing before vacating her room at the Crofter's Cottage. For one thing, that would even her stay there to a full fortnight, thereby easing the accounting for the two sisters. But for another, it would give Graeme the time to come to terms with the news that he was going to be sharing his living quarters with her.

"No point putting it off any longer," she said to the steering wheel as she took the keys from the ignition and slipped out of the front seat.

She glanced up at the narrow windows winking in the midday light from the castle tower and wondered if he was watching her arrival. Centuries earlier, the castle's inhabitants would have poured boiling oil down on intruders to keep them from gaining access to the keep. Then, enemies had come armed with battering rams and armies of fierce clansmen. She'd come armed with a mere slip of paper signed by the court.

As she approached the door, bags in hand, Libby wondered what she would say to him. Should she keep it casual? As if she were just some Highland tourist stopping in for a weekend? Or should she prepare herself with a list of reasons to cite as to why this was so necessary? Somehow, no matter what she said, she doubted he would think Hamish's idea that she take up residence was a sound one.

In the end, none of it mattered. Her knock on the door wasn't answered by Graeme at all.

"Hallo, Miss Hutchinson. I've been expecting you."

The woman had kindly green eyes and a face of the sort that was naturally beautiful without the need for any cosmetic enhancement. Her vibrant red hair was pulled back in a loosened knot that was now drooping at the back of her neck, with wisps of it loose and caressing her delicate chin. She wore an apron over the simple floral dress that draped her slender figure, falling to just above her knees. She was wiping her wet hands with a dish towel.

"You're Flora? Angus's sister?"

"Aye, that's me." She finished drying her hands and offered one to Libby in greeting. "Welcome to Castle Wrath. 'Tis grand to finally meet you after all my brother has told me about you. You're certainly as pretty as he said you were."

She hadn't said a word about having walked in on Libby and Graeme that night, and in fact acted every bit as if this was the first time she'd ever set eyes on her, even though images of Libby with her sweater hanging open must be flashing through her mind. Grateful, Libby smiled as the woman stepped back to allow her inside.

"I've set up Lady Isabella's room for you. I'm afraid 'tis on the topmost floor, a bit of a hike to get to, but well worth the effort. It really is the best room and has the prettiest view of the sea. Can I help you with your things?"

Without even waiting for Libby's reply, Flora took one bag while Libby lugged two others and followed her up the central oak stairway. As they went, Flora kept up a constant stream of chatter, filling Libby in on the basic arrangement of the castle, where to put any post she wished to send, when deliveries were made, if she preferred tea or coffee with her breakfast.

"Oh, you don't have to make my breakfast, Flora."

"Och, 'tis fine. I'm already doing it for Mr. Mackenzie. An extra spot of water in the tea kettle isn't any trouble."

On the first floor, they passed the doorway to Graeme's office and Libby glimpsed him inside, standing with his back to the door as he spoke into the telephone. He made no move to acknowledge them, and Flora said nothing as they climbed another set of stairs that led to the castle's north tower.

Lady Isabella's "room" was actually more of a suite that took up the whole of that part of the castle. There was the main bedchamber with its lofty carved ceiling and polished wood floor, a sitting room tucked in the rounded tower corner with views out to the sea and surrounding countryside, and a bathroom with both a shower and a claw-foot tub that connected the room to another equally large suite on the castle's other side.

"That's the laird's chamber," Flora told her, motioning toward the door. When Libby peered through, her concern must have shown on her face. "Ehm, Mr. Mackenzie prefers a bedchamber closer to his office on the floor below, in case any calls come in early. So 'twill be just you up here."

Libby smiled, nodded. Well, at least they wouldn't be sharing a shower.

Although they could both certainly fit in that tub . . .

The thought had come out of nowhere, but it only

served to remind Libby of what would now most certainly never be.

Back in the bedchamber, she started taking her things from her suitcases, hanging them in the tall rosewood armoire, which smelled of lavender and something else that was sweet but not quite floral—vanilla, perhaps?

The bed was enormous, a four-poster that would certainly require the small steps standing beside it just to get into. It stood in the middle of the room and was beautifully hand-carved along the posts with images of thistles and heather. The white sheets were freshly laid, smelling of lavender, the pillows goose-feather plump. It looked warm and inviting, as comforting as her mother's arms. Libby couldn't wait to curl up in it.

Flora had opened the windows in the sitting area to air the room, and the wind off the sea breezed inside, salty and cool, fluttering the gauzy white curtains. There was a woolen throw draped over the foot of the bed and a basket of fresh peat waiting beside the cozy hearth.

"It does get a bit chilly in here at night," Flora told her, pulling the windows closed. "If you run out of peat, there's more in the bin off the kitchen. Gil keeps us well stocked."

Flora reached toward the wall, flicking an inconspicuous switch that opened a small, nearly indistinguishable door built into the paneling. "These passages were built in case of fire, more for safety's sake than anything else, but they save you a bit of distance if you're heading for the kitchen. Mind yourself, though, the steps are small and the turnstile is quite narrow. Lady Isabella must have been a wee thing like yourself."

She ducked her head inside as if to demonstrate, until Libby realized she intended to take the stairs to leave.

"Dinna worry. I swept away all the cobwebs." Flora smiled, her eyes sparkling. "I was just after making a fresh pot of tea when you arrived. Why don't you come down to the kitchen when you're finished with your things and have a cuppa?"

Libby smiled and nodded, grateful that this woman had made her foreboding arrival at the castle so comfortable. She suspected that the other occupant of the house wouldn't be so pleasant.

It took about a half hour to arrange her things about the room and set up her toiletries in the bathroom. Libby ducked into the hidden stair, leaving the door open behind her to help light her way. But two turns onto the stairs and she found herself descending into complete and utter darkness. There wasn't any light anywhere on the stairs, so she had to flatten one hand against the wall as she continued, tentatively, to follow wherever the steps might lead her.

When she emerged into the kitchen, coming through an equally small door, it wasn't Flora she found waiting there.

"Oh," she said when she saw Graeme standing at the center butcher block, quietly munching on a sandwich.

He looked at her, but said nothing, turning his attention back to his lunch plate.

Libby crossed the room, took up the teapot Flora had left steeping for her and began straining off the leaves. She chanced a glance at him. "Do you know where Flora—"

But he had turned, taking up his plate as he headed for the hall door.

"Graeme . . ."

He stopped, turned to face her, silent as a stone.

"Is this it? Are we supposed to pretend we have never met, that we aren't living in the same house? Don't you think there are things we should discuss?"

"What could we possibly have to discuss?"

He was drawing an invisible line between them, choosing the path of avoidance over that of facing the situation head-on. But Libby wasn't interested in playing it that way.

"Well, Flora, for one thing."

From the expression on his face, Graeme clearly hadn't expected that response from her. "What about Flora?"

"Since I'm to be living here, I would like to contribute to paying for her services."

"That is not necessary."

"No, I really think—"

"I said it wasn't necessary."

His tone was stark, final, and utterly uncompromising.

Libby tried another approach, cutting straight to the very heart of the matter. "Graeme, I wanted to tell you the truth. In fact, I tried to tell you more than once, but I just couldn't. I couldn't risk it. Surely now that you've heard everything, you can understand the difficulty of the situation I was placed in."

Graeme looked at her. The truth was he *could* understand. He of all people knew what it was to be unable to trust. In fact, he'd begun to believe he would never trust another again.

The only problem was he *had* begun to trust.

He'd begun to trust *her*, only to discover that she, too, had deceived him.

"I've got to return to my work."

Graeme turned for the door, leaving Libby no choice but to watch him leave.

After half of a ham sandwich and tea in the kitchen, Libby found herself alone and wandering the halls of the castle. She had no idea where Flora had gone, but she was glad for the opportunity to acquaint herself with her father's childhood home alone, so she could take the time to take it all in—and to imagine.

What a place it must have been to grow up in. The castle was much bigger than it had at first appeared, running through a seemingly endless collection of rooms, halls, stairwells, and even several outbuildings. It took an effort just to try not to get lost. In one of the back hallways, she found a board fixed high upon the wall; attached to the board were a number of small bells of differing sizes with wires that ran the length of the ceiling. On the board, painted above each bell, were words like "Ld M'kay's Chamber," "Ldy M'kay's Chamber," even "Blue Room," "Green Room," and "Nursery." And those were just the main rooms. There were countless other bells that were merely numbered to distinguish them.

Walking the halls and opening doors as she came to them, Libby lost count of the different rooms she'd found at twenty-six. Imagine the games of hide-and-seek that must have been played by Lady Isabella and Calum's twelve children!

But most of the rooms—in fact almost all of them—had been closed up, the furnishings shrouded with dust-covers, and the windows shuttered against daylight for decades. *As if to forget the very lives that had been lived there.*

As she stood in the doorway to one of them, perhaps even the "Blue Room" noted on the bell board, since its walls were painted in a dull, fading periwinkle, Libby tried to envision a family, *her* family, spending quiet winter nights there. But she just couldn't picture it through the deathlike shrouds and darkened windows.

Seized by emotion, Libby started yanking away the covers, throwing back the shutters to allow in the sunlight.

Dust that had collected for years, undisturbed by human hands was sent flying. Libby unlatched the windows, some stuck from years of disuse, and threw wide the sashes, welcoming in the sea air as she continued her work. At some point Flora appeared in the doorway, no doubt wondering if Libby had lost her mind.

"Here," Libby said, handing her the corner of one

cloth that draped what appeared to be a very tall standing cabinet. "Give me a hand."

They worked up a sweat, attacking the furnishings and the floors with lemon oil and beeswax. They polished and dusted and scrubbed and polished more. Paneling that had been banished to darkness and layers of dust gleamed warm as honey beneath their diligent ministrations. They laughed as they rolled up the huge, worn carpets, sneezing from the dust as they carried them outside to beat against the old stable block with a broom.

As they worked, they talked. Libby told Flora about growing up an only child in New England, about life in America, about living in New York City. Flora, in turn, told Libby about growing up in a Highland village, about the carefree childhood she and Angus had had with the whole of the Highlands as their playground. Their father had worked on an oil rig in the North Sea, just as Flora's husband, Seamus, had. In fact it had been her father who had first brought Seamus home, a Glaswegian who'd had no family this far north. The MacLeiths made him family even before he and Flora had fallen in love and married to make a life together.

"He was a fine husband," Flora said, sitting with Libby a couple of hours later, sharing a pitcher of lemonade. "Och, I'd stand at the kitchen window and just watch for him to come home. Made my heart fly the moment I saw him sauntering up that cottage path. He gave me three beautiful bairns, he did, afore he . . ." Her voice dropped off. She breathed deeply. "The wee one was still in my belly when I lost him. I miss him, miss him like I'd miss my own arm if it were gone." Her voice dropped. "My own heart . . ."

Libby blinked against her tears, touched by the raw burden of this woman's loss and the obvious love that Flora still had for her husband, a love that reached beyond life, and even beyond death.

"And what of you?" Flora asked her, shaking the grief

away as she put on a smile. "How is it you've not been marched down the aisle afore now?"

Libby took a sip from her glass, hoping to ease the lump that had suddenly formed in her throat. "There was one. Back in New York, but he didn't truly love me for me. I suppose I was lucky I found out before the vows were said."

But Libby didn't feel so lucky.

Flora took her hand, squeezing it. Her eyes told of an unspoken understanding. "Oh, but there will be someone, someday. You must hold that hope in your heart always. Even I do."

At Libby's startled look Flora smiled. "Oh, I'll ne'er love like I did Seamus, that's for certain. But that doesna mean I winna long for someone just to hold me whenever I need the holding. Everybody needs holding once in a while, miss. And perhaps someday we'll each find us a man who'll do that holding, eh?"

Libby returned the smile, nodded. If it was all she had, there was at least that hope.

"So," she said, eyeing their most recent undertaking, freshly broom-beaten of dust, "we'd best get that carpet back up those stairs, then, hmm?"

They got through just that one room that afternoon, a drawing room complete with a Steinway grand piano. A pull on a wire fixed inconspicuously near the door revealed it was indeed the "Blue Room" from the bell board, and Libby made a mental note to call in at Ian M'Cuick's the next morning in search of a more vibrant shade of blue for the walls. Besides the fact that the color was graying from age, the far wall showed signs of having once featured a sizeable collection of hanging plates, the ghostly shadows of them still marked in precisely measured rows. Libby determined to find those plates, and after a great deal of searching, she did find them, packed away in crates under one of the castle garrets.

"They're beautiful," Libby said as she and Flora sat cross-legged on the garret floor, sorting through them.

They were Meissen porcelain, thin as eggshells, and decorated with a Scottish thistle trim around the edge. Together they carefully carried the plates down to the kitchen for a much-needed soak, leaving them to dry in the dish racks.

Much later that afternoon, around four o'clock, Flora had to hurry home to make supper for Angus and her children. She invited Libby to join them, but Libby asked if she could take a rain check. All she wanted was a long, hot bath to ease her aching muscles and wash away the layers of dust that she could feel even now coating every inch of her. After rooting around in the garret and crawling across floors and under chimney breasts, she surely had four hundred years of grime and soot smudged across her face.

Libby pulled out the barrette that hung limply in her hair and shook her tangled locks as steamy water filled the massive claw-foot bathtub. It was long enough for her to stretch out her legs, with a curved edge that allowed her to lean her head back as the decadent warmth of the scented bath enveloped her.

Heaven . . .

Turning off the tap, she closed her eyes and let the bathwater work its magic. She was too tired to even care that she'd forgotten her bathrobe in the other room. She simply lost herself in the magnificently simple pleasure, all the while wondering if there was a single muscle in her body that wasn't aching at that moment.

Graeme didn't surface from his office until he noticed the daylight fading outside the windows.

Where had the time gone? He'd been so caught up in working with his drawings, he hadn't even realized the hours were breezing by.

The hallway outside his office door was dark, cast in

the shadows of the ending day. Where the devil was Flora? She would usually pop in to tell him she was leaving. He had come to measure the passing of the day by Flora's appearances, bringing the day's post, usually around nine, lunch at noon, an afternoon pot of tea at two, then four or five when she was leaving for the night. Try as he might, he couldn't recall her having done so today, but then, he was beginning to lose track of what day it was, let alone whether his housekeeper had said good night to him, so anything was possible.

He walked downstairs, passing empty rooms and closed doors. He came across Murphy stretched out on the rug at the foot of the stairs, but found the kitchen curiously empty. Flora had left a plate for him warming in the oven, as was her custom. Roast beef and some small potatoes. There was a single dish of salad chilling in the refrigerator. There wasn't any indication that the castle's other tenant would be having supper in.

Apparently Libby had decided to go into the village, where she'd become quite the local hero, the native daughter come home at long last to save the village from ruination. Even he had to admit a certain admiration for her.

In the past several days while he'd been holed up in his office, Graeme had had a lot of time to think. He'd gotten past most of his initial anger. He wasn't at all thrilled about the prospect of losing the castle. Although he certainly wouldn't be homeless if the court ruled in Libby's favor, as he fully expected it to do, over the past months Graeme had grown attached to his remote hideaway and was more than a little reluctant to give it up to return to the glaring spotlight reserved for the dual heir of the Duke of Gransborough and the Countess of Abermuir. In fact, he fully intended to remain exactly where he was until he was legally obligated to leave.

But after learning the circumstances surrounding the estate, and Lady Venetia Mackay's plans for it, he had no choice but to admit that Libby was doing the right thing. The *only* thing. In her place, he would have done the same.

When he'd arranged for the purchase of the castle, he'd worked only through Lady Venetia's solicitors. He had never met the Mackay matriarch personally. He'd just figured her to be another absentee landlord, like so many across the Highlands, who left the administration of their estates to others and showed up once or twice a year. At no time had anyone indicated that the bulk of the estate was to be sold to any mineral drilling company. In fact, he'd offered to purchase the estate in whole, but had been refused, told that Lady Venetia didn't intend to part with it. In fact, they'd even assured him that if she did decide to sell, he would be the first to know.

As it was, he'd been among the very *last*.

Graeme brought his supper plate and a glass of Pinot Noir back up to his office, thinking he would put in a couple more hours of work before calling it a night. He was making good progress. It was as if ever since Libby had made the suggestion of working with the historical features of the building, a light had turned on in his head.

But as he reached the top of the stairs, he paused, looking down the hall. He found himself wondering which of the bedchambers Libby had chosen to take. If she came back from the village late, her room would be ice-cold. She wasn't used to living in a drafty castle with dodgy radiators. He rather doubted she had thought to light the hearth before she'd left.

He left his plate on the side table and walked the length of the hall, checking the doors as he went. But she'd taken none of the rooms on the first floor, and so he headed for the back stairs that led to the upper chambers.

As soon as he emerged from the stairs, the temperature dropped noticeably. Since he'd been at the castle, he'd kept the upper floors shut away to conserve the heat. In fact, he'd scarcely even looked at any of the other rooms since moving in.

But halfway down the hall he stopped at an open door and was stunned by what he found inside.

It was a drawing room with carved oak paneling that gleamed beneath an elaborate plasterwork ceiling. Furnishings of cherry and mahogany were freshly polished, revealing centuries-old craftsmanship, and the walls were adorned with gilt-framed portraits and mirrors. A stone mantelpiece featured proudly along one wall, surrounded by brocade-covered settees and chairs. Fresh flowers filled porcelain vases, and the scent of lemon perfumed the air.

He felt as if he had stepped back in time. At any moment he expected to see a Victorian-era butler come walking through, silver salver in hand. In all the weeks he'd been living in the castle, Graeme had yet to set foot in this room. Libby had been there but one day—half a day, really—and already had given the place her touch.

Farther down the hall, he was not at all surprised when he saw the room she'd decided to take up residence in. When he'd first bought the castle, this room more than any other had "spoken" to him. It was as if there was a spirit to the chamber, a soul that even the dustcovers had been unable to shroud. Now, fresh and clean and alive, the place virtually pulsed.

Had circumstances been different, he would have chosen this room for her himself.

The hearth was indeed cold, as he'd expected, so he bent to place a brick of peat on the grate, fueling it with kindling underneath. It lit easily and soon caught flame. He crisscrossed logs on top of the peat, watching as the wood began to burn. When he was certain the fire wouldn't go out, he headed for the bathroom to wash the soot and dirt from his hands.

He never made it to the sink.

She was there, asleep in the tub and utterly naked.

Graeme froze in the doorway, relishing the sight of her. Several times, when they'd been alone, he'd allowed himself to imagine what she must look like beneath all those bulky sweaters and shapeless trousers she favored wearing. And that night by the fire, he'd been on the very brink of satisfying his curiosity, until Flora and Angus had shown up unexpected. His imagination, however, hadn't been nearly so vivid as what he saw now reclined in that tub.

She was . . .

. . . beautiful.

Her dark hair, freshly washed, curled damply about her ears, one twisting tendril falling over her cheek, her darkly lashed eyes. Her skin was rose-petal pale, unblemished and pink from the bath. Her breasts were full, though not overly so, their rose tips taut from the cold. They were utterly magnificent. He felt his groin grow tight just looking at her, and his gaze moved down over the flat belly, gently flared hips, and shapely legs. One leg was bent, shielding him from a more thorough study, and he ached just to run his hand along that leg. Just once.

A gentleman wouldn't stand there staring at her like that, but he found he just couldn't deny himself the sheer, unadulterated pleasure.

Until the fire in the bedchamber behind him suddenly popped.

And Libby stirred, coming awake.

Chapter Sixteen

Libby opened her eyes and quickly realized she had drifted off to sleep in the bath.

How long had she been lying there, completely out of it? Apparently it had been some time since the sky was dark outside, and the water had gone cold. Just realizing it, she began to shiver and sat up, pulling the stopper from the drain. She stood, dripping, as she reached for her towel, wrapped it around herself, and headed for her bedchamber to retrieve her robe.

It was warmer there, and a moment later she realized why. There was a fire crackling in the hearth.

Who had . . . ?

She looked across the room to her chamber door, which was just slightly ajar. She knew Flora had left before she'd gone into the tub.

She glanced back to the bathroom door.

Had Graeme . . . ?

Libby felt a tingle race over her skin that had nothing to do with either the chill or the fire.

She got dressed, slipping on one of her oversized sweatshirts and flannel lounging pants. She combed the tangles from her hair and left it loose to dry, then went down to the kitchen to make a cup of tea. Flora, she discovered, had left a plate of scones.

The kettle was just starting to boil when Graeme came in. Libby looked at him and felt herself blush. She didn't dare ask him if he'd come upon her in the bath. "Would you like tea?"

"That would be nice, thank you."

He, too, was wearing a pair of lounging pants and an oversized T-shirt. Libby measured out the tea leaves while he took out jam and butter for the scones.

"I saw the room upstairs, that blue room. You did a brilliant job with it."

"The Blue Room," which was just down the hall from Libby's chamber.

He had come into her bedchamber.

A fresh blush stole across her face.

"Thanks. Seems a shame to hide all the furnishings and lock away all the rooms. I hope you don't mind that I . . ."

"It is your right, until the court may judge otherwise."

Libby frowned at his stiff reply.

Graeme must have noticed the look on her face and said, "I'm sorry. That wasn't very well done of me. To tell the truth, I had thought the same thing and intended one day to set about restoring the castle to its former condition, but just hadn't had the time."

Libby nodded, changed the subject. "How are things going with your project?"

"Very well. I'm working on some preliminary sketches right now. In fact, I'll be traveling to London tomorrow for a meeting at my firm."

"Oh." She hadn't expected he'd be leaving, and so soon.

"Would you—" Graeme hesitated, as if weighing his next words. "I mean to say, you had mentioned some London book dealers you were interested in speaking with. I'll be going down to the city only for the day. It wouldn't be any trouble if you wanted to go along."

"Oh," Libby said for the second time now. It was as

near a truce as she was going to receive. "That would
be—I mean, if you're sure you wouldn't mind, I'd love
to go. I'll need to make arrangements for an airline
ticket. Which flight are you on?"

"My un—," He stopped and said instead, "No need to
worry. I have a helicopter coming. Much easier than
waking at dawn to spend half the morning driving to Inverness and then the rest of the morning flying to
Gatwick."

"Oh," Libby said for a third time now. "What time
should I be ready to leave, then?"

"Half eight, unless you need me to make it later?"

"No, that's fine. Half eight it is."

Libby was in the kitchen and had prepared a pot of tea
by eight the next morning when Graeme came down.

Libby did a double take when he walked into the
kitchen. He was wearing a suit, a well-tailored dark gray
suit, crisp white shirt, and perfectly knotted burgundy
patterned tie. He was incredibly handsome, his dark hair
neatly groomed and his face freshly shaven.

She looked down at her own trousers and baggy
sweater, and L.L.Bean loafers and cringed. But digging
through musty bookshelves wasn't much suited to dressing smartly.

At precisely eight-thirty, Libby heard the distinctive
sound of a helicopter approaching outside. She looked
out the kitchen window just as the craft approached off
the North Sea.

"That would be our ride," Graeme said, and tucked a
cardboard tube that held his drawings under one arm as
Libby grabbed her purse.

Together they headed for the door.

The chopper touched down in the open field adjacent
to the castle, terrifying the sheep, which went bounding
off. Libby waited while Graeme greeted the pilot and
then introduced her. The helicopter was so loud, she

scarcely could hear, but was reasonably sure he'd said his name was Martin.

Graeme turned to help her inside, handing her a pair of headphones, which she slipped over her ears. Then he climbed onto the seat beside her, donning a matching set. Libby listened while the pilot did a series of checks in preparation for takeoff, explaining safety procedures and their intended flight path. They would be cutting east across the Highlands before heading south along Britain's east coast. "And if you start to feel ill, Miss Hutchinson, make certain you tell me. I can turn up the heat or turn on the vents for you."

Libby nodded.

"Are we ready, then?"

Libby looked at Graeme. He nodded. Martin engaged the engine and off they went.

Contrary to what she would have thought, riding in a helicopter was much smoother than being in an airplane. Libby had taken enough twin-engine puddle jumpers commuting back and forth across New England to expect to feel her stomach lurch the moment they took off. Instead, this was more a sensation of being lifted by some lofty hand and carried over the landscape.

She hadn't realized how low they would fly. As they soared over the village, Libby could see the villagers walking on the high street, stopping to shield their eyes as the helicopter flew overhead. The glorious mountain peaks of Ben Loyal and Ben Hope stretched out before them, ringed in mist beneath a brilliant morning sun.

The flight took just over three hours, and the changes in the landscape from Highlands to Lowlands, Scotland to England, were astounding. Libby didn't think she'd ever seen a countryside so beautiful, so truly in harmony with nature's hand. As they neared the British capital, Martin brought the helicopter down below a thousand feet because of the city's flying space restrictions, giving her a true bird's-eye view of such landmarks as the

Tower Bridge, the huge Ferris wheel called the London Eye, Big Ben, and even Buckingham Palace, all snaked through with the silty waters of the River Thames.

It was like living in a movie. By the time they landed at the heliport, Libby's pulse was racing.

"Did you see the river? Wasn't it amazing?"

Graeme enjoyed just watching her, her almost child-like delight in something he'd been doing almost all his life.

A private car was waiting at the heliport to convey them into the city.

Graeme cringed when the driver greeted him with "Good morning, my lord." But thankfully Libby was still so taken with by the flight and their surroundings, she didn't seem to have noticed.

Graeme offered to have the driver drop him at his firm so that Libby could have use of the car for driving and for carrying any books she might purchase. They would meet up later that afternoon when he was finished at his office.

He bid her farewell in front of the glass-encased high-rise that housed Clyne and Partners, Architects.

The security guard who waited in the inside lobby looked up when Graeme came in.

"Well, good morning, m'lord. Haven't seen you in this place in quite a while."

Graeme stopped to sign in. "Peter, how many years have I been walking into this lobby?"

"Ay'd haf to say must be five years now, m'lord."

"And for those five years, you knew me as Macken-zie. Graeme Mackenzie. Correct?"

"Aye, m'lord."

"Am I the same person who came here each morning for those five years?"

"Aye, m'lord."

"So doesn't it seem, well, for lack of a better word,

absurd to suddenly start referring to me differently after all that time?"

The guard hesitated, clearly uncertain, but finally admitted, "Aye, m'lord."

"I'm the same person, Peter," Graeme said, turning for the lifts. "Mackenzie will continue to suffice."

"Aye, m'lord Mackenzie."

Graeme sighed, waved a hand, shaking his head as he went.

Up on the thirty-second floor, the receptionist nearly dropped her morning coffee when she recognized Graeme coming around the corner. "Graeme—I mean, Lord Waltham."

"Graeme will do, Margaret," he said. "Is Philip in his office?"

She just nodded, her mouth still slightly ajar, speechless, apparently regretting the time she'd turned him down when he'd asked her out for lunch.

Before he'd fallen into line for his inheritance.

He started down the hall, hearing her on the phone behind him. "Yes, Mr. Clyne, Lord Waltham is on his way back to see you."

Philip Clyne was a distinguished graduate of Cambridge University. Forty-six, happily married, with three children ages fourteen to six, he'd established Clyne and Partners and built it into the top architectural firm in London, with project offices worldwide. The studio had received countless awards and citations for excellence and had won over fifty national and international competitions. Philip himself had been awarded the RIBA Royal Gold Medal for Architecture, the Gold Medal of the French Academy of Architecture, and the American Institute of Architects Gold Medal, otherwise known as an industry hat trick. A council member of the Royal College of Art and trustee of the Architecture Foundation of London, he was rumored to be on the shortlist in line for a knighthood.

But none of that mattered more to Graeme than the fact that Philip Clyne had taken him under his wing, serving as mentor, father, role model, and friend at various times during the ten years they'd known each other.

"Graeme!"

Philip clasped Graeme in a bear hug, clapping him on the back without any thought to the wrinkles he might bring to Graeme's Gieves & Hawkes tailored suit. "You look well. Seclusion agrees with you."

"Must be some healthy color has returned to my face, having not been under the ultraviolet glow of the press corps' flashbulbs these past weeks. People were beginning to think I must spend hours in a tanning bed."

The two men laughed as Philip's assistant, Gwendolyn, brought in a tray of coffee and pastries.

"Gwendolyn," Graeme said with a nod in greeting.

"My lord," she said as she hastened for the door.

Graeme simply shook his head. "It's as if I'm some sort of carnival feature."

"Pay them no mind. They only know what they read in the tabloids. Speaking of which—" Philip grinned. "Read you were out on the Riviera having banana-and-peanut-butter sandwiches with Elvis. So tell me, is he still 'nothin' but a hound dog'?"

Graeme had to appreciate his lightheartedness, remembering that ridiculous photo from *The Buzz*'s recent edition. Philip was one of only three who knew where Graeme had been living the past months, the other two being his mother and his uncle. All communication between Graeme and the office went through Philip directly. It was the only way Graeme had managed to stay hidden so successfully.

"Come on," Philip said then, looking at the tube of drawings Graeme had brought with him, "let me see what you've done with this wretched project."

They spent the next hour or more going over

Graeme's preliminary drawings, discussing every aspect of the job, and Graeme's undemonstrated plans.

"This is unlike anything we've ever considered before, Graeme. It's forward-thinking while at the same time remaining true to the past. The prince will almost certainly approve. Well done! I'll have a preliminary model made up and present the plans to His Royal Highness's offices as soon as possible. In the meantime, you need to continue to lay low until this project has been granted approval. We don't want anything, most especially any paparazzi high jinks, threatening this. If all goes well, I don't think I'd be exaggerating to say that a directorship with the firm would be well within reach for you. Think you can manage to avoid the spotlight until then?"

But the praise was bittersweet, since Graeme had agreed to give up his career as soon as the project was concluded. He hadn't told Philip that news yet, perhaps waiting for some sort of divine intervention that would suddenly occur, allowing him to be an architect and a duke and earl all at once.

They shook hands over the project's future success, and then Philip gave a glance at his watch. "It's early yet. Can you make time for lunch at the club before you need to head back?"

The gentlemen's clubs of London were a time-honored tradition that had remained virtually unchanged since their inception in the eighteenth century. Most of them had begun as coffeehouses, where men would gather to discuss politics, news of the day, and their mistresses. They soon became havens for gambling, with certain social and political sets squaring off into their own separate little societies. Their memberships were exclusive, and members could be assured of the utmost discretion and privacy once behind the hallowed doors of the noble and elevated St. James's Street mansions. Given his familial connections, Graeme had had his choice among them.

But it had been an easy decision, given the fact that the club of choice for all Gransboroughs since time immemorial was, had always been, White's.

The esteemed club had been housed behind the great columned facade at numbers 37–38 St. James's Street for well over two hundred years. Men like Beau Brummell, who had held court in its front bow window, and even the great Duke of Wellington had been admitted to membership. HRH Prince Charles was a member and had had his bachelor party at the club. Graeme suspected that was one of the reasons Philip had chosen the club for their luncheon that day. But no matter the reasons, Graeme was grateful he wouldn't have to spend the entire meal looking over his shoulder for a photographer's lens.

Philip's hunch paid off. The prince was just leaving the club as they arrived. Philip stopped, exchanged greetings and introduced Graeme as the latest project director of the prince's pet project.

"Wait until you get a look at the preliminary model, Your Highness," Philip told him. "I'm sure you'll be impressed."

The prince gave Graeme a lift of his eyebrows before making arrangements to have a look at the project the following week.

"So, tell me," Philip said as they sat down to the club's luncheon, "how are things in the wild, barbaric Highlands?"

"More beautiful than you can possibly imagine."

Unknown to Philip, it wasn't the picturesque scenery Graeme was really thinking about.

"I can't imagine Perpetua living more than five miles from Harrods. She'd never survive."

"I never thought I'd love it as much as I do. But I do. The place wraps itself around you until you're inextricably tied to it."

Philip nodded, taking a sip of claret. "Well, we'll have to come up some weekend and see for ourselves."

"You'd better make it soon. I may find myself having to vacate the premises."

Graeme went on to explain the whole story of Libby's arrival and the subsequent litigation to regain her inheritance.

Philip shook his head. "If the papers get wind of this, you'll be splashed right back on the front pages. I don't think I need to remind you how harmful that could be to this project, Graeme."

"I know. But you needn't worry. Libby's suit is against Lady Venetia, not me. And the castle's sale was through a trust in my mother's name, not mine. As far as anyone is concerned, I'm simply the caretaker. Any news it makes will be put at my mother's doorstep."

"Well, I can't think of a more able person to handle that imbroglio."

Lady Ardmuir was famous for her success in fending off even the most fervent reporter's inquisition.

"Let's see we keep it that way, hmm? And what of this American? An antiquarian bookseller, you say? She must be cut of some rather sturdy cloth if she thinks to take on Lady Venetia Mackay."

Instead of responding, Graeme simply blinked. Philip, who knew Graeme better than Graeme himself sometimes, instantly caught the hesitation.

"I see."

"You see what?"

"I see she's obviously more than just some American antiquarian bookseller."

Graeme looked at him.

"Be careful, Graeme."

He shook his head. "She has no idea who I am."

"That's not a charade someone in your position can keep playing too long."

"Yes, I am aware of that." Graeme frowned. "But that

doesn't mean I have to go out of my way to end it before I absolutely have to. I rather like being just Graeme Mackenzie again."

Philip merely looked at him. The unfortunate truth of it was, Graeme wasn't, would never be *just* Graeme Mackenzie ever again. A future of nothing but responsibility and duty to his family's noble lines stretched out before him like a prison sentence once the duke and Graeme's mother were no longer there to man their appointed posts. It was a life he wouldn't wish on his worst enemy. So until then, Philip could certainly understand Graeme's dogged insistence that life remain as it had been, even if it was only for a short while longer. And if hiding away in the Highlands provided that for him, then so be it. Philip would do everything he could to protect what small freedoms Graeme had left.

Chapter Seventeen

Graeme called ahead to his driver to ask where he might find Libby and had Philip drop him at the intersection nearest to it.

Out on the sidewalk, Graeme blended in with the eclectic pedestrian traffic of disoriented tourists, businessmen, backpacking students, teenagers emulating pop stars, and every other cosmopolitan imaginable. This section of the city, near Leicester and Soho Squares, was one of the busiest in London, both during the day and at night when the many restaurants and nightclubs kicked into high gear.

The bookshop that the driver had directed him to was near the church at St. Martin-in-the-Fields, tucked away in an alleyway called Cecil Court, a narrow cobbled hideaway packed with tiny shops featuring antiques, prints, but mostly books. There were shops just for children's books, another for the occult, even a shop for books written only by women. Graeme popped into three of them before he finally found Libby at the fourth, standing at the back counter flanked by two stacks of books.

She hadn't noticed him come in. He stood a moment to watch her at her work, impressed by her knowledge of the books and her shrewd negotiating skills as she bargained with the shop owner. Libby certainly knew her stuff, and by the time she was finished, Graeme expected she would be telling the shop owner he should be paying her to take the books off his hands.

As the shopkeeper went off to figure shipping charges to the States, Libby turned. It was then she saw Graeme.

"Oh," she said. "Hello."

The expression on her face was the sort any man would like to see after a day's work, an expression that said she was happy to see him. "I didn't know you were there."

"Just arrived." He motioned toward the back office, where the bookseller had disappeared. "I think you could have gotten him down at least another fifty pounds."

She grinned. "Probably, but I did want to leave him feeling he had made something in the deal. My generosity now will help give me a favorable edge should I find myself up against another buyer for a particular title from him in the future."

Graeme nodded. Shrewd and tactical.

"I'm just about finished here," Libby said, glancing at her watch. "I hope I'm not holding up our ride home. I sort of get lost when I'm around bookshops. Completely lose track of the time."

Her use of the word *home* sent an unexpected twinge through Graeme. Having been born to a life of country houses, city houses, boarding schools, and holiday getaways, and after having had to move from place to place over the past eight months, the word *home* suddenly left him a keen sense of longing.

"No, we're not late at all. In fact, I was thinking perhaps we'd delay our flight a few hours to take in some of the city sights. You said you'd never really seen London before. Perhaps we could even have dinner before we leave. I know of this brilliant little Polish restaurant, one of those places off the beaten path."

"Polish? I think I can honestly say I don't think I've

ever had Polish food. You mean like those sausages they sell at the baseball games?"

Graeme chuckled. "There's much more to Polish cooking than that. *Gołąbki. Pierożki. Mazurek.* My grandmother on my mother's side is Polish. My grandfather met her during the war and brought her home with him afterward. She always makes traditional Polish dishes for us at holidays. You're in for a definite experience."

The shopkeeper returned, and within a quarter hour they were on their way. Libby had left most of the books she'd purchased with the shop, filling out a packing slip to have them delivered straight to her employer, Belvedere Books in New York. She'd bought a few other titles for herself, tucking them into a canvas tote bag as they headed for the street.

Graeme took the bag and handed it to the driver, who had appeared almost as soon as they got to the main street. "So . . . we have a few hours left to explore the city before dinner. What would you like to do first?"

He'd expected her to name the usual tourist spots—the Tower, Buckingham Palace, or even Westminster Abbey. The answer she gave was not at all what he would have expected.

"I always thought if I ever came to London, the first thing I'd want to do would be to ride on a double-decker bus."

Graeme had never ridden on a bus, double-decker or otherwise. All his life he'd been chauffeured by private car, or those times when he'd been really desperate, he'd been known to hail a cab. But a bus? He wouldn't even know how to find one.

"You're quite certain that is what you want to do . . . ?"

"Look." She pointed down the street. "There's a bus stop there." She took his hand. "Let's do this. We'll get on the first one that stops and just see where it takes us."

Graeme's expression was less than enthusiastic.

"Come on," she said. "Where's your sense of adventure? It'll be fun."

Fun?

Adventure?

A London city bus?

Libby tugged a reluctant Graeme toward the red-and-white sign.

In only a few minutes, one of the red double-decker busses so distinctive to London came lumbering up to meet them. It looked like an antique, surely at least fifty years old. He wondered that it wasn't being pulled by a draft horse. Libby stepped up on the rear platform, quickly asked someone how to get a ticket.

"Jes' go on to yer seat, love. The conductor'll be 'round to collect your fare."

Grinning ear to ear, Libby scuttled up the stairs to the bus's top level, walking all the way to the front where they would have the best view.

A conductor wearing a change belt soon came seeking their fare.

"Where you off to, then?"

"That depends," Graeme answered. "Where does this thing go?"

The conductor recited what was obviously his daily litany. "Fulham–Chelsea–Victoria–Westminster–Aldwych–St. Paul's–Bank–Liverpool Street . . ."

Graeme removed his billfold from his pocket and pulled out a fifty-pound note. "Will this do?"

The conductor's eyes widened. "You're planning to pay for everyone on the bus, then? Otherwise, I can't change that."

Graeme pulled out a twenty.

The conductor frowned.

It was the smallest bill Graeme had on him. And he wasn't the sort of man to carry around a pocketful of change.

"My treat," Libby said, pulling a handful of coins from her purse.

After helping her to count out the correct amount, the conductor handed her two tickets, then went on his way, shaking his head.

"Now," Libby said, "just sit back, relax, and tell me what everything is."

And Graeme did. He spent the next three hours pointing out every feature on the cityscape they passed, describing the history of each building and bridge in architectural detail. He'd been running from it so long, he had almost forgotten how much he loved London, how around any corner a person could find themselves having a pint in the same pub that had once been frequented by Shakespeare, or standing beneath the oak where the eighteenth-century Duke of Hamilton had fought his famous duel against Lord Mohun (an event that, unfortunately, neither man survived).

Mostly Graeme talked about the buildings. He knew what they were, what they had been used for over the centuries, who had lived in them. About a half hour into their spur-of-the-moment tour, Graeme happened to look at Libby, half expecting to see her bored to tears by his commentary. But instead of the blank stare he usually found whenever he would start talking architecture, Libby was actually listening to him. More amazingly, she was listening with a keen interest, asking thoughtful questions, and seeming eager to hear more.

They spent the afternoon crisscrossing the city's various bus routes, eventually making a game of it. They'd get off one bus and board another, then do the same thing again. All the while, they talked and talked, discussing everything from shared interests in music (they both liked Clapton) and reading tastes, favorite movies (anything from Martin Scorsese) to their worst childhood schoolteachers. Graeme had never talked so honestly with another person in his life, nor had he ever laughed so freely. For those precious few hours, he was able to forget all about Libby's legal battles, the conflict of her moving into the castle, even his impending inheritances. He shed his suit coat, pulled off his tie, and let down his guard for the first time in months.

And it felt *bloody* good.

Finally, as the sun was dipping over the western suburbs, they got off the bus and ducked into the quiet, intimate café that was Graeme's favorite haunt in South Kensington.

The owner, a grinning, barrel-chested Pole named Jan, whose wife, Marianna, did all the restaurant's cooking, greeted him by name.

"*Dobry wieczór,* Mr. Mac! It has been too long since we've seen you, yes?"

Jan showed them to a candlelit two-seat table in a cozy corner that overlooked a cobbled courtyard mews that had centuries earlier been the stable block for the neat row of noblemen's town houses that stood around the corner. Now, in the twenty-first century, it housed a collection of studio flats, boutiques, an artists' studio, and this quaint café, which in summer was filled with the perfume of the fragrant wisteria bushes that clung to the wall outside. Faint strains of Polish folk music drifted from the speakers in the ceiling while the little terrier dog belonging to the restaurant's owner sat perched on his favorite rug by the bar.

Since Libby wasn't familiar with anything listed on the menu, Graeme gave their order in his grandmother's native tongue. Libby watched him, fascinated as he conversed with the waitress. She had no idea what he was saying, and it didn't even matter. There was just something about the sound of him speaking, even the gestures he made with his hands, that was all so incredibly sexy. In a moment he had gone from cultured, formal Englishman to sultry Eastern European. Even the expression on his face was different, mysterious, seductive. It was the most arousing transformation Libby had ever seen.

The food that was brought out in what seemed a continuous succession of heaping plates was truly out of this world. It wasn't overly spicy as she had expected, but flavored with herbs she recognized from her mother's garden—rosemary, chives, and thyme. They were simple entrées, but flavorful, and by the time they brought the last course to the table, Libby felt certain she couldn't possibly take another bite.

And then Graeme ordered dessert.

"No, I couldn't . . ."

But she managed a couple of bites of the chocolate-and-poppyseed cake that arrived at the table with their after-dinner coffees.

While Libby excused herself for the ladies' room, Graeme made two quick calls on his mobile. The driver was waiting for them when they emerged from the restaurant, and soon they were on their way.

"Will it take us long to get to the heliport from here?" Libby asked.

"We've one last stop to make before we leave."

"Oh. Where?"

"I should probably ask first—you're not afraid of heights are you?"

"No. Why?"

Graeme merely smiled in response. He refused to divulge anything further.

Libby had her face pressed against the window when, fifteen minutes later, the car rolled to a stop before one of London's newest and most visible landmarks.

"We're going on that?"

Standing at nearly four hundred fifty feet, the London Eye was the world's largest observation wheel, looking rather like a carnival Ferris wheel but built on a far grander scale. Instead of seats that swung in the breeze, there were thirty-two glass-encased "pods," each able to hold up to twenty-five passengers standing. The great spoked wheel, standing on the banks of the River Thames, turned at a snail's pace, taking thirty minutes to make just one rotation. On a clear day passengers could see as far away as twenty-five miles.

At night, however, the experience was truly breathtaking.

As they approached the boarding platform, Libby spotted the placard that read CLOSED. PLEASE CALL AGAIN DURING OPERATING HOURS.

"Oh," she said, turning to him. "We've arrived too late. It's closed."

But Graeme simply smiled and took her hand, leading her onward. "Let's just say I know someone who knows someone."

The pod was open and waiting as they walked up the platform.

"Evening, sir," said the operator and tipped his hat to Libby. "Miss."

Ten minutes later they were climbing to the stars with the torchlit streets of London stretching out before them.

It was a clear night, and Libby could see the Thames glistening beneath the moonlight while lovers walked arm in arm along the river's embankment beneath them. The higher they climbed, the more the rest of the world seemed to vanish, until people were no longer visible and they could see only the headlights of the cars driving along the Strand.

When they reached the highest point, the wheel drifted to a stop.

"Oh, Graeme, it's so beautiful."

And it was.

Just across the river, Big Ben and the Houses of Parliament were brilliantly floodlit in shades of blue, while on the other side stood the great noble dome of St. Paul's with the Tower Bridge in the distance, connected by a string of lights that stretched all along the curve of the

Thames. It was the most beautiful, most romantic sight Libby had ever seen.

And the sight of her face, the open delight and wonder, was the most beautiful, most romantic sight Graeme had ever seen.

She turned toward him. "Thank you. Thank you for this. All of this. It's just so—"

She never finished her thought. Graeme reached for her, cupping her chin in his hands as he tipped her face upward and captured her mouth with his.

He'd been wanting to do this all night, and all day, as he'd ridden with her on that bus, had shared a bite of cake with her at dinner, even when he'd been watching her haggle over the price of books at that shop. Truth was, he'd been wanting to do this long, long before that.

Here, high above the city, no one could interrupt them unexpectedly, and no photographer's lens could capture them for the morning edition. So Graeme took his time and kissed her slowly, deeply, pulling her close against him, wrapping her in his arms, making it last as long as he could as they stood virtually on top of the world.

When he finally pulled away, Libby was clutching the front of his jacket as if it were a lifeline. She didn't want to open her eyes for fear she had dreamed it. She had never been kissed like that in her life, had never even imagined being kissed like that. Her heart was pounding, and her legs felt as if at any moment they might buckle. And the only thing she could think was that she would do anything—*anything*—if he would just keep on kissing her.

Graeme nuzzled her ear, his breath hot against her skin. She closed her eyes.

"Graeme?"

He murmured into her hair. "Hmm?"

"Do you think you can delay our flight . . . "

He nodded. "I think so."

". . . till tomorrow?"

Chapter Eighteen

Graeme lifted his head, looked deeply into Libby's eyes. "You're certain?"

She looked back at him, and her voice came in a heavy whisper. "I've never been more certain of anything in my life."

Graeme crushed his mouth over hers, kissing her deeply, sliding his tongue against hers in long, sensual strokes. He felt her press her hips forward and felt a jolt that shot straight to his groin. It had been so long, perhaps his entire lifetime, since he'd felt so utterly, completely alive.

He groaned into her mouth, seeking release from the tension that was drawing his body taut as an archer's bow.

If he were the sort of man who prided himself on his conquests, he might consider taking her right there, four hundred and fifty feet above the rest of the world. But that wasn't him. And that was not this woman.

With Libby it would not be rushed or reckless. With Libby it would be a night to remember.

It took everything Graeme possessed to keep his hands off her as they slowly, and literally, returned to earth.

He led Libby into the car, and then made a quick call on his mobile.

He could have called Claridge's or even the Ritz, but Graeme knew a place, smaller, more intimate, unique, in fact, one that suited Libby much more.

The Cranbury was housed in two connected Victorian town houses on a quiet residential street in South Kensington. The rooms still bore their original paneling, marble-framed fireplaces, and tall bay windows. But a recent refurbishment had given it every modern convenience.

The manager had their suite waiting when they arrived, with a fire burning in the hearth.

"I'm just going to go down to arrange for a bottle of champagne," Graeme said. He could have easily used the phone, but he sensed that Libby would appreciate the few minutes alone.

When he returned, she was standing before the tall windows that faced onto the garden square in front of the hotel. She was wearing one of the plush white robes that had been hanging in the closet. It blanketed her, falling nearly to the floor, her feet, toes painted cherry red, peeking out from underneath.

She looked beautiful. Her hair was loose and curling around her shoulders, and tucked behind one ear. Her eyes were alive with light.

Graeme was feasting on her with his eyes when a discreet knock sounded on the door. He didn't take his gaze from her as he moved to the door and opened it.

"Your champagne, sir . . ."

Graeme simply pointed to the table, his eyes still fixed upon Libby. She smiled. Blushed.

The hotel concierge nodded, took the twenty-pound note Graeme held out in tip, then backed from the room.

Graeme poured them both a glass and took one to Libby.

She smiled, but he could sense a sudden nervousness.

"You're still certain? Because I can call the driver. We could—"

She put two fingers to his lips. "I'm very certain. Are you?"

Graeme's answer was a long, slow kiss.

They shared a sip of champagne, and then Graeme took her glass and set it on the windowsill. Wrapping his fingers around the thick lapels of her robe, he pulled her toward him for another kiss.

Libby melted against him, tipping her head back to meet his height. She flattened her hands against his chest and felt the drumbeat of his heart through his shirt, steady and strong. Slowly, as he kissed her, she started to loosen the buttons, impatient for the closeness of him, the heat of his skin beneath her hands. She pushed the shirt back and helped him to slip it off, running her hands over his shoulders, down his arms. Then she followed as he guided her away from the windows, toward the four-poster.

Libby could hear her own pulse thrumming in her ears as Graeme lowered himself onto the coverlet, then pulled her down beside him. He slipped away only long enough to loosen his belt and get rid of his pants. He left on his boxers, silk and hugging his lean waist, then pulled Libby to him once again.

He kissed her, and she eased against him, devouring his mouth just as eagerly as he was devouring hers. He kissed her in a way that made her completely forget where she was, what she was doing. She felt his hands slip down to the knot in the robe's belt, felt him loosen it. Uncertain, she'd left her panties and bra on underneath, and Graeme slipped the robe off one shoulder, kissing a hot path along her neck to where he nibbled at the satiny strap. It was then that he noticed the odd crystal stone hanging around her neck. It had a strange reddish glow to it, as if it were an ember of fire, but it was cool, he felt, to the touch.

He had seen the stone before, that night by the fire,

but then he hadn't thought, hadn't realized, hadn't put it all together . . .

"This is it, isn't it? This is that stone we read about at the Mackay Clan Centre."

Libby opened her eyes, nodded. "My father gave it to my mother. And my mother gave it to me. Without it, I wouldn't have come to Scotland at all. I wouldn't be here with you now."

While she spoke, Graeme slipped a finger underneath the satiny strap of her bra, sliding it off while his hands made good work of the hooked fastening in back and his mouth made good work of the curve of her neck.

Libby sucked in her breath as she felt the bra melt away, felt his hands slip against her to cup her breasts.

Oh . . . dear . . . God.

She arched her back, seeking more. She felt as if she might ignite from the heat that was burning inside of her. The more he touched her, the longer he kissed her, the more the heat grew, until it was consuming her.

"Graeme, please . . ."

She wanted him, wanted to feel him against her, over her, inside her, but Graeme had no intention of rushing.

He breathed in the scent of her perfume, the scent of her body, burying his face in her breasts. He flicked his tongue across one taut nipple, feeling her body sway in response. Her heart was racing; he could feel it against his hands, against his mouth, could see it in the rapid rise and fall of her chest as her breath hitched, held, and her fingers raked back through his hair.

Her pleasure was a heady aphrodisiac.

He moved his mouth downward, across her belly, nibbling at the soft curve of her hip as his hand dipped, delving beneath the lacy edge of her panties, easing them down, down, until they were there no more.

He was hard. He wanted her, wanted her more than he'd ever thought he could want a woman. And she lifted one knee, seeking his touch and he gave it to her, sliding his finger down to the slick center of her until she jolted and gasped. He felt her muscles quivering, saw her tighten her fingers into a fist around the sheet as he gently eased his fingers inside her, out, inside again.

She cried out, climaxing quickly, and from the expression of wonder he saw in her eyes as he rose up over her, he knew it had to be the first time she ever had.

It wouldn't be the last time that evening.

Her hands were desperate now, wanting him, seeking him, and she tugged at his boxers, pushing them away as he slid back up to take her mouth with his. Her fingers glanced him, caressing his hardness, and Graeme sucked in his breath, easing her back, lifting one knee, opening her to his first thrust.

It was almost too much for Graeme to bear, the tightness of her, the heat of her, the soft, struggled gasps as he drew back from her, only to fill her again . . . and again . . . and again.

He took her mouth with his, groaning against her. She lifted her hips to meet him, movement for movement, a perfect, age-old rhythm that grew like a crescendo, rising to a feverish pitch until the moment, the very moment that they surged together and she locked her legs around him, her pleasured cry muffled against his shoulder as the force of their climax rocked them both.

Libby awoke slowly, only dimly aware of the sound of the London street noise coming through the open window. It was a soft morning, and she was swathed in a nest of pillows and goose down, deliciously warm. She opened one bleary eye onto the steadily ticking alarm clock on the night table.

It read ten o'clock.

She stirred, lifting her head to a bed that was empty beside her.

She got up, retrieved her robe from where it was

draped over the chair, and slipped it on, knotting the belt at her waist.

"Good morning," Graeme said as she opened the French doors onto the suite's sitting room.

He was seated at a small table, wearing a matching white robe, the morning paper opened before him.

"Good morning," Libby mumbled, pushing her glasses up on her nose.

"Tea?" he asked, lifting a decorative china pot from the tray on the stand beside him.

She nodded and started for the seat across from him, but he grabbed the belt of her robe and gave it a yank, tugging her straight into his lap.

His mouth was on hers before she could say anything.

"Did you sleep well?" he asked when he pulled away from the kiss moments later.

"Have you noticed the time? I'd say I must have slept very well."

He smiled at her and then reached beside him where several shopping bags waited. "I took the liberty of having a few things sent over, since we hadn't expected an overnight stay. I hope I managed to guess close enough on the sizes. I took a look at your other things, but American sizes differ a bit from us Brits."

While she sipped her tea, Libby looked through the bags, taking out a pair of soft, pale khaki slacks and a beautiful red cashmere sweater with a matching cardigan. There was a pair of delicate skimmer shoes, from the designer whom Audrey Hepburn had helped make popular. And there was a soft ivory bra-and-panties set. Another bag contained toiletries, toothbrush, everything she could possibly need.

"Thank you."

She kissed him.

"I thought we really don't need to hurry back, so while you're in the shower, I'd like you to think about what you'd like to do today."

She smiled, tempted to pinch herself. Surely she must be dreaming. "Okay."

Taking up her shopping bags, and a flaky croissant on a plate, Libby practically skipped into the bathroom.

Graeme was humming over the financial section of the paper when a soft knock came on the door.

It was the hotel manager, and the look on his face immediately betrayed that whatever news had brought him to the door wasn't going to be good.

"Sorry to disturb, my lord. I just thought . . . , I mean to say, you would . . . , I'd better show you this."

He held out a copy of the morning edition of *The Buzz.* The headline, in big, bold, black lettering, read WALTHAM SPOTTED IN LONDON.

Graeme quickly read the article, which quoted an "unnamed source" in saying that he'd visited the offices of his architectural firm and had later ducked into White's club. "Attempts to ascertain his whereabouts after lunch were unsuccessful." *The Buzz,* however, had several correspondents combing the city as the story went to press.

Damn it!

His worst fears were confirmed by the manager a moment later.

"Ehm, I also spotted a photog camped out in the coffee shop on the corner, watching the front door. I assure you, my lord, no one here had anything to do with—"

"No, it's all right." Graeme thought of his early-morning shopping call. He'd had to use his name, or else he wouldn't have gotten the attention of the store manager, or the personalized service. "Must have been the delivery service who tipped off the paparazzi."

"I haven't let them past the front door, my lord." The manager shook his head. "You'd think they would have learned something after what happened to poor Princess Diana."

"Thank you," Graeme said, quickly forming a plan of

escape. "You wouldn't by any chance have a back service entrance?"

Graeme was dressed and waiting when Libby came out of the bathroom, showered and looking lovely in the things he'd bought for her.

"I like you in red," he said, taking her into his arms. He wondered how he was going to explain to her why they wouldn't be staying in the city after all.

He didn't have to. She instantly read the change in his expression. "Something is wrong."

"I'm afraid we'll have to change our plans and return to the Highlands sooner than I'd planned."

"Oh. Your work?"

"Something like that. I'm sorry, Libby."

She smiled. "Don't be. I had the most wonderful day yesterday." She looked at him. "And the most wonderful night."

He pulled her to him again, kissing her.

If she thought it odd that they left the hotel through the back service entrance, Libby didn't comment on it. The car was waiting, and they ducked in without anyone noticing. As they drove around the corner, Graeme spotted the photographer, recognizing him immediately from the months he'd spent avoiding him before, sitting in the café with his camera out and waiting for its prey.

It was midafternoon when the helicopter touched down at the castle.

There was an unfamiliar car waiting in the drive. Flora came out to meet them as soon as they approached.

"There's someone here to see you, miss. Was here yesterday, too, and was none too pleased to find you hadn't come back last night."

Libby looked at her, then at the car. "But I'm not expecting anyone. Who is it? Is it Mr. Brodie?"

"Nae." Flora frowned. "'Tis Lady Venetia. She's waiting in the parlor."

Libby looked at Graeme. She had expected this day would come sometime, just not right then, nor in that particular manner. She'd hoped to at least have time to prepare herself beforehand.

Turning toward the castle, Libby didn't say a word as she headed inside.

Chapter Nineteen

Libby was grateful to Graeme for the new clothes he'd bought for her. A certain confidence came with wearing nice things, and she suspected she was going to need every scrap of confidence she possessed to face the grandmother who had forsaken her even before she'd been born.

As she walked toward the front door, Libby tried to prepare herself for the coming confrontation. She stopped before the mirror in the entrance hall to check her appearance, smoothing back her hair from the tousle it had taken on during the helicopter ride. She didn't have the time to fix it properly, so she fished inside her handbag for a simple headband to push the unruly waves back from her face.

There, she thought, taking in the reflection. That was better. Her eyes looked bright and clear, and her face was nicely flushed from the outdoors. Despite the emotions that were swirling inside of her, she wanted Lady Venetia to see a poised woman possessed of the character and the strength of mind that had been passed down to her by her mother.

Taking a deep breath, Libby headed for the parlor.

Lady Venetia was standing at the far window, looking out onto the sea. She was more slightly built than Libby had expected, her figure appearing almost frail beneath the long skirt and tailored jacket she wore. Her white hair was swept up in a neatly pinned twist that suited the regal, Old World air that surrounded the woman like a mantle. For all the talk of her, and the terror she'd inspired amongst the villagers, she should have stood six feet, not barely inches over five. Despite this, however, the set of her shoulders said that this woman was still a force to be reckoned with.

Libby stood in the doorway until she summoned the courage to speak.

"Good afternoon."

The woman turned. Libby had already seen her image in the newspaper and in the portrait at the clan center, so she knew what to expect when they came face-to-face. The fact that Lady Venetia had not had this same advantage registered in her expression the moment she saw Libby. Though her dark gaze swept Libby from top to toe, and her face made a show that she clearly wasn't impressed, for the barest of moments when she first faced Libby, Lady Venetia Mackay blinked.

She'd seen her son Fraser's eyes looking back from the face of his daughter.

Libby seized that blink, and the vulnerability it implied, holding to it tightly.

"You look just like your mother," Lady Venetia said in a way that conveyed anything but a compliment. Her voice was faintly accented, a mixture of the adopted British and her native Dutch.

Libby came into the room. "I'm told I bear more of a resemblance to my father's side. Most specifically my namesake, Lady Isabella Mackay."

Lady Venetia's eyes narrowed at this impertinence, but she maintained her cool, detached composure. It was a trait she'd obviously perfected during her lifetime.

"So you think, just because that mother of yours alleges to have gotten you by my son, that it gives you the right to come here after all these years and claim this estate as your own? I'm no fool. She was probably bedding half the crofters in the village, and then thought to pass her ill-gotten mistake off on my unsuspecting son. You don't even have any proof that you are who you claim you are."

Libby felt the spark of anger, an anger she'd rarely ever felt. "I have every right to be here. In fact, some would say I have more right than you. I am a member of this family by birth. You only married into it."

Lady Venetia opened her mouth as if to say something, but then her eyes narrowed, as she looked just beneath Libby's chin to her neck. "Where did you get that stone?"

Libby lifted her fingers to the crystal her mother had given her. She had worn it outside her sweater that morning for the first time, no longer feeling the need to conceal it.

"It was given to me. By my mother."

"I always knew she'd stolen it. It belongs to this family. Give it back to me now."

She held out her hand, actually expecting Libby to do as she'd said.

Libby didn't move.

"Whether you like it or not, I belong to this family. And the stone is mine."

The woman's face reddened with rage, but it was only a moment before the decades of breeding and control overtook her. "Do you really believe you stand even the slightest chance of winning this absurd lawsuit? You have no idea who you are up against. I will make you regret having ever begun this nonsense. I will expose your mother for the strumpet she was, and I will expose you for the bastard child she used to blackmail my son into marrying her. I told him that. I told him she was nothing but a whore, that she would never love him like—"

She caught herself, stopping herself from what she'd been about to say. But it didn't matter.

"You told him that she would never love him like you did. It wasn't my mother you hated at all, was it? It was the idea that she had come to mean something to your only son. You would have hated anyone he'd dared to choose for himself."

Lady Venetia didn't even try to deny Libby's words. "That still doesn't make you his child. And he knew it. He'd listened to me. Even he had begun to doubt it before . . ."

"This is the twenty-first century, Lady Venetia. Any question of my paternity can be settled by a simple blood test."

A shadow clouded Lady Venetia's dark eyes, the shadow of a very real fear. It was then that Libby realized how this woman had managed to wield such control over so many for so long. She'd had a very privileged upbringing. From the moment she'd been born, she'd undoubtedly been raised to believe that anything she asked for, anything she wanted, would be hers. All she'd had to do was speak.

And she had.

But words were just that. *Words.* And nothing this woman could say now could hurt Libby, or her mother, any longer.

"You must have hated her very much," Libby said softly.

Lady Venetia's expression stilled. "I don't know what you are talking about."

"Matilde. My mother. The woman your son, Fraser Mackay, had dared to fall in love with. The woman he married, even against your wishes. Was it the first time he had ever gone against you? Had you held that much influence in his life before? You hated her so much, didn't you? And for what? For having made your son, my father, happy? Something you could never do."

"That's quite enough."

"No. It is not enough. I am not my mother. I am not afraid of you. You cannot threaten me as you threatened her and her family, as you have threatened all the people of this village for so long. All these years you've been left alone since my father was lost, and since your husband died."

"You don't know anything about me."

"Oh, but I do. You see, we are similar in that way. I know all about being alone. And it's sad, really, because like it or not, we're all that's left to one another in this world. All this time, instead of sitting here, choking on your anger and taking it out on others, you could have known me, your granddaughter. Your son's only child. Was it worth it? Was it worth forsaking your last chance for a family?"

Lady Venetia stared at her for a long, silent moment, her eyes brimming with unspoken emotion. She looked as if she wanted to say something in response, and would have, except that Graeme chose that moment to come into the room.

"Good day to you, Lady Mackay," he said politely. "We've never met personally." He held out his hand. "Graeme Mackenzie. I'm the caretaker of Castle Wrath."

She turned to him, narrowing her eyes. "What do you mean? I was made to think the castle was put into a trust, to remain uninhabited."

"And it was. The owners, however, have a keen interest in seeing it restored."

Graeme came to stand beside Libby, putting one arm around her waist.

Lady Venetia's entire countenance changed. "Of course. I should have suspected as much." She turned on Libby. "Well, you are certainly your mother's daughter."

"No more or no less than I am my father's daughter."

Lady Venetia took up her coat and her handbag. "I wouldn't get too comfortable here, Miss Hutchinson.

I'm not finished with you. You may think that by sleeping with him, you might succeed in getting this house, and it might work, but that will never make you a Mackay. You'll be hearing from my solicitors. That stone will be returned even if I have to have the constable do it for me."

Libby was physically trembling as, with that parting shot, Lady Venetia turned and sailed out of the room.

Graeme came up behind Libby and placed his hands gently on her shoulders. "Libby . . ."

She turned to face him, tears blurring his face before her. She drew a breath deeply, trying to take hold of her fragile emotions. Somehow, a small part of her had thought that perhaps when Lady Venetia saw her, realized that she truly was a flesh-and-blood person and not some bitter unwanted memory, her feelings might change. Perhaps she'd even dared to hope that they might find a way to bridge the enmity of the past, find a way to accept one another.

"I don't know which is the more difficult to bear. Her unjustified hatred of me, or knowing the only blood relative I have left in this world wishes I were never born."

Graeme enfolded Libby in his arms, and she gave in to the storm of her emotions, weeping, into his chest.

"Shh," he said soothingly, kissing her hair. "She's nothing but a wretched, embittered old woman."

"But she's something else, too. She's my grandmother. She's supposed to be sitting in a rocking chair, knitting mittens and spending her weekends gardening." She lifted her head, looked at him. "Is what she said true? Do you think I spent last night with you in order to get this house?"

"Libby, that doesn't even make sense. Don't do this. Don't allow her bitterness to tarnish what we shared together last night."

He cupped her face, wiping away her tears. Libby

looked at him and knew he was right. She nodded. "Thank you. Thank you for being here."

He answered by lowering his head and touching his lips to hers.

Behind them, Flora stood in the doorway, watching the two embrace. "Ehm, excuse me, Mr. Mackenzie?"

But they were oblivious to her.

"I . . ." She hesitated. "I just wondered if you would be needin' anything else afore I go home for the night? Ehm . . . excuse me?"

She waited another moment, then shrugged. "Good night, then."

Flora turned, a small, knowing smile lifting one corner of her mouth.

Libby was literally up to her elbows in soapsuds when she heard an unfamiliar voice calling up the stairs.

"Hallo . . . ? Is anybody home?"

"I'm up here!" she shouted to the door behind her and plunged the scrub brush into the bucket, yanking her hand out to slop soapy water over the floorboards. She was on her knees in one of the upper bedrooms, sleeves of her Boston College sweatshirt rolled up to her elbows, her hair pulled back in a lopsided sort of ponytail atop her head. She'd been working on that particular room all morning, moving out furniture, taking down window hangings before turning her efforts to the floor, setting her aching arms to the task of scrubbing what must surely be two hundred and fifty years' worth of dirt.

"Excuse me?"

Libby turned, pushing an errant lock of hair from her eyes with one dripping rubber-gloved hand. "Yes?"

"I'm . . ." A smartly dressed woman came into the doorway, staring at her with open curiosity. She wore a fitted navy pin-striped suit with a red silk scarf draped around her neck. Her hair, dark and dusted with silver, was cut in an updated, stylish pageboy.

"You must be Flora," she said in very refined, accented English.

"No, I'm Libby. Flora's not here."

"Oh. I was . . ." She looked at Libby closely. "I was
looking for Graeme."

Libby sat back on her heels. The knees of her jeans
were soaked from the floor, and she was barefoot. "Oh.
Graeme is out with Murphy."

"I see. And Murphy would be . . ." The woman took a
guess. "The gardener?"

Libby smiled, shaking her head. "No, Murphy's the
dog." She motioned toward the window. "They're down
on the shore playing fetch right now."

The woman turned, looked toward the beach beneath
the castle cliffs where two small figures were walking
near the shore. "I see . . ."

When she turned again, Libby stuck out her hand.
"Hi, I'm—" She stopped, yanked off the rubber glove,
then tried again. "I'm Libby Hutchinson."

The woman nodded and shook her hand. Libby had
never seen more beautifully manicured, elegant hands.
She wondered who she was. A business associate of
Graeme's, perhaps?

She had her answer a moment later.

"Pleasure to meet you, Miss Hutchinson. And I'm
Gemma Mackenzie. Graeme's mother."

Graeme tossed his windbreaker over the corner chair
as he strode into his office, heading straight for his drawing table. Libby had been right. A half hour in the outdoors had certainly helped to clear his mind. Now he felt
ready to tackle the last of his drawings.

He froze when he noticed the figure seated behind his
desk.

"Mother?"

She might as well have been the queen for as unexpected a sight as she was.

The countess looked at her son over the rim of her reading glasses with that same expression she'd given him as a boy when he'd gotten poor marks at school. She even shook her head.

"'Tis a sad, sad day when a mother has to learn from the newspapers that her son came to London and didn't even bother to call her."

"Mother, there's an explanation."

"I am aware of that, Graeme. I just met your *explanation*. Upstairs, scrubbing your floor."

"You met Libby?"

"Yes. I recognized her from her photograph."

Graeme narrowed his eyes. "What photograph?"

She tossed a newspaper on the desk before him. Graeme looked at it, his eyes catching on the headline.

WALTHAM'S SECRET NIGHT ON THE TOWN.

Beneath the text was a grainy photograph of Graeme and Libby sitting on the upper level of the red double-decker bus, laughing and looking very intimate. The caption read:

> *This chance tourist's snapshot confirms the rumors that Graeme Mackenzie, the Marquess of Waltham and future Earl of Abermuir and Duke of Gransborough, recently sneaked into town with an unknown young lady. Rumor has it he rented the entire London Eye for a private midnight rendezvous before stealing off to a cozy South Kensington hotel suite for the night.*

Graeme felt all color drain from his face. "Bloody hell!"

"Now, do you want to tell me what this is all about?"

He didn't answer her. Instead he reached for the keys to the Land Rover, grabbing the jacket he'd removed only moments before.

"Graeme, where the devil are you going? Am I to receive any explanation whatsoever? Graeme!"

"I'll be happy to explain it, Mother, in full detail, as long as it's during the drive to the village. Are you coming?"

Graeme did explain. He told his mother everything, finishing just as he pulled to a skidding halt in front of the village's newsagent.

He looked at his mother. "I'll be just a moment."

The bell dinged in protest as he yanked the door wide, striding straight past the racks of greeting cards and souvenir key chains to the newsstand. He grabbed up every copy of the paper his mother had shown him, along with every copy of every other London newspaper he saw, then dumped them on the counter before the astonished clerk.

"How much?" he asked.

"For all of them?"

"Yes."

"What in heaven do you want all those papers for?"

"I use them for wrapping fish. I've got a lot of it. I've been fishing." He didn't give her the opportunity to comment further. "How much?"

"I'll just need to total it up . . ."

She reached for the stack to count out the exact number of copies he had, and started punching buttons, one by one, into the cash register.

Graeme swept the papers off the counter, tossing a fifty-pound note at the woman. "That should cover it."

He turned for the door, leaving her openmouthed with astonishment behind him.

Graeme dumped the papers onto the backseat of the Land Rover, then started the engine, swinging the vehicle into reverse.

His mother waited until they'd driven out of the village before she spoke again. "Are you in love with this girl, Graeme?"

"What?!"

He pulled off the road onto the verge. He stared straight ahead out the windshield. "How the hell do I know? How could I possibly know? I can't even go out on a date without having to worry it will be broadcast across the entire bloody BBC!"

Gemma Mackenzie, known to most of the rest of the world as the Countess of Abermuir, the Iron Lady of the Lords, looked at her youngest son and felt her heart swell. She had never seen him so tied up in knots before. Even when he'd been seriously dating that Amanda person, he'd hadn't let it affect him like this. He certainly wouldn't have been running out to buy up all the newspapers over her. Whoever she was, this little American, she had managed to do something this mother had begun to think impossible.

She'd given Graeme Mackenzie back his heart.

Ever since the tragic deaths of his brother and father, Graeme hadn't just gone into physical hiding. He'd gone into emotional hiding as well. The losses had devastated him, devastated them both, but coupled with the pressure of his new future role, Graeme had simply buckled. Gemma hadn't confronted him about it, fearing that she might push him further still behind the protective wall he'd built around himself. Instead she'd tried to sort it out for him, making decisions, making appearances for him, even making the arrangements for him to get married, thinking it would help to pull him out of his lethargy.

But this—this was something different and wholly unexpected.

When they got back to the castle, Graeme looked at his mother across the front seat. "As I told you, Libby knows me only as Graeme Mackenzie, castle caretaker. I'd appreciate your not doing anything to have her think otherwise."

"But Graeme, surely you will have to tell her everything eventually."

"I am aware of that, Mother. And I will, as soon as I know she—"

He stopped himself before he could reveal the truth of his feelings. It didn't matter. The countess knew what he would have said anyway.

Graeme would tell her just as soon as he knew Libby loved him, too.

Her mother's heart twisted, knowing the dangerous game he played. "As you wish, my dear. As far as I'm concerned, I just came up to visit my son as I was passing through for a weekend in the Orkneys."

"Thank you, Mother. You're the best."

Gemma smiled, shaking her head. "Well, at least you have the good sense to realize it."

Chapter Twenty

The American girl came forward to meet Graeme and his mother the moment they exited the Land Rover.

Gone were the soap-soaked jeans, lopsided ponytail, and rubber gloves. She now wore a pale blue blouse that matched her eyes and a pair of smart wool trousers. Her hair was pulled back from her face in a modest barrette with bits of it curling softly about her face. Tiny silver earrings winked from her ears.

She looked lovely.

"Graeme, is something wrong?" she asked. "You tore out of here so suddenly." She stared at the stack of newspapers Graeme had just brought out of the Land Rover. "What are you doing with all those newspapers?"

"I, uh . . ." Graeme froze, words eluding him.

Gemma stepped forward to answer for him. "They're mine, dear. I . . ." She scrambled for something to say. "I just can't make a move without checking my horoscope. Have to read them, all of them, every single day."

She scooped the papers out of Graeme's arms and into her own, careful to shield the front pages from Libby's view.

Libby looked at her curiously. "I just made some tea."

"Splendid!" the countess said, and turned, vanishing

through the door, calling as she went, "I'll be there in a moment. Just need to check these first . . ."

Graeme looked at Libby and smiled, acting as if his mother's behavior were perfectly normal. "Would you please tell Flora we'll be having a third for supper tonight?"

"Flora? Oh, hmm. That might be a problem. I gave Flora the day off. She wanted to take her children to Inverness. The latest Harry Potter film is showing."

"Indeed? Well, I suppose we could go to the café in the village, then."

"Afraid we won't be able to do that either. It's Wednesday. Half-day closing in the village today."

"Oh. Hmm . . ."

"I'm sure I can manage something," Libby offered even as her brain was screaming, *No! Don't do it!*

Little did he know that the closest she'd ever come to reading a recipe was reciting the entrée numbers from the takeout menu of her favorite Chinese restaurant back home.

"Well," he said, "if you're sure it wouldn't be too much trouble . . ."

"No trouble at all. I'll just pop down to the village store before they close to see what I can find."

She wasn't totally without a plan. Libby knew that the Widow MacNamara sold pre-prepared meat pies and other quick-fix meals as a means of keeping herself busy while supplementing her monthly income. Prepared fresh each day, they were ready and waiting in the market cooler every morning, awaiting a convenient hour in the oven. And if there was one thing Libby did know, it was how to preheat an oven for a TV dinner. This would be virtually the same thing.

Graeme offered her the keys to the Land Rover, and in minutes she was off.

But at the store, the cooler that usually held the selection of Mrs. MacNamara's delicacies was ominously empty.

"Jamie," Libby said, calling to Ellie Mackay's teenage son. He worked sometimes weekends in the store so his mother could see to the office work. "Are you out of Mrs. MacNamara's pies?"

"Oh, aye, Miss Hutchinson. Cooler's on the fritz. Had to ask her to hold off for a few days. Won't have any more till Monday when the repairman comes."

Libby felt the beginnings of panic start her pulse to racing. Her only other alternative was the chip shop down the street, which was open all the time, but she really didn't want to serve Graeme's mother a takeaway meal for dinner.

"And I've got a guest for dinner tonight. Have you nothing else?"

"Ehm . . ." He thought about it. "My mum has a haggis in the fridge in back. Just made it fresh this morning."

Libby grabbed at the lifeline he offered. "She wouldn't be upset if you sold it to me?"

"Och, no, miss. But she'd be upset if I charged you even a pence fer it. You're like a cousin to us, Mackay to Mackay, and family helps family. Just wait here and I'll fetch it fer you."

Jamie vanished into the back of the store and came back a few minutes later with a parcel wrapped in white butcher's paper. "Just pop it in a pot of water and boil it for at least three hours. You can toss in some tatties the last hour to serve wit' it. Tha's what Mum always does."

Libby eyed the package doubtfully. "And this, what did you call it, *haggis* . . . it's good?"

"Och, there isna a Scotsman who doesna appreciate the warmth of a good haggis in his belly for his supper. 'Tis how my mum got my da to marry her. She makes the best haggis in all o' the Highlands."

It was all the convincing Libby needed. After all,

Robert Burns had composed an entire poem to a haggis, hadn't he? So whatever it was, it must be good. She leaned forward and kissed Jamie on the cheek. "Thank you, Jamie. You just saved my life."

The boy blushed, smiling broadly as she turned, grabbed up the sack of other things she'd purchased, and hurried out the door.

Three hours to cook it, he'd said. If she hurried, she'd have just enough time.

Jamie was still grinning when his mother came out from the back of the store a few moments later. "Who was that, lad?"

"Oh, just Miss Hutchinson. She was in a bit of a state without anything for supper for the laird and his guest. So I gave her your haggis. I dinna think you'd mind. She was most appreciative."

He rubbed his cheek where Libby had just kissed him. It was the first time he'd ever been kissed by a girl, other than his mother, that is. He couldn't wait to tell it to the lads.

With his mum having returned, Jamie was free to go off and meet his friends. He was already grabbing his coat and heading for the door.

"Does she know how to prepare it?"

But Jamie was already out the door.

"Jamie! D'you hear? I asked did you tell her how to prepare it?"

"Aye, I told her, ma. Told her to boil it at least three hours, just like you do. I'm off to meet the lads at the football pitch. I'll be home afore dark."

He turned, the door slamming behind him.

"Jamie? Jamie Mackay! You did tell her to prick the skin with a fork, aye?"

He was halfway down the street, running with his coattails flying behind him, but Ellie swore she saw him waving his arm in response.

He's a good lad, that Jamie, Ellie thought as she went back to her account books.

Graeme stood outside the kitchen and waited, listening at the door.

He heard:

A spoon stirring.

A drawer opening.

A pot boiling over.

And something that sounded rather like a very nasty curse word.

He knocked softly.

"Libby? Is there anything I can do to help?"

"No!" Her voice sounded frantic. "It's nearly ready. Why don't you take your mother into the dining room and open a bottle of wine?"

"Well, since I don't know what we're having for supper, I'm not certain which to choose, white or red."

He waited for her reply.

"Red. I think. Yes, definitely red."

Graeme looked at the door, shaking his head as he turned for the dining room.

His mother was already there, waiting.

"Is everything all right?"

"She assures me that whatever it is we're going to be eating is very nearly ready."

He took a bottle of Bordeaux from the wine rack.

In the kitchen Libby checked the stove timer. Ten more minutes.

Everything was going according to plan. She had the salad plates on the tray, ready to take into the dining room. The potatoes were cooked and mashed with butter and a dash of salt. There were freshly baked rolls (she'd found some in the deep freeze, bless Flora's heart) and a sliced apple cake for dessert.

All that remained was the haggis.

Libby lifted the lid off the pot, took a peek.

When she'd first gotten back from the market and had opened the white butcher's wrap, she'd thought perhaps Jamie had played a trick on her. First, the round, melon-shaped, meat-filled sack had looked too small to feed three people. But the longer it boiled, the more it expanded, so Libby had decided to allow it to cook the full three hours that Jamie had suggested just to make sure there would be enough.

As soon as the timer dinged, Libby grabbed the tongs, lifted the lid off the pot, and—

Graeme nearly dropped the wine bottle when there came a sound much like an explosion from the vicinity of the kitchen.

He turned and ran, with his mother falling in close behind him.

"Libby, are you . . . ?"

The scene that met him on the other side of the kitchen door defied description.

Libby was standing in the center of the room, the front of her pale blue blouse splattered with a dripping, brown, unidentifiable substance. That same stuff looked to have been flung across every wall and counter, every cabinet, and every window, reaching as high as the ceiling in some places. Even as he stood there, a blob of it dropped from overhead, landing on his arm. It was still warm. He swept it from his sleeve with a finger, took a sniff.

Haggis.

Libby wasn't saying a word. She just stood there, blinking as if she were shell-shocked.

Or perhaps the more appropriate description would be *haggis*-shocked.

The look on her face was so defeated, Graeme didn't know what to do or what to say.

Blessedly, his mother stepped forward, ever the able general.

"Oh, heavens. You forgot to prick the haggis before boiling it, didn't you, dear?"

When Libby just looked at her, the evidence of that very statement spewed across her nose, the countess took her hand and led her from the room, calling back as they went, "Graeme, can you see about getting a bucket of some soapy water and start scrubbing the stuff from the walls? We'll be back shortly."

Gemma led Libby up the stairs to her bedroom, then shoved her into the bathroom. "Why don't you let me have those clothes, dear, so I can get them soaking to keep the stains from setting?"

A few minutes later, the door opened a crack, and Libby's arm poked out, holding the haggis-splattered garments aloft. The countess listened for the sound of the bathwater running, then headed back to the kitchen, where she found Graeme on his hands and knees scrubbing the stuff from the tile floor.

She'd certainly raised him right.

She dumped Libby's clothes in the kitchen sink and filled it with cold water, then turned to her son. "Now, you get in your car and see if you can find something to salvage this supper. That girl will be feeling utterly dejected when she comes back down here, and so I want every reminder of this debacle gone before she does."

"The café is closed. But I think there's a chip shop."

"That'll do. Now go whilst I see to this mess."

As a long-standing member of the House of Lords, Gemma Mackenzie wasn't at all afraid of getting her hands dirty. She'd been raised on her father's Scottish estate, and he, knowing that she would be the one to assume his mantle when he was gone, had given her a childhood hands-on education that had even included the yearly dipping of the sheep. The floor was easy enough to clean, but when it came to the ceiling, particularly above the stove, Lady Abermuir had to use a bit more elbow grease.

By the time Graeme returned with three fish-and-chip takeaway suppers in a plastic sack, the place looked as if the past several hours had never occurred.

"All right," the countess said, wiping her wet hands on a towel. "You set those suppers up in the dining room as if they are a bloody Christmas feast. Use the best china you can find. Light some candles. I'll be right back down."

When she got to Libby's bedroom door, she knocked softly. "Dear, may I come in?"

She opened the door at the responding muffled "yes" and found Libby, freshly washed and dressed, sitting on her bed. She looked as if she wanted nothing more than to crawl under the duvet and hide.

Gemma sat on the bed beside her. "You know, when I was first married to Graeme's father, I wanted to bake him a birthday cake. Only I couldn't try just any birthday cake. Oh, no! It had to be a chocolate soufflé with whiskey crème sauce. So, of course, much to my horror, the thing came out of the oven flatter than an oatcake. But my husband, treasure that he was, insisted it was fine, even went on to suggest that I had created some wonderful new delicacy that would be the envy of the French culinary world. Oh, did I forget to mention that his entire family was there for the celebration as well? So what else could I do? He had to have something for his birthday cake, so I went along with it, drizzling this flat brown Frisbee of a thing in whiskey crème sauce in hopes to camouflage my dismal failure. Only, to compensate for the disaster of the soufflé, I had doubled the amount of whiskey, half thinking that if I could get them all drunk they'd never remember it. But when I went to light his birthday candles so he could make his wish . . ."

Libby looked at her. "It burst into flame?"

"Precisely, dear. Singed the poor man's eyebrows clear off."

Libby fought valiantly to hold back a smile.

"Go ahead and laugh. I've long since gotten over it. Lord knows, it's been told around the Christmas table every year since."

The countess looked at her. "So you see, dear, nothing is as bad as it seems. Someone, somewhere, has always done something far, far worse. I promise you, you will look back on this . . . this *haggisaster* one day and laugh, too."

Libby looked at her, smiled. "Thank you."

The countess gave her a hug. "Now, why don't you come downstairs with me, and I'll tell you about the time Graeme's brother, Teddy, convinced poor unsuspecting four-year-old Graeme that their father's prized polo cup was actually a tiny silver loo? And, even better, that he should make use of it smack in the middle of our summer garden party . . . ?"

Chapter Twenty-one

Two days later, when Graeme walked into "The Blue Room," he was greeted by a blast of bagpipe music blaring from a small portable CD player. Libby's feet, moving in time to the primitive drumbeat, were sticking out from underneath the piano.

"Ehm . . . Libby?"

She didn't hear him.

He tried a little louder. "Libby?"

Her feet just kept on air-dancing.

He knocked on the top of the piano as if it were a door. "Hello! Anybody home?"

"Oh . . . good morning!"

She wiggled her toes at him, their polish almost as shiny as the beeswax she was so diligently applying to the carved legs of the piano. The pipe music quieted to a dim bellow.

"Isn't this great? Young Jamie Mackay from the village store lent me his CD. I didn't believe him when he said the louder you play it, the better it sounds, but you know, he's right!"

Graeme stood back, crossed his arms, and smiled a wry grin. "It's always been my opinion that listening to music whilst standing next to an instrument is usually a more enjoyable experience than lying underneath it."

She poked her head out to look at him. "Oh, really? And have you ever actually tried lying under a piano?"

He thought about it. And a moment later, Graeme was sinking to the floor to join her.

A half hour, and some very rumpled clothing later, the CD came to a thundering finish and Graeme had to admit there was indeed a certain merit to the underside of a piano after all.

He was still smiling about it later that day as he rode along the rain-slick streets through London's Mayfair district on his way to Gransborough House, the ducal family house in town.

"Oy! Lord Waltham!"

Graeme turned on instinct as he stepped out of the car and was greeted by the all-too-familiar and unwelcome sound of the shutter click from a photographer's camera.

"Where's yer lady friend, aye, m'lord?" said the man with the Minolta stuck to his face who was clicking the shutter incessantly. "Come on now . . . give us a break, guv. What's 'er name?"

Graeme knew the photographer, Giles Gilchrist, by name, a particularly smarmy scourge who had been responsible for some of the most invasive, most inappropriate photographs that had ever been snapped of the royal family and various other members of the British nobility. No level of human decency had ever managed to curb his ravenous appetite for publishing images aimed at nothing more than pure titillation. In fact, his badge of honor came from being one of those responsible for Sarah Ferguson's downfall, by publishing those horrible photos of that Texan businessman sucking on her toes.

"Sod off," Graeme grumbled, pushing past the paparazzi's blinking lens, wishing he could plant his fist in the tosser's face. But he couldn't, because that would amount to an assault. Of course, the guy's camera shoved two inches from his face, snapping a shot up his nasal cavity, wasn't.

"We'll find out who she is, anyway, m'lord. So you might as well just tell it to us now and be done with it . . ."

Graeme gritted his teeth and made for the door, a volley of camera clicks popping behind him like rifle fire. The words "Take cover!" echoed through his thoughts, and he couldn't help but feel like one of those soldiers in the old World War II movies who scrambled across cinematic black-and-white French fields ducking sniper fire.

Thankfully, the Gransborough butler had been expecting him and opened the door to admit him the moment he reached the step.

"Thank you, Paul. Perfect timing as always."

"Good morning, my lord. Glad to be of assistance."

Graeme quickly shed his raincoat. "You're looking well, Paul. Have you been working out at the gymnasium again?"

Paul cracked a smile. "Not exactly, my lord."

Thickset and balding and dressed in his formal black-and-white waistcoated uniform, he looked every bit the quintessential British butler. He'd been a faithful Gransborough servant since Graeme had been old enough to drool. But a fitness buff Paul was not.

Graeme looked down the hall that led to the center of the house. "Is he . . . ?"

"In the library, my lord," Paul answered, already anticipating his question, "reading the morning paper. He said you should go right up. Might I bring you a coffee? Espresso perhaps . . ."

"That would be perfect. Thank you, Paul."

Graeme made his way through the arched central hall past a lineup of marble busts on plinths that stood like attentive soldiers, one to a tread, on the main stairway. Some families commissioned paintings of their ancestors. Others kept their relatives' memories alive through photo albums and videotape. The Dukes of Gransborough, however, went a step far beyond, immortalizing themselves in sculpture.

It had begun with the first duke, back in the late eighteenth century, who had been known to pace that same stairwell wearing knee breeches and periwig, seeking the counsel of his predecessors whenever he'd had a particularly perplexing dilemma to solve. Speaking to a marble bust had apparently proved more therapeutic than to a painting, and thereafter a tradition of committing the visages of all subsequent dukes to marble was born, a tradition that had stretched through more than two hundred and fifty years. If he ever felt inclined, Graeme could line his ancestors up around the dining table and have a bloody tea party with them, but he'd never seen the attraction in chatting with a bunch of bodyless heads. Still, they were all of them there, periwigs, mutton chops, and noble brows amongst them, and one day, God willing, there would be another added to the collection, one resembling Graeme. The fact that his place in the lineup would fall on the thirteenth tread was more disconcerting than he cared to admit.

Gransborough House was one of the few grand Georgian mansions remaining in London that hadn't been swallowed up by commercial office space or academic museums. Still very much a family home, the house edged Green Park along a broad, tree-lined thoroughfare known as the Queen's Walk. Begun by that same first duke in 1743, its neoclassical architecture was one of the finest examples of its kind in London, and the architects who'd worked on the house at various times throughout its history were a roll call of those Graeme had studied in his university textbooks—Kent, Adam, Holland, and Hardwick amongst them.

The house was built in the Palladian style, and the western facade, which faced the park, was a magnificent vision of classical pillars, elegant arches, and a beautiful

terraced garden replete with Roman statuary. But the
outside was just a whisper of the far more resplendent
interior. Adorned with friezework derived from Greek
and Roman temples and gilding as grand as any royal
palace, the rooms had been designed as an illustrious
backdrop for the elegant and distinguished lives that had
been lived there.

Over the generations (and subsequent dukes), it had
been renovated, remodeled, and redecorated more times
than could possibly be counted. For with each duke had
come a duchess who had seemed determined that she
would leave her mark.

There was the great room, which had once been used
to host fashionable Edwardian dress balls attended by
the most noble and royal personalities of the day. The
room stretched the full length of the terraced garden and
was hung with a huge glittering silver and crystal chandelier that had held hundreds of candles and had taken
six servants just to haul it up to the ceiling when it had
been lit. The dining room, with its lofty ornate domed
ceiling, had been his great-grandmother Euphemia's pet
project, a place to display her prized mahogany Chip-
pendale table that stretched over twenty feet between
Siena-marbled Corinthian columns.

All throughout the house were marble floors, and elegant furnishings filled the vast collection of rooms,
sweeping any visitor back through time to various eras
of grace and elegance gone by. It was the library, however, that had always been Graeme's favorite, not so
much for its impressive amount of books, which numbered in the thousands, tucked in neat shelves that ringed
the room, but more for the conscious restraint and lack
of ornamentation that seemed a stark contrast to the rest
of the place. The library had always been the duke's domain, and no woman's hand had ever succeeded in
changing a single feature of it. The furnishings were
simple and well used, the hearth always lit with a wel-

coming fire. In a house that had seemed like a live-in museum, this room more than any other had always felt like home.

Graeme arrived at the library, paused in the doorway, and cleared his throat discreetly.

Behind the great kneehole Sheraton desk, Albert George Trevelyan Charlton, the ninth Duke of Gransborough, looked up from his morning edition of *The Times*. He didn't smile. He didn't frown. He just looked, and then shifted his gaze back to the day's headline.

"Ah, good morning, Graeme," he finally said. "It is good to see you."

He was a man who had been born to be reckoned with, and everything about him was consistent with that image, from his heavy brow to the full shock of white hair he wore closely clipped to his collar. When he stood, he was a towering six feet three of broad shoulders, aristocratic bearing, and centuries of the very bluest blood England had to offer. His seventy-two years had only improved on those qualities.

The duke rose from his chair and came forward to meet his nephew, embracing him formally and briefly.

"The Highlands agree with you," he noted, taking a step back to scan Graeme from head to toe.

It was one thing Graeme had inherited from his father's side of the family, his height. He looked at the duke eye to eye.

"Come. Let us sit."

The duke waved a hand toward a pair of leather armchairs set before the huge arched window that faced out onto the terraced garden, and beyond that Green Park. As he took his seat, Graeme could see people strolling along the Queen's Walk beneath huge elms and oaks bursting with fall color. One pair, tourists, were snapping photographs of the Gransborough mansion over the box hedges, marveling at the golden Diana statue in the middle of the marble fountain. When they used their telephoto lens to try to sneak a peek inside the arched windows, Graeme knew a sudden unpleasant feeling, one he could only imagine was similar to what the caged beasts must feel on display in the Regent's Park Zoo.

What were they hoping to capture on film? A picture of a real, live English duke sitting on the loo?

Paul came in on cue, silver coffee service in hand. He prepared them each a demitasse, ministered them to each man's liking, then bowed out of the room on his silent butler feet.

The duke glanced at Graeme over a sip of his espresso. "I understand your latest drawings have garnered a preliminary nod of approval from His Highness, the Prince of Wales. That's quite an accomplishment, Graeme. Your firm must be overjoyed."

Graeme nodded. "I've a meeting there later today. There is still much work to do before the project can be finalized, but I'd say we're headed in the right direction."

"I see. Have you any thought for a time line?"

"I would guess six months at least before we can even begin to break ground."

The duke lifted a brow, breathed deeply to express his dissatisfaction with that comment.

"You know you won't be able to avoid it much longer, Graeme. Sooner or later, you'll have to accept your position as the heir to all of this. You must take the time to learn the ropes. Wins and Teddy both had the benefit of a childhood that had been geared toward their future positions. You, as the spare, I'm afraid did not."

Though Graeme bristled at the term "spare," he kept his countenance as the duke went on.

"I understand your commitment to your career, Graeme, and most especially to this project, and I commend you on your dedication to your work, but there's much we need to discuss about the estates, the inheritance. Out of respect for what you've suddenly found yourself flung into and for your dear mother's wishes, I agreed to give you this time, the time to finish this project as a period of adjustment to your new position in life. But I cannot wait forever, Graeme. I'm not a young man."

Graeme looked at him. "I know very well what is expected of me, Your Grace. And I gave you my word. As soon as I finish this project, my life is pledged to the dukedom."

The duke nodded. "Good. I'm glad to hear that. I was beginning to worry, although I must say I was pleased to learn that you've agreed to marry."

Graeme sat forward in his chair. "Yes, about that, Your Grace . . ."

"The sooner done with it, I think, the better. It will put an end to this media carnival that surrounds you and will allow you to return to the city as soon as possible, which would undoubtedly be better for you with your work. Now, I've already been in preliminary talks with Cleary—"

"Lord Cleary?"

"Of course. You always did get on well with his daughter, Amaranthe, so I assumed she'd be the most logical choice."

"Just how *preliminary* have these talks been?" Graeme asked, already dreading the response.

"Well, I had to try to discern if the girl was already involved elsewhere . . ."

Graeme closed his eyes. His uncle had never been one to mince words. When he wanted to know something, he asked. When he had an opinion, he gave it. Gruff, to the point, he was a living, breathing example of the word *outspoken*.

No doubt Amaranthe had already begun picking out china patterns.

That thought was confirmed a moment later.

"She's said to prefer a spring wedding, late spring.

Perhaps May, so the two of you can make your first appearance as newlyweds at Ascot in June."

"I'm afraid that won't be possible," Graeme said carefully.

"The Regatta in July, then. I don't care when it's done, just as long as it's done and done quickly."

Graeme drew a deep breath. "I'm afraid it's my marrying Amaranthe at all that won't be possible, Your Grace."

"I beg your pardon?" The duke betrayed a rare show of emotion. "Why the devil not?"

"Because I've met someone." Graeme looked at him. "Someone else."

The duke's face went from dark to pale white. A moment later, he lifted that heavy Gransborough brow, his voice dropping to a deadly calm. "What do you mean you've met someone else? Just who is this person?"

"Her name is Libby Hutchinson."

"Hutchinson? Never heard of the family. What's her father? A viscount? Tell me he's at least a viscount. Where is their family seat?"

"Outside Boston."

"Boston?"

"You wouldn't have heard of her, Your Grace. She's an American."

The Duke of Gransborough, for what was likely the first time in his life, was left speechless. He just stared at Graeme, blinking.

"She's actually Scottish, but was raised in America. Her family on her father's side own the Wrath Estate," and then he added to remind the duke, "that castle where I've been living the past weeks."

"I'm afraid I'm going to need a bit more of an explanation than that, Graeme."

Graeme decided to keep the details as brief as possible. He explained Libby's situation, her unexpected inheritance, and her legal battle with Lady Venetia. He added that he'd had every intention of marrying Amaranthe, or whoever his mother and the duke might have decided upon, until he realized he had more than just a casual regard for Libby.

"She's just different from anybody I've ever met before. She's independent, intelligent, someone I can actually carry on a conversation with. And she makes me laugh, something I've done precious little of in the past year."

The duke sighed with resignation. "And does this American return your feelings?"

Graeme looked at him, remembering his detour under the piano that morning. "I am led to suspect that she does."

"Of course she bloody well would. You're the heir to Britain's wealthiest dukedom! She'd be a fool not to."

"She doesn't know about that."

"Doesn't know about what?"

"The dukedom, my inheritance. She doesn't know anything about that aspect of my life at all. In truth, she just thinks I'm Graeme Mackenzie, the castle caretaker."

"She thinks you're a . . . ." The duke couldn't quite spit it out. ". . . a *caretaker*?"

"Yes. And amazingly, remarkably, she seems to like me in spite of it."

"Why on earth would you . . . ?" The duke just looked at Graeme as if he wanted to find a way to discredit what he was hearing, but then slowly he shook his head.

"This hasn't been easy on you, what with losing Teddy and Wins, and then your father so soon after that. I know you never expected, never dreamed you'd be your mother's heir, let alone my heir as well. But sometimes fate deals us unexpected turns for whatever reason, and we must rise to the challenge of them. You have put me in a most unappealing predicament. If I call off Lord Cleary, and this American decides she isn't up to the role of a future duchess, then what?"

Graeme couldn't answer him.

"And there are other things to consider as well. Amaranthe has been raised in The Environment, Graeme. She knows what it entails, what is expected of her, and she is well schooled for the task. You have to admit she is probably the most suitable candidate for the job."

Graeme couldn't deny that what the duke said was true. But was that worth staking the rest of his life on? To the duke, the role of duchess was more like a position of employment to be filled, with Amaranthe's bloodlines and boarding-school upbringing constituting her C.V.

To Graeme, a future duchess was the woman who would be his partner . . . for life.

The duke got up from his chair and went to stand at the tall arched window with his back facing the room. Graeme remained sitting, and waited.

"This has nothing to do with my thinking that this Hutchinson girl isn't good enough or British enough. But this is more than just finding someone who strikes your fancy, Graeme. An American is raised in an environment much different than we have here, and there are certain freedoms this girl might not be so willing to give up. And I have no intention of telling you who you must marry. I'd like to think we've moved a little beyond the Dark Ages and no longer arrange marriages in the cradle. I only began talks with Cleary because your mother told me it would be best to get the deed over and done with."

"My mother has met Libby, and she did not seem to think she wouldn't be up to the task."

The duke turned, faced Graeme across the room. He nodded. "Fine. I will talk to your mother. If this girl is the one, Graeme, if she is the one you wish to spend the rest of your life with, then I accept that and wish you very happy. But if she isn't . . ."

He didn't finish his sentence. He didn't have to.

"All I'm asking is for the time to find that out," Graeme said.

"Very well." The duke went to the desk, thumbed through his calendar. "I will try to hold Cleary off until mid-November. I won't be able to wait any longer than that, I'm afraid. If things don't work out with this American and there's to be a wedding with Amaranthe, the girl will need time to plan it. That will only be giving her five or six months."

Graeme nodded, accepting the arrangement. "Thank you, Your Grace. I appreciate your consideration. I shall be in touch."

Graeme got up to leave. He was anxious to be done with his business, anxious to return to the castle . . .

. . . and to Libby.

"Graeme?"

He stopped at the door, turned.

His uncle still stood at the desk, framed in the light of its magnificent arched window behind him.

"Good luck to you, son."

Chapter Twenty-two

Perched on nearly the top rung of the ladder, Libby stretched her arms and slid the portrait into place over the two hooks she'd just hammered into the wall.

"Is that straight?"

Behind her, Flora stood, arms crossed, cocking her head to the side. "A little to the right. No, too far. Now to the left. Wait. Can you duck down a wee bit? Yes, that's grand. Perfect. It's just perfect."

Libby descended the ladder and stood back to admire their handiwork. "Yes, it is, isn't it? It's absolutely perfect."

They'd found the portrait tucked away in one of the castle garrets, hidden beneath furniture and an old rug. Thankfully, the rug had protected it, leaving it virtually untouched. The gold plate affixed to the frame still read clearly, CALUM MACKAY OF WRATH, 1758. Painted by Sir Joshua Reynolds himself, it should have been hanging in a museum, not moldering away, forgotten, in an attic.

It was a magnificent image. He stood full length with one hand resting on the silver basket hilt of his sword, the other poised at his kilted hip. Dark hair, which looked to have been tousled from the blustery sky that was depicted behind him, was tied back over the high collar of his rich red coat. Gold braiding and a waistcoat of patterned sateen were buttoned over his trim figure. Legs corded with muscle stretched out at length from beneath the kilt he wore, the calves swathed in tartan hose and buckled shoes.

But it wasn't until Libby looked more closely that she saw past the embellishments, to the characteristics that told of the true Calum Mackay.

There was his steady chin that spoke of strength, a firm, uncompromising mouth hinting at stubbornness, with a stance that was confident and resolute as he stood above the tumbling sea. His castle, his domain, stood in the distance behind him, and there was sheer power in his potent gaze as he looked out at her. Intent, challenging, the longer she looked at him, looked at his eyes, the more Libby felt as if it were he looking out from that portrait onto her. This was a man who knew his place in the world, who had not merely posed to appear glorious for a painting. This was a man who had been glorious in his own right.

"I know he was my great-great-great-whatever-grandfather, but I have to say he was one handsome man, wasn't he?"

Flora nodded in agreement. "I certainly wouldn't be turning him out of my bed now. Lady Isabella was a lucky lass. I remember hearing once, when I was a child, that he was a twin."

"A twin?" It was the first Libby had ever heard of it.

"Aye. Can you just imagine two of them as fine as tha' walking about these parts? This one, Laird Calum, he was a pirate, too. You see that ship painted in the portrait?"

Libby hadn't even noticed the tall-masted ship depicted in the distance behind him until Flora had mentioned it.

"That was *The Adventurer,* and on it Laird Calum sailed the high seas. But he was not a pirate in the sense of a blackbearded cutthroat who pillaged villages and

raped innocent women. He raided English prison ships.
You see, after the last Jacobite rebellion, many Scots
were thrown into these big hulking boats and sent off to
the Colonies, never to see their homes or their families
again. The conditions were so bad, many of them died
afore ever reaching land. It was the English Crown's
plan for ridding the Highlands of the clan 'rabble,' but
Laird Calum, he sailed the seas and overtook the prison
ships, freeing the Scottish prisoners afore they could be
sent from their homeland. Many of those he freed are ancestors of the people who still live in this village. My
own great-great-great-great-grandfather was one of
them."

She looked at Libby then. "You know, in your own
way, you're doing the same thing in fighting to keep the
village from being sold out from under our feet. Must be
you've got some of that pirate blood in you as well,
aye?"

Libby looked at the image of her handsome ancestor
and beamed with pride. "I never knew that."

"Well, 'tisn't taught much in the history books, but it's
the stuff of legend around these parts of the Highlands.
Must've been such an exciting time, aye? Sailing the
high seas, fighting redcoats. They say there was even a
sword fight right here in this castle a'tween Lord Calum
and the British soldiers who had come to capture him.
'Twas only with the help of Lady Isabella's father, who
was an English duke, that he avoided hanging."

"Goodness!" Libby exclaimed. "I'm related to an
English duke?"

" 'Tis what they say. You know, you should talk to old
Gil. He would know more than most the auld stories of
the Mackay." Flora glanced at the clock on the wall.
"Och, is that the time a'ready? I'm afraid I've got to
leave a wee bit early today, if that would be all right with
you."

"Of course. Is something wrong with one of the children?"

"Nae, nothing like that. It's just I've promised to help in setting up for the *ceilidh* tonight."

Libby looked at her and attempted to repeat, "*Kaylee*?"

"Aye. 'Tis a traditional Scottish get-together. Back in the auld days, the villagers would come together to share food and, of course, drink, dancing, and stories. It was a means of keeping ties close within the clan."

"Oh, that's lovely," Libby said. "You go on, then. And have a nice time."

"What d'ya mean? You're not coming?" Flora shook her head. "Och, miss, it's not a formal sort of party, if that's what you're thinking. You don't need to have an invitation or anything like that. We have the *ceilidh* once a month, and everyone comes who wants to come. Backpackers, tourists, anyone who happens by. 'Tis just our way of keeping the village folk connected, especially the older ones who don't have much to keep themselves occupied the rest of the time. I thought sure someone would have told you about it by now. You must come and you must bring the laird, too. Old Gil will be there. You could ask him to tell some of the auld Mackay stories. The children always love that. You know, I've always thought it a shame no one has ever written those auld tales down, to save for the future generations."

Libby remembered something then, something she'd read in Lady Isabella's *Book of the Mackay*.

> *It is my hope that perhaps, God willing, my own descendant might one day continue this endeavor in a subsequent volume, setting down the lives and history of those who will follow after me.*

"All right, then," Libby said. "I will come to the *ceilidh*."

"Seven o'clock t'night, at the village hall."

"Seven o'clock it is, then."

After Flora had gone, Libby took a last look around the room they had just finished. It was the laird's suite, the room just off her own bedchamber. She'd been working on restoring it for nearly a week, and with Flora's help she'd aired it out, laundered all the linens, and polished every piece of furniture till it shone. On Gil's suggestion, she'd even employed a couple of the local villagers who had proved very capable carpenters and painters. The walls of the laird's suite were now a dark, rich green, setting off the elegant mahogany furnishings and the fine marble of the hearth. It was a room that exuded every bit of the masculinity portrayed in that portrait she'd just hung above the mantelpiece—all of the power, the potency, and the boldness befitting a pirate's den.

But as she stood back surveying the results of her hard work, Libby wasn't thinking of her pirate ancestor at all.

She was thinking of another handsome Scotsman. She was thinking of . . .

"Graeme!"

She hadn't noticed him standing in the doorway. "I thought you were going to be in London today."

"I was," he said, coming into the room. "And now I'm back. I finished early."

"Oh."

"What's all this?" he asked, taking a look around the room.

Libby had managed to hide their work on the room from him. She'd meant it to be a surprise for him. "This is the laird's suite." She looked at him, and added softly, "*Your* suite."

Graeme gave her a look that could have burned her, it was so intense. "Well, then," he said, sliding his hands around her waist, "the laird should like to see if that bed is as comfortable as it looks . . ."

He lowered his head and claimed the side of her neck with his mouth, sending a shock of raw pleasure jolting through her. Libby opened her mouth, sucking in a breath as he kissed along the column of her neck, burying his face in her hair.

"But Graeme, it's the middle of the afternoon!"

Graeme simply smiled and flicked the top button of her sweater open. "Indeed it is."

"But . . ." Libby momentarily lost the will to protest as his mouth resumed its work on her neck. "This morning . . . the piano . . . we already . . ."

Another button.

"I've been thinking about you all day," he breathed against her ear.

Another button.

"I've been *wanting* you all day," Graeme whispered, and pushed her sweater over her shoulders until it was sliding off her arms.

Graeme could tell from the uncertainty in her eyes and the way she crossed her arms over her breasts that she had likely never made love in the daylight before. He took her wrists, eased them down to her sides.

"Graeme . . ."

"Libby . . ." He stared into her eyes. "I want to see you."

"Yes, but . . ."

"Do you truly not realize how very beautiful you really are?"

She blinked, not knowing what to say. It was obvious from her expression that she didn't. Not by a long shot. But he intended to show her just how beautiful she was.

He led her slowly back to the bed, never taking his eyes from hers as he eased her down to lie on the thick coverlet. He reached up and loosened the clip that bound her hair, letting it fall over her shoulders in a tumble of dark waves. He watched her blink as he slowly traced a fingertip over her brow, across her cheek, rubbing it over the fullness of her bottom lip before he took her mouth in a slow, achingly tender kiss.

Slowly Graeme moved his hand down to the button of her jeans and loosened it, releasing the zipper. He lifted her hips, eased the pants down over her legs, pulling them away. A scrap of lacy panties that stretched across her hips, and a scrap of lacy bra were all that remained.

Libby sat up, kneeling on the bed beside him, and wrapped her arms around his neck, drawing his mouth to hers. He felt her reach for his tie, felt her loosen its knot and slide it from around his neck. He felt her loosen every button on the front of his starched white shirt. She pushed the shirt back, not even bothering to pull the tails from where they were tucked in his trousers, and moved her mouth along his neck to his shoulder, then to his chest. He sucked in a breath. He could feel her tugging at the buckle of his belt, felt her loosen his trousers, and helped her pull them away.

They lay back together on the bed, arms and legs and mouths locked in a hot, wet tangle. Graeme wanted to feel her against him, the heat, the silk of her skin, and it wasn't long before he had made good work of those two remaining scraps of lace. His senses reeled. He'd never known this—this need for another human being. All day he'd been thinking about her, missing her. It was new, this feeling, because he'd kept himself, his heart and his body, so closely guarded for so long. But this woman. Somehow she had reached to the very soul of him, touching him more deeply than he'd ever thought possible.

Graeme filled his hands with her breasts, saw her drop her head back and close her eyes as his fingers touched her, teased her, heard her gasp when he closed his mouth over her nipple.

Her hands raced over him, over his back, through his hair. "Graeme . . ."

She said his name as if she were beckoning to him, and she was.

And he gave.

Oh, did he give.

He could feel her heart pulsing wildly beneath his touch, and knew that same desperation, that same intense need. He slid one hand downward, stroking between her legs, to the slick center of her and worked and caressed until he felt her body rocking against him, climbing, striving to her climax. He could not bear the waiting any longer. With one powerful, unyielding thrust, he buried himself completely inside of her.

He knew she was close to her climax, and he grabbed her by her hips, drawing her higher, so that she would take him more deeply. He felt her muscles bunch as he moved with an ever-increasing rhythm of thrusts and strokes. He slid his hand between them and teased her until he had brought her to the edge. She arched against him. He watched her face as she found her release, saw the play of raw, sexual emotion, and took her mouth with his as he buried himself completely within her. His body rocked with his climax, his breathing trembled, and she held to him tightly while they soared.

They could hear the music echoing from the village hall even before they arrived at the *ceilidh.*

The day was mild, the sun just setting, and Libby and Graeme decided to walk the distance from the castle to the hall, fingers linked, taking the same path Flora always did, which cut across the pastures and wound along the cliff tops overlooking the sea.

They took their time, stopping more than once along the way to watch the color streaking across the autumn sky. They chatted, exchanging glances as lovers do. Graeme spotted a late-blooming sprig of sea pink and plucked it, tucking it gently behind Libby's ear. She thanked him with a long, tender kiss that wrapped them in the sea wind's soft embrace.

After they'd roused themselves from the laird's bed, they'd shared a bath in that great claw-foot tub. Libby had been right. It really had been big enough for the two of them, and as she sat cradled in Graeme's arms, he softly slid soapy hands over her still-tingling skin. They'd kissed, lingering in the warmth of the water that surrounded them, and Libby wondered at how her life had changed in the past weeks. How could it be that just a month earlier she had convinced herself she would never find anyone, that she would never be able to trust anyone again? She'd envisioned herself growing old, alone, with no husband and no children to comfort her.

Until she'd met Graeme.

She smiled to herself as she remembered their first encounter over the sight of his shotgun. Would it be a story they would tell their children, even their grandchildren someday? Libby reined the thought back, afraid to move too quickly, remembering the whirlwind romance with Jeff that had turned so quickly into a hurricane. It was a mistake she didn't intend to repeat.

As they walked the pathway that led to the hall, they could see some of the villagers milling about outside, chatting together and sharing a laugh over a pint. They waved to Libby and called to her in greeting, some nodding to Graeme, others giving him curious looks, for a good many in the village had never seen the mysterious caretaker of their castle other than perhaps a vague silhouette through the tinted windows of his Land Rover as he'd rolled past their cottage gardens.

Inside, the hall was fairly bursting, and the *ceilidh* was in full swing. Children were playing, chasing each other around the sea of grown-ups, and the ale kegs and whiskey bottles were thoroughly tapped. For those not old enough, or not interested in the stronger spirits, there was a punch bowl and pitchers of lemonade, and tables were lined against one wall, heaped with platters of sandwiches and meat pies, potatoes, cabbage, bannocks, oatcakes, and of course the ubiquitous haggis.

The floorboards thrummed with the footsteps of the dancers, who were turning and spinning about the room to the fiddles, pipes, and drums resounding from the makeshift bandstand at the far end of the hall.

Flora was one of the first to see Libby and Graeme come into the hall and came over to greet them.

"Good e'en to you both. You're lookin' lovely t'night, Libby. The dress suits you."

The soft cottony floral had arrived at the castle earlier that evening, brought by one of Flora's little ones, a red-haired darling named Rose who'd curtseyed after handing the dress over to Libby at the door. With it a short note: "Saw this in Effie MacNeil's shop window and thought of you."

Since she hadn't known about the *ceilidh*, Libby hadn't had the time to shop for something suitable to wear. But even if she had, the dress Flora had sent to her wasn't of the sort Libby would have ever considered for herself. When she wore dresses, which wasn't often with her working lifestyle, they were usually tailored, suitlike, and starkly professional. This dress could never be called any of those things.

It was unquestionably feminine, made from a simple cottony print with cap sleeves that skimmed her shoulders and a bodice that buttoned up the front, hugging her torso and ending in a sweeping hem that fell to just above her ankles. She'd worn her skimmer shoes and a pale blue cardigan to guard against the chill of the night. Her hair was down, hanging in a soft flip around her shoulders, with the narrow ribbon she'd threaded through it to hold it back from her face.

Libby had stared at her reflection and had been dumb-founded. She'd never thought of herself as very pretty, hidden as she usually was behind her working trousers and baggy sweaters. Passably attractive, perhaps, but wearing this dress made her feel unfamiliarly alluring.

"I have you to thank for it." Libby smiled. "And you likewise. You look lovely."

Indeed, Flora was a vision in a pale green frock that showed her slender dancer's figure to advantage. It was the first time Libby had ever seen her hair down and not wound back beneath a kerchief or in its usual knot. It was a riot of vivid red curls that fell nearly to her waist and shone in the low light inside the hall. She looked stunning, standing with her youngest tucked against the crook of one hip, an eighteen-month-old named Seamus for the father he'd lost while he'd still been in the womb.

Seamus had his thumb stuck fast in his mouth, and his eyes were the same brilliant green as his mother's, but his hair was dark and his lashes long and full. She could already see he'd grow up to be quite handsome, and she wondered if he had inherited those dark lashes from the father he'd never been given the chance to know.

"I don't see that brother of yours anywhere," Libby said to her. "Where is Angus? Is he on duty tonight?"

"Oh, Angus had a call from the chief constable just as I was leaving. He said he'd be along shortly." She scanned the assembly, looking for him in the throng. "I don't quite see him yet. I wonder what is keeping him. It's been a while . . ."

"Flora, lass!"

It was Ian M'Cuick who'd called out, and from the skewed angle of his necktie, the muss in his hair, and the look in his eyes, he'd apparently been sampling at the whiskey table for some time.

"Come now, lass. My wife isna looking. How about givin' us a wee turn about the dance floor, aye?" He looked at Libby, squinting at her from behind his eyeglasses. "Oh, hallo, Libby . . ." He made to tip his hat in greeting, a hat that he apparently didn't realize wasn't even there.

Flora laughed. "I'll take a turn wit' you, Ian, if you can convince Libby 'ere to take my wee one while we dance."

Libby needed no convincing. She didn't even need asking. She took Seamus into her arms and watched as Flora and Ian joined the other dancers on the floor. Despite his inebriation, Ian was a most coherent dancer as they turned and stepped in perfect unison around the crowded floor. When Sean MacNeish came up to cut in, Flora threw back her head and laughed, enjoying being the object of two men's admiration. It was a nice change from her usual role of housekeeper and frazzled single mother.

"See your mama, Seamus? Isn't she a pretty dancer?"

Seamus just stared at Libby, sucking furiously on his thumb.

Libby tucked his head beneath her cheek and swayed softly with him to the rhythm of the music, humming and breathing in the soft child's scent of his hair. She closed her eyes, losing herself in the warmth and closeness of him against her breast. She could feel Seamus's small body begin to grow heavier as he slowly drifted off to sleep.

"Oh, but she's a natural, isn't she?"

Graeme looked to where one of the twin spinster sisters from the B and B had suddenly appeared beside him. She was wearing a yellow dress, and he searched his brain, trying to remember which of the two, Miss Aggie or Miss Maggie, she might be.

Unable to recall, he simply smiled and nodded.

"You can always tell what sort of mother a lass will be when you see how she is with another woman's children. Our Libby there looks to have been born to it, she does."

The woman's hint was quite clear, even without the added wink she gave him. Graeme, however, had already been thinking the same thing. In fact he couldn't take his eyes off Libby as she rocked Flora's child gently to the music. She was beautiful, and the sight of her had him imagining her standing, holding and rocking another child—their child—and the feeling it gave him was more poignant than the swell of the sea, piercing him deeply inside.

It was a feeling that he now realized was love.

Chapter Twenty-three

Libby was standing beside old Gil, and as soon as Flora returned from dancing with Ian to claim her child, Gil swung a protesting Libby onto the floor.

"But I don't know any of the steps!"

Gil, however, would hear none of it.

"Come, lass. You've nothing to worry over. 'Tis in your Scottish blood, it is."

Libby took his hand and tried to follow his lead. She stumbled almost immediately and made to leave the floor, but Gil wouldn't let her quit that easily. He took her to the far side of the dancing floor and showed her the steps, walking her through them little by little. Soon she was performing the dance's measure, and tentatively they eased into the swirl of other dancers while the on-lookers called out encouragement from the sidelines.

"There, you've got it, lass!"

Gil had Libby by the waist and was leading her through the fast-paced turns and skips so quickly, she doubted her feet even touched the floor.

"My mother used to dance like this in our parlor with me when I was a little girl. Funny, I didn't remember it until just now."

"Och, Matilde was a fine dancer, she was. The village lads would all line up for a chance just to take a turn with her. You've inherited her natural step for it, I see."

They became separated by the steps of the dance, turning a circle around another team of dancers. Libby found herself with a new partner, Jamie Mackay, whose face was flushed and eyes wide with enthusiasm. His hands, as they locked with hers, were damp with a teenage boy's nervousness. Libby smiled and skipped through the next measure of the dance with him. She managed not to wince when Jamie accidentally trod on her toes.

They separated after another turn, and Libby danced with two more partners before joining up with Gil once again.

"So," she said as the music suddenly changed to a slower pace, "I'm told you're the one to ask about the old Mackay stories and legends."

"Oh, aye." Gil turned her in a wide, sweeping circle. "I've heard them all my life, I have. 'Tis an ancient clan, the Mackay. Made up of warriors, chieftains . . ."

"And pirates, too, I'm told."

Gil grinned. "You've heard of Laird Calum."

"I found his portrait in one of the castle garrets."

"Lady Venetia, she wasn't much fond of Scottish art. Called it antiquated. Preferred the style of her Dutch background, it seemed." He shook his head. "She moved most of the family portraits up to the garrets, except for Lady Isabella's in the hall." Gil grinned. "The old chief wouldna let her touch that one."

"I saw Lady Isabella's portrait the first day I visited the castle. It's mesmerizing."

"Well, from all accounts she was quite a mesmerizing lady. She brought royal blood to the Mackays, she did. Her father was an English duke, and his great-grandfather was the son of King Henry the Eighth himself."

Libby looked at him. "As in Anne Boleyn's Henry the Eighth?"

"Aye, one and the same. Wrong side of the royal blanket, o'course, back when Henry was a young man before his muddle of messy marriages. Pity that, considering he ended up the only surviving male child of the king."

"I found a book in the castle library written by Lady Isabella."

"Aye. *The Book of the Mackay,*" Gil said. "'Tis quite a special book, that."

"It is an incredible family record, but it only tells the clan history up until the time of Lady Isabella and Laird Calum. That seems like telling only half a story."

Gil nodded. "Aye, 'tis true."

"I thought perhaps I could try to finish telling it by writing down the rest of the clan history, from then until now. Might even see if it could be published, as a subsequent volume of Lady Isabella's original edition."

"Well, now, that's a grand thought, lass. I'd be happy to help you wit' it."

"I've a feeling I'll be making a nuisance of myself asking you about the stories."

"You could ne'er be a nuisance to me, lass. But why listen to the vague memories of an old man when you can hear it from Lady Isabella herself?"

"Lady Isabella . . . how?"

"In her journals. She wrote about everything in her life, from the time she was a wee lass, when she met Laird Calum, up until shortly afore she passed away. There's a whole collection of her journals up there at the castle."

"But I've gone through Lady Isabella's suite, and I haven't found anything that looks like any journals."

"That's because they aren't in Lady Isabella's suite."

Gil looked at her, his eyes sparkling as if he had something more to say, but he didn't. Instead the music ended, bringing Libby and Gil to the end of their dance. He took her hand, bowed over it gallantly.

"I'll come by on the morrow, lass, and show you

where you can find them. Come now, let me tell you about how Laird Calum and Lady Isabella came to meet one another. It's a tale that stretches all the way back to Paris, to the Palace of Versailles and King Louis XV and a mysterious comte. And it all started with that stone you wear about your neck . . ."

Libby and Gil found two empty chairs in one corner of the hall where Gil could continue with the telling of his story. Within minutes, most of the children had gathered at their feet to listen, surrounded by a good many of the adults. It was what the *ceilidh* has always been for, the retelling of tales, the passing down of history, and Libby's eyes were bright with interest as she sat perched on the very edge of her seat, hanging on Gil's every word.

Across the room, Graeme stood watching Libby from afar. He'd made the decision that he was going to tell her everything, the truth about him and his inheritance, that night.

And he was going to ask her to be his wife.

He glanced aside and saw Flora approaching. With her children sitting amongst Gil's rapt audience, she'd been given a few moments of quiet time.

"Old Gil has a way with the spoken word," she said. "He's the village's *seanachie,* you know. Our storyteller and historian. He can certainly mesmerize the wee ones."

"And the not-so-wee ones," Graeme added, nodding toward Libby.

Flora smiled. "She's a special lass, Libby is."

Graeme merely nodded. He was preoccupied, trying to think of what he would say to Libby, and—

"She's in love with you, you know."

He looked at Flora, startled at her frankness. He didn't know what he should say in response.

He didn't have to say a thing.

"Just don't hurt her. If you can't return her feelings,

then tell her. Libby needs a man who will be honest with her. She's been hurt once before. It's left quite a scar on her heart."

"I have no intention of ever hurting Libby."

"Grand." Flora smiled at him. "I dinna think you would."

A voice suddenly called out from the crowd. "How about giving us all a song, Flora lass?"

Flora reached out, squeezed Graeme's hand, and nodded to indicate the understanding between them before she headed for the bandstand.

The voices in the hall quieted the moment Flora took to the stage, as if every person there held their breath . . . and waited. The lights dimmed. A fiddle player came to stand beside her. He positioned his bow, slid it over the strings of his instrument to play the beginning notes of the song. A moment later, Flora opened her mouth and began to sing.

It wasn't just singing. Singing somehow didn't adequately describe the spell she began to spin with her voice. It was a mystical, captivating mixture of pitches and words, without the need of any musical accompaniment. She sang in the tongue of the Gael, a haunting song that enchanted everyone just as thoroughly as Old Gil had enchanted the children with his stories. Flora's voice filled the room, rich and throaty and pure, and though Graeme couldn't understand the words she sang, he knew it was a song of love. It was in her expression, and reflected in the faces of every person there as mothers took hold of their children and lovers stood together in each other's arms.

Graeme crossed the room, found Libby standing at the back of Flora's audience. He came up behind her and wrapped her in the circle of his arms. She leaned her head back against his chest, sighing softly. Nothing had ever felt so natural, so right, as just the two of them standing there, cloaked in the shadows of the hall.

He waited until Flora had finished her song, and then, while the others were cheering applause, he said into her ear, "I've something I need to say to you."

Libby turned to face him, blinking in the low light. The voices, the very presence of the others, seemed to melt away as he stared into those incredible gray-blue eyes. It was as if it were just the two of them standing in that hall. Just the two of them standing on the edge of the world—a world he hoped the two of them would share.

Graeme took Libby's hands. "First, I want you to know that the past weeks, since you came to the village, have been truly remarkable for me."

She smiled. "For me, too. I was just thinking, I—"

"Shh . . ." He put his fingers against her lips. "There's more. I need to get this said."

She nodded, suddenly nervous as she took a breath.

"Libby, I've never met anyone like you. You make me feel wonderful whenever I'm with you. When I'm not with you, I count the minutes until I can be again. But there is a part of my life that you do not know about. I am—"

"Excuse me, Mr. Mackenzie. I'm sorry to interrupt. Libby, I need to speak with you."

Graeme hadn't even noticed that the police constable had come up beside them.

"Can this wait, Constable?" Graeme said, his voice edged with annoyance. "We're in the middle of something."

"I'm afraid it can't. Believe me, I would rather be doing anything other than this right now, but—"

"Have you told her yet, Constable MacLeith?"

Libby blinked, trying to figure out how Angus and Lady Venetia had suddenly appeared when moments before she'd been lost in Graeme's eyes.

"Not just yet, Lady Venetia. I was just getting to it."

"Getting to what?" Graeme was not at all pleased.

Angus turned to Libby. "Libby, do you have on your person a crystal stone suspended from a silver chain?"

Libby lifted a hand in a protective gesture to her neck. "Why do you ask?"

"Lady Venetia has acquired an order from the Sheriff Court and I have been charged with recovering this stone from you. She has made a claim that it was stolen from her thirty years ago. By your mother."

Libby shook her head. "My mother did not steal it. It was given to her by my father!"

The other villagers had begun to take notice of the exchange. A crowd started to gather around them.

"Her mother was a maid in my employ at the castle," Lady Venetia said. "I dismissed her because she had been found stealing from us."

Libby rounded on her. "You dismissed her because she fell in love with your son! My mother was not a thief." She turned to the constable. "Angus, this is a mistake. My mother left me this stone when she passed away. It was a gift to her from my father, Fraser Mackay."

Angus looked as if he would have preferred to have been anywhere—anywhere on earth—other than right there, right then.

"Libby, do you have any proof that your mother received this stone from your father as a gift?"

She closed her eyes, fighting tears. She shook her head. "Of course not."

"Then I'm sorry, but she's gotten an order from the court. My chief constable has instructed me to retrieve the stone and return it to Lady Venetia. You can contact the sheriff and request a hearing to give your side of the story. But in the meantime, I have no choice. I have to take the stone."

"Just a minute." Graeme stepped forward, looking at Lady Venetia. "You would do this to your own granddaughter?"

"She is not my granddaughter."

"She is, and she is the only family you have. You might resent her mother for whatever wrong you feel she did, but what has Libby done to you? She only came here looking for the truth."

"You seem to forget, Mr. Mackenzie, she has begun litigation to take my home from me."

"You sold that home, and you're trying to sell the rest of the estate, putting all of these people here at risk of losing their jobs, their homes, and their lives. Libby is only trying to stop that from happening."

Lady Venetia looked around at the crowd of villagers, the same villagers she had held under the weight of her influence for decades. Only now, instead of looking at her with deference and even fear, they looked at her with open censure.

"I never wanted to live here. I thought after we married, we'd live in London or even Paris, come here in the summers for a week or two. But instead he stuck me out here in the middle of nowhere, surrounded with nothing but backward, simple people. I hated it here. I hated everything about this place. Because it was this place that brought her mother into our lives. And because of her, I lost my only son."

Lady Venetia took hold of herself, looked at Angus. "I want my stone, Constable MacLeith. And I want it *now*."

Angus looked at Libby. "Libby . . ."

"How much?" Graeme said, still unwilling to give in. He knew how much that stone meant to Libby, and he would pay anything to keep it for her. "You were willing to sell this estate for money. How much for the stone? I'll pay you whatever you want for it."

But Lady Venetia merely smirked. "This isn't about money, Mr. Mackenzie."

"No, it's not, is it? It's about revenge. Your need to get revenge on Libby's mother, and in absence of her, Libby herself, for the tragic loss of your son, even as you refuse to admit it is a loss for which you were the more responsible."

Lady Venetia stared at Graeme, her eyes stony, untouched. "Constable . . . I'm waiting."

Angus said defeatedly, "Libby."

Libby reached for the chain and slid it over her head. Almost as soon as she took it from around her neck, the stone seemed to color, brightening to a sharp, burning yellow. Some of the people gathered around them gasped. Others murmured, shaking their heads. Someone whispered "no" as Libby held the stone out, her hand trembling. Angus took it quickly from her.

Lady Venetia snatched the stone even before he could give it to her and dropped it into her pocketbook. She pointed a finger at Libby. "I warned your mother that she would regret interfering in my life."

Libby stood there, saying nothing, staring at Lady Venetia in disbelief as tears rolled down her cheeks.

"You've gotten what you came for," Graeme said. "So why don't you go now? I'm sure I speak for everybody here when I tell you that you are not welcome at this gathering."

The villagers nodded, murmuring their agreement.

"Believe me, Mr. Mackenzie, I am more than happy to see the last of this godforsaken place."

And with that, Lady Venetia turned and walked from the village hall.

When Graeme and Libby got back to the castle that night, they could hear a telephone ringing insistently inside.

They'd accepted a ride back from the village with Angus, who felt terrible about the part he'd had to play in that evening's events. As Libby stood on the drive, assuring him he'd had no choice in the matter, Graeme went running for the door to answer the still-ringing call.

They were still standing on the courtyard outside when Graeme returned ten minutes later.

"I've got to go to London," he said abruptly.

"Now?" Libby said. "But Graeme, it's after midnight!"

"I know. I've got an emergency meeting at eight o'clock in the morning. I don't even have time to call for a charter. I've got to leave for Inverness now so I can catch the five a.m. flight."

"Do you want me to go with you?"

He tossed a bag in the back of the Land Rover. "No. I'll be back by tomorrow afternoon. I'm sorry, Libby. I wouldn't leave under any other circumstances. Especially after everything that happened tonight." He looked at her. "Bloody hell, I'll just call them back, tell them I can't be there."

Libby shook her head. "No, no. This project is too important for you. Please. Go. Everything will be fine."

"Are you certain you'll be all right here? I really don't like leaving you alone."

Angus stepped in. "I'll take her back with me to spend the night with Flora and the kids. I know Flora would love it."

Graeme looked at Libby. "All right?"

She nodded. "Yes, yes. That's fine. Don't worry. You'd better go, or you'll be late."

Graeme kissed her quickly and then turned for the Land Rover.

He was gone in seconds, tearing down the drive in a cloud of gravel and dust.

Chapter Twenty-four

When Graeme returned to the castle late the next after-noon, Libby wasn't there.

"She must still be at Flora's," he said to his mother and his uncle, who had both accompanied him on the flight back from London. "I'm sure she'll be back soon."

They retired to the drawing room for a glass of claret and to wait for her return.

When she didn't return by six that evening, Graeme picked up the phone to call Flora. She answered on the third ring.

"Hallo?"

"Flora. It's Graeme Mackenzie. Is Libby still there?"

"Ehm . . ."

Graeme knew immediately that something was wrong. "What is it? What's happened?"

"Haven't you seen the newspaper today?"

"Which newspaper, Flora?" And then he realized it didn't matter. "What did it say?"

"It was an announcement of your engagement to the daughter of some nobleman. Or should I say the engage-ment of someone named Lord Waltham, who looked very much like you, to the daughter of some earl named Cleary."

Graeme responded with a word he rarely ever used in

public. He dropped his head forward and took a breath, realizing his worst fear had just come true. It was then he noticed the newspaper, sitting on the hall table. He took it up, scanned its front page, and found the headline almost immediately.

GRANSBOROUGH HEIR TO WED THE EARL OF CLEARY'S ELDEST DAUGHTER.

It was an exclusive interview that had been granted by Amaranthe herself. The text stated that negotiations had been opened and that a formal announcement was imminent. "We're planning for the ceremony in early May," she'd been quoted as saying, "with a honeymoon in France." When asked how she had managed to snare the elusive and much-sought-after Lord Waltham, she replied merely that they'd known each other since they'd been children and had always been quite close, making it seem as if "catching" Graeme had never been an issue at all.

According to her, she'd already "caught" him long, long ago.

A photo of Graeme appeared beside the story with a caption that read, "The prospective groom: Graeme Mackenzie, Marquess of Waltham." It was set beside another photo, this one of Amaranthe, smiling and looking practically engaged.

Bloody hell.

Graeme picked up the receiver again, not even sure if Flora was still there.

She was.

"Where is she, Flora? Where's Libby?"

"Before I tell you, I want you to answer me something. Is it true?"

"Damn it, Flora!"

"I mean it. I'm not going to say another word until

you give me the truth. Are you going to marry that other girl?"

"No, I'm not. This is a mistake. A big, unbelievably badly timed mistake. Please, Flora. I need to talk to Libby. I need to explain this to her. Now."

Flora fell quiet for a moment, considering. Then she said, "Don't make me regret this. She's at the village hall, making arrangements for Ian M'Cuick and Sean MacNaeish to stand in her stead with the legal proceedings in Edinburgh. She's also meeting with all of the villagers to offer to sell them their plots of land from the estate. Her attorney has arranged for financial help through mortgages and grants with the Highland Council. She's leaving for Edinburgh just as soon as she's finished, and then, after the arrangements have been finalized for the estate, she'll be returning to the States."

"Bloody hell she will."

Graeme didn't even bother to say good-bye.

He strode into the drawing room and shoved the newspaper under the duke's nose. "Just tell me you didn't have anything to do with this."

The duke looked at the article, registering genuine surprise as he shook his head. "Of course not, Graeme. I would never do something so underhanded. Cleary must have thought he could force your hand by announcing it prematurely to the press. Devil take him."

"Graeme." The countess, his mother, came forward. "I take it Libby saw this."

"Yes."

"Do you know where she has gone?"

"Yes. Presently she's at the village hall. However, she's planning to leave for Edinburgh, and then eventually return to the States."

"Well, what are you standing here with us for? Don't you think you ought to stop her before she does?"

*   *   *

Libby was sitting at one end of a long table in the center of the village hall when Graeme, his mother, and the duke came striding in. A number of the villagers were sitting along each side of the table, filling out paperwork and asking questions of Libby and a man who was undoubtedly her attorney. When Graeme came to stand at the foot of the table, voices quieted. All eyes turned to him at once.

"Libby, can I speak to you, please?"

When she looked up at him, he could tell she'd been crying. Her eyes, those eyes he'd come to love, were red and puffy and utterly forlorn. The expression on her face tore through him like a shot. He didn't even wait for her reply.

"Libby, it isn't true."

"Oh. So, you're not really a nobleman?"

"No, that much is true. I am a marquess, my mother is a countess, and my uncle is indeed a duke. I will eventually inherit both of their titles."

She frowned at him, shaking her head. "Why would you have me believe you were a caretaker?"

"I can't expect you to understand any of this, but in the beginning, I didn't think it would cause any harm. I wanted you to know me as me, just Graeme Mackenzie. Not as a bloody marquess, or the heir of a duke. I was looking for anonymity and came to the castle to escape the attention of the press, who were hounding me daily. When my brother and then my father both died, I became heir to two noble titles. It was something I never expected, and something I wasn't prepared to have to live with, but it was a responsibility I had to assume, like it or not. It is my duty to my family. I knew that I was going to have to return to that life someday, but I just wanted to hang on to the last bit of privacy I had remaining a little longer."

He looked at her. She was listening. Thank God, she was listening.

"As for Amaranthe, yes, I had told my mother and my uncle that I would marry for the sake of the title. To be honest, when I agreed to it, I didn't care who I ended up with for a bride. That was before I met you."

Graeme came around the table, knelt beside Libby's chair. "After I met you, after I *fell in love with you*, I knew I couldn't take just anyone for my wife. I knew there was only one person I would want to spend the rest of my life with. In fact, I told this to my mother and my uncle just a few days ago. I told my uncle I had no intention of marrying Amaranthe, or anyone else, for that matter. But I still had one more thing to take care of. I had to tell you the truth of who I was. And I was going to tell you everything last night at the *ceilidh,* but then Lady Venetia came in, the time wasn't right, and well, then I was called to London this morning. I didn't want to just blurt it out on my way out the door. I wanted to make sure to do it properly. I brought my mother and my uncle back with me from London now because I wanted them to be with us when I told you the truth and when I asked you if you would consent to be my wife."

Libby looked at him. "What did you say?"

Graeme reached inside his coat pocket and took out a box, the distinct sort of silk-covered box that came only from a jeweler. He took a deep breath, opened the box, took out a ring from inside. It was a beautiful square-cut diamond, surrounded by smaller round diamonds on each side.

"Libby, this ring was my mother's ring, and her mother's ring before her. It has been in our family for generations. I brought it back from London with me to give to you."

He took her hand, felt it tremble in his. He prayed that tremble meant she would say yes. "I would like to ask you to accept this ring from me, and do me the honor of being my wife."

Libby looked at him. "But you're a duke."

Graeme nodded. "Yes. Yes, I am."

"And I'm just an antique bookseller. I live in a studio walk-up on the Upper West Side."

"Even if that was all there is to you, it wouldn't matter. But, Libby, you're so much more than that. Look around you. Look at what you've come to mean to the people of this village. Look at what you're doing right now to help them."

The others sitting around the table nodded in agreement.

"And dinna forget, lass," said Gil, who had been standing behind her. "You are a Mackay. Your ancestors were great Scottish clan chiefs. Your namesake, Lady Isabella, was herself the daughter of a duke and carried the blood of an English king. You carry that same blood, lass."

"But none of that matters more than what you mean to me." Graeme looked into Libby's eyes. "I may have a title attached to my name, but before you came into my life, I was incomplete, like a forgotten piece of a puzzle. When I'm with you, that is not longer true. You fulfill me, Libby Hutchinson. When I'm with you, the puzzle just fits. No one else, no daughter of an earl, no royal princess, could do that. Only you. I want only to be the same to you, if you'll just say yes."

Libby knew just what he meant. She'd known that same lost, detached feeling as well, until she'd felt she was drowning in it. But Graeme had been the one to throw her a lifeline, pulling her back from that dark abyss.

She looked deeply into his eyes. Graeme held his breath, waited until she answered a softly tearful, "Yes, Graeme. I will marry you."

The entire hall broke out in a resounding cheer.

Graeme scarcely heard them. He took Libby into his arms and kissed her with all the love he felt for her in his heart.

He was still kissing her moments later when Angus MacLeith suddenly appeared in the hall.

"Ehm, excuse me . . . Libby?"

Graeme groaned. "Has anyone ever told you that you've got the very worst timing, PC MacLeith?"

Libby eased from Graeme's embrace. "Angus?"

"Libby, there was an accident. Last night. A car drove off the A839 into a gorge just outside the village of Tunga." He paused, looking at her. "It was Lady Venetia's car. Her body has just been recovered."

Libby stared at him, trying to grasp what it was he was telling her. "You're saying she's . . . she's dead?"

Angus nodded.

It felt as if the very ground suddenly shifted beneath her feet.

She shook her head. "I don't know what to say."

She didn't feel anything, except a profound sense of loss, and the sting of regret that she had never been able to bridge the gap that had stood between them. Perhaps, however, she never would have.

"It was to have been expected."

Ian M'Cuick came forward. "You remember when I told you the legends surrounding the Mackay stone, lass? You remember when I told you how, like a person's heart, the stone can never be taken, that it must only be given? Every other time throughout history, whenever the stone was taken unlawfully, misfortune befell the person responsible. It has been this way for centuries and has continued now into the very present."

The other villagers murmured in agreement.

Libby looked at him, at Old Gil, at the other villagers. "So are you saying this happened to Lady Venetia because she took the stone from me?"

Angus answered her. "Ehm . . . I don't know about all that, but I do know that this was found lying on the verge of the road at the point where Lady Venetia's car went over." He shook his head in a way that indicated his bewilderment. "It was lying with its chain in a perfect circle. Lady's Venetia's handbag, the same bag in which I'm quite certain I remember seeing her deposit the stone earlier last night, was lying on the floor of the car, unopened."

Angus held out the stone . . . to Libby. "I think everyone here will agree, there is only one person who should have this."

Before nearly the whole of the village who had adopted her as one of their own, and with the man she loved at her side, Libby took the stone and slipped the chain over her head.

Years later, there was some disagreement about what exactly had happened that October night. Some said the stone sparked like a flint to a fire. Others said it had flashed, as if within its mystical crystal it had captured a bolt of lightning. The colors they'd all seen had ranged from blue to red to green and even gold. Some had heard a sound. Others had heard only the sigh of the Highland wind.

But one thing they all were able to agree on was that after having been missing for more than three decades, the Mackay stone had indeed finally come home . . .

. . . and it had brought with it a new Mackay lady, to the laird who held her heart.

Epilogue

The Village of Wrath, Scotland

It was a perfect day for a wedding.

That April morning dawned to a brilliant sunrise that defied the television weather predictions, brushing an artist's palette of pinks, reds, and oranges across an uncommonly peaceful North Sea.

All throughout the day, the groom's mother had been nervous, worrying that the ceremony, which was to be held outdoors on the shore of the bay and in the ruins of the old church, would have to be moved indoors. The bride, however, would hear none of it. She knew in her heart that nothing would ever dare to spoil this long-awaited day.

She wore a gown of the palest ivory silk that was sleek and simple in its design, its only adornment the crystal stone that hung over the modest bodice, and the sash made of the tartan of the Mackays which draped across from shoulder to waist. A piper stood on the high bluff and dusk was falling as the bride walked along the candlelit pathway that led to the church's altar.

Standing, waiting for her in his kilt and tailored black coat, the groom found himself sucking in his breath.

She was a true vision.

It was a ceremony much like another which had been performed some three decades earlier. Only this time, instead of nesting birds for witnesses, the entire village was there. When the minister declared them man and wife, the whole assembly let out a cheer. The piper played, hugs and kisses were exchanged, and the villagers started back up the hill toward the blazing lights of the castle where the celebration would continue on into the night.

The bride and her groom, however, lingered behind.

Holding Graeme's hand, Libby bent to place her bride's bouquet before the new granite headstone that bore her mother's name.

The decision to have her mother brought back to Scotland, back to take her final rest at her *home*, had been a simple one. There had been a special service months earlier, where various people from the village had shared their memories of Matilde. She'd been laid to rest beside the granite obelisk that bore the name of Fraser Mackay, marking the final resting place of Libby's father. Though he had been Matilde's husband only in name during her lifetime, Libby was determined that they would spend their eternity together.

"These are for you, Mom," Libby whispered, blinking back the tears that had begun pooling in her eyes.

And as she stood again, with the wind rushing in off the sea, Libby would have sworn she heard her mother's whispered sigh as the scent of her lavender drifted by.